Praise for P9-DVF-967

"Richly woven."   —*True West*

"A cleverly planned and beautifully written piece of Western literature."   —*The Oklahoman*

"A good portrait of an age and a place as well as a man, briskly narrated and engaging."   —*Kirkus Reviews*

"Eickhoff presents a poetic, yet violent fiction account of Wild Bill Hickok."   —Elmer Kelton

"A brilliant, mysterious, and in the end poetic capture of that romantic American figure, the Western gunfighter of old. Wild Bill Hickok comes fully alive in these pages—and dies with equal force."   —David Nevin, *New York Times* bestselling author of *Meriwether*

"In this majestic epic, James Butler Hickok, better known as Wild Bill, is seen through a kaleidoscope of mythologies. He is God's Avenging Angel, Odysseus, and Sir Lancelot, Charlemagne's perfect knight, the hero of gaudy dime novels, and an American legend. In his Prince Albert coat and red sash he is also the great pacifier of hungry women from Elizabeth Custer to Guinevere, as well as a killer extraordinaire who offs barmen with aplomb. This is a great psychedelic novel, and Randy Eickhoff is a top banana."   —Richard S. Wheeler, Spur Award-winning author of *The Exile*

And Not to Yield

A NOVEL OF THE LIFE AND TIMES OF
WILD BILL HICKOK

RANDY LEE EICKHOFF

A TOM DOHERTY ASSOCIATES BOOK
NEW YORK

NOTE: If you purchased this book without a cover, you should be aware that this book is stolen property. It was reported as "unsold and destroyed" to the publisher, and neither the author nor the publisher has received any payment for this "stripped book."

This is a work of fiction. All the characters and events portrayed in this book are either products of the author's imagination or are used fictitiously.

AND NOT TO YIELD: A NOVEL OF THE LIFE AND TIMES OF WILD BILL HICKOK

Copyright © 2004 by Randy Lee Eickhoff

All rights reserved, including the right to reproduce this book, or portions thereof, in any form.

A Forge Book
Published by Tom Doherty Associates, LLC
175 Fifth Avenue
New York, NY 10010

www.tor.com

Forge® is a registered trademark of Tom Doherty Associates, LLC.

ISBN 0-812-56776-5
EAN 978-0812-56776-2

First edition: June 2004
First mass market edition: April 2005

Printed in the United States of America

0 9 8 7 6 5 4 3 2 1

for Raelene

ACKNOWLEDGMENTS

I WOULD like to thank the Deadwood Public Library, for helping with research for this book, and Leon Metz, who generously gave me free access to his wonderful library.

I owe a great debt to Barbara Wild, the copy editor, whose careful work on the manuscript kept many errors from the reader.

Sing to me, Calliope, Muse of Epic Poetry, and tell me the story of the man whose own wisdom and trickery wounded him and caused him to languish far from the loving arms of his wife. Sing to me the story of that wanderer who sacked Troy and sundered her heaven-built wall only to be forced to roam uncharted seas and visit strange lands where he faced many trials. Sing to me his adventures among nations of all manners, minds, and fashions. Sing to me of a man, abandoned by the gods . . .

—Homer's *Odyssey*
translated by Randy Lee Eickhoff

S'il faut choisir un crucifié, la foule sauve toujours Barabbas.
If it has to choose who is to be crucified,
the crowd will always save Barabbas.

—Jean Cocteau
Le Rappel à l'ordre

More are men's ends marked than their lives before:
The setting sun, and music at the close,
As the last taste of sweets, is sweetest last,
Writ in remembrance more than things long past.

—*Richard II* II.i.11–14

A brittle glory shineth in this face:
As brittle as the glory is the face.

—*Richard II* IV.i.287–288

PART ONE

Youth

Of arms and the man I sing

CHAPTER

1

"ONCE UPON a time a long, long time ago, a good knight loped gently over the plain on his faithful horse, and this good knight felt badly in his heart because he had a terrible deed to face. . . ."

Papa told me that story. I was five. He told me many stories. His face always smiled. His face was always tired.

The knight came over the green fields. He went into a forest. Everything was dark and scary. He was looking for the Green Knight. The Green Knight had let him chop off his head. It rolled on the floor of King Arthur's castle like a bright green and hairy ball. But the Green Knight picked up his head. He got on his green horse.

" 'I'll be waiting for you to come to me in a year and a day for your return blow,' the Green Knight said, and he galloped away. Now Sir Gawain, for that was the good knight's name, had to let the Green Knight chop his head off. . . ."

* * *

Here is the house. It is white and red. Papa says red is more dura . . . dura . . . lasts longer.

The trees in the grove are green and brown.

The road is dusty. When the buggies and wagons go by, the dust hangs in the air. I cough.

Papa and Mama and me and Oliver and Lorenzo and Horace live there. There was another Lorenzo. He died. Papa said that the name hadn't been used up. That's why Lorenzo is Lorenzo.

> *Rock of ages, cleft for me;*
> *Let me hide, myself in thee.*

He sang me to sleep with that song.

"Sleep time, little Jim," he said. "Close your eyes. Nod your little head."

And I pretended to close my eyes.

Then I came awake.

Mama made biscuits for breakfast. I poured syrup on them. The syrup came from Papa's store on the first floor of the Green Mountain House. I used to watch the men play dominoes. They sat by the stove in the winter and they played dominoes.

I liked the store.

Then Papa got sick and lost it.

We went on a trip and Papa got a farm in a bunch of trees and Lorenzo teased me and hid among them and I couldn't find him and then Celinda was born and Lydia was born and

> *Lor, Lor, my pretty little Pink,*
> *Lor, Lor I say,*

We had a hidden cellar where Negroes used to hide when the bad men came looking for them. It was filled with hay so they could sleep on it.

"Your Uncle Aaron was at Bunker Hill when the British attacked. And there they stood, brave men holding their fire until Israel Putnam shouted out, 'Don't fire until you see the whites of their eyes!' And Aaron held his fire, kneeling there as the Redcoats marched up the hill . . ."

> *Old Dan Tucker was a fine ol' man,*
> *Washed his face in a frying pan,*
> *Combed his hair with a wagon wheel,*
> *Died with a toothache in his heel.*

CHAPTER

2

WE WERE hiding in the branches of the trees near the dirt road leading down to Homer. Horace and me. We had been there since noon. Mr. Dewey came by in his wagon. Horace shot one of the horses in the butt with his slingshot. He hit that gray mare solid with a buckeye. She gave this high whinny and took off like Ma's cat the day she stumbled and poured hot water over it. We laughed at Old Man Dewey. He sat up there on his buckboard seat. He pulled back on the reins for all he was worth and shouted, "Whoa! Consarn you! Whoa!" And other words that we didn't expect a deacon to be shouting. That buckboard went racing lickety-split down the road. Horace and I near fell out of the tree, laughing as we did at the way Old Man Dewey bounced around in his seat.

"Jim!"

"Uh-oh," Horace said. He shoved his slingshot in my hands, shinnied down that chestnut tree, and hightailed it toward the barn as fast as he could run, which was pretty fast, 'cause he always won the races at school when Mr. Deasy made us run them on the last day of school when our parents would come to see what we had learned and—

"James Butler Hickok!"

I peeked out from the branches and saw Pa coming hard down the lane from the house toward the road. I sighed, wedged Horace's slingshot between two branches, and climbed down.

"Yes, Pa?" I asked as he came up.

His eyes were wrathy and he had tiny white lines around his mouth. His forehead shone with sweat. His butternut shirt had dark sweat patches under his arms and on his chest. He held on to the tree for a moment, breathing deeply.

"You all right, Pa?" I asked. He had been sickly again lately and Oliver and Lorenzo were doing most of the farm work.

Pa gulped for air and waved his hand at me. I stood by quietly. The sun was warm on my shoulders and meadowlarks were singing in the field over the split-rail fence behind me. I watched a gray squirrel scamper across the ground with a buckeye in its mouth. It saw me and raced up the tree Pa was leaning against.

"Did . . . you shoot . . . Mr. Dewey's horse . . . with a slingshot?"

I frowned. "No, sir," I said. I didn't add that it was Horace who shot the horse. I didn't want to wake snakes. Horace was almost three years older than me and could hit like a mule could kick. I was no fool.

Pa stared hard at me for a second. "Mr. Dewey says he saw you in the tree just after his horse was hit. He was almost thrown from his wagon. Now, why would he invent a story like that, Jim?"

"I don't know, sir," I said. I tried to look away from Pa. But his eyes pulled mine back like magnets did nails.

He nodded slowly. "All right, Jim. I believe you." And just at that moment, that damn squirrel bounced on the branch holding Horace's slingshot and it fell like a divining rod right at Pa's feet.

He looked down at it a moment. Then he looked back at me. I could see the disappointment in his eyes.

"Pa—"

He turned and walked away from me. He trudged down the dusty lane toward the house, his shoulders bowed as if he carried the whole world upon them. I sighed and picked up the slingshot. I looked up at the barn and saw Horace peeking out the door, laughing. I shook my head and grabbed the slingshot by the Y and held it up so he could watch while I pulled the two arms apart.

"Hey!" he shouted, and came running down toward me. His face looked grim. I threw the slingshot in the middle of the road and took off running for the grove. I glanced once over my shoulder. I saw his grim face. I ran faster into the shade of the grove. I ran toward the middle, then hid behind a tree, lying flat on the ground, watching.

Horace ran into the small clearing, then paused, trotting uncertainly around in a circle. But he couldn't find me. He stopped and put his hands on his hips, yelling, "All right, Jim! I know you're around here! You might as well come out and take your lickin', 'cause when I find you I'm gonna beat the crap outta you!"

He had big hands. I crept backward until I was another tree line back. Then I got to my feet and slipped back out of the grove. I ran back to the house. I went into the house. My shoes rattled on the puncheon floor. Ma was making molasses cookies.

"Can I have one?" I asked.

Ma gave me a hard look. "What's this I hear about you shooting horses with your slingshot?"

I sighed and shook my head. "Didn't," I mumbled. But I knew she wouldn't believe me, either. She was nice, but she had a hard look in her eyes that hurt when she turned it on you.

"Then who did?"

I looked up at her. Her eyes were looking hard at me and I looked away and hoped she couldn't see Horace at the back of my mind.

"Don't know," I mumbled again.

She sighed. "James Butler Hickok, you stand up straight now. Hear?"

I straightened my shoulders and looked up at her hairline.

"Now, who shot Mr. Dewey's horse?"

I swallowed and shook my head.

"It wasn't you, was it?"

I shook my head again.

She sighed again. "I didn't think so. It was Horace, wasn't it?"

I shrugged.

"All right." I looked at her eyes. They were softer now. A tiny smile hovered around her lips. She nodded at the table. "You can have one cookie. *One!*" she emphasized as I reached for it. I studied them carefully, then picked the biggest one I could find.

"Thanks, Ma!" I shouted, and ran back outside.

Right into Horace.

"So. You squealed on me, didja?" he snarled. He looked at the cookie in my hand. "Gimme that!"

He snatched it from me.

"Give it back!" I said hotly.

He sneered and took a bite. "What you gonna do about it?"

"I'll . . . I'll—"

"You won't do nothing," he scoffed. He crammed the rest of the cookie in his mouth.

A sudden madness came down upon me. I slugged him in the stomach. A look of surprise came over his face as the breath *whooshed!* from him in a mouthful of cookie crumbs. He bent forward at the waist, trying to suck air back in. He got cookie crumbs as well and gagged. I hauled off and smacked him again on the nose. Blood smeared itself over his cheek. Tears came to his eyes. I took a deep breath and came into him, windmilling my arms, not paying attention to where my fists landed, just feeling a savage pleasure when they did.

"Momma! Momma!" he cried. He tried to push me away. But it was useless. A strange happiness came over me. His hand grabbed my face. I bit his thumb. He howled.

Something grabbed me from behind. I turned and started hitting again. Pa stepped back in surprise. His boot caught the threshold and he stumbled backward and sat down hard on the floor. *Whomp!* He stared, startled, at me.

I was breathing hard and turned back to Horace, but he was down on all fours in the dirt, bawling, blood spotting the dirt beneath him.

"What in the world?"

I looked back over my shoulder at Ma standing in the doorway, looking from Pa to Horace to me and back to Pa.

"He—" I started to say, then clamped my mouth tight.

Ma looked down and saw the half-chewed cookie in the dust and nodded slowly. "Horace, you should be ashamed of yourself!"

He lifted a tearstained face. "He hit me when I wasn't looking!" he cried. "Unfair!"

"You were too looking!" I said hotly.

"Liar! I wasn't!"

"Well, you're looking now!" I shouted, and stepped forward and smacked him again as he started standing. He fell backward. I jumped on top of him and began to pummel him as hard as I could hit.

"That's enough, boys!" Ma said.

I looked up at her just as Pa pulled himself up off the floor and came out. His hand grabbed the back of my collar and pulled me off Horace. I stumbled, trying to get my balance, when Pa released me, and fell into the dirt. I looked up at him. His face was furious. Behind his head, a gray-white cloud floated over the sun. I watched a hawk swing low under the cloud and fold its wings as it dived down toward the field.

"Go to your room!" Pa said.

I rose, dusted my pants off, and walked into the house to my room. I closed the door and sat on my bed. Dimly I heard Pa giving Horace a tongue-lashing and knew I would be next. I lay down and pulled a book out from under my pillow. I glanced at the title: *The Last of the Mohicans.* I found my place where I had put the hickory leaf and began to read. I had to work to make my way through some of the sentences, but it was worth the trouble.

"Softly, softly," said the scout, extending his long rifle in front of the eager Heyward; "we now know our work, but the beauty of the trail must not be deformed. A step too soon may give us hours of trouble . . ."

It would be nice to be reading this on the braided hearth rug over the patterned oilcloth covering the floor in front of the fire with the wind howling outside, I thought. I shivered as the thought came close to me. Lorenzo read the Bible aloud once like that. The story of David and Goliath. Pa sat on his deacon's bench. He nodded and listened quietly as Lorenzo read. Pa didn't have to look at the word to correct Lorenzo when he made a mistake. Ma sat in her slat-backed rocker. It had ivy painted along the back. She had a lard oil lamp on a small spool-turned table beside her so she could see to sew.

I guess that served Horace rightly for taking my cookie. But Ma looked mighty mad. Horace had it coming. Why, back last spring Horace had thumped me in the school yard when I wouldn't let him use my shooter after he had lost all his marbles to Ben Allison. That wasn't right, 'cause I knew Horace would lose mine, too. We were studying about the Revolutionary War then and that was when Mr. Deasy had told us about James Fenimore Cooper and his books and—

I heard Pa's boots thump on the puncheon floor and hastily slid the book under my pillow. I had my hands clasped behind my head when he opened the door and came in.

"Jim, do you know what you've done?" he demanded.

"Yes, Pa," I said. I kept my eyes on the ceiling.

"Look at me," he said sternly.

I looked at him, then watched his lips as they puckered and bent, pushing the words out.

"We cannot have you boys fighting amongst yourselves. Remember what the Good Book says: 'Whosoever smiteth you upon the left cheek turn to him also thy right.' "

"Yes, Pa," I said automatically. Pa was always quoting the Bible. He had a lot of that crammed up in his head, although sometimes he got to where he was confused and couldn't remember it. Pa had wanted to be a preacher and was studying to be a Presbyterian minister at Middlebury College back in Vermont. It was there that he met Ma. Her father had been with Ethan Allen's Green Mountain Boys in the Revolutionary War. But then a typhoid fever epidemic came along and Pa caught it while nursing the sick and then near died from brain fever. Sometimes he remembered everything; then sometimes it all went away from him and he would wander around with this vacant look in his eyes for days. But this wasn't one of them days.

"Remember that he who troubleth his own house shall inherit the wind," Pa said. "He who fights with his brethren by his brethren will he be slain and his body will roll in the dust and dogs will lap his blood. Absalom! Absalom!"

He closed his eyes and struck himself in the chest softly with his fist.

"You all right, Pa?" I asked.

He stood still for a moment, then opened his eyes and looked down at me. His eyes looked glazed and I waited to see if he would remember where he was and what he was doing, but then a look of puzzlement came into them and he frowned.

Ma's voice called from the kitchen, "William? Will you come here?"

Pa half-turned toward the door, then looked down at me and frowned again.

"William?"

Her voice sounded a little higher.

He turned and left, blundering into the doorjamb with his left shoulder.

CHAPTER

3

I HEARD the voices on the playground.

"Your pa's an ijjeet!" Rody taunted. His big yellow teeth grinned down at me. His breath smelled like onions. He laughed and poked me in the chest with his fist. "He walks around like this!" He walled his eyes and puffed out his cheeks and stomped stiff-legged around me. The others giggled. Horace told him to quit it because Mr. Deasy was looking.

Rody stopped and turned to Horace, jeering, "And we know why you know that, Ho-race!" He made his name sound like *whores*. "You spend enough time smooching his butt." He puckered up and made kissing noises. The others laughed nervously.

The word sounded bad the way he said it. Sarah McLaughlin had once kissed me on a dare and the kiss sounded like that: *smooch*. Only softer and nicer. *Smooch* was a strange word. It could sound pretty or it could sound ugly. When Rody said it, it sounded ugly and Horace's face turned red clear up into his hair. His hands curled into fists, but he turned and walked away from Rody.

"Smoochsmoochsmooch," Rody called, mocking him. He made that kissing sound with his lips.

"The Hickoks," someone said scornfully behind me.

I turned and stared into Dotje's pimply face. His big buck teeth had ridges on them and looked green. He smirked.

"Ain't a backbone among 'em," he said. He poked me in the chest with his dirty finger. "You a kisser, too? Do you kiss your mama before you go to bed?"

"Yes," I answered.

"Hey, everyone! He says he kisses his mama every night before he goes to bed."

Everyone turned to look at me. Someone sniggered, and then everyone laughed. I felt my face grow warm.

"I do not!" I said.

"Oh. Hey, everyone, he says he don't kiss his mama every night before he goes to bed!"

They all laughed and he laughed and stuck his finger in his nose, digging.

I glanced at the door to the classroom, but Mr. Deasy had gone back inside. I looked back at Dotje, then hauled off and smacked him. His finger rammed into his nose. He cried out and jerked his finger away. Blood gushed from his nose. I smacked him again for good measure. He fell to the ground, bawling. Blood dripped onto the ground, a curious red against the brown dust.

CHAPTER

4

I FELT warm and rose from the bed and walked on tiptoes to the door and peeked out. Pa was sitting in his slat-backed rocker and Ma had wrung out a cloth and was laying it across his forehead, saying, "There, there, William. Deep breaths. That's right: deep breaths."

Pa obeyed, taking long, slow deep breaths, although I could see in his face that he didn't know why he was doing that. "Polly," he said. He frowned. His face looked white and cool but pinched. He was trying hard to get the answer to what he couldn't remember. He looked up at the mantel over the fireplace where daguerreotypes of my grandmas and grandpas sat. He shook his head. He glanced at me and shook his head. I could see he didn't recognize me. I turned away and went back to my room and picked up the book again.

One moccasin is so much like another, it is probable there is some mistake.

"Jim! Wash up and come to supper, now!" Ma's voice cut through the words and I marked my place in the book and rose and went out. I stepped to the basin and ewer next to the deacon's bench beside the door. I splashed some water into the basin and scrubbed my hands hard with a bar of gray soap that felt like it had grit in it.

"Cleanliness is next to godliness," Pa said. His eyes twinkled as he rubbed my hands pink with the towel. "Always remember that, James. Cleanliness is next to godliness. You can't have one without the other."

I dried my hands on the damp towel and turned to the room. Horace was already at the table, glowering at me. Lorenzo sat across from him. He gave me a half smile as I sat next to him. He poked me in the ribs with his finger and I squirmed away from him.

"Cut it out," I mumbled. Pa gave me a puzzled look from his place at the table.

"This is supper time," Ma said sharply. "You boys straighten up! We've had enough of your gamboling around this day. We'll have some peace now. Understand?"

I glanced once at her blue-gray eyes and nodded quickly. "Yes, ma'am," I said. Lorenzo and Horace were quick to come on the tail of my words. We had been tomfooling enough for the day, she seemed to say. I had heard that tone of voice enough to know that all issues were hereby settled by the grace of God and Ma's firm hand, which could raise a welt on a person's dignity with the help of a willow switch she kept standing in the corner by the fireplace as a silent reminder for one to mend one's ways before they got a chance to be unmended.

I glanced down at the table. The tablecloth was clean and white and pressed. The small brown crock holding the milk for the table stood near Pa's hand. A pattypan holding biscuits stood next to it. A bowl filled with Boston baked beans in thick molasses was in the middle of the table next to a platter of chicken fixin's.

Ma took her place at the end of the table and sighed deeply. She held out her hands. Horace took one. I took the other and Lorenzo took mine. He held out his other hand. Pa took it gingerly. His eyebrows twitched. My sister Celinda shook her curls and cocked her head at him. He smiled and took her tiny hand in his. Lydia laughed and smashed a spoon on the small table in front of her chair next to Ma's right hand.

"William?" she said. Pa looked at her. "The blessing?" she said. He frowned, trying to remember. A soft sigh escaped her lips. She glanced at Horace.

"All right, Horace. Give us the blessing."

He pouted and glared at me.

"Horace," she said again, a bit more sharply.

He bowed his head and mumbled, "Thou hast again remembered us, O Lord, and we would not forget thee. Bless this food, we pray, and help us to serve thee well."

"And?" Ma prompted.

I watched him glance from the corners of his eyes at Ma. His eyes shifted over to mine and he heaved a deep sigh.

"And forgive us our transgressions and let us forgive others as we would have them forgive us. Amen." He rushed the last and glared at me as I worked hard to keep from laughing.

"Amen," the rest of us echoed.

Ma straightened and handed Lydia a piece of biscuit soaked in honey. Lydia squealed and began smearing her face with it.

Lorenzo took the brown crock and filled Pa's glass with milk, then his. He handed the crock to me. I poured my glass full and handed the crock on to Ma. I took a sip, tasting a hint of cream behind the milk.

Briefly I see Lorenzo crouching by our patient cow at daybreak in the barn after bringing her in from the lush green pasture next to the orchard, his fingers tugging at her dugs in an old and secret ritual of the morning world.

Pa took the glass in his hand, looking at it questioningly. He sipped it. His face brightened. "A miracle!" he said. He beamed as he looked around the table at us. "If we all live on good drink as this, why, we won't have a rotten tooth in our heads and our stomachs will know great comfort! Eh, what do you say, Polly?"

"Of course, William," she answered. She glanced at Horace. "Straighten up and stop looking daggers at James. You received nothing more than you asked for and now it is over and done with. No more." She glanced warningly at me.

"Yes, ma'am," I mumbled. I grabbed a biscuit and stuffed it in my mouth to prevent myself from having to say more. I looked boldly across at Horace. His eyes met mine, furious for the moment. Then they wavered and slipped away, glanced back, then away again. He bent his head, studying his plate as he ate silently.

CHAPTER

5

"YOU ARE named after the great Roman poet and lawyer Horace," Papa said. He smiled at Horace. *"Ira furor brevis est."*

"What's that?" Horace asked.

" 'Anger is a short madness,' " Papa said. "It would do you well to remember that."

"And me, Papa?" I asked. "Who am I named after?"

He smiled. "Why, you are named after King James who gave us the new Bible."

I looked at Horace. "You're named after an old poet. I'm a king."

Horace pouted. "I wanna be a king, too!" His lower lip trembled as if he was going to burst into tears.

"And me, Papa?" Lorenzo asked eagerly.

"You, Lorenzo, are named after a man who saved a woman's soul by bringing her to our Lord Jesus Christ!"

Lorenzo's face fell. I grinned at him.

"I'm still the king!" I crowed.

"And Oliver? What about Oliver, Papa?" Lorenzo asked.

"Oliver? Why, Oliver is named after the man who brought true Christianity to England and threw the evil people who pretended to love God out. He was a great man. A truly great man."

"Tell me where I was born," I said importantly.

"No, tell *me*," Horace said.

"I'm the king," I said. "I go first."

Horace pouted.

Papa smiled. He had a nice smile when he smiled that way. "Horace, you were born when we lived at Union Center. James, you were born in Homer."

"Who was Homer, Papa?" I looked importantly at Horace. Anyone could be born at a Union Center. There wasn't anything special about that name. But Homer?

"Homer was a great, great poet," Papa said. "He wrote the *Iliad* and the *Odyssey*. Stories about great heroes." He closed his eyes.

> " 'Sing to me the story of that wanderer who sacked Troy
> and sundered her heaven-built wall only to be forced
> to roam uncharted seas and visit strange lands
> where he faced many trials.
> Sing to me his adventures—' "

And I sat, openmouthed, listening to the adventures of a man whose name was that of my birthplace. Even Horace and the others listened, and great envious looks were cast my way by Horace because no such legends came from a place called Union Center.

CHAPTER

6

ON SUNDAYS, Pa loaded us all into the wagon and we made the journey down Little Vermillion Creek to the Presbyterian church. We passed the McLaughlin farmhouse and I watched eagerly to see if Sarah or Josephine would be standing at the half door to wave at us as we drove by in the buggy. Pa would give me the whip so I could wave it at them. Sarah was a sweet one, but Josephine had a strange look in her eye whenever she was around me and she would stand real close to me so I could breathe the vanilla that she put behind each ear and on her neck. I would sniff real hard and suddenly I would get this hungry feeling in my stomach that would leave me so weak that all the cookies in the world wouldn't fill it.

Nahum Gould would see us coming and limp around in a state until Pa pulled the team to a halt and handed Ma down to one of us.

"William! William!" Gould would exclaim. (He always addressed Pa with both names—"William! William!"—as if he was having a hard time making Pa understand that he wanted to talk to him.) Gould would come to our wagon, swinging his game foot around in a half circle and giving a little hop. He had lost part of that foot when he had stopped to clear a stone from his plow and something startled the team (a snake was usually given as the cause) and the team bolted, dragging the plow blade over Gould's foot, cutting it in half. There was a sternness about him that disturbed a lot of people, but he was always kind toward us. I just think the others weren't willing to look beneath the Quaker name to the man himself before gouging his name. This was usually done by someone wanting to be the biggest toad in the puddle, who would put warts on another to make himself look more important to others.

"Nahum," Pa would say calmly. Then he would step down and Gould would grab Pa's arm just above his black-coated elbow and draw him aside, whispering urgently to him. We weren't supposed to know what the urgency was about, but we all did. Gould was a rabid Abolitionist and belonged to the Quaker church across the road. He would keep Pa until our church bell rang and Pa gently excused himself to join the rest of us standing by the door waiting for him.

I didn't care much for our church, a white clapboard affair with a steeple and bell. The church stood on a small knoll, surrounded by locust trees and tall elms, above Tomahawk Creek not far from a wooden bridge that seemed to always have a pall of perpetual gloom thrown over it. In the fall, the whitewashed walls shone like ideal Christian purity in the morning sun. But there didn't seem to be much Christianity practiced there other than lip service to the deity and memorized prayers that one could mutter absentmindedly upon command. There always seemed to be a night-musty smell to it like old men. Reverend Robert Cowley did his best to bore the young boys there. He started each service the same way:

"O Lord, open our minds, we pray, that we might receive thy noble wisdom. Hasten, O Lord, to guide us through these terrible times that we might do thy bidding and carry thy message to those who need it most."

That was about as far as any of us got in the service except for the times when our mothers would elbow us up to join in a hymn or two when Reverend Cowley ran out of steam and decided he needed a minute or two rest to gather his thoughts in order to purge us more of our sins, real and imagined. We set **off on** our own journeys until we came to the familiar end:

"Come down into our hearts, O Lord, we beseech thee. Drive away from us all the snares of the enemy and may thy holy angels dwell among us to keep us safe in peace and may thy blessing be always upon us, O Lord. This we pray in thy name. Amen."

And then there would be a mad scramble for the door despite our mothers' heavy sighs. But only Mrs. Beaufoy took exception at our mass exodus from the altar of the Lord.

"You boys are setting down the long road to hell and damnation!" she complained loudly once when Horace accidentally stepped on her corns.

That caused all of us to laugh when we got outside, for every boy in the county (and some of the girls as well) knew about the collection of drawings her husband, Philip, kept hidden in the tack room in the barn. When he stood up to do the reading in church *"Visit, we beseech thee, O Lord, our homes and drive away from them all sin . . ."* why, we kids would stuff our fingers in our mouths to keep from laughing. Petey Sweeney got the giggles once and stuffed his fingers so far in his throat that he gagged and vomited in the pew. We all left church early that day to keep from getting the bug that Petey's mother swore he had. We all met later down at the swimming hole at Tomahawk Creek to discuss this windfall. We thought that we could make this a regular thing. But no one wanted to follow Petey's example, so that ended that.

CHAPTER

7

I LIKED the Fall, the best 'cause that was when there would be this smoky smell to the air, sharp and cold: rainy and wintery and leaves burning and the corduroy of our churchgoing clothes. The woods that Tomahawk Creek cut through would be full of color and turkeys and squirrels were plentiful for hunting. I didn't have a gun. But I had a good slingshot that let me stun a few squirrels and once a turkey, but when I ran up to throttle him or cut his throat with my barlow knife he suddenly came awake and took a chunk out of my arm. Gobbling angrily, he chased me through the woods, jabbing at my backside. I came out of the woods howling and running for all I was worth. That turkey should have stayed in the woods. But I guess I had really made him angry. He chased me all the way to the house. Pa heard me howling and came running from the barn. He had been splitting wood and still had the ax in his hand. He stopped, wide-eyed at the turkey chasing me around and around Ma's clothesline post. Then Pa caught the turkey up by his neck and quickly upended him. The turkey gobbled angrily. His wings thrashed and beat at Pa's chest.

"What on earth?" Ma said. She came to the door and I ran to her and buried my face in her apron, bawling. "What's going on?"

"I reckon Jim's brought us dinner," Pa said somberly. He held the turkey up. "Looks like a nice one." He smiled down at me. "Good job, Jim." He took the turkey around behind the house. The turkey gobbled and suddenly there was a squawk and a loud *clunk!* and then the turkey didn't gobble anymore. Ma smiled down at me. She smoothed my hair back.

"Well, Jim, I guess you've earned a cookie for this day's work," she said. She took me into the house and gave me a molasses cookie and a glass of buttermilk.

Ever green summer keeps changing to autumn. . . .

At Christmas, there would be lanterns in the windows as we drove by for early service, rumbling over the wooden bridge in the wagon, listening to the echo of the wheels off the wooden planks and wishing we were back home instead of making the trip to hear Reverend Cowley tell us the story of Christmas one more time. It wasn't so bad going back home or stopping at homes along the way to sample early baking. I remember the ropes of green branches and the holly and ivy that had been wound around the pier glass and holly and ivy, green and red, looped around nails tapped around doors and windows. Christmas was a good time of the year. That was the year I got a fiddle for Christmas and Pa showed me how to finger it a bit and then arranged for Dan Tucker to teach me what he couldn't teach me.

CHAPTER

8

DIMLY I dreamed footsteps creaking on the floorboards of my bedroom and was already fighting awake through black night to the dim light of a lantern when Father called softly, "Jim, boy, wake up."

I rose on my elbows, blinking in the lantern light. Over against the wall, Lorenzo turned restlessly on his side to face the wall away from the light, grumbling in his sleep. Soft shadows danced on the rough-hewn wood walls where our clothes hung on nails to keep crickets out of them. I yawned.

"Yes, Father?" I said. I knuckled the sleep from my eyes and yawned again, tasting the thick night in my mouth. I shivered as the blanket slipped down from my naked chest to gather at my waist.

"I need your help, Jim," Father said quietly. He glanced over at Lorenzo, indecision working on his worried face. He looked pale and drawn in the yellow light, but then Father always looked pale and drawn, thanks to the typhoid fever he caught while helping nurse the sick when he and Mother were visiting North Hero on the shores of Lake Champlain in Vermont shortly after they were married. Father had been a seminary student, studying for the Presbyterian ministry at Middlebury College, but after he came down with typhoid fever his mind was never quite the same again. He had gotten better—or so Mother said—since we came to Illinois, but there were times when he lapsed into a bewildered confusion. When that happened, we just had to go along with him to keep him out of trouble until he came out of his fog. On his good days, he could still split a chalk line with an ax even though he looked tall and stringy.

"Leave him be, Father. I'll help you," I whispered, throwing the covers off and swinging my legs off my bunk to the floor. I stood, moving my feet gingerly to keep from sliding a sliver into my foot. I didn't want Mother digging around in the bottom of my foot with one of her needles to get the sliver out. The last time that happened, I hurt for a week.

Father frowned for a moment, then nodded. He waited while I pulled on my pants and shirt and heavy woolen socks. I picked up my boots and nodded at the door. Father turned and I followed him out into the kitchen. I pulled a chair from the table and sat, working my boots on, tucking my pants into the tops. The kitchen was still warm from the banked fire in the small cast-iron stove. I could smell the yeast in the bread dough rising beneath a clean dish towel in the heavy stoneware bowl. Mother always set the dough before going to bed so she could bake fresh in the morning.

"What's wrong?" I asked, rising and settling my feet in my boots. I worked the left one around a bit to ease it. The boots were new and stiff and pinched painfully just above my instep where I had a small bump growing on each foot. Doc Simpson said that was because I had worn boots too small when I was growing, so my feet never filled out with the rest of me.

"We have to go over to Nahum Gould's place," Father whispered. He raised his thumb and forefinger and massaged his eyes, the bridge of his nose.

"Now?" I asked. "It's still dark out. Nobody'll be up."

"Sh. Not so loud," he whispered. He glanced at the closed

door that led to his and Mother's room. "I don't want to wake your mother. She'll only worry."

My stomach felt queer as I stared at him. "Why would she think that? And why are we going over to Nahum's place this time of night?"

"One of Nahum's boys rode over and asked if we could collect some Negroes from their place. Some bounty hunters came through Wedron yesterday afternoon looking for some runaways. Nahum's afraid that someone might have seen them being brought over to his place. His boy rode on up the line to Bill Dewey's place to warn him. We're to collect the Negroes and bring them back here, then take them on up to Dewey's place in a couple of days."

I frowned and shook my head as I crossed to the door and slipped my canvas jacket off its peg. I took down my hat and set it firmly in place, pulling the brim down to my ears. I flinched as it rubbed across the sunburn on my forehead, and took it off. I had been hoeing weeds all day without a hat and was paying the price. I glanced in the small mirror, looking at the red on my nose, the freckles standing out. The sun had brought out red glints in my auburn hair. I resettled the hat gingerly and looked at Father, fidgeting in the middle of the room, shuffling back and forth from one foot to the other.

"What's wrong?" I asked.

He blinked, then looked away, troubled. "I think we should take Lorenzo, too. Oliver has to cut back trees in the morning so he should sleep."

"Let him sleep, Father," I said gently. "He was up at four this morning, plowing."

Father's lips narrowed into a thin line, his face setting stubbornly. "I think Lorenzo should come. We might need him."

"All right, Father," I said resignedly. "You wake him. I'll go hitch the team."

He nodded and turned back to the bedroom. I opened the door and stepped outside into the cold fall air. I shivered as the cold struck my exposed face, making me feel cold even though I was well bundled in my flannel shirt and jacket. I pulled a pair of gloves from my pocket and slipped them on. My breath appeared as tiny clouds of mist.

"Frost on the pumpkin come morning," I muttered as I walked across the yard to the barn. Then I remembered it *was* morning as I touched the iron hasp covered with a light sprinkle of frost. I slid the door open and walked inside, pausing to feel for the lantern beside the door. I lit it and carried it down to the end of the barn where the wagon harness hung on the wall. The horses watched me as I passed their stalls, their hooves moving on their straw bedding.

"It's going to be a cold one," I said to them as I came down the line. I slipped the harness over them, fitted the bits, then walked them out of the barn and backed them into place. Sam grumbled as I hooked the traces. "I know," I said soothingly. "I don't want to be up, either."

I climbed into the wagon and drove the short distance up to the house. Father came out with a sleepy Lorenzo beside him. They climbed into the wagon and I clucked to the horses and pulled out into our lane leading down to the dirt road and turned south, heading down to Gould's place.

"Damned inconsiderate—" Lorenzo began.

"Don't take the Lord's name in vain," Father said mildly, interrupting him.

"Sorry," Lorenzo mumbled, and huddled on the floor of the wagon, bracing his back against the seat. "This couldn't wait until morning?"

"No," Father said. "Best we get them moved under darkness."

Lorenzo sighed and fell silent, but I could feel his resentment at being shaken awake in the wee hours. Or maybe it was mine. Father had been moving Negroes up through our place as a stop on the Underground Railway for the past three years, but recently it had become very risky. More and more bounty hunters were out on the road with blank warrants that allowed them to seize any Negroes on suspicion and take them to the nearest authority until proper ownership could be established. But "the nearest authority" was vaguely defined and most bounty hunters would simply seize any Negroes they found off a private property and take them back down across the Mason-Dixon Line and put them back on the market. Some farmers down south would hire bounty hunters to find runaways when they didn't have any, paying a dollar a pound for any Negroes brought to them, claiming ownership. It was a way of getting fresh slaves cheaply.

We drove past the McLaughlin farm and I turned to watch the black windows, half-hoping the creaking of our wagon in the frosty night would rouse the McLaughlins and I would see a light come on in one of the windows and the figure of Sarah slip behind the curtain. But the only thing that stirred was their rooster, who crowed indignantly at being awakened as we passed. I sighed, my breath puffing gently out in front of me in a small cloud. I glanced down at Lorenzo, grinning up at me, reading my mind. I shook my head and his grin grew wider. As Father patiently held the reins on the horses, I turned back to the front and watched the black limbs of the trees, still half-covered with fall leaves of gold and brown, stretching out over the white ribbon of road stretching in front of us. The brush along the roadside seemed dark and threatening in the white moonlight. No sign of life flickered near us outside of strange night sounds that seemed like the chirp of crickets and the whirring of locusts in the trees. But crickets and locusts would not have been out at that time of year, and I shivered, wondering what the sounds I thought I was hearing were. The guttural twang of a bullfrog rolled up from beneath the wooden bridge over Tomahawk Creek as we rumbled across the worn planks and past the church, its white sides glowing ghostly in the pale light.

It was a night made for ghosts and goblins and suddenly I imagined the night growing darker and darker and the stars colder and colder. We rounded a bend in the road and saw the twisted limbs of a sycamore that had served as a hanging tree a few years back for Cage Harpe—who passed himself off as a second or third cousin to Wiley and Micajah Harpe, the two brothers who butchered about thirty men before they were killed. But no one paid much attention to Harpe's claim until he tried to rape Dolly Beaufoy (there was some question there, as quite a few boys and men had sampled Dolly's charms) in the grove and was caught by her cousin who was looking for a stray cow at the time. The cousin locked Harpe in the corn bin and went to get the sheriff, but his brothers took Harpe from the bin and hanged him before the sheriff could get back. The sycamore always seemed dead after that. Even when sparse green leaves dotted its dark limbs. I watched uneasily as we came closer and closer to it, then breathed a silent sigh of relief as we passed by safely without hearing Harpe moaning.

Lorenzo heaved a quiet sigh of relief behind me. I grinned and glanced over my shoulder at him. He shook his head and burrowed deeper into his heavy coat. Father cleared his throat beside me. I looked at him, sitting easily beside me, quietly contemplating the moving haunches of the horses in front of us.

"Ghosts and goblins and witches won't harm you unless you let them," he said quietly. He smiled gently. "That is a promise we are given in Psalms, Jim. 'Thou shalt not be afraid for the terror by night; nor the arrow that flieth by day.' Set your mind at ease. What we do is right and for that we won't be harmed." His eyes turned toward me. "We are told that, too."

"Yes," I wanted to say. *"Yes. I know. But do those who want to harm us know that as well? The Good Book provides comfort to those who don't have a good right cross. Or a pistol."* But I didn't voice my words. Father took a dim view of those taking the teachings lightly. I heard Lorenzo moving uneasily behind me and knew that he shared my thoughts. Hadn't Dotje's father one night when he was riding home from the Green Mountain come across Harpe? At least,

Henry claimed that when Father found him blundering along the road on foot, stinking of whiskey and his pants stained from where he had soiled them.

"Where's your horse, Henry?" Pa asked.

Henry squinted, trying to focus upon Pa's face, weaving back and forth from his place in the road. "I tell you, William, he was after me. As certain as that tree bears apples"—he pointed to the hickory tree—*"he was after me. It was horrible. His tongue hanging out all black and his eyes bulging out and I could smell the earth of the grave around him and he was mumbling and howling and—"*

"Who, Henry? Who stole your horse?"

Henry swallowed and glanced wild-eyed around him, then leaned forward, saying, "It was Cage Harpe, as I stand and breathe, William. Cage Harpe. I tried to run away, but my horse threw me"—I nearly chuckled at that, for I knew Henry's mare was nearly toothless and the best one could whip her to was a shambling trot—"and then he was on me leaning over me and I smelled his stinking breath," and Pa leaned back here from Henry's own stench as he started to gabble, "andthenhegrabbedmeandshookmeandhiseyeswere-allbloodshotand—"

The horses turned into Nahum's lane and I shook the memory away as Father guided the horses up to the barn door. Nahum was waiting and threw the doors open and we drove inside. He swung the doors shut and stood nervously around, wringing his hands as we climbed down, stiff from the cold ride over.

"William, William, thank God you've arrived!"

"Don't have a conniption fit, Nahum," Father said soothingly. "We're here. Now what's the problem?"

Nahum took a deep breath, trying to calm himself. His eyes were bright with anxiety and angry righteousness. "A couple of bounty hunters were in Homer yesterday—"

"There are always bounty hunters in Homer," Father said mildly. "Since when has that bothered you?"

Nahum sighed and wiped his hands across his eyes. He suddenly looked tired and old. His beard was a gray stubble against the soft flesh of his cheeks and jowls. His fingers trembled as he tugged at his lower lip. "I've had words with Hiram Jenkins. You know this, of course, William."

Father nodded. Everyone in the county had heard about how Jenkins had taken a shipment of grain from Nahum and then tried to short him on bushel measure. Nahum had a warrant served on Jenkins, who settled out of court to keep a black mark off his business. But people still found out about Jenkins and his business practices and began to take their business to a mild-mannered Quaker in Utica.

"All right, Nahum," Father said.

"It's just that I'm afraid—"

"Don't worry about it, Nahum," Father said. "We're here now. We might as well take them back with us. How many are there?"

Relief showed on Nahum's face. He sighed deeply and turned to limp to the back of the barn. He had a false room built in the back there by the corn crib. He had finished picking a couple of days before, and dry leaves hung like pieces of parchment between the slats. The door was hidden by bales of straw on a dead roller. He took a hay hook and tugged the bales aside. The door was still barely visible. He took the hook, placed it in a small hole, and turned it. The door swung open. A man and a woman looked out at us, silent, waiting, their black faces shiny with expectation. The man held a small girl on his lap. Her eyes were big with fright. The man wore a stained butternut shirt and canvas pants. The young girl was in a soiled blue-white checked dress. The woman wore a black dress. She was pretty; her negroid features softened her café au lait skin.

"It's all right," Nahum said soothingly. "These are the Hickoks. They will take you on to their place."

"Ah thought we'd stay heah for a couple of days," the man said suspiciously. He held the young girl away from us.

"Yes," Nahum said. "That was the plan. But something has come up. It will be safer to move you earlier than we thought."

The woman nodded and looked at the man. "You know we

have no choice. Now don't be pigheaded and let's go. Trust in God, Jethro. Trust in God." She smiled down at the little girl. "Now don't you worry, Sarah. Y'papa won' let nuthin' happen to you."

"A family?" Father asked.

"No, suh," the woman said. "This man is Jethro." She nodded at him. "His master sold his wife downriver. The girl was to go to Alabama. But—"

"Ain't no man got no right to break up a family," Jethro said angrily. "Jus' 'cause we niggers don' mean we ain't family."

"Yes," Father said. "And your wife?"

The man's face fell. Tears filled his eyes with hopelessness. "Ah hope she can join us. We tryin' to ge' to Chicago. Her sister lives there."

"Can you help Momma?" the little girl asked. Her eyes were as big as liquid brown pennies in her thin face.

"We'll try," Father said. He looked at the woman. "And you?"

"Ah'm Hannah," she said. She smiled, suddenly shy. "Ah came 'long to help." Her face clouded. "But it time Ah was leavin'." She looked at me and Lorenzo significantly. Then she looked back at Father. "But Ah don' think this is the time for that."

Father nodded. He turned to Nahum. "We'll trouble you for a couple of blankets, Nahum. And some straw to spread over them. I'll have Horace bring the blankets back in a couple of days."

"No need," Nahum said. "Clara's almost finished quilting new ones. Keep them. I think you'll have more than enough need for them before this is all over."

Father nodded. "Thank you," he said politely. He turned back to the Negroes. "Get ready."

"We's ready," Hannah said. The man nodded and picked up a flour sack in one huge hand. He rose, balancing the young girl on his hip, holding the flour sack in the other. Father glanced at Hannah. She smiled faintly and held her hands open. "All Ah have y' is seein'."

Father turned to Lorenzo. "Get a fork and spread some straw over the bottom of the wagon." He turned to me. "Go up to the house with Nahum and get some blankets to put over the straw and over our friends here. Then help Lorenzo cover them with more straw."

"Yes, Father," I said.

I slipped out of the barn with Nahum while Lorenzo began spreading straw over the bed of the wagon.

"Best to use the back door, I think," Nahum said lowly. I followed him as we made our way carefully through his garden. The pumpkins glowed like large orange balls in the cold white moonlight. I waited by the door while Nahum went inside the house to gather the blankets. I looked around uneasily, feeling the night pressing in hard upon me, shivering slightly against the cold. The door opened and Nahum handed an armful of blankets to me, then disappeared, returning with a small box filled with glass jars.

"Clara put up some jam," he said. He smiled half-apologetically. "We were planning on bringing it over, but"—he grimaced and looked down at his foot—"I've been feeling gimpy lately. You might as well take it with you now." I took the jam. I knew he was feeling awkward about putting us out this way and was trying to make up a little for calling us out on such a cold night. We always had at least a day's notice before a group of Negroes was brought to us even though they would usually be brought in the dead of night. We had never had to go and collect them before.

"It's all right, sir," I said politely. "We don't really mind. And thank you for the jam. Mother will appreciate your thoughtfulness."

He cleared his throat and looked away as he patted me clumsily upon my shoulder. "You're a good boy, James," he said gruffly.

I followed him back through the garden and to the barn. Lorenzo had spread the straw evenly over the bed of the wagon. I climbed into the wagon and spread the blankets around on the straw and climbed down. Jethro placed the young girl in the wagon, then helped Hannah into the bed.

They lay down and I covered them with the extra blankets while Lorenzo started pitching the straw over them to cover the blankets.

"That really won't keep anyone from looking in your wagon if they want to, William," Nahum said.

Father shrugged. "I guess we'll have to cross that stream when we come to it. I don't know what else to do on short notice."

Suddenly I remembered the pumpkins. "Father, I have an idea if Mr. Gould will go along with it."

They turned to look at me questioningly. "What is it, Jim?" Father asked.

I faced Nahum. "I couldn't help but notice that you have a good pumpkin crop," I said. Nahum frowned, nodding. "Well, I expect they're about ready for market." He nodded again, impatiently. "I reckon we could haul them there for you, if you like, couldn't we, Father? After all, we already got the straw bed prepared, so they won't bruise."

Father and Nahum stared at me; then Father laughed gently. "Why, yes. It would be the neighborly thing to do." He turned to Nahum. "In fact, we *will* take them on into Lowell or Homer for you, if you wish. That way, you would only have to make one trip yourself with your corn."

A light dawned in Nahum's eyes. His eyebrows rose and he looked at me respectfully. "You've got a good head on your shoulders, James." He nodded and said, "William, I don't expect you to take those pumpkins on in for nothing. I'll be willing to pay."

Father shook his head. "There'll come a time when I may need your help, Nahum. Let it ride until then."

"I don't like being obligated," Nahum began, but Father interrupted.

"This isn't the time to be debating, Nahum. Dawn's coming and it would be best if we were on the road by then."

Nahum opened his mouth to protest, then changed his mind. "Of course, of course, William. You are, as usual, right. All right. Pull around to the side and we'll load those pumpkins on top of the straw." His face began to gleam with excitement. He laughed and rubbed his hands together glee-fully. "I'd like to see Jenkins's face if this ever gets out."

"We'd better hope that it doesn't," Father said dryly. "We're still breaking the law." He coughed suddenly and grabbed the wagon side for support. He took a deep breath, forcing himself to be calm.

"Father—" I began, but he smiled wanly at me.

"I'm all right, Jim. You and Lorenzo pull the wagon around to the patch and begin loading those pumpkins. Gen-tly. Remember we have people beneath the load."

Hannah's muffled voice came from beneath the straw. "We 'preciate that, suh. They's 'nough load heah now."

I couldn't help but smile admiringly at her stoicism. I climbed into the wagon and took the reins, clucking gently to the horses as Lorenzo slid the doors open. I guided the team around to the side and reined in next to the garden. We loaded the pumpkins swiftly, piling them gently upon Han-nah and Jethro and his daughter, then carefully stacking the pumpkins along the sides to give an illusion of a full wagon.

"We'll meet you in town tomorrow afternoon, Nahum," Father said as he climbed onto the seat beside me. Lorenzo stepped carefully in over the tailgate and settled down in one corner. He huddled deep into his coat.

"I don't know why I always get the tail end," he complained.

"You'll be warmer there," I said. "At least you're out of the wind."

"Ah'll trade places if'n y'want to," Hannah said.

We laughed and Father took the reins, clucking to the team. We pulled out of Nahum's lane and turned back to-ward our farm. "All right," Father said softly. "We're on the road, now, so no more talking until we get home."

False dawn began to appear in the east with soft streaks of pink and purple. The breeze began to pick up as we neared Tomahawk Creek. I shivered as its frosty fingers felt their way down the collar of my coat. I glanced back at Lorenzo, muffled to his eyes with his coat, arms wrapped around him and hands tucked under his armpits as he huddled for warmth. I rubbed my nose upon the sleeve of my coat.

Father laughed softly. "I'll bet they're a lot warmer than we are despite being beneath those pumpkins," he said. He cocked an eyebrow as he regarded me. "Sometimes I think the good Lord is always working to help man out in his time of difficulty. Man just can't see the good for all the suffering around him. Now, you take Hannah and Jethro and Sarah back there." He raised his head, indicating the wagon bed. "God has seen to make them warm despite their misery."

But I was cold enough that I didn't want to see the lesson behind his words. "God didn't pitch that hay into the wagon, Father. And God sure didn't put them pumpkins over them to hide 'em."

" 'Those' pumpkins, Jim," he admonished gently. "A person who lets his words get away without care is one who will be hurt by them." He sighed. "And as for God—" He paused, leaning his head back to look at the tops of the trees as we moved slowly down the road. "It's all a matter of your point of view. If you think you are miserable, then you are and always will be. But if you look at the small things that God gives you for comfort, you might be surprised how happy you are. Jethro and Hannah and that little Sarah are forced to flee and to live in hidden places. But they are free," he said quietly and firmly. "And they are warm and fed and have each other. There are a lot of people in this world who are not."

"But—" I started to object, then fell silent as two men rode out of a small stand of willows, blocking the team.

Father reined in and straightened in his seat. He gathered the reins through the fingers of his left hand, straightening the back of the reins with his right, holding them beside him. The men were bearded and filthy. One of them rode up to Father's side of the wagon. "Morning. You appear to be out early." He glanced into the back of the wagon. He gestured at the pumpkins. "A good crop, it looks like."

"God's been good with his yield," Father said quietly, but I recognized the iron behind his words. I had heard it enough whenever I got into mischief. I half-turned to watch the other as he rode up to my side.

"What you looking at, boy?" he asked gruffly. His eyes were hard and gummy.

"Nothing," I said, meeting his stare.

"Something, I think," he said harshly.

"No," I answered recklessly. A thrill began singing its way through me. "Believe me. I'm looking at nothing."

A dull flush began to creep up from under his grimy collar as my taunt finally crept through the muddle in his mind.

"Be quiet, Jim," Father said.

"Better listen to your pa, boy," the leader said. "We don't need no lip from a weanling."

"Oh?" I raised my eyebrows. "Then who do you need it from?"

The leader stared hard at me, his lips thinning into a hard, straight line. "I think we should take a look in that wagon," he said. "It's too early, I'm thinking, for any farmer to be taking crops to town at this hour."

"Not when he has to make more than one trip and a full day ahead of him," Father said calmly.

"Uh-huh. And pigs might fly, but I gotta see one before I believe it," the leader said. He looked over our heads at the man who was trying to stare me down. "Get down, Clem, and make certain that's only straw under them punkins."

Clem started to swing down from his saddle, but Father suddenly whipped the slack reins across the face of the leader's horse. "Yaaah!" he yelled.

Instinctively I threw my arms up and shouted, and Clem's horse reared and lunged, away from me, sending Clem spinning head over heels into the ditch beside the road.

"Goddamnit!" he roared, and yelped with pain.

"Sumbitch!" the leader hollered as his horse began to buck and plunge.

Father slapped the rumps of our team with the reins. They lurched forward. He slackened the reins, slapping them again over the horses' backsides, and they lifted into a gallop.

"Stop! Stop! Goddamnit, I'm ordering you to stop!" the leader shouted, but Dad ignored him and leaned forward, urging the team into a faster gallop. I glanced back at Lorenzo, clinging white-faced to the sides of the wagon to keep from tumbling over the tailgate. An angry bee whizzed by; then I heard a sharp *pop!* and realized the man in the ditch was shooting at us.

"Get down!" Father said sharply. His arm hit me like an iron bar in the chest. I tumbled backward on top of the pumpkins. I heard Hannah yelp beneath me and the pumpkins as I sprawled over them.

Several shots sounded; then Father slid the wagon around a curve and rumbled over the wooden bridge. "Hold on!" he yelled. I raised my head, watching as he pulled hard on the reins, turning the team sharply into a small trace running through a grove of oaks along the side of the creek. The horses high-stepped awkwardly to keep from falling as they worked against the bits in their mouths, but Father straightened the team and wagon and pulled them to a halt behind a willow stand by the creek.

"Father!" I exclaimed, but he shushed me with a wave of his hand. I turned to look behind us as I heard horses galloping over the wooden planks of the bridge. But the men didn't turn into the small side road and galloped on toward Wedron, the sound of their passing slowly disappearing.

Father clucked to the team and guided them carefully through the oak grove until we caught the Utica road. Then he worked his way back to our farm, following the back roads and trails that only the farmers knew.

The sun stood halfway to noon by the time we turned into the lane leading up to the home place. Father drove around to the back of the house and reined in. The team stopped and hung their heads, their lathered sides heaving for breath. Father slumped suddenly in the seat, the reins going slack in his hands.

"Father!" I said, alarmed, and climbed back over the seat. I grabbed his shoulders, but he waved me away, his face white, drained.

"Get the others in the cellar," he said. "Be quick about it!"

The door opened and Mother stepped outside. Alarmed, she stepped forward to the side of the wagon to help Father down. He took her arm and stepped down. He stumbled and would have fallen had she not slipped her shoulder under his arm. He tried to smile.

"We have guests," he said faintly. "In the wagon. Under the pumpkins."

She took in the situation at a glance, then turned and called, "Horace! Oliver! Come quickly!"

My brothers appeared to her call, Oliver shoving a slice of bread into his mouth and chewing vigorously. She pointed at Lorenzo climbing stiffly out of the back of the wagon.

"Unload those pumpkins!" she commanded. I started toward the back of the wagon, but she stopped me, saying, "Jim, you leave them to that! Come and help me with your father."

"Yes, ma'am," I said. I stepped forward and took Father's other arm. Together Mother and I helped him into the house and to their bedroom. He fell heavily upon the mattress. The springs of the old iron bed squeaked in protest. Mother rolled him to his side and started to tug off his boots. She glanced up at me. Her ringlets hung over her angular face.

"All right, Jim," she said quietly. "I can take it from here. You help your brothers. How many did you bring back?"

"Three," I answered. "A man and his daughter and a woman."

Her eyebrows rose as she gave a hard tug and pulled one boot off. She dropped it on the floor and started tugging on his other boot. "The man and the woman aren't married?"

"No, ma'am," I said.

"Uh-huh," she grunted as she gave a hard yank on Father's foot. "I guess you'd better put the man in the cellar and the woman and the young girl in Oliver's room up in the attic. He can move in with you and Lorenzo for a while."

"I don't think the girl will want to be separated from her father," I said. Mother eyed me appraisingly. I shook my head and continued. "She seems to cling to him. Her mother was sold down the river and I think she's afraid of losing her father, too, now."

"What do you suggest?"

"I'd say put the father and the girl together in the cellar. It's warm and dry down there and it won't be long before we move them over to Panton's Mills. A day or two at the most."

"That soon?" I nodded. She frowned. "All right. What happened?"

I grinned and shook my head. "You know, don't you? Nahum said that he's afraid that Hiram Jenkins may have associated him with the Underground. If Nahum's right, it won't take much for someone to connect Dad and us with it, too. Everybody knows Father's a deacon close to Nahum's church." I shrugged. "I think we'd better act as if we know somebody knows about us."

Mother gave a tiny smile. "You're thinking now, Jim. Good. Put the man and the little girl in the cellar together. But be certain there's plenty of blankets and a couple of lanterns down there. Little girls are easily afraid of the dark. Put the woman—what's her name?"

"Hannah," I replied.

"Hannah, then, in Oliver's room up in the attic. Tell Oliver to go over to Panton's Mills and tell Mr. Panton that he needs to stay over there and pretend that he's working for him. That'll free up a room. Mr. Panton will go along with that. Besides," she added dryly, "he'll have a bit of free labor."

"Yes, ma'am," I said.

"We'll say that we took Hannah on to help me take care of your father," she said. She glanced at Father lying half-awake on the bed. "May be that I'll need her, too," she muttered half to herself. "If anyone asks, we'll say that your grandfather sent her out here."

And so Hannah became a part of the family. She stayed with us long after the others left and when still others came through to stay a few nights with us. When I came down with a sore throat and my tonsils swelled to the size of hazelnuts (*"Lord, child! Ah don't see how y'can breathe!"*) she brought honeyed tea to me and played checkers when I tired of reading Washington Irving's *The Sketch Book of Geoffrey*

Crayon, Gent. Sometimes she would sing the simple songs that I could saw out of my fiddle. Sometimes she would just sit quietly with me. And I would know that she was there and that was enough.

CHAPTER

9

"JIM! TIME to get up!"

Mother's voice came strongly through the door to our bedroom. I pulled myself up from a nightmare and glanced over at Lorenzo, but his bed was empty. I frowned and rolled my head to look out the window at pale sunlight shining brightly through the muslin curtains. How had I slept so late? My bed felt hot. My face was damp. I felt slimy and cold. I swung my legs over the side of the bed and sat up. I felt dizzy. I reached down and got my stockings. I pulled them on. They felt rough on my feet. A bead of sweat rolled down my nose. My mouth was dry.

"Mother!" I called. My voice sounded like a crow cawing. "Mother!"

But it was Hannah who opened the door and came in.

"What's the matter wit' y', boy?" she said. She put her hand on my forehead. It felt cool and I grabbed it and held it. "Here!" she said. "'Nough of that!" She tried to pull it away, but I wouldn't let it go. Then I felt her cool cheek against mine. She smelled faintly of cinnamon. I saw the side of a brown breast between buttons on her blouse. I didn't care.

"Boy, y'burnin' up! Y'get back into bed!"

"Gotta—" I mumbled. She pushed me by the shoulders. I fell back against my pillow. The room moved around and around. I gagged and tried to vomit. But couldn't. I had nothing to throw up. I felt her fingers pressing around my neck. It hurt.

"Mizzus Hickok!" she called. "Y'better come! Jim's ailing!"

Beside Hannah, Mother appeared wiping her hands on a towel. She touched my forehead. Her fingers were dry like paper. She frowned. "Your throat hurt?" I nodded. She looked at Hannah. "You stay with him. I'll get Horace to ride into town for the doctor." She handed the towel to Hannah and left.

Hannah sat down on the edge of my bed. She used the towel to wipe the sweat from my face. "Y'just lay there now and everything will be all right."

"I'm dying," I mumbled miserably.

"No, Ah don' think so," she said. But I knew she was worried. She always got that syrupy sound to her words when she was worried.

I closed my eyes and saw black shadows dancing between dead trees.

I felt another hand on my forehead. I opened my eyes and stared into Doc Simpson's eyes. I saw a huge wart beside his nose. Two black hairs grew out of it. He smelled like medicine. Like hoarhound drops and castor oil. Peppermint. All mixed together.

"Scarlet fever," he said. He craned his head around to talk over his shoulder. "There's a lot of that going around now. There isn't much we can do for it. Just have to let it run its course. Keep him covered and make him drink lots of water with a little peppermint and carbonized petroleum jelly in it."

He rose and looked down at me. He shook his head and

sighed. "We lost the Adams baby over at Homer to it just yesterday."

Mother made that *tch-tch* sound with her tongue. "So sad. Harriet and Harvey must be taking it badly. I'll send a pie over."

"No other way to take it," Doc Simpson said. He sighed again. "Just wish I knew what all we could do for it." He patted me on the head. It hurt. "You take it easy, James."

He left with Mother. Hannah came over and looked down at me. "Scarlet fever. Keep y'warm and y'burning up and all. Humph! Keep y'cool to brings yer temp-er-achur down, that what needed! A touch of belladonna and some calomel and aconite, I think. Mix it with a little bacon rind. That what y'need." She bent and kissed my forehead and gently patted my cheek. "Y'jus' lay there an' leave ev'r'thing to me."

She left and I looked out the window. Cold sunlight. In the books no one died when the sun was shining. But I knew that wasn't right. You could die just the same if the sun was shining or not. I closed my eyes and imagined my friends at my funeral. Yellow candles on the altar. My coffin. And Hannah singing.

> *"Amazin' grace! How sweet the sound*
> *That saved a wretch like me!"*

Pretty and sad. I shivered. I wanted to cry, but I didn't want anyone to come in and see me crying. I liked that song, though. The words were pretty and sad. And that made me cry. The pretty and sad words.

"Here." I opened my eyes. Hannah stood beside my bed. "Sit up." She put her arm under my shoulders and lifted. I sat up and leaned my head against her soft breast. It felt better than my pillow and I wished she would lie down with me and let me lay my head there and sleep there. I tried to tell her that, but she laughed and said, "Y'too young for that. Here. Take this." She shoved a spoon in my mouth. It tasted terrible.

"Yuck," I said. I tried to spit, but my mouth was too dry.

"Drink this, now," she said. She put a cup to my lips and I

drank, tasting beef broth. It felt warm and good as it slid down my throat. She put the cup on the floor and leaned me over. She tugged at my nightshirt. "Let me get this off y'all."

"I'll be naked!" I croaked. I wrapped my arms around myself to keep her from pulling it off. She laughed.

"Y'all ain't got nothing Ah ain't seen before," she scolded. "But we gots to rub this lotion on y'rashes and get a clean nightshirt on. This one's done soaked wet."

And I let her pull it off me. I shivered as she spread lotion over my back and under my arms and across my neck. She pushed me back on the bed and spread lotion over my chest and stomach. I felt myself moving when she spread the lotion in my groin.

"Y'all ain't that sick y'can do that!" she said. She laughed again. Deep. Like a man would laugh.

"Hannah," I said, embarrassed.

"Don't worry," she whispered. "Ah won't tell. Now, sit up again so's we can get this clean nightshirt on y'all."

It felt cool and clean on me, and when she left I closed my eyes and thought about my friends at school doing their sums and stuff and wished I was there instead of laying in my bed. The light was soft in the window. But it was nice. And then the darkness came again upon me in long, rolling waves. I heard the mumble of people's voices riding on the waves. I saw a small boat sailing toward me, rocking over the waves. Two people were in it. One was a woman with curling coppery-red hair and sparkling green eyes. The other was a short man with a great hooked nose. His eyes burned. They scared me.

> *"Sing, little sparrow, let me hear*
> *Your song now for all the year"*

I opened my eyes. The curtains had been drawn back and gold sunlight poured in upon the puncheon floor. Hannah sat in a spindly-backed rocker. She stared out the window, singing. I felt cool. I smelled lavender and lemon verbena, and the sheets beneath me were fresh.

"Hannah," I said. My voice sounded normal. She turned her head and smiled. She rose and came to me, laying her hand across my forehead. It felt warm.

"Well, y'feelin' better," she said.

"I'm thirsty," I said.

"Uh-huh. Ah just bet y'are." She walked to the window and took a glass off the sill. She came back and helped me up. She held the glass to my lips. I drank thirstily. I lay back down. I felt hungry. I told her so. She beamed at me.

"That's good. Ah'll get y'some soup." She turned to go and I stopped her.

"Hannah." She looked back at me over my shoulder. "I love you."

She smiled. "Ah knows y'do, young Jim. Ah knows y'do."

CHAPTER

10

A GREAT fire, banked high and flickering, rose and fell on the wall. The smell of fresh bread was heavy in the room, and beneath it I could smell the cinnamon of fresh apple pie. Father sat in the slat-backed rocker in front of the fire. He looked thin and pale, his beard a gray shadow over his gaunt cheeks. He held his Bible in his hands. His fingers looked pale and translucent and I imagined I could see the bones under them as he slowly turned the pages, reading passages at random. Mother moved quietly in the kitchen. My sisters played with rag dolls on the braided rug in front of the fire. I sat on the deacon's bench with Lorenzo, listening to Father read in a reedy voice.

" 'For rebellion is as the sin of witchcraft, and stubbornness is as iniquity and idolatry—' " He paused and stared into the flames. His eyes looked vacant for a moment; then he seemed to bring memory back as he looked over at Lorenzo and me. He tried to smile, but the smile looked terrible. The slack flesh of his jaws hung down. "That doesn't mean that you owe blind obedience to another, boys." He was upset by what Reverend Cowley had preached at Christmas services, a stern warning to those rumored to be helping slaves escape from their legal masters.

"The law," he had intoned, his eyes burning righteously out at his congregation, "is the law. If one transgresses against it, then one is defying authority. That cannot be. Man must have order in his life or he is nothing more than an animal, lurking around in the dark woods! God warns us to be obedient or we shall suffer the lion out of the forest and the wolf of the evenings and a leopard will come among us and tear us to pieces, because man's transgressions are many and his backslidings have grown to abominations. Destruction upon destruction will come down upon us and the whole land will become spoiled. The trumpets of the Armageddon will sound and the light of heaven will no longer shine upon the plains. The Lord says that the land shall become desolate and every city will be forsaken!"

Father shook his head. "No, boys, Reverend Cowley was wrong. When something is wrong, you must not blindly follow it. You must remember what is right and believe in yourself. Can you do anything less than Jesus?"

I glanced at Lorenzo and frowned. He caught my look and shook his head slightly as if to warn me not to question Father at the moment. I didn't need his warning. Father had been slipping in and out of the present for the past couple of weeks. A lump came into my throat. I hated to see his mind wandering around in dark places where none of us could go. I wished Oliver was there to help us, but he had left home and gone to California along with others, looking for gold. Horace and Lorenzo had taken over the running of the farm, doing the chores, while I spent my time in the woods and fields, hunting meat for our table. Horace resented this but had to acknowledge that I was the better shot and since powder and ball was expensive, it was sound practice to leave that to me.

I had traded squirrel and raccoon skins from animals I had caught with a couple of double-springed No. 4 English Rattraps for an old flintlock pistol three years before and discovered that I could hit about anything I aimed at. From that it was a practical step to Father's rifle and shotgun. I began wandering the hills, hunting squirrels, rabbits, and prairie chickens and, at least once every two weeks, a deer that I hung in the smokehouse behind the barn. Mother and Father were not pleased—Father most of all, as he wanted me to study for the law, and Mother because she wanted me to be a preacher—but we needed meat for the table. I learned what I could from *The Trapper's Guide* and *The Life of Kit Carson*, reading at night in my attic room after the others had gone to bed. I traded the furs and Father's rifle at the Green Mountain House for a better one and a cap-and-ball revolving pistol and practiced as much as I could.

"You must remember that, boys," Father said, and I brought myself back to the present, listening to him as he warned us about the evils of slavery. His eyes looked fever-bright in the firelight. "Do not sacrifice your beliefs because another tells you that the law forbids you to have them. Man makes laws, but God gave you good sense to figure out if the law is just or not."

Then his eyes glazed again and he frowned, groping for the thought he knew he had. I let my mind wander again as he bent his head and began to awkwardly rifle the pages of his Bible, searching for a passage to help him remember. The winter had been harsh and wolves had moved in from the hills and deep woods. Nahum had lost a milch cow and a new calf to them and other farmers had complained about losing stock as well.

"William, William. We need your boy James," Nahum said after church while we huddled in the cold on the wagon, waiting for Father to climb in and drive us back home. Nahum glanced up at me. He sighed, his breath coming out in a frosty cloud. He clapped his gloved hands together. "I'm sorry, William, but your boy is the best shooter in these parts and these wolves have gotten out of hand. Mrs. Wilson lost five of her best layers just last night."

"James has school, Nahum," Father said mildly.

"William, William," he said, shaking his head. "I

wouldn't ask, but we"—he paused to indicate a small group of silent, somber-faced men dressed in black who had gathered around them—"we can't afford to lose any more stock. Times are hard, William. Sometimes, we just have to do things we don't want to."

"No," Father said. "I won't compromise James's schooling. Once you leave school, Nahum, it's twice as hard going back to it."

I knew what he was talking about. He had lectured all of us many times on the need for us to take responsibility for our own actions. But, he had emphasized, we also had to remember that some things took a great amount of self-discipline and the moment we relaxed that discipline, we would find it twice as hard getting back into the swing of things.

"The devil just watches for such moments, boys," he'd said. "Then he pounces upon you. The minute you relax your discipline, you'll find it almost impossible to get your nose back on the grindstone. That's why we have so many ne'er-do-wells along the road today. They never got the gumption back to make something of themselves after they slipped away from self-discipline." Father had been reading Mr. Emerson's essays with great relish.

Nahum eyed him steadily for a moment, then shook his head. "William, I don't know any other way of putting it. There isn't one of us here who wouldn't do it if we could. But the pure fact is that we can't. We have to stay back and protect what we have. But we can't keep an eye on everything all the time. We need James. We *need* him, William. He can carry the fight to the wolves, track them, get rid of them while we guard our stock. Can't you see that that is the only possible solution? Can *you* afford to lose any stock, William?"

A low grumble came from the others around Father. He turned his head and studied the others; then his shoulders slumped. "All right," he said. "I'll give James a week." He raised his head and fixed me with his piercing blue-gray eyes. "But *only* a week, understand?" He was speaking to the others, but I knew that he meant me.

I nodded. "Yes, Father. I'll do it for a week. Then I'll go back to school." I looked down at Nahum. "I'll start tomorrow, sir. But today is Christmas. I'm spending that with my family."

Relief spread over Nahum's face. He nodded vigorously. "Yes, that will be all right. Certainly, James, we don't want to take you from your family. By all means."

Father climbed into the wagon and looked down, studying the men. "All well and good, gentlemen. But there are costs to this, as well." A cautionary look came into the eyes of all. "There's powder and shot to be considered. And James should be rewarded for his time."

"There's the bounty," Nahum began, but Father cut him off.

"That's to be understood, Nahum," he said sternly, and all there knew that there would be no arguing with Father on this matter. "But his powder and shot are operating expenses you can't expect James or his family to bear."

"William, William. You will benefit just as much as the rest of us," Nahum said, frowning.

"Yes, that's true," Father said. He gathered the reins. "But I have no intention of bearing all the expense. We shall split it among all of us. *All* of us," he added, staring hard at Beaufoy, who was known for his stinginess. Beaufoy looked away, then back at Father, and finally nodded.

"I'll pay the first foray," George McLaughlin said, stepping forward. He looked up at me. "You swing by the farm tomorrow, James. I'll give you a horn and some shot to get you started."

My heart leaped as I glanced over his head to where Sarah and Josephine sat, waiting in the wagon. Sarah looked away from me, her cheeks reddening, but Josephine smiled and a devilish look came into her eyes. "Thank you, sir," I said, looking back to him. He nodded.

"That's good of you, George," Father said. He glanced at the others. "I think that's the way to do it. When James needs more powder and shot, he'll go to the next one on the list. In alphabetical order. That's only fair, I think."

The others nodded grudgingly, but Beaufoy spoke up, saying, "Is that *after* McLaughlin?"

A look of quiet disgust came over Father's face. He lifted his chin. "No, we'll start with the beginning of the alphabet, I think. You'll be after Adams, Beaufoy."

"That don't seem right," Beaufoy complained. "I mean, Nashe should rightfully come after McLaughlin. Seems to me, anyway."

"You objecting to the terms, Beaufoy?" Nahum asked dangerously.

Beaufoy took a quick look around at the grim faces of his neighbors and sensed them pulling away from him. He shook his head. "No, no. That ain't what I'm saying. It's just that—no, nothing. All right." He looked up at me and said sourly, "You come by my place next, Jim." But I could see the angry glare in his eyes and made a mental note to watch myself when I went around to his farm. I didn't know what it was, but I sensed something not right with him.

"Yes, sir," I said.

Father nodded curtly, flicked the reins over the backs of our horses, and pulled away from church, heading home. A strange exhilaration swept through me as I contemplated the brief vacation I would have away from school. It was a boy's dream! Freedom to wander through the woods and fields, hunting. Father glanced at me and shook his head slightly. Immediately I wiped the smile off my face, but he had seen my pleasure at being given permission to be truant from school.

"Priorities, James," he said softly. "Always remember your priorities. All other things are momentary and temporal. Joy is fleeting. It comes to us only in brief spurts." He coughed, a hard, wracking cough that wrenched his back into a crooked question mark. "And then," he managed in a strangled voice, "you are left with reality. With life." A bitter smile flashed across his lips and then disappeared. But in that smile I read the future. And it was black and grim.

CHAPTER

11

A GREAT fire, banked high and red, flamed in the fireplace, but dinner was not yet on the table. Mother bustled around in the kitchen with Hannah, both stepping nimbly over and around my sisters, who played at helping them prepare Christmas dinner. The cooking smells wafted into the room where we sat before the fire, I on a small stool beside the hearth while Oliver and Horace and Lorenzo lounged around on the floor. Father sat in his slat-backed rocker, his feet resting on the toasted boss.

"You will be careful tomorrow, James," Father said suddenly, sternly, startling me. I looked over at him and nodded.

"Yes, Father," I said. "I'll be careful."

He cleared his throat, started to speak, then sighed and shook his head. "I don't know what to tell you, James, other than to be very careful. Wolves aren't like other animals. They're like people. Crafty, and you don't know what they will do until they do it. But if you always expect the worst, then you'll be ready for anything that happens." He grinned wryly. "Not a very good endorsement for man, though, is it?

Still, one has to wonder what man has become over the years, and I suppose this is as good a time of the year to do it as any other. I don't see much where man has really progressed. There is a lot of hatred out there, boys. A lot of hatred. You'll have to work with it the best that you can."

"Mizzus Hickok sent me in with some hot cider for y'gentlemens," Hannah said, coming into the room with a tray filled with cups of steaming cider. She passed among us, bending forward to let us select our own. She smiled at me and I smelled baking upon her. My head swam suddenly and I stammered out a "thank you" as I lifted a cup from the tray, cradling it in my hands that suddenly felt big and awkward.

"Thank you, Hannah," Father said. He sipped and nodded appreciatively. "This is very good. Just the right touch of cinnamon and clove."

"Little brown sugar does it good, too, Ah think," Hannah said. She nodded at us. "Dinner'll be ready in a few more minutes. Soon's we get the fixin's ready."

She left and Father leaned back in his rocker, resting his cup upon the arm of the chair. "I think that was a propitious delivery, boys," he said. "This is not the time of year to be talking about the frailties of man. James, would you hand down my Bible for me? I think it is time that we remember what this time of year is about."

I rose and took his Bible from its resting place on the mantel and handed it to him. He took another swallow of the cider and placed the cup on the small table at his elbow. He took his glasses from the table and slipped them on, placing the wire hooks carefully over his ears. Then, he slowly, lovingly, opened the Bible and began to read.

" 'There was in the days of Herod, the king of Judaea, a certain priest named Zacharias . . . ' " and I let my mind slip away from his words, sipping my cider as I thought of the morrow and where I would start my hunt—at the McLaughlin pasture where wolves had brought down a mother that had tried to defend her newborn calf.

Then Mother came in with Hannah, both bearing the Christmas dinner, and I watched as Father rose painfully from his chair and crossed to his place at the head of the table. We all crowded around at our usual spots with Hannah sitting on my left. She had a small puff of powder clinging to her dress just above her breast. She caught me looking and smiled at me and my stomach gave a kind of lurch as it did when I swung out from a hanging rope over a deep hole in Tomahawk Creek just as I let go.

"Now," Father said, and I took Hannah's hand in mine and Lydia's small hand in the other as we formed our circle around the evening table. Father cleared his throat and closed his eyes, raising his face to the ceiling. I knew he was looking beyond the ceiling to the heavens and imagining God on his throne. I knew it, but I pushed the thought aside for the moment, concentrating on the plump turkey, trussed and skewered, its skin a basted golden-brown. I had collected that turkey within an hour of taking my stand in the woods above the tiny salt lick above Tomahawk Creek where I had prudently scattered a couple of handfuls of corn every day for a month.

"Bless us, O Lord, and these thy gifts which through thy bounty we are about to receive through Christ our Lord. God grant us peace; God grant us wisdom; God grant us patience that we might do thy work as we walk through thy world. Give us the strength to avenge the persecuted and—"

Why did Mr. Beaufoy refer to his tallywhacker as a turkey?

"—lead us not into temptation. Amen."

We all "amened" after him and pulled out our chairs, sitting. For a few minutes we busied ourselves, passing our plates up to Father, who carefully carved the turkey, filling them with whatever was in front of us as we passed them back down to their temporary owners. Then we ate, being careful to chew our food and not gulp it lest we draw a stern rebuke from Mother about the healthful need to chew each bite twenty times before swallowing.

Once, Lorenzo asked if that included water and was given the chore of washing and drying everything on the dining table to familiarize him with the peculiar attributes of water and why his question was a sarcastic rejoinder and not a serious one despite his protests after the penance was pronounced.

"Father?" Lorenzo said. Father looked up, fastidiously wiping his mouth on a napkin. "Do you think I could go along with James? I mean, he might need someone to watch his back in case another devil of a turkey creeps up on him." He smirked at me. I shook my head.

"A tree'll do that job just as good as you, I reckon," I answered. Lorenzo laughed.

"Well, James, I don't know. Seems to me I remember—"

"I would think you all would do better if you focused on what this day is all about," Father said quietly, but with enough authority in his voice that we knew better than to push the issue. Whenever Father didn't get enough time to complete his Bible thought for the day, he would stubbornly hold it in his mind until he had exorcised it, even if it took the daylight hours to finish it.

"William," Mother said politely. "It's Christmas. I think the boys are all old enough to know the day without being reminded of it."

"It's only one day out of the year, Polly," Father said patiently. "And I don't think it hurts them one bit to recall purpose over pleasure. The Lord is patient, my dear, but patience is not endless."

We glanced at one another, trying to recall the reason for Father's words. Horace shook his head slightly and I sighed and glanced at Hannah out of the corners of my eyes. She caught my look and smiled again. I felt my face grow warm and took a large bite of sweet potatoes. Too large. I started coughing and grabbed my water glass to wash the bite down.

"Moderation, James!" Father snapped. "How many times have we told you—"

"Sorry, Father," I managed between coughs. "Wrong pipe. That's all."

"The wrong pipe comes from the lack of attention. I hope

that you pay closer attention tomorrow when you are alone out there."

Lorenzo cleared his throat. "Uh, Father, about that—"

"I think James will be able to handle the problem quite well on his own," Father said quietly. "Besides, I'm not about to lose two sons to this adventure. You have school, Lorenzo."

"Not for two more days!" Lorenzo objected.

"And that time can best be put to studying after you finish your chores," Father said firmly. "That is enough about all of this. Now, who can tell me the parable about the Prodigal Son? Horace?"

CHAPTER

12

THE DAY came up cold and gray, with swollen clouds hanging low over the grove. The dampness of the day clung to me as I moved into the trees, following the frozen path of the wolves. Behind me, the crows cawed urgently as they came back to the feast of a doe they'd pulled down after I had frightened them away with my approach. I noticed that a fresh track had been added to the old ones. One wolf had come back for a couple of feedings. I moved cautiously through the trees, making my way slowly through the brush to minimize the scratching of branches against my canvas trousers and coat. I held my Hall-North percussion rifle at port with a gloved hand while my right hand I kept naked against the time when I might need it urgently.

Halfway through the grove, a prickling sensation began on the back of my neck. I eased across a clearing and placed my back against a tree, carefully searching the underbrush for the reason for my unease. I frowned, listening to the deep silence. *Deep silence! Where were the squirrels? The jays? Sparrows?*

I stared all around the shadowy order of the clearing, moving my thoughts in time with my eyes. For a brief moment I felt panic as a shadow moved; then I relaxed as it came stationary again and I could see it was only a small bush. Fat flakes of snow began to fall, but I remained where I was, shifting my weight slightly, working my toes beneath their two layers of socks in my boots, willing the cold outside my body.

And then I smelled the wolf, a musty, deep smell that seemed to gather at the back of my throat. I swallowed and tasted the smell and knew he was close and that he was watching me, waiting, waiting—

I straightened and dropped my arm holding the rifle, half-turning to the clearing to make it look like I didn't know he was there. Still he didn't show himself. My hand moved along the barrel of my rifle. It was icy cold. A strange melancholy settled over me as if I was half-awakened from a dream and didn't know the passing of time. I shivered. Then, somehow, I knew he was coming. I took a deep, quick breath and turned, bringing the rifle up to my shoulder as I did so. The wolf was halfway across the clearing when I came around. He growled low in his throat at my sudden move and tried to turn, but the force of his rush was against him. I brought the bead of my rifle down upon his chest. He half-turned, giving me his shoulder, and I squeezed the trigger. I didn't hear the sound of the shot behind the rush of blood pounding in my head, but I felt the thump of the rifle as it recoiled against my shoulder. The ball took the wolf in the shoulder, knocking him over. He yelped and his paws scrambled in the snow, trying to push him erect. His head twisted and he snapped at his shoulder where the bullet had taken him. Then his eyes glazed and he stretched out slowly, his paws digging at the snow in the last panic of life. I took a deep breath and leaned back against the tree. My head felt suddenly clear and I became aware of the fine outlines of the trees, the twigs on the undergrowth, the dead leaves that had yet to fall from their twigs.

I waited until his legs stretched out stiff, then slowly approached and nudged him with the toe of my boot. Suddenly I remembered that my rifle was empty and I hastened back to the tree and placed my back to it as I reloaded the Hall-North. I had to try twice to place the percussion cap on the nipple, but at last I finished. Again I approached the wolf and nudged him. A wave of disappointment came over me along with deep regret and, strangely, a small sense of exhilaration. I took a deep breath, smelling the harsh bite of the wolf's blood. I dragged the carcass of the wolf close to the tree. I leaned my rifle against the tree, close to hand, then took out my skinning knife and squatted over the wolf.

Heavy snow had begun to fall before I was finished, and I could feel the cold working its fingers deep under my coat. My toes were numb and my hands mottled blue. I rolled up the wolf's coat and scrubbed my hands as clean as I could with the snow, then took a pair of gloves from the deep pockets of my coat and pulled them on. I rose, stamping my feet until they began to tingle, then gathered the wolf's coat and my rifle and began to make my way back home. The woods had become dark and deep as I emerged from their depths and forced my way through the gathering drifts across the home pasture. By the time I stumbled into our front yard, I could barely see the outline of our house through the blowing snow.

I stepped up onto the porch and dropped the wolf pelt onto an old hide-bottomed chair, then tried to open the door, but my hands wouldn't turn the knob. I knocked on the door with the butt of my rifle. The cold had found me beneath my coat by now. I felt chilled to the bone. I knocked again, swinging the rifle butt hard against the door. Suddenly it opened and heat rushed out, nearly staggering me. Hannah stared at me as if Harpe's ghost had suddenly appeared in front of her.

"Why, James!" she exclaimed. "What in the world?" She stepped forward, taking my rifle from me. "Y'look frozen half to death! Y'get in heah! Come on now!"

I stumbled and nearly fell over the threshold. My feet felt like two lumps of ice. I took a deep breath and winced as hot air rushed into my lungs.

"Where . . . Where's Mother? The others?" I managed. I tried to unbutton my coat, but my fingers couldn't feel the buttons and I couldn't push them through the buttonholes of my coat. Hannah pushed my hands away and quickly unbuttoned my coat, hanging it on a hook beside the door. She pushed me toward the fireplace. I stumbled over the rug and would have fallen had she not grabbed me by my arm and held me up.

"Y'daddy took a turn to the wuss shortly after y'left for the woods," she said. Her finely arched eyebrows pinched together in a frown. "Y'brother Horace was goin' to ride foah the doctor, but y'mama thought it better if they jus' hitched up the team and took y'daddy into town. Save time that way. She right, of course; by the time Horace rode in and back agin, why, they-all would have been in town an hour at least. Ah don' know what to tell yuh. But Ah don' think they'll be back tonight." She glanced out the window where the thick flakes had turned to hard snow rattling against the panes. The wind began to moan around the eaves. "Ah think they'll stay over at the Green Mountain House. If not there, then somewhere in Homer."

My teeth began to chatter.

"An' heah y'is freezin' in them wet clothes! Tch. Tch." She clucked her tongue in disapproval. "Y'get out'n those wet clothes right now while I gets y'a blanket to wrap in!" She bustled into Mother and Father's room and came back with a bolster while I was still trying to work the buttons on my shirt.

"Heah," she said impatiently, brushing my hands away. She ignored my protests and within seconds had my butternut shirt unbuttoned and was pulling it off my shoulders. She wrapped the blanket around me. "Now, y'slip outta them pants. Whilst Ah gets y'a hot drink! Men!" she snorted derogatorily as she headed with my wet shirt to the kitchen. "Not one-a them's got the sense the good Lord give a jackrabbit!"

I slipped out of my pants and wrapped the blanket around me and pushed a small stool in front of the hearth and dropped thankfully on it. Slowly, I began to thaw, but the wind whistling around the eaves made me huddle deeper into the blanket. Hannah appeared with a cup of hot tea. She shoved it into my hands, commanding me to drink. I sipped, tasting peppermint and honey. I drank deeper.

"Good. That's good," she said with satisfaction. "Warm yer insides up and y'won't catch pee-no-mea." She disappeared back in the kitchen and reappeared with a small jar of Balm of Gilead ointment. She opened the jar and the odor of wintergreen spread in the room. "Open that blanket so's Ah kin rub this on y'chest an' back," she ordered.

"It's cold," I complained, teeth chattering.

"James Butler Hickok, y'do as Ah say!" she commanded sternly. Her black eyes held that no-nonsense look.

Automatically I opened the blanket. Her fingers swiped a generous amount of the ointment on her fingertips and rubbed it on my shoulders and back, moving in small circles as she worked cold knots out of my muscles. Her hands slipped over my shoulders and down onto my chest, rubbing. Slowly, my muscles began to relax as the warmth from the ointment and the fire worked their magic. My eyelids began to droop.

"There!" she exclaimed with satisfaction. She stepped away from me. "Now y'get y'self inta bed. Go on now, y'hear?"

Obediently I rose and stumbled toward the stairs. I nearly fell and again she caught me. "Now y'stop this nonsense, y'hear, James? Y'gets y'self up to bed!"

"Yes, ma'am," I said sleepily. I didn't remember ever feeling that tired. I forced my feet up the stairs and fell onto my bed. Dimly I was aware of Hannah covering me with blankets. Then I slept.

CHAPTER

13

GRAY DAYLIGHT shone through the muslin curtains Mother had hung over the small attic window when I awoke. Wind still moaned around the eaves and the rafters creaked and popped overhead. I took a deep breath, smelling the faint odor of wintergreen and balsam from the ointment that Hannah had rubbed on my chest. I sighed and stretched beneath the blankets piled on top of me, squirreling deeper into the warm nest I had made while I slept. I felt drowsy and content.

The stairs creaked and I turned my head to watch Hannah peek over the top. She saw me awake and smiled, coming the rest of the way up. She came across and put her hand on my forehead, feeling for a fever. She nodded, satisfied.

"How y'feel this mornin'?" she asked.

"Fine," I said. "Is it still snowing?"

She nodded. "Yes, and it don' look like it gonna let up for another day. Maybe two."

"I wonder how Father is," I said, frowning.

She hesitated, then shook her head slowly. "Ah don' know,

but—" She shrugged. "It only a mattah of time, James. But Ah think y'know that, don' yuh?"

I sighed, feeling a lump beginning to form in my throat. "Yes, I know it. It's just that not knowing is worse than knowing."

She nodded. "Ah knows. But we kin only wait. Nothin' more kin be done. 'Cept take care of what's heah. Now, if'n y'feel up to it, the cow needs to be milked and fed and other chores needin' to be done. Ah kin gather the eggs—"

"No," I said, interrupting her. "There's only need for one of us to go outside. That should be me. Some hay'll need to be pitched down and I reckon I'd better muck out a couple of stalls."

"Y'dress warmly, heah?" she said.

"The work'll keep me warm," I said. Without thinking, I threw back the covers and sat up before I realized I was naked. Hannah took a step backward, then turned her face away. Her face grew darker. I blushed and grabbed my blankets, covering myself. "Sorry, Hannah," I said.

She made a shoo-shoo gesture with her hands and turned back to the stairs. "Ain't seen nothing Ah ain't seen befoah," she said. "Ah'll get y'breakfast ready while y'dress."

Hannah had eggs and bacon on a plate waiting for me by the time I got dressed and made my way down from the attic. I was ravenous and wolfed everything down, wiping the last of the egg yolk and grease from my plate with a piece of fresh-baked bread. Hannah nodded approvingly as I pushed back from the table, well sated.

"Y'did a fair amount of damage to that," she said, clearing my plate from in front of me.

"It was great, Hannah. Thank you," I said. I glanced out the window and sighed reluctantly. "Well, that cow isn't going to get milked or the stalls cleaned with me sitting here."

I rose and crossed to where my coat hung on a peg beside the door. I shrugged into it, buttoning it tightly against my chin. I wrapped a scarf around my face and pulled the flaps of my hat down over my ears. I pulled a pair of leather gloves out of the pocket of my coat and opened the door, gasping as the wind struck me hard. I stepped outside and quickly shut the door behind me. I could barely see the barn through the swirling snow. I lowered my head and forced my way through the deep drifts.

I reached the barn and had to kick snow away before I could open the door. I hurried inside and pulled the door behind me. The barn was cold and dim, but I could see Jenny, our cow, waiting in her stall. She heard me and lowed, telling me she wanted to be milked. I glanced at the other stalls and saw that Horace or Lorenzo had already mucked them out and spread clean hay. I silently thanked my brother as I took a stool and pail and made my way to Jenny's stall.

"There now, old girl," I said soothingly as I slid into the stall beside her. "I'll bet you're glad to see me."

She lowed again and I laughed and sat beside her and began pulling on her teats. The milk came in a long, hissing rush and I leaned my forehead against Jenny's warm flank as I settled into milking motion. When I finished, I threw some hay for her, shoveled out the manure from her stall, and gave her a small bait of corn in celebration.

"There, old girl," I said, patting her rump. "I'll see you around supper time, all right?"

She grunted and lowered her head, methodically working her cud. I laughed again and picked up the bucket of milk and walked to the door. I braced myself and swung the door open just enough for me to slip out. Again the wind seemed to take my breath away. I shut the door hurriedly behind me and pushed my way again through the drifts back to the house. I went around to the kitchen door and opened the door, stepping inside, pulling the door shut hard behind me to make it latch.

"Oh!" Hannah exclaimed, and squirmed in the zinc bathtub she had pulled over to the fire, trying to cover herself with a washcloth.

I stood, staring openmouthed at her full breasts, her heavy thighs tapering into well-muscled calves.

"I-I-I'm sorry," I stammered. I gestured with the milk pail. Milk slopped over onto the floor. "I finished milking," I said lamely.

"An' y'were goin' to clean the stalls, too," Hannah said, huddling down in the bathtub. It did little good, though. I could still see the tops of her naked breasts and knew the rest of her was naked, too.

"Horace or Lorenzo already did that," I said. I tried to look away, but her gleaming nakedness drew my eyes back to her like nails to a magnet. My temples began to pound.

"James!" she said.

"Sorry. Sorry," I mumbled. I forced myself to turn around. I became aware of the milk pail in my hand and automatically turned again to place it on the counter.

Hannah had just stepped from the tub. She exclaimed and hurriedly tried to wrap a towel around her. In her frustration, the towel kept slipping away. Before I knew it, I was next to her. She stopped, staring at me her eyes big and luminous. Gently I took the towel from her and wrapped it around her. She smelled like cinnamon. My cold fingers touched the skin of her shoulder. She shivered. I bent and kissed her. For a moment she stood stock-still, shocked. Then she tentatively kissed me back. I kissed her again.

And again.

The towel dropped.

She stood naked in front of me, her eyes downcast.

A tiny pulse beat rapidly in her throat.

I touched it gently.

CHAPTER

14

I OPENED my eyes to moonlight streaming in through my window. I rose and walked naked across the wooden floor and pushed the muslin curtains aside. A full moon stood high in the sky. Behind it I could see the cold glitter of stars. The storm had passed. I sighed and stretched in the cold of my room, then hurried back to my bed. Hannah raised herself up on one elbow as I slid in beside her. Her naked breasts pressed against my chest. I caught my breath and I took her in my arms and kissed her. I slid my hands over her back and felt welts.

"What happened?" I asked.

She leaned back away from me, then sat up and turned away. The blankets fell away from her shoulders to gather in folds around her hips. I saw the criss-crossed marks on her back and touched them gently.

"What happened?" I asked again.

"That what a blacksnake do when a woman sasses her master," Hannah said harshly. "Ah was took down to the barn with all the other niggers standing around and the master had another nigger lay it on me. Then he salted me."

"Salted?" I asked.

She sighed. "They's rub salt over my back. After they's done wi' whippin'."

She looked over her shoulder at me. I sat up and wrapped my arms around her and kissed the welts on her back. My hands cupped her breasts. She moaned.

"I'm sorry, Hannah," I said hoarsely.

She shook her head. "It take two to do this, James." She rolled over on top of me and pulled the blankets up over us. She looked down into my eyes. "But Ah don' think there'll be much of this later."

"No," I answered regretfully. A great sadness filled me. "No, I don't expect there will be."

Two days later, I awoke, trying to figure out what had awakened me. The night seemed still, dark. I glanced at the silver moonlight coming through the window. I listened hard. Then I heard excited cackling. I threw back the covers and leaped from bed.

"What—" Hannah said groggily, raising herself.

"Something's in the henhouse!" I exclaimed, pulling on my pants. I stamped into my boots and hurried down the stairs. I paused to shrug into my coat, then grabbed Father's shotgun from the corner of the kitchen and stepped outside.

I paused to let my eyes adjust to the dark. Whatever it was, the hens were in a right ruckus. I stepped down off the steps and hurried as fast as I could through the drifts toward the house. I could smell the hot, sickly, rich smell of live chickens on the cold air. Halfway there, I saw a shadow dart from the edge of the house and run lightly over the snow. I recognized the brush and raised Father's shotgun, sighting carefully, swinging the barrel slightly. I squeezed the trigger and felt the shotgun kick against my shoulder. A gray cloud rose from the barrel. I took a step to the side, my finger automatically sliding to the second trigger. Then I saw the fox lying on the snow, his legs kicking weakly in his last tremors.

I pushed my way through the snow, keeping the barrel of the shotgun up. His blood was black on the snow in the moonlight, his coat red rust. The chicken lay a short distance away. I sighed, lowering the barrel of the shotgun. The moon cast an eerie white light upon the snow, making it almost like daylight. I felt a strange sense of regret as I bent and picked up the fox. His head rolled back and his tongue lolled out the side of his sharp teeth, dripping blood.

I turned and trudged back to the house, being careful to hold the fox away from me so the blood wouldn't spatter against my pants or coat. Hannah, wrapped in a quilt, was waiting at the door when I came back to the house. Moonlight played off her coffee-colored skin. She seemed one with the night and I paused, staring admiringly at her. She glanced from the fox in my hand to my face, and I read the admiration in her eyes. She smiled softly, sadly, then turned and went back to the steps, climbing slowly to my bedroom. I heard the rustle of the blankets and the creak of the rawhide webbing as she settled back into my bed. I looked down at the fox. I sighed and took a piece of old rawhide lacing hanging from a hook on the back porch. I made a quick loop and hung the fox from the hook by his front paws.

I turned and looked to the east; the sun had yet to throw false morning into the sky. I took a deep breath and let it out slowly, watching the mist rise up in the cold. I glanced again at the fox. A glaze had settled over his bright black eyes. Yet they seemed to be looking into me, and for a brief moment I imagined him saying, *You have killed me, but the brief life I lived, wild and free, is a life to be remembered.* I shivered and went into the kitchen. I stood Father's shotgun back in the corner and went up the stairs. I climbed into bed and Hannah turned to me. Tears glinted in her eyes. She rested her head upon my chest and I felt the warmth of her tears slide onto my chest.

And I held her close.

CHAPTER

15

I WAS in the barn, finishing the milking of Jenny, when I heard the wagon slow and Lorenzo's voice call out in the clear, cold air. I rose, taking the bucket of milk with me, and walked outside the barn, squinting my eyes against the hard glare of the sun off the snow. I waved and came down to the front of the house. Lorenzo looked tired, with purple half moons under his eyes. Mother looked as if she had been pulled through a thicket by her curls. Father was pale and hollow-eyed.

"James," Lorenzo said, nodding. I placed the milk pail on the ground and took the reins as he handed them to me. "Did you get any wolves?"

"One," I admitted. "And a fox that got into the henhouse one night." Mother looked up quickly at that, concern showing in her face.

"How many did we lose?" she asked.

"One," I said. "But I got it back. Hannah fixed it the next night for supper," I added casually, nodding as Hannah came out the door.

Mother nodded and sighed. "One. Well, long's it didn't go to waste. I guess we should be thankful that more weren't lost."

"Yes'm," Hannah said. She nodded shyly at me. "James took care of that right away. Next morning, he repaired the coop so no more foxes could get in."

Mother frowned, glancing between the two of us. Hannah's face turned a shade darker. I glanced up at Father, pretending not to notice how Mother's lips compressed into a hard, straight line.

"Father, how are you?"

He looked at me, puzzlement showing in his eyes. He looked at Mother. "Polly? Where are we?"

"We're home, William," Mother said, sighing. "Home." She glanced back at Hannah, frowning.

Hannah pretended not to notice and bent, picking up the pail of milk. "Ah'll just bet y'all could do with a bite to eat. Ah'll go an' take care of that."

She nodded pleasantly and left. I reached up to help Father down from the wagon. He gave me a quick look of fear and clutched Lorenzo's arm. Lorenzo looked down at me and shook his head.

"He's been like that ever since we took him in," Lorenzo said. He stepped down and reached up, helping Father as he stepped clumsily out of the wagon box and stumbled over the wheel to the ground.

"What happened?" I asked, standing back so Mother could take his other arm.

"Well, we don't know," Mother said. "That day when you went out hunting he got to watching the weather, and when it started to snow he got to fidgeting and worrying about where you were. When the snow began to gather and you still weren't home, he started pacing back and forth in front of the door and window, fussing about how you might be lying out there, hurt, in the woods someplace. Horace tried to tell him that you were all right. So did Lorenzo." I glanced at him; he nodded. "But he just wouldn't believe them. Then he started to get himself ready to go out and find you and bring you home. We tried to stop him, and then he just sort of, well"—she shrugged—"collapsed. There isn't anything else to say about it. Horace was going to ride in after the doctor, but I figured it would be faster if we just took your dad in to him."

"That's what Hannah told me," I said.

"Uh-huh," Mother grunted as they helped Father over the threshold into the living room. He stood still as she began to take off his hat and coat. "Speaking of which"—she eyed me sternly—"you two were alone out here together. Everything okay?"

"Sure," I said, feeling my ears grow hot.

Her lips grew harder. "You sure, Son?"

"What couldn't be right?" I asked.

She studied me for a long moment, then sighed and slowly nodded. "All right. I guess I'm just jumping at shadows. The past few days have been hard, being in town with your father and not knowing how you were."

"Where are the girls?"

"We left them off at the McLaughlins' on the way past," Mother said. She shook her head. "They're too young for this sort of thing. They don't understand what is wrong with your father."

"I'm not certain I understand, either," I said.

Mother sighed. "Well, we can only place our trust in the Lord and hope that he will guide us and make all things right."

I didn't answer. I was beginning to have a pretty dim opinion of the Lord lately. Father had lived his entire life trying to help others and now the good Lord was making him go through life like a child. I remembered Mr. Deasy reading to us about how man went through seven ages—

"It would behoove you all to listen a bit instead of carrying on like a bunch of hooligans and harlots!" he said, fixing the class with a stern look over the tops of his steel reading spectacles. "And if you don't, I'll make certain that your parents find out about your behavior in school!"

We settled instantly. Most of our parents needed little excuse to whale a bit of learning into us with razor strops or broomsticks. Or silence. I didn't mind the occasional whip-pings so much as I did the silence that came for days when I did something that brought Mother or Father's disapproval. Botje started to sass Mr. Deasy back, but Lorenzo nudged him and gave him a warning look and Botje dropped his chin into the palms of his hands and propped his elbows on the plain plank that was his desk.

"That's better," Mr. Deasy said. "Now, class, pay atten-tion. This comes from Shakespeare's As You Like It—"

"Short and sweet is how I like it, but I don't think we're gonna get it," muttered Botje.

"What's that?" Mr. Deasy said, raising his voice sharply.

"Nothin'," Botje said sullenly.

"Very well." Mr. Deasy cleared his throat, then began:

> " 'All the world's a stage,
> And all the men and women merely players:
> They have their exits and their entrances;
> And one man in his time plays many parts,
> His acts being seven ages. At first the infant,
> Mewling and puling in the nurse's arms.
> And then the whining schoolboy, with his satchel,
> And shining morning face, creeping like snail
> Unwillingly to school. And then the lover,
> Sighing like furnace, with a woeful ballad
> Made to his mistress' eyebrow. Then a soldier,
> Full of strange oaths, and bearded like the pard,
> Jealous in honour, sudden and quick in quarrel,
> Seeking the bubble reputation
> Even in the cannon's mouth. And then the justice,
> In fair round belly with good capon lined,
> With eyes severe, and beard of formal cut,
> Full of wise saws and modern instances;
> And so he plays his part. The sixth age shifts
> Into the lean and slippered pantaloon,
> With spectacles on nose and pouch on side,
> His youthful hose well saved, a world too wide
> For his shrunk shank; and his big manly voice,

Turning again toward childish treble, pipes
And whistles in his sound. Last scene of all,
That ends this strange eventful history,
Is second childishness, and mere oblivion,
Sans teeth, sans eyes, sans taste, sans everything.' "

But Father, as near as I could figure it, had been cheated of a few of those ages. So much for God.

He had not made this life sweeter than that of a painted pomp. And I, I determined, seeing Father shuffle on his forgotten feet into the house, would not find myself a player in that show.

I turned and looked across the fields a blinding white from sun glancing off the unspoiled snow. *No,* I determined, *I will not end like this, shuffling through life and not knowing it.*

CHAPTER

16

THE WIND moaned around the eaves and I could hear the dry rustle of the autumn leaves shuffling off from where they had fallen and rustling in the trees where they stubbornly clung to the branches. I shivered although I was warm from my place beside the fire. I looked at the hot coals and watched, fascinated at the motion of the heat swirling slowly, forming images that appeared in strange succession among the glowing embers.

"Jim?"

I blinked and turned to Father, sitting in his rocker near the corner of the fireplace. My cheeks felt warm from the heat pouring from the fireplace. He bent forward and I felt his hand cool against my cheeks.

"Are you all right?"

"Yes, sir," I said. I glanced back at the fire. "It's just that—"

I stopped and stared in fascination as a ghostly figure formed itself, writhing, hollow-eyed, and mouth-gaped.

"Yes?" Father prompted. I shivered again and turned

away, searching for and finding his eyes bright with concern. I took a deep breath and shook my head.

"Nothing, Father. Sometimes I get these strange feelings. I can't explain them, but they make me uneasy."

He pursed his lips, contemplating me searchingly. Then he sighed and ruffled my hair and leaned back in his chair. He locked his thumbs under his jaw and stared, brooding, into the fire. His thin face was drawn and white, and firelight flickered on the deep hollows of his cheeks. He remained silent for a long period. Time passed and still he stared silently into the fire, his eyes distant and seemingly focused upon nothing.

I sighed and turned away at Mother's voice gently reminding me that it was time for bed. Lorenzo complained and she stared at him with her unblinking hawk's eye. He rose and moved quietly toward our room. I pushed myself to my feet to follow him, but Father spoke out, stopping me.

"Jim, wait a moment. I wish to speak with you."

"It's his bedtime," Mother murmured.

Father smiled at her. "I know, Polly. But I wish to speak with him for a minute or two. We won't be long."

Mother shook her head at the suggestion that Father wanted to speak alone with me. She sighed and put away her knitting in the small carpetbag in which she stored her yarn and sewing supplies at the side of her chair.

"Don't keep him too late," she said to Father. "Tomorrow is a busy day. Boys grow while they're sleeping."

"They are all busy," Father said quietly.

Her lips tightened as she studied him; then she shook her head and took herself silently away.

I stood, waiting while Father studied me carefully. Then he gripped the arms of his rocker and said, "Jim, you must always fight against those dreams you have."

I shuffled my feet nervously. I knew he was concerned about me. But I didn't think my occasional reveries were much more than the mystical wanderings of a boy's mind filled with visions of adventures he had read about and wanted badly to experience.

"It's nothing, Father," I said. "I'll make sure it doesn't happen again."

Father stared searchingly into my eyes. Slowly he shook his head and said, "No, James, I don't want you to stop reading and thinking about what you are reading. But I think it is time that you realized a few things that dreams can only suggest.

"There will come a time when you will have to make a choice about what to do. Sometimes a man has to forget himself to help others who cannot help themselves. There are times when the law is not enough. Remember the story I told you about Samson?" He waited until I told him that I did; then he continued. "Some men are wily enough to escape justice. Others are strong enough to avoid the law's reach or powerful enough that the law cannot touch them. These men cannot be reasoned with and . . ."

He paused again, frowning as he gathered his thoughts.

"You must remember that good men are often blind to what they *know* they should do but are reluctant to believe. Jacob had to have his thigh broken by an angel. Paul had to be knocked off his camel and struck blind on the road to Damascus and suffer that blindness until he saw with his inner eye the truth he was meant to see. Even Jesus had to resort to violence a time or two when reason failed— remember when he lashed the moneylenders out of the Temple?"

A strong gust rattled the windows in their frames. Father glanced toward them. "This will blow a good storm down from the north—if I don't miss my guess."

He fell into a silent reverie for a long moment. His eye appeared to be studying something in the distance. I sighed. Father had slipped again into the other world. I rose and started toward my room. My hand was upon the doorknob when his voice stopped me.

"Jim."

I turned. "Yes, sir?"

"You're a good boy, Jim. Read Mark thirteen before you go to bed."

I sighed. Father was getting more and more insistent upon assigning reading passages from the Bible to one of us who happened to catch his eye. Tonight, it appeared, was to be my turn. "Yes, Father," I said, resigned.

He nodded. "Good night, James," he said, and rose.

"Night, Father," I answered.

He pressed his palm to the small of his back, stretching, then shuffled to his bedroom. He closed the door quietly. I sighed and walked to his chair and took his Bible from the small walnut table next to his rocker.

I opened it to Mark 13 and settled down in front of the fire to read it. Twice. But still I didn't understand it. I read the chapters before and after but could not understand why Father was so insistent that I read that particular chapter. I knew the words and the warnings Jesus gave his disciples, but I couldn't connect those words with Father's words.

I closed the Bible irritably and sat, staring into the fire, trying to comprehend why Father wanted me to read Mark 13. I brooded upon the reading and tried to work it out carefully in my mind Still the reason eluded me.

Sighing, I opened the Bible again and turned to the story of Samson—always one of my favorites, enjoying the strength of Samson, his dedication to his people, Delilah (I had a few secret dreams about that woman!), and his betrayal and his nobility in the midst of that betrayal and his death.

"What is it you do not understand?"

The voice startled me. I sat up and looked around. A long-haired man—blond hair—sat in Father's rocker. He was clean-shaven and wore a white robe. He was barefoot and I wondered how he could stand going unshod in that weather.

"I do not feel the cold as you do," he said.

"Oh," I said, then leaped to my feet, heart thudding frantically in my chest. "How did—"

"I hear your thoughts," he said easily.

"Who are you? What are you doing here?" I asked, working hard at controlling the sudden surge of fear in my belly.

He smiled. "You know who I am. You have read enough about me."

I shook my head, puzzled. A look of boredom flitted over his face.

"Tch. Tch. I thought you were wiser beyond your years. But apparently I was mistaken."

"I think," I said slowly, edging toward Father's gun, "that you'd better explain yourself, sir."

A twinkle came into his frost blue eyes. He leaned back in Father's rocker and studied me with a bemused expression.

"Or you will do what?" His eyes flickered to Father's gun and back. "Use that? Well, go ahead; take it."

I took a long step and reached for the gun, but when my fingers closed upon it I found I could not lift it. I strained, but it seemed as if the wood of the stock had taken root or merged with the very wood of the house itself.

I whirled and threw myself at him. His eyebrows rose in surprise and he raised his hand to stop me. A smile played teasingly around his lips.

"Are you wanting to wrestle?" he asked mockingly. "I wrestled a couple of times before with man."

I stepped back and frowned at him. What was this nonsense? "If you aren't a man, then who are you?"

He nudged the Bible on the floor with his toe. "Genesis thirty-two," he said.

I ignored his gesture. "When Jacob wrestled with an angel? It's one of Father's favorites. We all know it well." I looked at him closely, ready to give him the lie back in his throat. "Now you want me to believe you are Jacob? Try harder."

He smiled gently. "Not Jacob. The other one."

I felt my jaw drop as the meaning of his words seeped into my tired mind. I shook my head in disbelief, but even while I was denying him, the stray moments began to slide neatly into place. Yet I didn't *want* to believe him, because that would give meaning to all I had been prepared to deny.

"Yes," he said to my silence. "My name is Gabriel."

Without thinking I said, "You're an angel."

"Thank you," he said, smiling.

"I mean—" I stopped, flushing with embarrassment. I didn't know what I meant.

"I know," he said. I started at his words. He shook his head. "Don't think anything about the impossibility of things, James."

"What do you want?" I blurted, then bit my lip, as the tone of my voice was sharper than I intended.

He laughed, though, and I breathed a deep sigh of relief, for I remembered the story told how Zacharias had doubted Gabriel's word and been struck dumb for his trouble. A brief vision of what it might be like walking through the rest of my days struck mute flashed across my mind. I cleared my throat, uncomfortable with the thought.

"Why do you suppose your father asked you to read Mark thirteen?" Gabriel asked.

I sighed and shook my head. "I don't know," I confessed. "Sometimes he does things like that to me or Horace or Lorenzo and we don't know why."

"Then why do you do it?" he asked.

"Because he's my father and asked me to read it."

"*Asked* you?" he said gently.

I nodded. "Oh, I know he tells us to read it, but he wouldn't say anything if we didn't. It's one of those things that"—I paused—"you just do," I finished lamely.

"Yes, I know. You've said that before. But *why*?"

"Because he's my father," I said again. I shook my head. "That's enough for me."

"Because your father asked you to," he said, smiling. "That's all you need to know, isn't it?" I nodded and a satisfied expression came over his face. "That's all our Father asks," he said. "That you do what he asks."

"Yeah," I grunted. "I picked that up. But there's something there that I really don't understand as well. I don't pretend to know everything about why I'm told to do this or do that. It's enough that I'm told and do what I'm told."

"Yes," he said. "But you would like to know, wouldn't you?"

I shrugged. "Yes, of course."

"Your father was about your age when he was told to read Mark thirteen," he said conversationally.

For a moment I didn't comprehend what he was saying; then understanding came to me. "You mean, *you* told him?" He smiled gently. "Why?"

"Because we wanted him to know that there are times when men like that are needed. The world needs the peace-makers, but it also needs the warriors who will let the peace-makers work. Sometimes a strong hand or fist is needed to make people see reason." He shrugged. "And in some instances, the left hand of God must go to work."

"The left hand of God?" I shook my head, puzzled. "I don't understand."

He shook his head. "That's the dark side, the terrible vengeance that rises from the anger of God. There are some who must do that work, too. Sometimes a rare man comes along who must walk in that darkness and do the Lord's work among the violent. David was one of those. Sometimes the darkness swallows those men up and they become that which they once fought. Saul, Absalom, others." He shook his head, his lips pressed grimly together. "It isn't a place for some, either. Your father was one of those."

"You mean—" I shook my head. "No, not Father. He's a kind man—"

"Now," Gabriel said gently. "But for a time he was one of the left hands of God. But it takes an unusually strong man to do that work. One who is not afraid of walking through the darkness. That's why I suggested that your father have you read that passage."

"*You* suggested?"

He nodded. "Oh yes. We are seldom far away from your father these days. This is the time when he needs us the most."

"What time is that?" I asked, but he shook his head.

"It is not given to man to know the comings and goings of time yet to be spent," he said. "But this I will tell you: There is a need for you. There will be times when you will have to stand alone against great odds. There will be times when you will have to walk alone in darkness and live among those who have fallen away from God's grace. Remember always that where good lives, evil is a neighbor. But never forget that you are human, James. That is the most important."

"I won't," I said softly.

He nodded and then disappeared. I blinked and looked around, but I was alone.

And then I awoke, stiff with cold. The fire was long gone out. I shook my head; dreaming again. I had better get to bed before Mother came out and found me still up. I looked down at the Bible lying open in my lap: Mark 13.

I had been reading the story of Samson.

A chill went through me that had nothing to do with the cold.

CHAPTER

•━━━◦◦◦◦◦◦━━━•

17

ABOUT TWO weeks later, Mother acted queer. I recognized the mood early when I came into the kitchen for breakfast. She glanced at me, surly, her thin mouth pulled tightly down at the corners, her blue-gray eyes stony. I sighed and took my place at the table, sitting straight, my hands in my lap, holding myself as quiet as a shadow and hoping to get through breakfast before her tongue scraped the flesh off my bones.

She cleared her throat and I sighed inwardly, mentally flashing over yesterday, searching for anything I might have done that could result in a coring.

"You were late coming home last night, James," she said, and my heart sank at the brittle tone in her voice.

"Yes, ma'am," I said carefully. I glanced at the door, willing the others to come in. Sometimes Mother eased off a bit when all of us were in the room together. That didn't mean that we were automatically exempt from one of her forays; it was just that there might be such a clamor that she would temporarily forget her intentions as she tried to keep up with all the goings-on around her. Time was our friend, for Mother kept herself so busy that something would happen to distract her and occasionally one of us could escape her intentions.

"You know when you're supposed to be in," she said. It wasn't a question, but I answered it anyway. Silence wasn't golden when Mother was in one of her moods. She took such a tactic as a weakness, and her tongue would get wagging harder than ever as she lathered herself up and took to waxing eloquent.

"Yes, ma'am," I said, and braced myself for the battering.

"Why?"

For a moment I was dumbfounded as I stared open-mouthed at her. She glanced over her shoulder. Not a muscle twitched.

"Why?" she repeated.

"I—I was helping Old Man Josiah load his wagon with apples," I said. Her eyes narrowed and I rushed on. "His man went into town Saturday and didn't come back on Sunday. Josiah needed to get the apples before they began to turn. He asked if I would help."

She cast a quick reproving look at me. "*Mr.* Barnes, James," she said quietly.

I shivered and stammered defensively, "He told me to call him Josiah."

"He was just being polite. You should never take advantage of a man's politeness, James. You respect your elders. Your turn will come. There's no need to hurry it along."

"Yes, ma'am," I said. I knew better than to press my argument when those deep lines drew down at the corners of her mouth.

"Did you get the apples loaded?"

"Yes, ma'am. We finished late by lantern light. J—Mr. Barnes said he would drive them over to Troy today."

"He pay you?"

I hesitated and she turned from her place by the stove to stare at me, waiting for my answer. I wasn't quite certain how to answer her. But I knew it wasn't the time for one of my stories. This was the time for truth.

"No, ma'am," I said.

She nodded. "He offer?"

"Yes, ma'am. But he's had a run of bad luck lately and I figured he needed it more than we did."

A small tic pulled her lips into a grimace, and she pushed her shoulders back, rolling her head slightly to help remove a crick in her neck. For a moment I thought that I was going to be given another tongue-lashing; then the tic spread into a quiet smile.

"You're a good boy, Jim," she said quietly. My cheeks began to burn and I looked back at the doorway, hoping Lorenzo would come in. "Good boy" usually followed an admonition to always walk in the footsteps of the Lord, to mind the Ten Commandments, to—

"Jim, there comes a time when you're going to have to make a choice," she said. I perked up. This was a new one I hadn't heard before. "There are going to always be a lot of Mr. Barneses around who can't do for themselves. They're good people, but they just can't help themselves when others come against them. I have a hunch that's what the good Lord put you here on this earth for—to be helping others."

I flushed deeply and looked down at the table. I didn't want to say what needed to be said at this point, but I couldn't let her go on about my becoming a missionary or a preacher. I knew that Father had hopes that one of us would go in that direction, but I sure didn't have any inclination for filling that dream. I had read Cooper's *Leatherstocking Tales* through half a dozen times and Carson and Boone and, well, just about everything I could get my hands on that told the doings in the Far West. The West was yanking hard on me each day and I knew that someday I would have to go there. Some nights I even had dreams about adventures there—me and Carson, usually—but a couple of times nightmares pulled me up out of sleep and I awoke drenched in sweat, my heart pounding like I'd sprinted a mile or two, but I couldn't manage to recall what had frightened me so, even though I would lie awake there until false dawn came and the sky was painted with pink streaks.

"Mother," I said carefully, "I don't think I'm cut out to be a preacher."

She nodded solemnly and said, "Nor do I, Jim. You got too much devil in you for that. But I think you're strong enough to turn that devilment into good. You just have to remember purpose. But be careful, Jim. Be careful. The devil is a sly one. He's a trickster that hides in the shadow of good. A slick one. That's why I said you have to remember purpose and look for what his suggestions might bring upon you and others. It isn't going to be easy going for you and I think a lot of the time you're going to have to be unhappy, but don't let your sadness take you down the wrong path. Don't go looking for the easy road. If the Lord wanted life to be easy, we'd still be in the Garden of Eden. But we aren't. It isn't Matthew, Mark, Luke, or Peter that you have to read, Jim. Look at Revelation. It's there you'll find your purpose in life. John's your man. Follow what he says. And remember that there are some among us who aren't meant to turn the other cheek but to help those that do. There's always going to be someone who will pop them on that cheek no matter how many times they turn it, and they get tired of hitting them, why, they'll more than likely take a knife or gun to them."

She paused, looking away from me off into the distance. "Your father was like that once, James. And he still is—to a degree. But sometimes when his mind strays he forgets purpose. That doesn't mean he's a weak man, though. I've seen strength in him when others walked away. But there's a lot of goodness in him, Jim. Now I know he likes to read to you and tell you some things. What was that book he was reading to you and Lorenzo the other day out under the sycamores?"

"Blake, Mother. He was talking about Milton? You know, *Paradise Lost*?"

"Oh yes," she said, and this time a broad smile lifted the light into her face and her eyes softened. "Oh my, yes. I remember him going on about that. He doesn't care much for Blake, does he?"

"No, ma'am," I said. "Leastways, not that I can see. He was going on about how Blake was wrong and Satan wasn't the strongest character in *Paradise Lost*."

"Uh-huh. Well, do you know why Milton has that fellow seem more interesting than others?" I shook my head. "It's just what I've been talking about. Satan likes to hide behind a screen of good. Sin is always far more beautiful than good, Jim. Always. That's why it gets folks to go to the left rather than the right. Milton was a smart one, Jim. He weaves a sense of goodness around you, then socks you *wham!*" She brought her hand down hard upon the table, making me jump in surprise. "Just when you least expect it. But you read on and you discover just how hard the devil can be and how the goodness just overcomes him all the time. But it takes a special person to resist him all the time."

I cleared my throat when she paused to reflect some, and said, "Yeah, I know, but Reverend—"

"I know what he says," she said, breaking in impatiently. "But he's wrong. Oh, there's strength in his words and they're good words, but he's wrong about always turning that cheek. Remember what I told you. There's always someone going to pop you when you do it if you're fool enough to keep turning. Even Christ resorted to violence on occasion, and there hasn't been a better man walking this good earth. Remember when he whipped those money changers out of the Lord's Temple? He wasn't too gentle that time. And remember when Satan came to him and tried to tease him into walking in the devil's footsteps instead of the Lord's? Why, he wasn't too gentle then, either.

"No, Jim, history is full of men who walked in the Lord's footsteps and carried a big stick or sword or club." Her eyes became distant and a soft smile came across her face, making the hard planes disappear, and for a moment I saw the young girl who had drawn Father's eye and made him camp on her doorstep until she said yes. I think that was the closest I ever felt to Mother, for I sensed a soft goodness to her and a certain girlish giddiness that made her seem . . . vulnerable, I guess. I don't know how to explain it any other way.

"There's going to be a time, Jim, when you will have to be the left hand of the Lord." A sadness came into her eyes and, for a moment, I thought I saw the glimmer of tears gathering, but she turned away and busied herself at the counter, cracking eggs and whipping batter in a heavy mixing bowl. "I know you're young for this talk, Jim, but I've seen how you stand up to those that try to take advantage of the others. That Botje boy, for example. He's a bully, a no-account that isn't ever going to amount to anything. But he'll make life miserable for any he senses to be weak. I know you've had a few spats with him and you'll have more. But always watch your back. People like him won't come straight on to you when they discover they can't beat you. They're sneaky and not worth the spit to drown a grasshopper. He isn't ever going to change; you only have to look at his father to know that—and his mother," she added as an afterthought. "The fruit doesn't fall far from the tree and that fruit was spoiled at birth—carried that rottenness right from the core into the fresh ripening. I know what the Good Book says about goodness in everyone and always looking for the good and having patience—I guess I know Job as well as any—but, Jim, that doesn't mean that the Lord doesn't have his folks on this earth as well as the devil does. The Lord put Samson down here to help his people and Joshua to help his. David was a great warrior as well as a great king. Alas, Absalom! Absalom! I see no reason why you think you have to be a preacher to do the Lord's work, Jim. There's a wildness in you, but that wildness can do his work as well." She shook her head. "I wish it could be otherwise, but there you have it. Your father should have been the one to give you this talk and maybe he will yet. But what you did for Mr. Barnes you're going to have to do for others as well. There are those who just won't listen to reason, and those are the ones you're going to have to put reason to. Someone has to do it. No reason why that someone isn't you. Remember that the Lord didn't spend his time in the Temple but went down in the city where the sinners were. He knew that those who were good didn't need his help as much as the sinners—although there's a lot of whited sepulchers among those who pretend to good—and that's probably where you're going to have to go as well, where you'll find the sinners. But watch your back," she said again warningly. "I have a bad feeling about that. A premonition, I think, and I hope to God I'm wrong. Now how do you want your eggs this morning? And how many?"

I reckoned about a half-dozen and she could whip them all up together, if she wanted. She smiled and pulled fresh bread out of the warming oven and put it on the table with a saucer of fresh-churned butter, heavy yellow with rich cream. I pulled the pitcher of buttermilk to me and filled the heavy glass by my plate and drank thirstily. I buttered a few thick slices of bread while Mother readied my eggs. She slid them off on the plate, and by the time she added a few slices of hickory-smoked bacon I already had half of them settling comfortably in my stomach. She reached across and ruffled my hair and I nearly choked on a mouthful of bread at the suddenness of her gesture. Mother just wasn't free with hugs and kisses among us menfolks, although there was a tenderness there that ran deep. She laughed delightedly at the startled look on my face, and for a brief moment I felt close to her and smiled at her girlishness as she relaxed the stern role she had to hold against those times when Pa's weakness came over him. I knew then that she had had to grow older before she should have and take a hard line in life where she should have been able to laugh and dance and enjoy spring instead of always walking in the fall. But because she had to shoulder the burden of Job I knew that she had given me words I needed to ponder on and think carefully about before I became another Kit Carson or Andy Burnett or "Broken Hand" Tom Fitzpatrick or Jedediah Smith, that quiet, Bible-toting mountain man whose sobriety had made him as much a legend as had his adventures.

CHAPTER

18

SPRING CAME quickly that year, the ice breaking from Vermillion Creek and Tomahawk Creek in late March, and a sudden warming spell displaced April showers. Mr. Deasy celebrated spring the way he always celebrated spring, taking his classes through his Chaucer, pronouncing with relish the opening lines, slowly, with great pomp,

> " 'Whan that Aprill with his shoures soote
> The droghte of March hath perced to the roote,' "

while staring with dreamy eyes around the room and out the windows to where the sun shone brightly upon the new grass.

By the end of April when the showers had still not come to lift the sun's heat, we discovered as we had each spring the joys of truancy and swimming in Tomahawk Creek. Oliver had left for California to find his fortune (and we hoped ours) and I had taken his place, working on Dan Carr's farm near our own while Lorenzo and Horace managed our place. We needed the money, what with Father spending more and more time staring vacantly into the fire and holding his Bible in his hands but seldom reading from it. He had his good days when he would do small chores around the house, but we always had to check Jenny if he had been milking, as he sometimes would not finish the job. We couldn't afford to let Jenny get milk fever.

On May Day a heavy rain fell, and the next day a bunch of us went swimming down at Tomahawk Creek. Botje's cousin, John Betts, was visiting from Peru. He was bigger than most of the other boys and took great pleasure in swimming underwater and pulling the younger boys down, dunking them. I took an immediate dislike to him. Wylie McKenzie had come with us to the creek. Although he couldn't swim, Wylie liked to paddle in the shallows, looking for freshwater clams.

I was lying on the thick grass of the bank, letting the sun dry me, when suddenly Wylie screamed. I sat up and saw Wylie in deep water, flailing his arms wildly as he went under. I glanced over and saw Betts dressing quickly.

"Help!" Wylie bawled.

I leaped up and ran to the edge of the creek. I cleared the shallows with a low dive and swam to Wylie. I grabbed him, tucking his chin under my arm, and pulled him to shore. He lay, crying and puking, on the shore.

"Good work, James," Lorenzo said quietly. He nodded to where Betts was tying his shoes. "He threw him into the deep pool after Wylie told him he couldn't swim."

"He—hurt me," Wylie sobbed.

"Little punk," Botje sneered. "You wanted to come along and play with the big boys. It's your own fault."

"Leave him alone," I said quietly.

Botje glanced at me; then his cousin came up to stand by his shoulder, placing his hands on his hips, smirking. Botje laughed. "And what you gonna do about it, Hickok?" he challenged.

I lashed out, popping him on the nose. Blood spattered against his face like a ripe tomato. His cousin stared openmouthed; then I grabbed the collar of his shirt, spun him around, and reached between his legs, grabbing.

He howled with pain and tried to push my hand away, but I jerked, bringing him up on his tiptoes, and crow-hopped him down to the edge of the bank. His shrieks went up the scale until he sounded like a young girl screaming at a ghost. I took a deep breath, then lifted and threw him forward. He flew over the water, his hands going immediately to cup his groin. Then he landed with a flat *splat!* in the water.

"Pa'll get you for this, Hickok!" Botje bawled, holding a dirty handkerchief against his nose.

I moved toward him, but he turned and ran away into the woods. I turned to watch as his cousin dragged himself like a drowning rat from the creek and lay, crying, on the bank, holding himself tenderly. I brushed the water from my arms and legs. I glanced at Lorenzo as I dressed. A wide grin split his face.

"Well?" I challenged. "You got something to say?"

He spread his hands, shaking his head. "No, no. Not me. I expect his old man"—he nodded toward Botje's cousin—"will, though. And you know Botje's dad will."

"Let them," I said, finishing dressing. I walked over to Wiley. "Come on," I said gently. "I'll take you home."

"Thanks, Jim," he said, eyes shining. He snuffled and wiped his nose with his hand. "When I get big, I hope I'm just like you."

"When you get big"—I smiled—"you might be better than me." I glanced at Lorenzo.

He nodded toward the woods where Botje had disappeared. "Better watch your back. He won't come at you to your face, but I don't doubt he'll get a bunch of guys together and come after you."

I laughed and punched him gently on the arm. "I've got you to do that," I said.

"I won't always be around, Jim," he said seriously. "I'll do what I can while I'm alive, but I won't always be with you. Best you remember that."

"I'll remember," I said. I turned to Wiley. "Come on; let's get you home."

Word spread quickly about what I had done. The next day at school, Mr. Deasy handed back the spelling test he had given us. I sighed as I saw all the corrections marked on my paper. I could read the words and understand them, I could speak them, but I never could spell them. It was the damnedest thing, I thought wryly.

"Good job," he whispered, bending close to my ear. I smelled the peppermint on his breath and the faint hint of tobacco beneath. We all knew he smoked, but we kept it quiet for fear our parents would fire him for his "weakness."

I frowned at the paper. "But I failed."

"I wasn't talking about the test," he said. He smiled. "*Arma virumque cano*. Spelling is something that you can correct with time, Mr. Hickok. Courage and care are not."

I glanced over to where Sarah McLaughlin sat. Her face was shining as she smiled at me. I ducked my head, feeling my cheeks beginning to burn.

When I got home that evening, Mother met me at the door. She gave me a slight smile and said, "We had a caller today."

"Oh?" I said casually. I shifted my books from one hand to the other.

"Yes," she continued. "It seems Mr. Botje came by to complain about you."

"Sorry, Mother," I said.

She shook her head. "Don't be, James. Lorenzo told me everything. You did what was right. Although," she added, "I don't think you should have hit his boy in the nose. I understand that it's broken and they had to take him into Homer to get the doctor to look at it."

"Well"—I looked away from her— "I guess I didn't think."

She folded her arms and studied me for a long moment.

"No, James, you didn't think. You just acted. But there are times when action is better than procrastinating. I think this was one of those times. A person can't help being what they are." She paused, then nodded toward the bedroom. "Your father wants to see you."

"Father?" I said, surprised. She nodded.

"Yes. He's aware of things. For the moment."

I heard a click in her throat and saw tears spring to her eyes before she could turn away. I glanced over her shoulder into the kitchen and saw Hannah looking at us. She nodded and smiled. I walked into the bedroom, pausing just inside the door. Father lay on the bed, gaunt, his beard showing a salt-and-pepper stubble against his hollowed cheeks. But his eyes looked clear. He gestured and I walked over to the bed and sat on the edge. I could smell the sour sickness on him. He reached for my hand. I let him take it. He smiled and a lump came into my throat.

"Well, James, I hear you have been at it again."

"Yes, sir. I guess I have."

He squeezed my hand gently. "I heard what your mother said. You mustn't ever think that we are disappointed in what you do." He sighed and took several short, shallow breaths. "James, I know I haven't had much to do with you lately—"

"It's all right, Father. I understand," I said quickly.

"—but I want you to know that there are a few people in this world who are put here to do what you did the other day." He smiled. "Christ tells us to turn the other cheek, but God doesn't mean for us to be alone and defenseless, either. He puts people here to help those who cannot help themselves. There comes a time when evil must be faced by someone who is not meant to turn that cheek. Those are special people, James. Special people. They don't come along except once in a rare while. For all of his greatness, Charlemagne only had twelve of them for his entire world. I think that God means for you to be one of those men, James. You will not have many friends. You will be alone much of the time. But I think God put you here for doing what you did the other day."

"Yes, sir," I said.

He coughed, a long, wracking cough that shook the bed. "Be careful, James. Be very careful. You have a special gift and there will be many temptations to misuse that gift. Be certain that you use it only for right. And be careful. Don't unleash the fury upon anyone unless it is the only resort left. Remember this, James!" He squeezed my hand fiercely.

"Yes, sir. I'll remember."

"Good. Good," he said. A great weariness seemed to come upon him. "I think I'll sleep for a bit, now, James."

"All right, Father," I said.

I rose and left his bedroom. Mother looked at me, but I shook my head and took my rifle and went outside. I went across the pasture to the trees and made my way to a small glade in the middle where a tiny spring bubbled past a salt lick. I settled back, out of sight in the bushes where I had sat so many mornings and evenings, waiting for a deer to come. I waited there now, not for a deer so we would have venison, but because it was something to do. Waiting in the stand gave purpose to thought. But I didn't know what to think about Father's words. His dying was in the way of quiet contemplation. *There will be time later,* I told myself. *There will be time.*

I settled in to wait.

I saw a flash of brown and gently brought my rifle up, waiting. A doe stepped out into the small clearing, head up, nostrils working as she tested the breeze. But I knew she couldn't smell me, as the breeze was into my face and she had come from the west, where my scent wouldn't carry to her. She crossed to the small stream and bent her head, drinking daintily. I waited, knowing that a buck would follow her in a few moments. That was the way nature worked; the male waited, watching for danger.

I heard him before I saw him. A slight scraping of twigs brushing against his side. A soft hoof fall. Somewhere a squirrel scolded. A jay chattered. Then he was there, almost by magic, head up, eyes watching. Six points on his rack. He moved forward gingerly, almost regally. I waited until he was beside the doe and she stepped back from the stream. When his head started down, I eased the hammer back, muffling the sound with my hand. Still a tiny *click!* sounded, almost inaudible. His head came up swiftly, twisting as he glanced from side to side. I centered the sights just behind his right shoulder and gently squeezed the trigger as he took a step back away from the spring.

The bullet took him high above the shoulder. He staggered, then turned, leaping away, the doe running in front of him. I reloaded, then came out of the thicket and crossed to where he had disappeared from the clearing. A bright splash of blood lay on the dead leaves. I glanced up at the green leaves and saw a few bright drops of blood. I nodded and moved forward, trailing him cautiously.

I tracked him for an hour through the woods before finding him lying upon the ground where he had finally dropped. A small pool of blood lay near his shoulder. I approached cautiously and nudged him with my foot. He didn't move. I looked around but couldn't see the doe. I sighed and squatted on my heels, studying him. A whitetail buck. Big. It was a long ways back to the house, and I wasn't certain if I could drag him that far through the thick woods. But the McLaughlin place was just past the line of woods. In fact, I could just see the outline of the split-rail fence that marked the edge of their west field. Perhaps I would be able to borrow a horse from him to take the buck home.

Meanwhile, I field-dressed the buck, then took a small rope and hoisted the buck well into a tree and high enough off the ground to keep the varmints away from him. The carrion birds I couldn't do anything about, but the offal I left should keep them occupied until I could return with a horse.

I hurried through the woods and climbed over the fence on McLaughlin's pasture. I called out as I neared the barn, then went inside, in case Mr. McLaughlin was there. But the barn was empty. I stood my rifle against a stall and went back to the tack room, thinking he might be in there, repairing harness, but it, too, was empty. I had shut the door behind me when a husky voice spoke from the front of the barn.

"Good morning, Jim."

I glanced around and saw Josephine standing in the doorway, one hand on her hip, the other braced against the door. Wisps of crisp dark hair blew gently around her face; her eyes were big and wide and dark, sardonic. Her lips were full like strawberries. Sunlight shone from behind her, outlining her curves. She glanced down at my hands, then exclaimed. "You're hurt!"

She rushed forward before I could explain, taking my hands and looking closely at me. I smelled rosewater on her. Her brunette hair fell softly around her face and over her shoulders in natural waves. She had a tiny mole on one cheek—a beauty mark, some called it. Her green eyes rose to mine as I said, "No, I just shot a deer and need to borrow a horse to get it home."

"Pa's not here," she said, but she didn't drop my hands as she stared intently into my eyes. I began to feel uncomfortable, awkward. I was conscious of her breasts pushing hard against her dress. The tip of her tongue appeared redly between her full lips. Then she stood on tiptoe, throwing her arms around me, kissing me hard.

"Jim—" she panted.

"Josephine, I don't think—" I stammered, but then she kissed me again and pushed me back to a stall where we fell onto a mound of soft hay. I slipped my hands around to push her away and froze as they cupped her breasts and she moaned. She rose to her knees, her long white hands going behind her back, releasing the buttons to her dress. She shrugged her shoulders and her dress fell in folds around her waist. She stood and pushed the dress down over her generous hips. She kicked her dress from her and slid her undergarments away, standing naked before me.

"Josephine," I said hoarsely.

She smiled and stretched languidly, her large breasts moving slowly. Then she lowered her white hands and slid them down over her hips. My eyes were drawn hypnotically to the thick curly black triangle between her legs. She spread her legs and I swallowed heavily and reached for her.

The gloaming had begun by the time I emerged from the trees, leading the horse I had borrowed from the McLaughlin place. The buck lay over the back of the horse. Lights were on in practically all the windows, and several buggies and wagons were in the yard. I frowned and led the horse around to the back porch. I tied it to a post and entered through the kitchen. Hannah was making coffee. She looked up, relief spreading over her face.

"Where y'been?" she asked. "Horace and Lorenzo both went out looking for y'and come back hours ago empty-handed."

"Hunting," I said. I gestured toward the door. "I got a buck on a horse out there. I had to go to the McLaughlin place to borrow a horse to bring it back. What's wrong?"

"Y'daddy," she said. "He died about two this afternoon. He was calling for y' all morning up to the time he went." She came over to take the rifle from me. She took a deep breath; then a hard look came over her face and I saw hurt in her eyes. "I reckon it was deer y'was huntin' all right. I can smell it all over yuh. Roses?"

I ignored her and started for the living room.

"Y'better wash some of that smell off yuh," she said sharply. "There's enough smell of death in this house today. We don' need no moah."

I turned toward the pump and splashed water over my hands, scrubbing the blood from them with a bar of gray soap. I splashed water on my face, dried with a towel Hannah silently handed me, then went into the living room.

The low murmur of voices stopped when I entered as heads swiveled to meet me. They stared curiously. I saw at a glance that George McLaughlin was there, standing by the door, a cup of coffee in his hand. Nahum Gould, Abner

Westgate, the Wixons, and others stood in tiny groups in the room.

Mother sat in her rocker before the fire. Lorenzo and Horace stood at her shoulder. She looked up; quiet fell over the room. I saw the relief leap into her eyes. "James," she said. "We were afraid something had happened to you."

"No, I'm all right," I said. My ears started to burn. I crossed to her and bent to kiss her cheek. She smiled wanly and patted my cheek. Her nose twitched, and I knew she smelled Josephine on me. I rose and turned toward the room.

"I'm sorry to have caused you all to worry. I shot a buck but had to track him down." I glanced at George McLaughlin. "He made it all the way through the woods to your north line. I had to borrow a horse from your place, Mr. McLaughlin, to bring him back. He's tied up out there."

"We'll take care of him, James," Abner Westgate said, putting his cup on a small table. He looked at Beaufoy. "Come on. Least we can do is hang the deer for him in the smokehouse."

Beaufoy looked unhappy at the prospect of work, but he obediently placed his cup on the sideboard and followed Westgate from the room. I glanced at Mr. McLaughlin. He nodded.

"That's all right, James. You're welcome to the loan. No harm done."

My cheeks felt hot, but I held his eyes as I thanked him. I turned back to Mother. "I'm sorry I wasn't here, Mother."

"Well, who knew he would go this quickly?"

Tears threatened to spill from her eyes. We had been prepared for a long time for Father's passing, but no matter how long you've had to prepare for it, death is always a surprise. I guess it's because we really hope in our hearts that it won't come even though common sense tells us it's going to happen. We still hope for miracles, regardless of how old we are, because we still have lingering doubts about the promised land our preachers insist is going to be ours when we die. I remember once I asked Father that if everything was going to be so good for us once we died, why didn't we hurry up and get it over with so we could enjoy the better place? Father looked at me, his brow furrowed in thought, and said, "You know, James, I've thought about that a lot. I guess it's because this is supposed to be sort of a training ground for us so we can prove to God how worthy we are."

I let it go after that. Whenever Father got into his teacher's voice I knew it would be a long time before he got out of it, and the sun was shining that day and the shad flies were out along the creek and the bass were jumping. There were more things for a boy that day than dry, dusty words. But I sensed a hesitance to him, almost as if he was telling me more what he wanted to believe than what he believed.

CHAPTER

19

I PAUSED, leaning on my shovel, wiping perspiration from my forehead. I glanced up at the hot sun. Noon. Or close enough to it, I thought, and took a deep breath, arching my shoulders back to relieve the tightness in my muscles. I glanced at the others near me, working on the Illinois and Michigan Canal. I shook my head ruefully. It was a long way from the quiet woods where I once wandered with a rifle, hunting. But work was where one found it these days. I frowned and glanced down the long shovel line to where the straw boss, Charlie Hudson, stood in the shade of an elm tree. He wouldn't move from there in this July heat except to bully one of the smaller men on a whim when he thought the man wasn't working as fast as he should.

I shrugged and turned, staring down the long line of the canal laid true by a surveyor's plumb. A lot had happened since Father's death. We had been forced to move back to Homer, where Lorenzo and Horace put their money together and bought a small house for us. I had planned on following Oliver out west, but Lorenzo had taken me aside one day and quietly laid out our finances. The family couldn't afford to have me move. Father's sickness and funeral and all had been costly to the family and we needed every hand working to bring in money.

Work was scarce around Homer, so I went up to Utica and found work as a driver on the canal—except for those times when everyone had to lend a hand to dredge the bottom after rains filled the canal with silt. Then we all had to dig a section free.

I shook my head and sighed, turning back to the side of the canal. I started to work my way back into the rhythm, bend, lift, scoop, throw. It was easy work once one caught onto the rhythm, and I let my mind stray back to the weekend when Lorenzo had shown us a clipping from a Kansas newspaper about an argument between the Kansas "Free Staters" and the Missouri "Border Ruffians" who were squabbling over the land claims in the Kansas Territory.

"I think we should give some thought to this," Lorenzo had said quietly.

"What?" I asked. I leaned back against the porch railing, shading my eyes against the sun to look at him. He sat in Father's old rocker, studying the newspaper. He turned it so I could read the headline. I shrugged. "We have enough fights right here with the whites and the blacks. What do we want to go to Kansas for and mess in that trouble?"

"I don't care about that," Lorenzo said. "But there is land available there for the taking."

Interest struck me and I turned back to look at him. I nodded. "Go on."

"According to everything I've read, Kansas land is deep and rich. Good land for farming," he said. "Level and not rocky. In most places," he added. "And it's cheap land, right now. Prices are bound to go up once the place gets settled. I think maybe we should take a little trip over there and check it out. If the price is right, we might consider moving the family over there." He glanced at the village and shook his head. "There sure ain't much here for the Hickoks anymore.

I think it's gonna get worse, too. Stock and grain prices are starting to fall a bit."

"Well," I sighed, "I sure could use a break from that canal. When do you think of going?"

"I don't know," he answered, snapping the paper in his hands. "Soon, though. The longer we wait, the more prices are going to change."

The shovel struck a stone, jarring me clear back to my shoulders. I stepped back and worked the blade under it and stepped hard on the lug, levering upward. Slowly the stone rolled up from the ground and over, rolling down the bank to land with a splash in the water. The noise caused the others to look up from the work questioningly.

"You there!"

I turned and looked back toward the elm where Hudson lolled. He was looking in my direction. I waited.

"We're taking things outta the water, not throwing 'em in!" he said harshly.

"An accident," I said quietly.

He cupped his hand around his ear and leaned forward from the waist. "Eh? What's that, Hickok?"

I drew a deep breath, feeling resentment creep in. "An accident," I said louder. "A rock rolled into the water."

"Well, get it out, you damn fool! Don't just stand there lickering around on your shovel. You ain't gettin' a dollar a day to lollygag at water lilies! Put some back into it!"

I turned back and started shoveling. Anger worked in me, destroying the rhythm, and I found myself beginning to pant in the heat as sweat trickled down from my brow, stinging my eyes. The blade struck another rock, turning the shovel in my hands. I tried to work the blade under it, but the rock was too big. I sighed and began digging around it, exposing it. The rock was too big to lever out. I jammed the shovel into the freshly turned earth and turned, starting back to where we had a team hitched to a drag bar.

"Now where the hell do you think you're going?" Hudson demanded as I walked past him.

"I need the team to pull a rock," I said without pausing.

I stepped down to the team and ran my hands along the back of the wheel horse. "Good boy," I said softly, stepping behind him and picking up the reins. I clucked softly, pulling gently on the reins, turning the team toward the canal path. I flicked the reins lightly across their backs. "Let's go, boys," I said.

Obediently they stepped off, moving slowly down the path, the links on the traces jingling musically. I walked behind them, taking care that they didn't get too close to the edge.

"Jesus Christ!" Hudson exploded as I started to pass him. "You gonna take all day? Get those horses moving!" He stepped forward and grabbed the reins from my hands. He gathered the slack and started whipping the leather across their backs. "Hey! Haw! Haw! Goddamnit! Move, you bastards!"

He lashed out again at the horses. Startled, the horses lunged forward. The drag bar whipped forward, smacking Hudson's ankle. He howled with pain.

"You sumbitches!" He sawed the reins back, pulling viciously on the bits, stopping the horses. They stood trembling, confused as he kept the reins tight and started to whip the horses with the long leather straps trailing behind in the dust. They grunted from pain.

I stepped forward and yanked the reins from his hands, easing the tension. "Shh. Easy, boys," I said soothingly. The horses shuffled nervously, then relaxed. I felt a blow on my shoulder and stumbled. I dropped the reins and turned to face Hudson.

He was red-faced with fury, and tiny bubbles of spittle gathered in the corners of his mouth. "What do you think you doing, boy!" he shouted. "Who the hell do you think you are?"

He jabbed a stiff forefinger in my chest. I stepped back, stumbling over the drag bar. I caught myself and stood, staring hard at him.

"Keep your hands to yourself," I said warningly.

He laughed and stepped forward, jabbing me again with

his hard forefinger. "Goddamnit, boy! You telling me what to do?"

I took another step backward to gain my balance. He misunderstood the step and contempt spread in his eyes. He stepped forward again and started to jab me in the chest. I slapped his hand away and used both hands to push him away from me. He stumbled backward, lost his balance, and fell, landing square in a pile of fresh horse apples. Laughter rolled up and down the bank of the canal as he pushed himself up.

"Sumbitch!" he shouted, and swung a fist at me.

I slapped his hand away and stepped in close, swinging a short hard right to his jaw, knocking him backward into the horse apples again. Laughter rose from the men gathering around us. He lay stunned on the ground, gathering his wits.

"Serves him right," someone said.

"Get him, Hickok," another said.

"He's had it coming for a long time."

Hudson pushed himself up, shaking his head to clear it. He glared at me, then lifted his shoulders and settled his feet. His fists came up.

"All right," he said. "You want a piece of me? You got it!"

He feinted and I turned to catch the blow on my arm, but he pulled the punch back and hooked low for my belly. I tensed my muscles just as the blow landed, but he was a large man and the air *whuffed!* from my lungs. I saw his knee coming up for my face but couldn't turn away as he caught me on the nose. Something snapped and I felt blood on my face.

"Shit," someone said. I heard it dimly through the roaring in my ears. I took a step to the side as Hudson tried to slam a fist into my ear. I felt the wind as it passed my cheek.

I caught his arm with my hand and jerked him forward. He staggered and tried to butt me with his forehead, but I ducked under him and shifted my grip to his shirt, bunching it in my hand. With my other hand I grabbed him between the legs, squeezing. He yelped with pain. I took a deep breath and hunched my shoulders, lifting. He squealed like a pig. I felt his hands trying to push my arm away. I bent slightly at the knees, then shoved him toward the sky.

"Gawd!" I heard someone breathe. "That's gotta hurt!"

I turned toward the canal and took a short run to get momentum, then threw Hudson into the water. His arms and legs whirled for a moment; then his hands went automatically between his legs. He belly flopped into the water and went under. Immediately he came back up, splashing his arms around him.

"Help! Help!" he roared. He went under again and came back up, strangling from a mouthful of water. "Help! . . . Can't swim—" He went under again.

"Let him drown," someone said.

"Hell," another said, and sat down, pulling off his shoes. He took a deep breath and jumped into the water as Hudson went down again. He came up splashing his hands weakly as the other man grabbed him by the hair and started pulling him to the bank. His face went under and he started strangling. The other man grabbed a tree root hanging out from the side of the bank and pulled Hudson to it, keeping his face out of the water. Reluctantly others reached down to pull the straw boss up onto the bank. He sprawled on the canal path. His stomach worked and water vomited out of his mouth as the other man pulled himself out of the water with the aid of the root.

"You'd better get away from here, Hickok," someone said. I turned and recognized Adams, a small man who had been the butt of Hudson's viciousness a few days back. He gestured toward Hudson lying in a pool of his own vomit, panting for breath. "He'll press charges against you. Bet your life on that!"

"It was self-defense," I said quietly. I looked at the others around me. They looked away, embarrassed. "You all saw that."

But no one would meet my eyes except Adams, who took my arm and led me away from the small group. He paused beneath the elm tree, his lips pressed tightly together. His eyes were hard and angry, but I could read the resolution in them.

"Yes, it was self-defense," he said lowly, so I had to bend forward to hear the words falling softly from his lips. "But these men need their jobs. They have families to feed. If Hudson presses charges, they won't jeopardize their jobs."

I recognized the finality to his words and shook my head ruefully. "I don't know what you all expected me to do," I said.

"About what you did," Adams said. "None of us would have, but that's because we can't afford to, much as we'd like to. You're young; you can find work elsewhere. There ain't nothing keeping you here. Go, now! Before he has a chance to get the law down on you."

I took a deep breath, looking back at the knot of men standing around Hudson. No one bent to help him, but neither did they look in my direction. I nodded slowly and turned without another word and headed down the canal path, away from the group.

PART TWO

Kansas

Regions of sorrow . . .

CHAPTER

20

I SHRUGGED my back around to ease the strain where it had settled in the hollow of my shoulder. My feet felt puffy, and I was a bit worn from the long hike in the sun. Lorenzo and I had been on the road for a spell, making our way to St. Louis. It seemed the logical thing to do, as work was getting scarce to find around home.

Lorenzo wasn't as itchy as I was to leave home, but the prospect of the good land fairly cheap in Kansas was appealing. We needed to do *something,* as Father's death had left us in poor straits. So that June Lorenzo and I set off on foot to make our way over to Kansas and file for a homestead. We hoarded our money carefully along the way, laying up off the road at night to keep from being robbed while we slept. But I hadn't expected St. Louis to be as big as this.

We walked down into town, trying to stay out of everyone's way as we made our way through the streets. Hunters and trappers made their way along the street while the townsfolk held to the wooden sidewalks. Lorenzo gawked at the sight of a couple of simpering ladies who batted their eyelids coyly from beneath the parasols they twirled in invitation.

"Look out!" someone shouted.

I turned and saw a wagon bearing down on Lorenzo and pulled him out of the way just as the driver sawed on the lead horses, swearing a blue streak at us as he careened down the street in front of us. Lorenzo turned to look at me, shaking his head.

"This ain't for us, Jimbo," he said.

"No, Billy Barnes, it *is* for us," I said, trying to joke him with his nickname. But he just shook his head and turned back to the street, hugging the side as close as he could get.

We made our way without further incident down to the post office to see if we had any news from home and were surprised to find a letter waiting us.

"This ain't good," Lorenzo said worriedly. We found a bench against a storefront and sat down to read it.

Dear Brothers,

Mother isnt well and took her bed when you two left after 3 days. We dont no wat to tell you more the doctor said he aint certain wat ails her. But you no Mother she dont want you to worry and says that you aint to come home but to go on about your buzness and try and find a good and decent christian place where we can make a new home.

Luv, yr sister
Lydia

Lorenzo looked up, his eyes narrowed in concern. "What you think we ought to do, Jim?"

I pointed at the letter. "Well, we don't know what's wrong with her and we have her words that we should be setting out to find a new place for the family. I think we should go on and do just that."

Lorenzo rubbed his hand along his jaw. "I don't know," he

said doubtfully. He fingered the letter and opened it and read it again. "Anything could be happening to her."

"Yes, that's right," I said impatiently. "She could even have a bellyache or just a bit of that womanly thing that took her to bed once in a while. In the meantime, I say let's get on with our business."

I rose and picked up my pack, looking down at him. "Let's go on down to the riverfront and see if we can find a way upriver that isn't going to break us."

Lorenzo shook his head but folded the letter carefully and stuck it in his pocket. He rose and picked up his pack and gave a deep sigh. I grinned at him.

"You look like the portent of doom, Billy Barnes," I joked.

"I can't help worrying about Mother," he said somberly. "She's alone now that Father's gone."

"She's not alone," I objected. "She has Lydia and—"

"And?" Lorenzo paused in the street, raising his eyebrows. "And what about you or me, or Oliver could come back from California or—"

"You want to go back?" I asked quietly.

He turned away from me, his face a study in pain, gnawing on his long lower lip. "It's just that I've gotta hunch that one of us should stay back there to keep an eye on things." He faced me. "Times are changing fast, Jim. Too fast, I'm thinking. There should be a man at home."

I stared at him silently for a long time, then squared my shoulders. "All right then. One of us goes back and the other goes on. That way we got both ends covered." I dug into my pocket and pulled out a coin. "Should we flip for it?"

He shook his head. "No. I know you don't want to go back. It wouldn't be long until you found some other reason to move away. You got a restless spirit, Jim. I'll go back and take care of things at home until you find something."

Slowly I put the coin back in my pocket. "You sure about this?" I asked.

He nodded. "Yep. Just as sure as I am it's gonna be a hot one the rest of the day." He made an exaggerated sweep of his brow and pretended to shake sweat off the palm of his hand. I laughed and clapped him on the shoulder.

"All right then! Let's head on down and see if we can find me a way to get to Kansas. We'll take our leave down there."

Together we marched down to the river. I knew that Lorenzo felt bad about leaving me alone in that strange town, but rather than feeling dejected, I felt my blood sing with relief at the prospect of adventure that lay before me.

CHAPTER

21

THE WHISTLE blew long and hard and I clambered eagerly over a pile of cotton bales to stare at the dock where the *River Queen* was putting in. Finding a ride upriver hadn't been as easy as I thought. Most boats were too expensive and fare would have put a big dent in what little money I had. Lorenzo had given me most of what we had brought with us so I could prove up on a claim somewhere, and I was reluctant to place a large chunk of that on floating wood. The pilot, however, took a good look at me and said I could ride as far as Leavenworth as long as I was willing to help load cargo. That seemed like a fair exchange to me and I took him up on that.

"Well, Bill," a voice said as a rough hand clapped me on the shoulder. "It looks like this is gonna be the end of the line for you."

I turned to grin at Jim Voorhees, the cargo master. He was about as round as he was tall, but there wasn't much fat on that frame. For some strange reason, though, he had taken to calling me "Bill" and the rest of the crew followed right along regardless of how many times I corrected them. I guess he had heard me calling Lorenzo "Billy Barnes" and somehow thought I was Lorenzo since we looked alike although we were a few years apart.

"I guess so," I replied. I looked back at the crowd gathering at the dock. "It looks like we've got a greeting party. Is that usual?"

Voorhees frowned as he studied the growing crowd. He shook his head. "Well, we always draw some—all boats do—but this boodle don't look quite chirky." He glanced up at the wheelhouse. "I think I'd better see what the cap'n wants to do about this."

"What's the matter?" I asked. But he was gone before I got an answer.

I turned back to watch the crowd draw nearer as the steamboat edged closer. They milled around, staring at us as we approached, their faces sullen. Some shook their fists. And then I heard them shouting, demanding that we pass by. I frowned, wondering what resentment they could possibly have against a steamboat docking. Then I saw that the people in front held those in back away with cudgels. I stepped back in the shadows under the second deck and lounged against the wall, watching.

As the captain carefully placed the steamboat against the dock and the loading planks were let down, a heavily mustached man came aboard, blocking others from leaving.

"Say, what is this?" a salesman asked irritably. "What do you think you're doing?"

The man shook his head. "Sorry, sir. But the folks here have decided that no passengers are going to disembark here. We already got enough trouble hereabouts with Abolitionists and proslavery folks tearing at each other's throats that we don't need no more adding more fuel to the fire." He lifted his head to look at the other passengers waiting to leave and said, "I'd appreciate it if you folks would just go on back to your cabins now. You all are gonna have to go on to the next stop. Leavenworth ain't for you."

Angry murmurs rose from the passengers. A few of the

crowd shook raised fists at the men on the steamboat. I turned to a well-dressed man leaning casually against the cabin wall, smoking a cigar.

"Excuse me, sir," I said politely, and waited while he turned his head and looked carefully at me before nodding.

"What is it, boy?"

"I don't understand why those folks don't want to let us off the boat. It seems to me that if we paid our fare to get here, why, then we should be allowed to leave if we want."

He nodded, a small grin working its way around his cigar. "Yes, it does seem that should be the way of things, doesn't it? But"—he pointed his cigar at the dock—"those folks are a bit more interested in their wants than others' rights. There's gonna be a few elections around here soon and a lot of people are trying to make Kansas go proslavery. They figure by eliminating the competition they have a better chance at getting that to happen."

I frowned. "Doesn't seem right to me. A person should be able to make up his own mind about what he wants."

The man gave me a quick look up and down, then shrugged. "Doesn't matter, though, does it? It doesn't look as if you are getting off the boat anyway." He flipped his cigar over the side of the boat and, turning, thrust his hands into his pockets and strolled toward the back of the boat away from the sunlight.

I glanced around, then noticed that a team of roustabouts had elbowed their way aboard and were beginning to carry cargo ashore. The people stepped aside, ignoring the roustabouts as they came ashore, shouldering their burdens. I nodded and made my way down to the cargo. A large white man with a stump of a cigar clenched tightly between his teeth stood directing the men, glancing occasionally at a clump of papers he held tightly in his sweaty fists. He scowled at me as I came up to him.

"What you want?" he asked.

"To go ashore," I said bluntly.

"Yeah," he grunted. "And souls in hell want ice water. Don't look like you're gonna get your chance, though, does it?"

"There are ways," I said, shrugging. "What needs to be taken ashore?"

He glanced at my bag, then raised his eyebrows. "Boy, you're just asking for trouble."

"No, sir," I said. "Just a box to carry ashore."

He placed his hands on his hips and considered me, his eyes beginning to crinkle at the corners as the thought pleased him. "I sorta like your style. A bit wild, but that'll carry you a ways, I'm thinking. What's your name?"

"That's Bill Hickok," one of the rousties said as he huffed his way past, carrying a load awkwardly over his shoulder. "He's a good lad."

"Jim," I corrected automatically. "I'm Jim."

The foreman shook his head. "Bill suits you. Well, Wild Bill, let's see if we can get you ashore." He glanced around. A man was struggling with a wooden crate just too big for him to get his arms around it. "Soakey!" The man turned his head. "Let this fellow give you a hand."

Soakey gave me a quick look, then ducked his head with thanks. "It ain't heavy, but I just can't get a grip on it."

"That's all right," I said. I tossed the sack containing my belongings on top of the box and took the back end. Soakey turned around, knelt, and lifted the edge of the box against his own back.

"Let's do 'er," he said, and together we made our way out of the hold and up to the gangplank.

"Just a minute," the foreman said. He pulled a rangy man over and whispered into his ear. The man grinned, glanced at us, then nodded. He grabbed a light box and scurried ahead of us.

I watched as he made his way onto the gangplank, then pretended to lose control of the crate and bump hard into the center of the group of citizenry stubbornly holding tightly to the center of the wharf. They stumbled, a few arms windmilling, hands clutched and grabbed at one another; then a small knot tumbled off the edge of the pier into the water.

Shouts of laughter and curses rang up through the air. A couple of men took issue with the man who had lost his balance and started to swing their fists at him, but he ducked, lowered his head, and swept forward like an angry billy goat, piling another bunch of onlookers into the water.

In the confusion, Soakey and I made our way ashore and into the warehouse. I helped him stack the crate on top of a pile, then reclaimed my sack of belongings.

"Thanks," I said, shaking his hand.

He grinned and wiped the perspiration from his forehead with a red bandanna. "Good luck to you," he said. He pinched his nose between thumb and forefinger, snarkled, and blew a clump of snot on the weathered boards of the warehouse floor. "We gotta put up with that crap all the time. Does a man good to see some of those do-gooders get a bath and it not even being Saturday."

I laughed, waved, and cautiously made my way out of the warehouse, shouldering my war bag as I went.

Outside I saw an old man, wild-eyed, wringing his hands and flinging them wide. "Oh, by God," he cried. "I forgot him. I forgot little Paul Williams! I left him out there for the Injuns to scalp, and him only seven years old! Another apple of God's eye gone to wild! Gone!" He lowered his arm and pointed at me, his eyes boring madly into mine. "Right is needed upon the plains! Right and God's good strong hand! Needed! Before any morality and religion can come upon that sand of Gomorrah!"

"I wouldn't mind him much, if'n I were you," came a voice from my shoulder. I turned to look at a man dressed in homespun, his pants held up by canvas gallowses. He heaved a sack of flour into a buckboard and paused, eyeing me carefully.

"If'n I don't miss my guess, you're not far from the plow," he said. He grinned to take any sting from his words. "I'm Bill Williams. I gotta small place just west of here." He glanced at the madman dancing now in the streets to the music of his own madness. "And I ain't seen an Injun out there for most on six years or so. The cavalry keeps them pushed farther back in the hills so's they don't come down onto the flats much a-tall."

"Jim Hickok," I said, returning his smile. "And you'd be right about the plow. 'Cept that was mainly my brothers, although I took a turn or two when time was needed, and harvesting everyone was needed. Rest of the time"—I shrugged modestly—"I got the meat for the table."

"Good shot, are you?" he asked, eyeing me shrewdly.

"Yes, sir," I said. "Just seems to come natural-like to me."

"Ah-huh," he said skeptically, placing his hands on his hips and turning his head so he could stare at me. He was a full head shorter than I and much thinner, more rawbone and rawhide than muscle. But I could see the deep yellow calluses upon his hands and knew that he didn't farm sitting in the kitchen and sipping coffee. "Well," he said dryly, "I reckon you have come to the right place for that natural ability. But if you're looking for work, I'm falling behind upon my plowing, thanks to these rains." He shook his head. "A farmer can't do without rain and can't do with too much." He laughed. "And right now, we're in between. If you can handle a double-blade and don't mind early and late hours, I can use you. Give you room and board and five dollars a week. It's only temporary, mind!" he cautioned, holding up a dirt-begrimed finger. "Only till the plowing and planting's done. Wish I could keep you on full-time, but"—he shook his head—"these aren't the times for making that sort of commitment. But it'll give you the time to look around and see where you are and what you want to be doin'."

I was grateful for his offer and took him up on it at once. I threw my war bag into the back of his buckboard and followed him into the store to help him load the rest of his purchases. The inside of the store was dim, and it took a moment for my eyes to clear. I saw where Williams's purchases had been bagged off to the side with old flour sacks and gunnysacks. Mr. Lewis, who owned the store, was busily working his account books, pretending to ignore the other customer who stood leaning against a post, working something from between his teeth with a dirty thumbnail. His hair hung long and greasy to his shoulders, and scabs showed above his dirty cheeks and beard where lice had been working freely. He had big wrists and hands that hadn't been washed in a month of Sundays. He wore Bulchers, the left one flapping free of its sole, Kentucky jeans, and a linsey shirt that had started out blue-striped but now appeared muddy. He had a big knife stuck in his belt and snickered when his eyes fell upon me.

"Well, whatta we got here? You just get off the boat, boy?" His voice was harsh and grated upon the senses like a plow blade rubbing across a granite stone.

Williams threw him a look as he shouldered another bag. "He's working for me, Casey, so leave him alone."

"Don't look like he'd be much trouble," Casey said. He tapped a dirty fingernail against the handle of the big knife. "Tell me, boy, you pro or against?"

"I don't want any trouble in here," Mr. Lewis said worriedly. "You two just take your differences out into the street to settle them."

"We ain't got no differences. Yet," Casey said lazily.

"And we won't have," I said, taking up two of the sacks and following Williams out the door.

Williams stepped into the back of the buckboard and packed his sack tightly against the boards. He leaned in close to take the ones I carried and said in a low voice, "That man's trouble when he's been drinking and I ain't never seen the time when he wasn't. You stay out here while I get the rest. There ain't much more."

He climbed out of the buckboard and went into the store while I stood on the boardwalk, waiting awkwardly for him. At last I reentered the store and found Williams, both arms loaded with sacks, being confronted by Casey. Mr. Lewis was nowhere to be seen.

"You hired a boy and you don't know where he stands, Williams? Seems a bit careless to me. Especially the way folks are feeling around here," he said.

"Kansas has always been a free state, Casey," Williams said evenly. "It don't take no piece of paper in Washington to change that. Besides, I mind my business and I expect others to mind theirs."

"Well now, I don't know about that. Senator Atchison says—"

"Makes no difference what Senator Atchison says," Williams interrupted. "He's in Missouri and this is Kansas."

I knew what the argument was about. Or what it *should* have been about, except Casey was obviously spoiling for a fight with anyone he could taunt into meeting him. Senator David Atchison was the leader of the proslavery forces in Missouri and had been speech making up and down the rivers claiming that it could be a disaster to have a free state as Missouri's western neighbor. I had read one of Atchison's *Platte Argus* editorials on the boat coming up the river in which he'd said: "Stake out your claims and woe be to the Abolitionists who shall intrude upon it or come within range of your long rifles or within point-blank shot of your revolvers."

"Damn me if I don't think you are one of them no-acccount Free Staters yourself, Williams," he said.

"You know what I am, Casey, and I know what you are. Now get out of my way."

"Anything I can do to help, Mr. Williams?" I said.

Casey turned slowly, grinning, to face me. "Well now," he said, leaning forward, and I could smell the Old Mononga-hela on his breath and knew that he wouldn't be listening to reason, filled up with Dutch courage the way he was and all. I also figured there was no reason to stand there listening to him talk himself up into courage, so I simply reached forward and plucked the big knife out of his belt. His mouth dropped open. "Hey!" he began, but I didn't let him finish. I flipped the knife over so I gripped it by the blade and smacked him with the heavy handle right between the eyes. He stood for a moment, his eyes crossing to see where the hurt came from; then he crashed forward, falling face-first onto the board planks of the store. I reached down and grabbed the filthy collar of his shirt and lifted him. A bright red splotch showed on the floor where he had broken his nose in the fall. I dragged him out of the store and around the corner to the alley, his heels bumping down the steps. I left him there with the knife buried in the dirt beside him. Then I thought better of it and stepped on the knife from the side, snapping the blade from the hilt.

I went back to where Williams had finished loading the buckboard and was already on the seat, holding the reins between his fingers. When he saw me, he slid over to make room. I climbed up beside him and he clicked his tongue against his teeth and pulled the off rein, turning the team in the middle of the street. He clicked his tongue against his teeth again and the team broke obediently into a trot, their harness jangling musically with their movement.

He glanced at me. "What'd you do with him?"

I shrugged. "Just pulled him into the alley in the shade where he won't get sunstroke. He'll have a sore head when he wakes up. I broke his knife, though. Accident."

"Ah-huh," Williams said. He spit over the side of the wagon. "Surely must've had a hard head."

"I reckon," I said.

CHAPTER

22

LEAVENWORTH WASN'T much more than a spit on the map about that time, and I felt little inclination of staying within its boundaries of muddy streets and warped boardwalks. It was a forbidden country where human passions were venerated to excess and restraint pushed to the limits. Most of those who lived in Leavenworth were of one hard slant or the other: either for slavery or against it. Either way, one was certain to come to blows at one time sooner or later if he stayed in the town. I couldn't see much future in that, so Williams's offer was a good one for me.

He had a nice little farm just southwest of the town where a creek bent in a wide oxbow as it meandered its way down toward the Missouri River. Primroses and elderberry and plums stood along its banks. I could see why he had chosen it for his homestead. It was just below a good stand of walnut and just up from some hickory and oak. Willows dangled leafy tendrils over the creek amid some buttonwood, and his house had been built beneath a huge cottonwood to give it shade during the hot summer days. I knew there was game there, for we had chased up prairie chickens and I had heard wild turkeys gobbling back along the creek. The road we followed took us over unbroken prairie, and I couldn't keep my eyes off the western reaches, where I saw blue lupine and wild strawberry.

"Yes," he said, and I glanced at him and realized he had been reading my mind.

"It's beautiful," I said.

He smiled sadly and shook his head. "For now it is, but there will be enough coming like me who will plow all that under. Can't stop progress, and I suppose there's good about that, too. A man digs down into that black earth and sees how it's been veined with water for hundreds of years and he feels a certain sacredness about him. But by then it's too late."

I nodded as the wagon rumbled over a wooden bridge. I took a deep breath, smelling the water flowing under the bridge, a perfect distillate made of spartina and the albumen of eggs. A stream of mallards coasted in with the current, and a bass jumped beneath an overhanging willow where dragonflies hovered. Spotted butterflies fluttered around the bank along with bluebottles. Near the reeds growing next to the bridge I could see the warm, thick slobber of frog spawn growing like clotted water and heard the croaking of bullfrogs sounding their maleness arrogantly to one another, calling for their mates. I could understand why Williams farmed here; he had found his paradise, and I felt a tug at my spirit at the possibility of emulating him. Yet even then I felt the fantasy of the moment as a bright porcelain of my soul. I ached for the serenity of the life Williams had, but the moment was a strange, wandering wisp of desire, for I could not see myself hunched over the plow or my children and their children rolling around my heels on the puncheon floor of my house, a copy of the home that I had just left.

I felt, instead, the need of the land and the people in it and knew that I would not be able to live a life of any normalcy for long despite my desire. I heard, in the middle of all that Eden, the distant echo of my father's voice and looked to the horizon, expecting to see a knight on horse making his way over the plain. But then I saw only blue sky and endless prairie filled with patches of walnut, hickory, oak, elm, willow, some buttonwood, and mostly cottonwood around the creeks and tanks. The water here had cut through a limestone hill, giving a slight tang to the taste, and the flowers across the prairie were brilliant, with blue lupine, primroses, wild strawberry, elderberry, and plum blossoms and chokecherries along the creek banks.

I heard the call of a quail, the challenging tom-tomming of a prairie chicken, the nervous gobble of a wild turkey. A strange peace fell over me and I found myself wanting to throw myself down on the long-stem bluegrass and inhale the virgin beauty of the prairie, to smell the acrid dark soil. I felt not as if I had come home but that I had at last found home. It didn't take much for me to see myself living my life fully and quietly and contentedly on the wide steppes of the Kansas prairie for the rest of my life.

CHAPTER

23

AS YOU plant the harvest row, you implicate the mellowed silence in hopes that the crop will not be diseased, the wheat will not rust, the corn will be knee-high by June, and the north will not send down drifts of snow until the crops are brought in after the first frost. The sun seems to brighten as you build each row, straight as an arrow behind two bow-necked Percherons, your hand callused from gripping the oak handles of the plow, guiding it carefully through the rich black earth that rolls up with a musty smell of the ages that have passed through time and time again.

I paused in the noonday heat of the field to drink cold water from the oaken bucket Williams's boy brought out to me. Perspiration dripped freely from me and my muscles felt loose and relaxed, although there was a steady ache across my shoulders that I knew would go away in time after the first rows were readied. I looked across the neatly turned furrows to where blue smoke rose lazily from Williams's chimney and past him to where Richard Budd's fields butted against Williams's fields and where the smoke rose from Budd's chimney straight up in the windless air.

For a brief moment I felt lonely and ached for my home and Mother's cooking, Hannah—but then I sighed and turned away, my hands again gripping the plow handles. I clicked my tongue against my teeth and slapped the reins gently across the Percherons' backs. Peace replaced the loneliness in my breast as the plodding hooves of the great beasts moved rhythmically across the land.

I guided the plow, turning at the end when we came to a split-rail fence and retracing my way over and over again. There was a certain music in the monotony and I listened to it, feeling it within me. And then it was over before I knew it and the sun seemed to drop below the horizon with a soft *whoosh!* I pulled the Percherons to a halt and eased the harness over their shoulders, walking them back across the black furrows to the house. Already I imagined I smelled the dew, but it would be hours before the moon would come up, at first red, then softening to white as it traveled over the prairies, and then the dew would begin rising from the warm earth. I sighed, contented with my lot, already regretting that my work here was only temporary, as it would be over at Budd's place. And then—

I shrugged with the unconcern of youth. Something would offer itself; something always offered itself to the youth. Uncertainty belonged with the aged. I was foolish enough to believe that and yet wise enough to know the frailty of the moment.

Memory is the country of the usable past when one is aware of mistranslations, mistakes, the inevitability of misinterpretation of experiences, leaving man in his age with an imperfect view of his life and the momentary importance of his actions. And his regrets for those actions. And then he realizes the strength of those battalions filled with malignant subterranean demons of dreams and then the black indwelling spirits come to him and he realizes the forlornness of his past as he plays out the hallucinatory placement of our days.

CHAPTER

24

RELUCTANTLY I rode back to Leavenworth with a farmer going in for supplies. After Williams had no more work for me, I moved over to Budd's place and finished plowing his fields for him, planting, repairing fences. I split enough firewood to carry him through the winter, and then he ran out of things for me to do. I debated about making my way farther west, but something made me realize the futility of that. The planting season was almost over and little would remain for a farmer except to quietly tend his crops and take care of the odd jobs around his farm that are little more than routine. Reason told me that I would quickly find myself out of work with increasing rapidity as the summer moved toward its rendezvous with fall. I thought about trying to file on a hundred and sixty acres of land that had easy rolling hills to it with a heavily timbered creek running a loop halfway around it. Kansas took you prisoner and never considered amnesty or an early parole. There was a quiet sense of insinuation to the land that once you stepped onto it you belonged to it forever.

Leavenworth had become a town filled with sullen individuals who stared suspiciously at one another, trying to decide who was pro- or antislavery. I thanked the farmer and stepped down from the wagon, easily shouldering my bag as I pondered my next move. I turned to make my way toward the land office. A man stumbled out of a bar and nearly knocked me into the street. I grabbed a post for balance as he bounced off me, missed his step off the boardwalk, and sprawled into the street. He lay still for a moment, then pushed himself up, cursing, and turned to face me.

"Watch where you're going, bud!" he exclaimed, slapping dust from his shirt and pants.

I stared at him coolly. "You're the one who ran into me," I said quietly.

His eyes narrowed. "I don't take no sass from someone still wet from his mother's milk!"

I placed my bundle carefully against the wall of the store behind me as he made his way back up onto the boardwalk. He came close to me, his face inches away, and I realized he was not as drunk as I had first supposed.

"The question is," he said, "what I should do with you."

"Walk away," I suggested. "If you're wise."

Laughter went up from a small group of laggards and layabouts who had gathered with hopes of seeing a fight. I glanced around quickly, noticing where they were, and took a half step to my left to keep my back free. That half step caught my opponent unaware, and his fist slashed through the space where I had been, throwing him off-balance. I quickly set myself and struck him hard on his kidneys, straightening him.

He grunted and swung around, trying to backhand me, but I had been through this with my brothers and many schoolyard scraps. I leaned back away from him, then stepped in close, hunching my shoulders, swinging quick, short blows into his midsection. His breath *whooshed* from him and he bowed forward. I took a step back and laced him with a hard uppercut I brought from my hip. He straightened, his eyes glazed, and for a moment he appeared balanced; then he fell backward, senseless, into the street, his arms outflung as if he'd been crucified.

"Break it up, boys," a voice said behind me.

I turned quickly, taking a step back and to the side in case a blow followed the words. But the speaker stood quietly, staring at the others. He wore the uniform of a colonel and the others sneered at him and a couple spit at his feet, but they were moving away when they did and he ignored them. He turned to me, eyeing me speculatively.

"You have a good set of shoulders on you, lad," he said. "I'm Colonel Harvey." He nodded at the man still lying senseless in the dirt of the street. "And obviously you can handle yourself quite well."

"Jim Hickok. I wanted nothing to do with that," I said quickly, thinking that he might consider me the instigator of the fracas. But he smiled at my words.

"I know," he said. "I could see it coming when he"—he nodded at the man in the street—"collided with you. It was quite deliberate, you know."

"Deliberate?" I frowned, shaking my head.

"Oh yes," he said, folding his arms over his chest. He tapped his left shoulder with his gauntleted fingers. "Quite deliberate."

"But why?"

He shrugged. "They wanted to see what side you were on."

"Side?"

"Pro- or antislavery," he said. He glanced around Leavenworth. "That issue has been brewing in the town for quite some days now." He laughed dryly. "I'm afraid that the whole town—if not the country—is going to erupt over this slavery issue. And other things," he added as an afterthought. "The slave issue is just the spark for the powder keg. But things are going to get worse since that John Brown episode. Where do you stand, by the way?"

His question nearly caught me off-guard, but I had been

watching the others as well, the woodsman in me attuned to the temper of those around me, feeling the tension like a tautly strung fiddle bow.

"My father used to be a part of the Railway," I said quietly. "Until he died. I do not believe anyone has the right to own another. John Brown?"

He nodded at my words. "A self-styled minister. Has his own idea about religion, though. Very Old Testament. You didn't hear about the Jeremy Ridge Massacre?"

I shook my head, frowning. "I didn't know the Indians were up."

He laughed shortly. "They aren't. That was Brown and three of his sons. After a little altercation between the anti- and proslavery forces here in Leavenworth, Brown took his sons to Jeremy Ridge and brutally hanged and burned three proslavery men he caught there. According to what I heard, he preached a long sermon while they were burning on their ropes, saying he was sending them to the fires of hell with a head start on burning. That's why I'm here: to catch Brown. If I can."

He sighed and clapped his hands together. "But it turns out that both the Free Staters and proslavery folks don't like the military stepping in. You'd almost think it was a private feud and no outsiders are allowed by mutual agreement. Yet we are about the only law that is here now."

"What about the marshal?"

He shook his head. "He varies from day to day, depending upon his strength and the amount of backing he gets from whichever side he favors. Law!" He nearly spit the word. "This is a huge joke. The law is whoever is in charge."

"Isn't that the normal way of things?" I asked.

His eyebrows rose. "A bit of education as well as a strong back, I see. Well, the governor, Wilson Shannon, resigned and Daniel Woodson, the territorial secretary and staunch proslavery supporter, took his place. He promptly proclaimed the territory to be in open rebellion and had Dave Atchison bring in his so-called Grand Army of Missourians to help him keep the peace."

Atchison, a florid, sociable huge man who was inordinately fond of horses, hunting, and fishing, accompanied his pleasures with frequent nips from a bottle of whiskey he kept near him at all times. He liked to brag that he was born in Frogtown, Kentucky, where he was the "biggest frog in the puddle."

I nodded at this. "I've heard about him. They say he won't listen to any reason or argument that doesn't support his own feelings."

"He's an extremist. In all things," the colonel added. "At any rate, he got into a battle with Brown, and while he fought with Brown and his people Jim Lane took an army of Free Staters to Lecompton. It looked like a war was going to get started, but Colonel St. George Crooke stopped it with troops from here.

"That kept an uneasy peace alive until the new governor, John Geary, could arrive. He promptly dismantled the militia and forced Atchison out of Kansas."

"And how do you figure into this?"

Colonel Harvey gave me another appraising look. "I command a small force of Free Staters. We could use a scout."

For a moment I didn't understand his meaning; then I shook my head. "I don't have a horse or a gun or anything. And what makes you think that I would make a good scout?"

A wintry smile touched his lips. "I can tell," he said quietly. He glanced down again and I felt a momentary embarrassment at the poorness of my person reflected by my homespun shirt, worn pants, and laced boots. "You may dress like a farmer and you may have worked as a farmer, but you are no farmer." His eyes touched mine. "It's in the eyes," he said.

I nodded sagely, although at that moment I didn't understand what he meant. Much later, after Ellsworth, I knew that he had seen the hunter in me and that was enough for him. What else I needed to know I could learn later, for there are some things that come only with experience. But for that experience to take there needed to be a foundation, and although I was young, I had that foundation from my roamings through the woods, learning the various songs and calls of the birds and how to read the silence that falls at man's approach, knowing the body of the woods, the lobe and larynx of bushes that are as familiar as my own palm, the sound of quail and grouse taking flight and tail feathers drumming poetry into the slipstream of the wild geese. I knew the golden days of the woods when leaves turned varnished yellow and rattled fall's music to those who paused to listen to it.

And so I became a scout, and a man who lived on Crooked Creek gave me a horse and rifle and revolver because he was too stumped up with arthritis to take his place with Harvey but still felt the need to make an obligation for his beliefs. I scouted for Harvey and narrowly missed being captured by the federal troops at Hickory Point when Harvey sent me to Lecompton for supplies.

After that Harvey disbanded his Free Staters and I became a pilgrim for a while and wandered from town to town with my fiddle and a dog that picked up with me on the road to Mill Creek. I played for my supper at many dances and the dog—I named him Fritz for no particular reason—would yawn with boredom until I played "Buffalo Gals," at which point he would rise on his haunches, lift his head to the ceiling, and yowl the chorus along with me:

"Buffalo gals, won't you come out tonight,"

much to the amusement of the merrymakers with me.

It was at Mill Creek that I met up with John Owen, who gave me a pallet in his cabin after a dance, and it was at his place that I improved myself with a pistol, a heavy Dragoon revolver, using oyster cans for targets. Owen had married a Shawnee woman, Patinuxa, a descendant of Logan, chief of the Mingo who turned against the settlers after the Yellow Creek Massacre in 1774 when most of his family was wiped out. They had one child, Mary Jane, but fever took Patinuxa and Owen never quite got over losing his wife so young.

Together Owen and I made our way around the countryside, squandering our days at church socials and town gatherings where I fiddled and he plucked at his banjo, feeling the wildness of dark juices working to keep us from sainthood as blushing young women flirted with us beneath the stern and watchful eyes of their mothers safely behind tables laden with cakes and pies and decorated with wild cherry blossoms and prairie flowers in bacchanal glory.

Kansas, however, was an unstable place as arguments became bitter between those wanting Kansas to be a free state and those wanting it to be a slave state. The slightest mention of politics in a saloon—and sooner or later talk always comes around to politics where men bend an elbow—would draw a fiery rebuttal from someone and a fight would commence with friends and neighbors joining in on one side or the other.

The strange thing was that I had lived long enough by this time to see the thinking on each side. The South needed the slaves for economic prosperity—the slaves had become such an ingrained part of that society and culture, both founded on agriculture that needed cheap labor to prosper. The North believed firmly in Jefferson's words that all men were created equal. The hot-blooded Abolitionists, however, were trying to ram their one-sided opinion down everyone's throats—not a good way to try to win an argument. Still, I always remembered Hannah and the look and feel of her back heavily scarred where a blacksnake had been used to try to teach her docile acceptance of her betters. But it was hard, very hard, especially when I saw what people like the self-appointed "reverend" John Brown did to those who disagreed with their position.

Despite the newspaper columns that lauded him as the greatest Abolitionist hero of his time, Brown was a vicious fanatic—preaching against slavery and insisting on rigid adherence to the Old Testament—and it was, in my opinion, due to him that Kansas soon became known as "Bleeding Kansas." It was his sons, however, that started the whole affair. Five of his twenty sons came to Kansas and staked out claims south of Lawrence and set up Brown's Station to suit their purposes. When a group of bushwhackers came across from Missouri and harassed them, one of them sent word back east to their father and "Goodman" John Brown hastened west with a wagon loaded down with rifles and sabers.

By the time Brown got there, the "Wakarusa War" was in full swing, with the Missouri boys raiding in Kansas one night, the Kansas boys raiding in Missouri the next. All given, no one really knew who was one up on the other. Goodman John immediately formed a group of men he called the Pottawatomie Rifles, named after a creek that ran through his boys' properties south of town where proslavery riders raided free-state settlers.

Now I don't rightly know what happened next, but I have a hunch the lid blew off the simmering pot when an assassin wounded the Douglas County sheriff, a staunch proslavery fellow. Goodman John led his rifles to Lawrence to help protect the town from a proslavery group—renegades, bushwhackers, many of whom later rode with Quantrill and Bloody Bill Anderson—that threatened to come across the river from Missouri to retaliate. It wasn't long after that Senator Charles Sumner from Massachusetts delivered his speech "The Crime Against Kansas" and was savagely beaten with a cane by Preston Smith Brooks, a member of the House of Representatives.

Sumner's beating settled things in Brown's mind, and through some twisted reasoning Brown led his sons down to Pottawatomie Creek to regulate matters. They slaughtered five men there, hacking them to pieces with their sabers, in the name of freedom for the slaves. From there, Brown started out on his holy war against Missouri and all who opposed his views.

I disagreed with Brown's tactics—Lord, but anyone with common sense would have disagreed with him—but I always remembered Hannah and that formed a restlessness in my spirit and when Owen and I heard about Jim Lane put-

ting together a tatterdemalion free-state army near High-
land to fight against those ruffians coming across from Missouri, more of a peacekeeping force, really, we decided to
join him.

CHAPTER

25

WE HEARD the crackle of gunfire, steady though sporadic, as we came into town. Owen frowned and glanced over at me.

"Sounds like a spat going on," he said.

"I don't think so," I said. "It sounds too steady for that. Let's take a look."

We followed the sound down an alley to a stable. Behind the stable, a shooting contest was in process. We dismounted and stood on the outskirts of the crowd, watching. A short, squat man stood, arms folded, watching critically as the men took turns firing at targets set up fifty yards and staggered from them. Each time one of them missed, he shook his head and spit a long stream of tobacco juice. The ground was soaked brown in front of him. Impulsively I walked up to him. His gray eyes flickered toward me, then back at the contest. I could see he was not very impressed.

"Your boys don't seem to be doing very well," I said.

One of his eyebrows jacked itself high and he turned, glowering, toward me. He spit, narrowly missing the toe of my boot. "Well, young'un," he said. "You think you can do better, there's your chance."

I shook my head, grinning. "Sorry. I didn't mean to upset you. It's just that they look like they could use a lot of practice."

"Uh-huh," he said, his jaws working furiously on the plug of tobacco that bulged his left cheek. "Well, son, out here, you be critical about a man's shooting, you better be willing to show your own. And," he added, reaching inside his pocket, "to make it interesting, what say thirty dollars says you can't beat the best of 'em?"

"Take it," Owen said from my elbow. I turned and looked down at him. He nodded. "I'll cover it."

I took a deep breath, feeling my blood sing with the challenge. I nodded and slipped the Dragoon from my belt. The man grunted and stepped forward waving his arms.

"Cease fire!" he barked. The men paused, dropping their weapons down by their sides, turning to look curiously at him. "Men, we have a young'un here who doesn't think you are any great shakes when it comes to marksmanship."

Eyes swiveled angrily toward me. I felt myself go red under their stares but met their gazes calmly.

"Well, Colonel Lane, let's see what he can do with that hog leg he's holding!" a voice yelled from the crowd.

"Colonel Lane? Jim Lane?" I said. The man turned to me, nodding. "Well, it's you we came to find," I said, feeling my embarrassment grow.

"Well, you found me," he said. He glanced at Owen standing behind me. A tiny smile tugged at the corners of his lips. "But we still have a little matter to settle before we engage in amenities, I think. Now," Lane said, turning back to the men. "Where's Fitzpatrick?"

"Here, Colonel," a voice answered, and a tall, thin man with black hair stepped from the crowd of men. He wore a pair of pistols belted high around his waist, butts forward. His trousers had been stuffed into the tops of his high boots. He wore a linen shirt with a patchwork vest over it. A high-crowned hat, dented in the middle, had been pulled low over his eyes. He glanced at me and smiled faintly.

"Well, Fitzpatrick, what do you say? You want to take this young'un on?"

Fitzpatrick studied me for a moment, then shrugged. "Makes no difference to me," he said. "Whatever you want."

"All right," Lane said. He folded his arms and nodded toward Fitzpatrick. "Let's see what you can do."

Three men grabbed fresh targets and ran downrange to set them up.

I stepped forward and held out my hand. "I'm James Hickok," I said.

He took my hand briefly. His hand felt soft in mine and I knew instinctively that he was no farmer. "Fitzpatrick," he said. "Most folks just call me 'Fitz.' " He looked me up and down. "This could be costly. You got the money?"

Annoyance swept over me and I grinned at him. "I reckon I can afford a dime or two." I nodded downrange. "You want to go first?"

He turned and drew his pistols quickly. I noticed that he didn't cross his arms across his chest to grip his pistols but drew them with a flickering twist of his wrist. When his right hand came level, he fired, then alternated left and right until he had ten shots off. He lowered his pistols and nodded and a man ran down to check his target. I glanced down at his pistols.

"Navy Colts," I said admiringly.

He nodded, looking automatically at the Dragoon in my hand. "That's pretty heavy for infighting. You might think about going to a lighter caliber."

I flushed and raised the Dragoon, conscious of its weight but holding it as negligently as I could. "I can handle one of these."

"Didn't say that," he said. "Just said that sometimes a smaller caliber and lighter gun is better." He held one of his pistols up. "The charge don't mean nothing if you can't hit what you're aiming at. And if you can, then a Navy works just fine. And it's lighter. You can get at it quicker."

"Seven out of ten in the eye!" the man called from downrange.

"Not bad," I said.

Fitzpatrick nodded. "Could've been better, I suppose." He looked again at the Dragoon. "You got an extra cylinder for that? Or we going to wait while you reload?"

"I have an extra," I mumbled, stepping past him. I raised the Dragoon, firing rapidly. Then I slipped the lever and palmed the cylinder out, replacing it with another I took from my pocket. I snapped it tight and raised the pistol, firing rapidly four times as I brought it level. I lowered the pistol, feeling the sting of the back charge in my hand as the man raced down.

"Not bad, I'm thinking," Fitzpatrick murmured from beside me.

The man turned slowly, shaking his head. "Ten outta ten!" he called.

I heard a rumble of disbelief from the crowd behind me. Fitzpatrick smiled down at me. "Think you can do it again?" he asked.

"Why not?" I said, emboldened by what I had just accomplished. "Should we stretch the distance some?"

His eyebrow twitched, but he nodded, and two men raced off to move the targets back. We walked back to a small table that had been laid with powder and ball, and reloaded our pistols.

"How's your arm holding out?" Fitzpatrick said conversationally.

"All right," I said.

"Uh-huh," he said, rocking the hammers to test the action. "But I'm betting that you feel the weight if you fire long, right?"

I didn't comment, suddenly aware of the weight of the pistol. Then I realized the subtlety of his remarks, calculated to turn my mind from shooting to the discomfort the Dragoon caused. I shifted the weight of the pistol to my left hand and clenched and unclenched my right to work the tension from my arm. Together we walked back to the firing line. The men slipped to the side after placing the fresh targets. Fitzpatrick nodded.

"No reason we both can't shoot," he said. "Unless you think you might be bothered by my noise."

"Nope," I answered. I raised my pistol and began firing.

Fitzpatrick followed my lead, but I noticed he took more time to aim this time than before. We stepped back after setting our shots and a man ran down, counting first Fitzpatrick's target and announcing that he had nine out of ten in the bull. A satisfied roar rose, congratulating him. Then the man turned and looked at my target. The uproar died as he slowly backed from the target and looked back at us.

"Ten out of ten again," he said disbelievingly.

The crowd fell silent. Fitzpatrick shook his head. "Well, I'd say that you've beaten me and beaten me square, by God!" He grinned and offered his hand.

"Shoot again!" someone yelled, but Fitzpatrick again shook his head.

"Nope," he said. "There's no sense wasting powder. This 'Wild Bill' has beaten me and done it properly. None here's gonna object to that, far as I'm concerned." He turned to Lane, who stayed at the side, impassively watching us. "Colonel, you could do worse than signing this one up."

"Both of us," Owen said. He came forward, clapping me on the shoulder. He looked at Lane. "And I'd say you owe us thirty dollars for that. Give it to Jim here."

"Good going, Wild Bill!" someone shouted. I flushed at the nickname given to someone good with pistols.

The crowd clapped and someone gave a wild shout and a hat went sailing up in the air. I felt myself blushing and looked over at Lane. He came forward and handed thirty dollars to me.

"I think you're right, Fitzpatrick," he said. He looked at Owen and nodded. "There's a place for both you and Bill here. How old are you, son?" he said, turning toward me.

"Nineteen," I stammered. Suddenly I felt as awkward as a schoolboy in his presence and glanced down at the toe of my boot. "And I'd sure as certain like to be with you and your boys!"

"Then you shall be," he said, shaking my hand. "You're the best shot in three hundred."

And on that we were enlisted in his Frontier Guard, as he liked to call them. I sort of attached myself to him as his bodyguard along with Owen and we traveled around the countryside together, with Lane stumping for election to the U.S. Senate part of the time and the rest of the time patrolling the border. Once in Grasshopper Falls when Lane was delivering a particularly fire-breathing speech denouncing the so-called Border Ruffians as the spawn of Beelzebub, I noticed a dirty man with a beard start to slip his pistol from his holster. I stepped forward with the Dragoon in my hand and stared at him for a long moment before he replaced his pistol and slunk away. Lane never noticed, caught up as he was in his oratory.

Not long after this, a territorial grand jury, made up solely of proslavery folks, indicted some of the folks in Lawrence, citing them for treason along with a bunch of other crimes so vaguely stated as to be ridiculous. They sent a U.S. marshal along with a posse of Missourians to arrest them. But after the marshal served the warrants and told the posse to go home, they went on a rampage instead, tearing Lawrence apart, setting fire to the buildings, looting the stores, and shooting at anything that moved. Whiskey flowed like a river among them.

We heard about what was happening in Lawrence and headed that way as soon as we could get horsed. So did Goodman John Brown along with his sons and a few others who believed along with him that slavery was an abomination against God. But we were too late. The Missourians had slipped back over the border after drinking Lawrence dry and pretty near leveling the town. Brown took it all personally and declared "those barbarians have to be shown that we, too, have rights." He ordered his men to horse and they took off for Pottawatomie Creek, where they dragged five men from their beds and hacked them to death with swords already bloodied from the time before. They washed their swords free of blood in the creek and I guess it ran red. After that, people began to refer to our place as "Bleeding Kansas." But Lane's army had nothing to do with that. Brown went his own way; we went ours. I think Brown was really more interested in spilling blood to show the South that they couldn't be riding across the border and messing around with Kansas politics. He was more of an "eye for an eye" man instead of "turning the cheek" and forgiving.

We found out that many of those who had come across into Kansas joined up or were from Atchison's Grand Army of Missouri—not much of an army, really. More a group of men who had decided the unsettled times were ready-made for their unsettled ways—a bunch of hell-raisers out to have a little fun. I don't think they were much better than Brown and his boys. But then again, we weren't, either, I reckon now with a bit of hindsight—the calf wouldn't get out of the barn if the door had been shut properly in the first place, Father always said, and thinking about it now doesn't shut it then. But we didn't think then. We reacted just like Brown, although, I think, with a bit more civility.

Lane's men finally met up with Atchison's Grand Army of Missouri on Bull Creek, fifteen miles north of Osawatomie. But before we could engage in anything other than a few minor skirmishes on the flanks, Colonel Philip St. George Crooke came up with a squad of troops from Fort Leavenworth and demanded that we all disband and go home. None of us wanted to take on those troopers, who were better armed than we were and had the look of seasoned veterans about them, so we slunk away with our tails between our legs, much to the name- and catcalling of the troopers. But Lane allowed that there was a time when discretion was called for and that there wasn't any reason to be ashamed. There would be plenty of other chances, he said, for us firebrands to earn our spurs.

And he was right. I soon learned that the Third Commandment could be suspended on occasion. The border broke out in a series of barn burnings, lynchings, and killings from ambush. A rightly named guerrilla war that Brown and others like him took to with relish. We had our moments, too, but I could see that things weren't going to amount to much after a few months and soon Owen and I found ourselves back in Monticello, Kansas, where Owen became a supervisor and I the town constable, thanks to a commission issued by James Denver, who was acting as the territorial governor.

I also filed a claim on a hundred and sixty acres, and between being a constable and working my claim I felt subsumed by function. But I still had time for Owen's daughter, Mary.

Ah, Mary! When I first saw her, I felt as if a mule had kicked me in the stomach and Hannah's memory slipped into the background. I remember standing face-to-face with Mary in the moonlight and watching the pale light shimmering silvery off the prairie grasses rolling gently in the night breeze like dark waves. We put our arms around each other and the future seemed spread out before us in a familiar intensity. My hands curved as if seeking the handles of a plow and I smelled the rich Kansas earth and imagined the crops that could be planted and raised from it.

CHAPTER

26

SHE LAUGHED and I was aware of being involved in her laughter and being a part of it. Her teeth were accidental stars in the night and I felt my breath slip from me in short gasps, inhaled automatically in momentary recovery. I lost myself in the dark cavern of her throat where her heart beat, pulsing in the night like a gentle ripple in a backwater stream.

I dreamed the dreams of a farmer with Mary lying beside me in the pale moonlight, watching the annealed stars and low-hooked moon. Her lips trembled beneath mine and her bronzed skin seemed to glow from an inner fever and together we made plans to wed. I built a cabin on my claim, taking great pains to make it as comfortable as possible. I bought a milch cow and put up hay, planning to serve one year as constable before settling down with Mary. I wrote to Mother and told her about Mary and that, I imagine, was the beginning of hard times between Mother and me. She dispatched Lorenzo to talk me out of marrying beneath her station.

* * *

The last fingers of leaves clutched and sank into the wet bank of the creek while the wind blew lightly, rattling the dried limbs of the trees like old bones. An uneasiness seemed to stalk the land in the cruelest month and I lay in bed, mixing memory and desire, half-asleep, half-dreaming. Mary was visiting her folks and broken images slipped through the dimness and I saw again the disapproving face of Mother, thin-lipped, hollow-cheeked, wearing a mobcap and widow's weeds and looking like the dried husk of a spinster. Broken images slipped across the land of my dreams where the eyes of Jesus saw nothing.

I heard footsteps shuffling, a cold wind suddenly wafting under my door, an exclamation and sudden hush.

I awoke, momentarily confused, then rose and crossed silently to my window and peered out. Torchlight ran red on sweaty faces grim with determination. I recognized some of them—proslavery men whose hatred steamed in the night. I thought I smelled the whiskey on their breath that gave them the courage to come to my cabin like rats creeping through back alleys. The first torch flew toward the roof of my cabin and I turned, grabbing as many possessions as I could, crossing the cabin to the back, where I dived through a window and rolled like a log into the darkness. I cocked the Dragoon and fired at a dim shadow. It staggered, then howled like a gut-shot dog.

"Jesus! He's out!"

I fired again, deliberately holding low as two rushed in to help the first. A leg snapped backward as the heavy ball struck it and the figure tumbled onto the ground. I worked my way backward, down to the creek, and slipped over the bank and through the shadows away from the cabin while curses and screams of pain dented the night.

Morning dawned, gray in the early light with a milky fog rising from the creek bed. I came cautiously out of the buffaloberry bushes where I had hidden in the night. I carried the heavy Dragoon pistol loosely in my hand, ready for whoever was foolish enough to show himself. I paused before the smoking ashes of what had been my cabin, listening to the birds sing themselves awake, and knew that I was alone.

A few charred timbers still stood, but even the stone fireplace had cracked from the heat of the fire and fallen in on itself. A self-pitying lump came into my throat, but I swallowed it away and stared at the remains of my cabin while cold anger seeped through me, settling like ice in the pit of my stomach, forcing emotions away. I wanted the anger now, *needed* the anger now, to justify the burning of my cabin as a personal attack upon myself and not upon my beliefs. To believe otherwise was to admit being naïve, and I was vain enough to want to believe I was important enough for others to want to destroy. But I was deceiving myself by making myself a martyr to the cause of antislavery. I felt noble, enriched, bitter, working myself into a justification for the morality of my intentions. I fully intended to find the men responsible for burning my cabin. But deep down I knew such intentions were futile, for the men I wanted would have witnesses that they were nowhere near my cabin when misfortune struck.

"Jim?"

I dropped to the ground, spinning around, cursing at my carelessness at not hearing him approach. I rocked the hammer back, automatically aiming at the figure in the mist. He threw up his hands, backing hastily away.

"It's me, Jim!"

I took a deep breath and let it out slowly. I gently lowered the hammer and pushed myself up from the ground. "Hello, Lorenzo. Bad timing to come up on me that way."

Lorenzo dropped his hands and moved in to me. "Damn it, Jim! You took seven years off the backside of my life!"

"Lucky I didn't take *that*," I said defensively. "What are you doing creeping up like that without announcing yourself?"

"Why the hell are you so touchy?" he retorted.

I gestured at my cabin. "That's why. Some boys came around last night and burned me out. Almost got me as well."

"Yours?" I nodded. "Looks like it was a pretty one. I knew you had registered a claim, but I didn't know you had built already."

"Yeah, well, I had a reason," I said, sighing. "Now I reckon I'm just going to have to start again."

"Uh-huh," he grunted. He glanced at me sideways. "The Indian girl?" he asked deliberately offhandedly.

I bristled at the tone of his voice, recognizing the distaste under his question. I turned toward him. "What do you mean?" I asked quietly.

"You know what I mean," he said defensively. "Mother almost had a stroke when she read your last letter, thinking that you were contemplating marrying her."

"I am," I answered.

"Jim," he said solemnly. "She's an Indian."

A wave of anger washed over me. I had been fighting against this prejudice for almost six months—nearly being killed a couple of times—and now I was hearing the same words from my brother that I had been hearing from the pukes and crackers I had been chasing into Missouri. I felt the heat of my anger flood up into my cheeks, and the copper taste at the back of my throat told me I was close to losing control. Somewhere a jay called, raucous and loud. A squirrel answered angrily. I took a deep breath and turned back to face my brother, willing the anger away.

"I never thought I would hear that from you, Lorenzo," I said, shaking my head. "After all we did with Father, running the Negroes back and forth to get them away from their owners. Why, we even took in Hannah, if you remember." I felt a twinge of memory at the mention of her name and looked away. Lorenzo caught it.

"I remember," he said, giving me a hard look. "And don't think I don't know about the two of you. I never said nothing, but you can bet I wanted to ream your butt. What would Mother had said if she'd a-had a baby? Would've destroyed her. She wouldn't have been able to lift her head up at all in town or church, what with people snickering whenever she passed."

I flushed. "You don't know what you're talking about," I mumbled. But I knew he could tell I was lying. Unless I was spinning a story, I never could tell an out-and-out lie. I always flushed redder than a first-kissed schoolgirl at a church social.

"Yeah, you keep saying that. All licorice and horehound drops."

"Does Mother know?"

He shrugged. "I don't know. I *think* so. But with Mother you can't rightly tell everything. Sometimes she gets that prim twist to her mouth and you know she's holding her tongue although the words wanna burst outta her." He held his hand up warningly as I felt my eyes grow hard and harsh words leaped to my lips. "Now, Jim, remember that she's a bit old-fashioned. She's willing to help folks, but she don't think chickens should mate with eagles—the chickens cannot fly that high and might get hurt. Some people are like eagles; they are made to fly high. Others are made to be part of the earth. Your little Indian girl belongs there, Jim. You belong up among the eagles."

"Very literary, Brother. But what makes me so that I should fly among the eagles? Because I'm white?"

He hesitated and, I have to give him credit for doing so, blushed. But his lips were tight with resolution as he met my eyes. "Yes, that's part of it. Being white, you come from a different world than she does. You don't fit in her world and she doesn't fit in yours."

"What are you talking about?" I exploded, waving my arms around at my burnt cabin. "I built this for us. I planned on farming this land. If this wasn't becoming a part of the earth, I don't know what the hell it was! I thought I was far enough from the border to keep those Missourian ruffians away." Suddenly I felt as if the air had been punched out of me. I waved my hands awkwardly, limply. "Hell, they spent most of their time raiding the river bottoms east of here. There's a Blue Lodge not far from here and those damn Ma-sons always raid to the southeast. But I reckon that's no insurance that they would continue to do that."

"It isn't a matter of what you *want* to do but what you're *meant* to do, Jim," he said. A hint of sadness seemed to touch his eyes for a moment, and in that moment it was like looking into a mirror and I saw myself in the unhappiness behind his solemnity and behind that solemnity I felt the distance that I was going to have to ride and the loneliness with that distance.

I turned away and stared at the charred timbers of my cabin. A half wall still hung blackly together with the stark frame of a window balanced precariously on top of it. I looked through that frame and a low fog seemed to rise from the creek. In the fog I saw the shadows of aging soldiers in an ancient war, and a great sorrow descended upon me and I knew that sorrow would be with me constantly and I would know joy only briefly. The changing seasons would bring little relief, and the little happiness I would feel would be taken away quickly by bitter time. Faintly I heard Lorenzo clear his throat, and I took a deep breath, facing him once again.

"Did you recognize any of them?"

"Thought I did," I answered slowly. "I winged a couple, maybe hurt 'em a little more seriously, but there's gonna be my mark on more than one who came here."

"Word has it that you've joined the Free-State Militia—the Redlegs. If there's any truth to that, you've got reason enough to have some of those boys coming to your house for a bit of Hickok barbecue." Lorenzo frowned. "Those boys are nothing but trouble, from what I've heard. I hope you haven't thrown your lot in with them."

I shook my head emphatically. "I rode with Jim Lane for a while *before* he formed the Redlegs, but I didn't like him. Couldn't trust him. I found out later that when he first came to Kansas he boasted he'd just as soon buy a nigger as a mule. But he changed his tune when he took a hard look at the Free Staters. No, I won't join a man who can't make up his mind or changes it when the wind blows differently. Man's got to be constant. I left him months ago."

Lorenzo watched me hard for a few moments before relaxing and saying, "All right. Let's leave it at that. I heard from a letter you wrote to Mother that there was a section with about a hundred of acres on it you thought we should go after."

"There was," I said. I took a deep breath, trying to push the anger down inside of me. "But right now I want to rethink that."

He frowned. "But—"

I shook my head. "I mean it. You can file on it if you want—I'll show you where it is—but what Mother said needs some thinking over."

"You have to remember what Mother is like," he said.

"I do remember and that's the trouble," I said. "I remember how many nights you and me rode with Father to pick up some Negroes and take them on to the next stop. She never said anything against that. So why now is she all of a sudden set against Mary Jane? No," I continued when he started to argue with me, "no, don't say anything right now. I'm angry." I gestured toward the smoking ruins of my cabin. "I don't think I want to build another cabin right now. There's just too much hatred going on. Both at home and here."

Lorenzo said he could wait a bit while I thought it over. He took a job working for a farmer north of Monticello. I found a job driving freight between Independence and Santa Fe.

Still a restlessness within my spirit dug away at me like spurs in the flanks of a restless gelding. The prairie hills rolled away from the wagons slowly, like brown waves upon an endless sea, lulling me into a certain lassitude that drugged my mind sometimes, making me feel like I was a sailor lost upon the Sea of Galilee. A couple of times I almost fell off my horse as I guided the wagons from one town to another.

One day I rode out a ways ahead of the freight train, checking the coulees and gullies for renegades who had been preying upon the wagons near Leavenworth. I rode over a small hill and saw a young man struggling against a couple of bearded buffalo hunters. His horse stood ground-reined a few yards away. As I watched, one of the hunters dug a fist into the youth's stomach. He leaned over, gagging, as the two of them bore him facedown upon the ground. One of them sat on his head as the other pulled his pants down, skinning them off as smoothly as a skinner's knife cutting through a buffalo hide.

I shook my head and nudged my horse with my heels, riding down to them. They were so intent upon their purpose that they never heard my horse's hooves moving through the long bluestem grass. The youth kept struggling gamely, but it was a losing battle against those men who were intent upon having their sport with him.

"Ain't nothin' like a fresh one, eh, Luke?" the one standing between the boy's legs said. He hooked dirty thumbs into his belt and pushed his pants down around his ankles. His legs gleamed like dirty ivory in the noonday sun. "Hold 'im now. I'll return the favor."

"Ain't fair, Ned," the other complained, trying to grab the boy's hands. "You allus seem to get the fresh'ns while I come in second."

Ned grinned. "This here one looks fresh enough that it won't matter none."

"There's that," Luke snickered obscenely.

I slid the Dragoon from its holster hanging from the pommel of my saddle and rocked the hammer back. The hunters froze, then turned slowly, craning their necks up and squinting against the sun to where I sat on my horse.

"What you want?" Ned demanded, hawking and spitting. His teeth gleamed dirty yellow in his bearded face. I could smell the buffalo stink on both of them—like meat left too long in the sun. The day seemed to narrow down to a small world that held only the four of us.

"Anything I hate is a buffalo man taking advantage of a boy," I said, feeling the anger burning through me like hot oil. "Let him up."

"Now," Ned whined.

"Your choice," I said. "Let him up or I'll knock you off him. I'll put a bullet through you big enough to let a jackrabbit find daylight."

"Better do it, Luke," Ned said.

Suddenly the two of them moved left and right, their hands scrabbling for their weapons. As Ned came up with a long skinning knife in his hand the Dragoon roared, knocking him back onto the ground. He screamed and his hands gripped the hole in his belly as he curved into a fetal position against the pain soaring through him. Luke turned white and started to run, but he forgot his pants gathered around his ankles and sprawled on his belly across a scrub prickly pear cactus. He yelped and rolled away, then dived for his rifle lying where he had carelessly dropped it in the grass. I waited until he tried to bring it up, then shot him in the forehead. His head jerked backward, the top of his skull fragmenting.

I glanced over at Ned, who convulsed once, his legs twisting in agony; then he lay still. I sighed and lowered the hammer on the Dragoon and looked at the boy still stretched on the ground.

"You can get up now," I said. "They won't be bothering you anymore."

He rose and kept his back to me as he picked up his pants and stepped into them. He tucked his shirttail in, keeping his face down and away from me. His hair was long and yellow-white and fell forward in twin curtains that covered the sides of his face. I could see the red on the back of his neck. I sighed and stepped down from my horse, taking a water bag with me.

"Well," I said, walking up to him. "I'm James Hickok." I pulled the wooden stopper from the canvas bag and took a long drink, then reached around and handed it to the boy.

"Go ahead," I said. "Have a drink."

Wordlessly he took the bag and tilted it up. He had fine features and was older than I first thought but still looked about ten years younger than me. His eyes, I noticed, were blue-gray. He poured a little water into his hand and splashed it across his face, then handed the bag back to me.

"Thanks," he mumbled. His cheeks were still pink beneath a soft furze that was the beginning of a future beard. I could see the embarrassment taking a hard hold upon him.

I took the water bag from him and walked back to my horse, draping it over the saddle horn. "You know," I said conversationally, "there are some things a person just can't help. There comes a time when you do everything you can and if the numbers are against you, you're still going to come up short."

I stepped into the stirrups and swung up onto my horse. "You did everything you could," I said gently. "There's nothing to be ashamed of."

He turned and lifted his head, his eyes shining. "Thanks," he said gruffly. "I appreciate what you done."

I shook my head. "You'd do the same if things were the other way around. And they could have been that way." I looked at the boy's horse still standing patiently to the side. I didn't see any weapons. "Especially if I wouldn't have had a gun, either." I pointed down at the bodies. "But now you do. Get what you want from them. They aren't going to be needing anything, keeping the devil company the way they are now."

I turned the horse as he called out.

"I'm Bill. Bill Cody!" he shouted.

I looked over my shoulder and smiled at him. "Pleased to meet you, Bill Cody," I said. "Maybe we'll meet again." I touched the brim of my hat and lifted the horse into a trot away from them.

"I'll remember this!" he shouted, and I waved again.

I was certain that he would remember it, but I didn't think that I would see him again despite my words. The land was big and empty, with nothing but miles and miles between homesteads and towns, and the chances of coming upon a person twice in a lifetime seemed as remote then as those of reaching the full harvest moon.

I soon pushed the matter from my mind as I turned my thoughts back to Mary Jane. Like I told Lorenzo, I needed time to think about what had happened, and that was a mistake on my part. Maybe I was trying to follow Mother's way or maybe I was trying to make up for her about not being there the day Father died while I was spending that time with Josephine, tumbling around the barn on spread hay—I don't know. Either way, it was a mistake to stay gone so long away from Mary Jane. I had made up my mind to settle down again on the acres I had claimed despite Mother's concern and take Mary Jane for my wife. Mother could sort the problem out herself. But when I came back from my first trip, Mary Jane had already decided for me: she had married a doctor named Harris. At first, I tried to bury my disappointment in a bottle of Old Hickory, but that didn't last long. Her image soon disappeared from my memory until I could only remember her name and a faint outline of her form. When I could no longer remember what she looked like, I took a job on a stage line.

CHAPTER

27

I CAME to like the work along the Old Santa Fe Trail that wound up into the hills of the upper reaches of the Arkansas River before turning along the River of Lost Souls and climbing into the Raton Mountains in New Mexico. That became a little hairy, working the stage along those steep gorges and ravines, but smelling the jack pine and spruce in the early mornings and when it rained made it all worthwhile. I had never seen such hardness in a land before, but there was something intoxicating about it that pulled me right into its bosom and made me love it.

Somehow, my name got lost along the way and everyone took to calling me "Bill." I don't really remember when it became permanent, but I guess it was when I took to raising the teams I was driving into a gallop when we came to the outskirts of Santa Fe in order to shake the kinks out of the passengers' spines after they had been sitting for so long.

One day, we came rolling into Santa Fe in a cloud of dust, a lady in the coach screaming that we were going to be killed at that speed. I nearly ran over a little sandy-haired man dressed in buckskins who had been crossing the street, but he skipped nimbly out of the way as I pulled the team to a stop in front of the station.

"Oh, God!" the woman inside said loudly. "Oh, God! We made it! We made it! Praise be the Lord!"

"Yes, ma'am," I said, stepping down and opening the door for the passengers. "But he didn't have his hands on the reins. I did."

She gave me a murderous look, indignantly slapped my hand aside, and descended to the ground. She nearly stumbled when her knees buckled, but the small man leaped over and steadied her by the elbow. She jerked her arm away with a decisive and dismissive, "Men!" and, throwing her chin out in front of her like a logger's elbow, stormed on down the street toward the hotel.

"You really should be ashamed of yourself!" a drummer in a dusty bowler squeaked as he stumbled out of the coach.

"Oh, shut up," said a burly man dressed like a banker, with a heavy gold chain across his vest, pushing himself out of the coach. "It relieved the boredom." He stepped down and brushed the dust from him, nodding at me. "You sure woke us up, son. Good job."

"Thank you, sir," I said. He reached into his vest pocket, removed a dollar, and handed it to me before crossing the plaza toward the bank. I watched him as he moved away, then felt a gentle tap on my shoulder. I turned around and found the small man facing me. His eyes met mine steadily.

"That was quite a trick," he said softly, musically. "But you damn near rode me down."

I glanced at the dollar in my hand and stuffed it into my pocket. I grinned at him. "Well, you managed to get out of the way, didn't you?"

"I did," he said. "But there are some who might not have been able to. You need to start thinking about them instead of the fun you're having at the time."

I started to retort hotly, but he had a bearing about him made me draw the words back, considering, before I threw them out to the air. I think it was in the eyes; yes, it was in the eyes. No fear or apprehension showed, which was unusual, as he was fully a head shorter than I and looked to be about as big around as my thigh. If not for the buckskins and his square shoulders, I would not have given him a second glance. But his eyes—that is where the character lies, where the truth lies, and although I didn't know this at the time, I sensed it and had learned enough in my short time on the plains by then to pay heed to my senses.

"You're probably right," I said tactfully—words cost little but can gain you much, I thought—"but after a time on the trail, it seems just natural to want to let the horses out. They know they're near the end, too, and look forward to getting the harness off. But I apologize."

He stood silent for a long moment, studying me to see if I was being sarcastic or my words were sincere. Then he relaxed and a faint smile touched his lips beneath his sandy mustache. "You know," he said, "few people would offer an apology to someone out here even if they were wrong and knew it. It signals to most that they are weak—they think—and so they stubbornly maintain they are right."

I grinned at him. "So I shouldn't apologize?"

"No"—he shook his head—"that's not what I'm saying. A man needs to be honest to himself at all times. He should be honest to others as well, but most of all he has to be honest to himself and willing to admit when he's made a mistake. I'm just giving you a bit of advice, that's all. Not," he hastened to add, "that I'm free with it, normally, but I've got a hunch that you haven't been out west long. Most people see apologies as a weakness. You may have to fight someone sometime when they try to take advantage of you for apologizing."

I shrugged. "No sense worrying about it. When it comes, it comes."

"Uh-huh," he said, his eyes studying mine carefully. Suddenly he held out his hand. "I accept. I'm Christopher Carson. Most people call me Kit."

I could feel my mouth dropping open as I took his hand. "*The* Kit Carson? I've read about you so much I think I could recite your life backward. Why, when I was a boy"—I felt the silliness of my words as I spoke them and the red burning my cheeks, but I couldn't stop myself from gushing—"I tried to imitate you in the woods back home. I read your autobiography until the pages wore out."

"Yes, well, uh, thanks," he stammered softly. He looked around quickly as if searching for a way to escape. He pulled gently on my hand and I suddenly realized that I was gripping it as if I intended on owning it forever. Sheepishly I released it and rubbed the back of my neck and wiped my hand down the leg of my trousers, not really knowing what to do with it but feeling like I never wanted to wash it again and feeling stupid for feeling that way. I never had many heroes in my time, but here was one standing in front of me as plain as day, although he was smaller than I thought he would be and looked like he could drown in a cup of water.

"Sorry," I said. "There I go again: apologizing. It's just that I never thought—well, hope I didn't make you mad."

"No, no, you didn't. It's just a bit much, you know, when people treat you like you're something special when you ain't."

"But, Mr. Carson—"

"Kit," he reminded me gently. "Kit. Please."

"All right. Oh." I shook my head. "Sorry. I'm James Hickok."

He cocked his head, squinting quizzically at me. "Any relation to a Bill Hickok I'm beginning to hear about?"

"Oh, some people call me that," I said, feeling my cheeks redden again. "Look, can I buy you a drink—or a cup of coffee—as a way of apologizing? Maybe we could start over?"

He glanced up at the sun, pressed his lips together thoughtfully, then nodded. "A cup of coffee would be nice. I don't drink much. I kind of like knowing what I'm doing and saying. Drink can grab a man by the throat and make him a fool, and I don't seem to have much trouble doing that by myself without the help of drink. But come on, I know a small place where we won't be bothered, and tonight I'll show you the Santa Fe that appeals to your age."

He led me to a small restaurant run by a Mexican just off the plaza. The coffee was strong but seasoned with cinnamon and rich cream. I finally relaxed in his presence, and slowly he began to share his adventures with me—or, at least, what seemed like adventures to me but were regarded by him as just everyday occurrences in his life as a mountain man. I began to ache for a share in his nostalgia, but I knew those days were gone and there was no way I could bring them back by trying to live in the past. Dreams, I know, are fine, but they are only dreams to be enjoyed and not the mystic revelations of a possible life.

That night, he was as good as his word—he always was—and we began our night sojourn around Santa Fe with a stop in the bar of the United States Hotel. When we pushed our way into that smoke-filled room, I saw immediately that it had become the meeting place for the mountain men. Most in that room were more Kit's age than my own, and I knew that he had made this the first stop to show me the life that had been and the stubborn men who refused to acknowledge the passing of time.

Hunters and trappers, wearing old smoke-cured and fringed buckskins, crowded the bar, drinking and bickering among themselves about the relative merits of various traps. Hawkin rifles were held carelessly or stood in corners and leaned against the bar within easy reach of callused hands. Bowie knives bristled at their belts along with small hatchets. Beneath the smoke I could smell old grease and a faint hint of pine needles. A few hailed Kit and motioned for him to join them, but he shook his head, politely declining their offer of drink, and nodded in my direction to show that he had already committed himself to my company.

On second glance, I had to amend my first opinion, recognizing merchants from Santa Fe, traders, freighters and teamsters, and Mexican entrepreneurs arguing softly in the corners away from the mountain men. The room was loud with noise as people bargained and quarreled, some singing raucous and sentimental songs. The noise began to infiltrate my senses and slowly I became aware that English wasn't the only language being spoken in the room. I heard French and Spanish and against a door leading to a back room stood four or five red-faced men arguing in German. I realized that this was the cosmopolitan center of Santa Fe, a refuge for lonely men, some of whom had made their way from the trail and mountains, all seeking a brief respite from their loneliness in the river of whiskey and warm beer that they poured liberally down parched throats.

Here Kit had a short drink—indeed, I don't think he would have been allowed out of the room had he not had one—and then we proceeded to an L-shaped flat-roofed adobe house down in the Mexican quarter. It was much darker down here and we walked in the center of the street as a precaution against suddenly being accosted from the shadows of the alleys. The room was filled with poker tables and a roulette wheel and high-banked dicing tables. Monte seemed to be the favorite game, for four of the tables had been designated for that play. The banks there were stacked with Spanish doubloons and Mexican gold and silver along with paper script.

A man threw up his hands and stepped away from one of the tables. On an impulse, I took his place. Kit gave me a questioning look but stood near my elbow as I placed some money on the worn green felt covered with the faded painted face of a snarling tiger in front of me. I lost the first round, then the second, as the bored-looking dealer slapped the shoe in front of him, slipping the losing and the winning cards from its lip. I decided to try once more when a woman came up and dropped a hand on the dealer's shoulder, leaning down to speak lowly in his ear. Her voice carried to me, but she spoke in Spanish. Kit nudged me and I bent toward him, listening as he said, "That's Señora Dona Gertrudis Barcelo. She's in charge of the monte play here." I glanced over at the woman smoking a small cigarillo. She wore a black satin dress, her shoulders bare, hair piled in curious curls held in place with a ruby-crested band. A black velvet band was around her waist and neck. Her black eyes danced toward us and caught and held mine boldly. I nodded politely toward her. A tiny smile moved her full and painted lips, bringing dimples into each cheek.

"Be careful there," Kit murmured from beside me.

"Why do you say that?" I asked quietly.

"She just told the dealer to let the handsome young American win," he said quietly.

"Then we should play a little more, don't you think? I would hate to disappoint her," I said as a recklessness came over me. I reached over and coppered my bet. I glanced at her and saw her fingers tighten on the dealer's shoulder. She gave me a tiny nod as the dealer slapped the shoe and slipped the cards out smoothly. I won and placed another bet on the king of spades, letting my winnings and original bet ride. Again the dealer slapped the shoe and swiftly drew two cards, the first the loser and the second the winner. Again I won.

"You'd better stop while you're ahead, Bill," Kit said softly. "I wouldn't take advantage of her. She's letting you win now, but you go much further, you're going to have to oblige her."

"Would it be all that bad?" I asked.

He nudged me gently with his elbow. I followed his gaze toward the side of the room where a young man in a suit sat on a chair placed on a small platform high above the crowd. He held a Greener, the twin muzzles pointed in my general direction. He glared at me, the muscles working in the corners of his jaw.

"Who is he?" I asked.

"Her current lover," he said. "Funny thing about her lovers: They don't last long. She's sort of like a black widow. Of course, it depends upon how good they are, I expect. Both in bed and out. That one's got a shotgun, though. Man would have to be quick and good to beat that. Besides," he said dryly, turning to me, "cards are the devil's prayer book. Haven't you heard that before from a parson somewhere?"

I laughed, feeling the recklessness moving up from my belly to my shoulders, that feeling a man gets when he figures he can whip his weight in wildcats. The room became suddenly bright and clear and I smiled across the room at the young man on the chair. I raised a finger to my hat and saluted him mockingly.

"Don't be a fool!" Kit said sternly. "You won't win down here. Maybe uptown, but not down here. Look around you."

Obediently I looked around. At first I noticed nothing; then suddenly I became aware that with the exception of a couple of mountain men and a muleskinner, Kit and I were the lone white men in the room. A few had become aware of the young man's interest and were staring, openly hostile, at me. I glanced across at Señora Barcelo. She smiled faintly back and I could read the invitation in her eyes. But then I noticed the fine, hard lines at the corners of her eyes, the rough skin scarred by smallpox beneath the rice powder she had used liberally on her face and shoulders. I imagined what she would be like beneath me in bed—*if you get that far without being cut in two by the Greener,* I thought. I tried to tell myself that he would not be stupid enough to use it in a crowd this size, since a shotgun doesn't recognize a particular person but treats all the same, impersonally and deadly. Then again, infatuation makes a person do dumb things. *Just like you were about to do.*

"You know," I said to Kit, "I think you have a very valid point there." I scooped my winnings up from the table and weighed them carefully in my hand, then placed my winnings in my pocket. "Man really shouldn't tempt fate when he's already had a look at the other man's cards." But I stepped back reluctantly from the table, feeling the pull of the cards and aching to buck the tiger again.

"Glad you see it that way," Kit said. "You can always come back later, you know. I wouldn't—but then, I'm older than you and been that way before."

"What way's that?"

"Letting your pecker do your thinking for you," he said dryly. Then he raised his voice so all at the table could hear. "Come on. There's a couple of other places I want to show you."

I nodded politely at Señora Barcelo. She raised her left

eyebrow, and her full lips curved as she gave a tiny sigh. I smiled and followed Kit to the door. But I made a mental note of the narrow adobe-lined streets we had taken to get to the casino. I knew I would be back; discretion may be needed, but opportunity will always come to the patient man. And I knew that Señora Barcelo and I were not finished. Yet.

Kit and I took a small, dark alley smelling of acrid piss and rotting garbage to move over one street. I noticed we turned in the same direction and admired Kit's cautiousness. If we were being followed, they would follow the other street in one direction or another, not thinking that two *gringos* would take a narrow and dark alley in Mexican town.

"Where we going?" I asked.

Kit laughed. "Well, I figure if you're getting an itch, I should take you to a place where you might be able to scratch it without gettin' yourself cut into with a scattergun." He nodded in the direction we were walking. "Not far down there is a *cantina*—a dance hall, really—and although you gotta be a little careful about which *señorita* you move with, you might get away with it."

"They don't have scatterguns there, I suppose?" I said.

He shook his head. "No, but they do have knives. And most know how to use them. That happens, don't be a hero. Just draw your pistol and point it at them. There may be a hothead or two down there, but usually that cools them off."

"Sounds like you have a lot of experience in this," I said.

"I have a lot of experience *living* here," he said. "That's all. Remember that you are dealing with humans, with people, and not with patterns. You can never predict with a certainty what others are going to do. It's best that you remember that, Bill. It will do you good later. You may *think* you know someone, but it's always best to be cautious and think that you ain't got the slightest idea what the other fellow is going to do. That way, you won't be surprised when you're wrong—and I have a hunch that you're going to be wrong-thinking more ways than one. Best not to be wrong-actioned, too."

I walked quietly beside Kit, thinking over what he had just told me. There was a lot of philosophy in that, enough to hold a man a lifetime if he paid attention to it. I figured coming from Kit Carson, it was something to do, and made a mental note to remember everything that he said and apply it to whatever it was that I was doing.

We arrived at what appeared to be an adobe house. Kit didn't knock, however, but threw the door open and strolled in. Music poured out, striking me in the face with the intensity of its scales. I took a step inside, nearly stomping on Kit's heels. The room was smoky and heavy with perfume and sour sweat. Over in the far corner, a couple of men plucked guitars and another sawed on a fiddle while a fourth squeezed a concertina enthusiastically. Kit said something and I bent down closer to his lips. Heels thudded hard against the pegged wood floor as young men and women danced the fandango, their feet going a mile a minute while they stared hard into their partners' eyes, their faces set in a disdainful manner. The women swirled their skirts back and forth with a practiced hand, exposing a flash of a crimson or bright yellow petticoat and slender calves. A few bolder ones brought the skirt up a little higher to tease their partners with a flash of dusky thigh. One, I noticed, had a red ribbon tied around her thigh and her breasts bobbled like scoops of brown sugar dropped into boiling water.

"You'll have to be a bit careful here!" Kit said, nudging my side with his elbow.

"I thought this was different than the place we just left!" I protested.

"It is. Except tonight there's gonna be a bit of trouble!" He nodded over to our right. I turned and noticed a young *señorita* waving a fan ineffectually in front of her. She wore a bright red dress with a white off-shoulder blouse that plunged nearly below her brown breasts bulging over the top. She had a red comb seated high in her glossy black hair gathered on top of her head to leave her slender neck exposed. Men clustered around her like dogs who'd cornered a bitch in heat. She laughed, enjoying their antics as they pressed against one another, each trying to force the other out of the tight circle. A lull came in the music and two rushed away toward a table where a huge punch bowl stood to get her a drink.

"Yep," Kit said, shaking his head. "It was a mistake coming here. There's gonna be trouble there."

"How do you know?"

"I know her," he replied. "That's Lupe Garcia. She'll play those boys till one of 'em gets hurt. Then she'll go sparkin' with the winner." He spit as if a foul bug had suddenly darted into his mouth. He nearly struck the foot of a man who turned angrily toward us, his face set in righteous indignation. But the expression hastily left his face when he recognized Kit, and he turned away from us, forcing a path through the pressing crowd. "That's her usual game. I've seen it happen too many times, but"—he sighed heavily—"there's nothing to be done about it."

As Kit spoke, a flurry of excitement broke out between two hotheaded men dressed alike in short, highly embroidered jackets and tight pants that flared at the ankle. Their black hair, slicked back straight off their high foreheads, gleamed in the yellow light from liberal applications of macassar oil. They were quickly separated, but their black eyes flashed deadly signals and challenges at each other.

"That didn't seem to take long," I answered.

"I don't know," Kit said doubtfully from beside me. "I got a funny feeling that this ain't over yet."

He proved prophetic. One of the youths said something and the other laughed and taunted him. I don't know what he said, but I could recognize scorn and ridicule in his tone. The other youth flushed and, turning, strode furiously out, to the amusement of others clustered around the woman. A few minutes later, the youth reappeared, his face set in marble lines, cold fury seeping from his black eyes. He called across the dance floor. The other youth looked up, then said something to the young one standing next to him. He hitched his pants higher and swaggered out the door, slipping a hand behind his back. He staggered back in almost immediately, his hands pressed against his chest. He tried to call out for help, but the words were lost in bubbles of blood bursting from his lips. He dropped to his knees, then slowly fell forward onto his face and lay still.

The music stopped and everyone pushed forward around the young man to see what had happened. But there were too many of them and interest quickly lagged. The fiddle player began a bouncy tune and the dancing began again. A couple of men picked up the body and carried it outside and returned so quickly that I knew they had dumped the body in an alley to get it out of the way until they felt like dealing with it later.

Kit sighed again. "This was a mistake. Come on; let's get out of here before the usual riot begins. This is no place for a white man. I don't relish a knife in my ribs. Especially if I can avoid it by simply leaving." He looked up at me and smiled at my frown. "You've spent too much time reading those damned dime novels. Don't believe a word of them. If I had killed as many men as they claimed I have, why, we'd be standing here talking alone."

"But you did kill some," I said quickly.

He threw his head back and stared up at me, frowning.

"I didn't mean that the way it sounded," I added.

"Yes," he said slowly, "I've killed some. But there ain't a night go by when I wish I hadn't. At least," he corrected himself, "some of them. A few needed killing. There was no way to reason with them. Best to have gotten them out of the way when I did."

We left the dance hall. I heard rats scurrying and squeaking and fighting over something in the alley, but I didn't look to see what it was. I had a feeling I knew and think Kit knew, too, for he turned up another street. I followed hard on his heels, our feet kicking puffs of dirt high so flecks shone briefly like quartz flakes in the light pouring out of windows.

"I don't mean to say that I served up myself as judge and jury and executioner, but sometimes a man has to do just that." He glanced up at me and nodded as if to confirm his thoughts. "You stick around here long enough and you'll know what I mean by that. There's some people who just won't live and let others alone. Those are the ones that you are going to have to take care of so other folks have a chance to make a life." He shook his head. "It ain't right, but sometimes you just have to weigh the balance of one wrong against the other and decide which one will do the least amount of harm."

I turned his words over and over in my mind, committing them to memory as we made our way through the warm and humid Santa Fe night. We worked our way back uptown to where the money flowed easier and the liquor was better. The women were prettier in these places—for the moment— but in some I could already see the hardness of their lives setting in behind their eyes. A few had already attained a slate-hard blankness that gave the lie to their curved lips and flashing teeth when they smiled automatically at the men around them. I noticed it was the drunkest men who went with them into back rooms and up the stairs. To this day I can remember that, my first walk on the wild side of life— glasses clinking, sometimes bursting; out-of-tune pianos spranging tinnily; chips rattling along with dice; and a pretty, hennaed-haired woman singing in a whiskey-husked alto. She wore a black dress with a yellow crinoline under it that whisked around her thin calves as she strutted back and forth across the stage. Marabou feathers curled from a fer- ronniere around her high forehead and barley-sugar curls to drape across one cheek. I saw a fiddle and bow lying on top of the piano and walked over and picked them up. The piano player, a colored man with red garters pulled up on the sleeves of his crisply starched white shirt, never missed a beat as he grinned up at me and asked if I could play. I plucked the strings, testing the notes, then nodded, waited to hear the melody line in his song, then slipped rapidly into it with him, sawing softly in the background before taking the lead. The woman glanced in surprise at me. I winked back at her and a brightness came into her eyes as she hip-swung her way over to me and leaned down from the small stage. I glanced down her bottle green bodice at the creamy tops of her round breasts and felt my face grow hot and nearly bumbled a measure but caught myself and grinned up at her.

She winked and hip-swung her way saucily back across the stage, her blond curls bouncing in time with her bubbling breasts, drawing cheers from those men paying attention. But her eyes kept flickering back to mine.

"I think you made your conquest tonight," Kit said from beside me. "And it's a lot safer."

I glanced down at him and laughed, feeling delight make my cheeks burn rosy, and I nodded. He clapped me on the shoulder.

"I'm leaving you for now. No, no, stay here," he said as I went to lay the fiddle aside and go with him. "I need some sleep. I'm taking a pack train up to Taos tomorrow. If you're up that way, stop by. Everyone knows where I live."

"I'll do that," I said. I smiled down at him. "And thanks for what you've done. I appreciate it."

"Don't think on it," he said. He clapped me on the shoulder again, then turned and slipped easily through the crowd. Few noticed him leaving, most seeing him and ignoring him as they would their shadows on the ground on a hot summer day.

I turned back to my playing. Someone placed a drink near my shoulder and I nodded my thanks. The colored piano player glanced longingly at it.

"Help yourself," I said.

Surprise washed over his face, and he maintained the rhythm in the bass while he took the glass and sipped a large mouthful of the whiskey. He replaced the glass and swished the whiskey around in his mouth, swallowing it in stages. He smacked his lips.

"I'm thanking you," he said. His voice sounded musical, a soft drawl on his words. I grinned at him again.

"Why, think nothing of it," I said. "How about 'Louisiana Gals' next?"

Effortlessly he slipped into it. The woman onstage gave us a startled look but slipped into the song, sashaying around as if someone had oiled her hips. The room was becoming decidedly warmer.

"That's Rose," the piano player said. "An' I'm Ned."

"Hickok," I answered. "Jim Hickok." Then for some reason—I'm still not sure why—I added, "But folks call me 'Bill.' "

He gave me a quick look, then nodded. "Bill it is, then." He lifted his head and called out, "Rose! This here's Bill."

She winked at me. "And a wild one he is, I'm betting."

I winked back and knew the night was mine.

CHAPTER

28

SNOW WAS beginning to fall, thick flakes floating lazily down, but it hadn't begun to gather yet, and I knew that over Raton Pass and down in the valley the snow hadn't begun to fall. It would—that I knew—but it always came first high up. I shivered and tried to burrow deeper into my coat. My gloved hands held the reins tightly as my legs gripped the gelding's ribs. I had gotten the first wagon over the pass and down onto the flats, but there were seven more to guide up and over. I had found work with the freight company of Russell, Majors & Waddell as a wagon master after tiring of driving the stage. At first, I had nearly refused their offer when they told me I had to take a pledge not to drink or quarrel or fight with another employee and be honest—did they want a saint or a wagon master?—but then I figured it was only sound business and an old-timer with the company laughed and said that as long as anything I did didn't come to their attention or cause them any trouble, they would pretend I was living up to the letter of the pledge. I signed on and was sent first to Platte Crossing up on the Nebraska flats near Fort Kearney. There I met Jack Slade and knew that the old-timer was right: As long as the work was done the way they wanted it, they would turn a blind eye toward the deed.

Slade was a short, slim man with long black hair and a certain madness lurking deep in his black eyes. He always wore a black shadbelly coat and low-heeled Wellingtons. I felt his eyes upon me as I swung down from my horse near the watering trough. I dusted my shirt and pants, easing the pistol in its sheath at my waist with my elbow. I took a tin cup from the pump at one end of the trough and drew water. I drank deeply, tasting the cold, sweet water, poured another cup, and drank it. The day was hot—the sun nearly boiling my brains out through my ears—and I had ridden a long and hard trail up from Julesburg.

I lowered the cup and placed it back on the bent wire hook wrapped around the mouth of the pump. I took a bandanna from my neck, washed it out in the trough, and used it to wipe my face and neck. I tied it back around my neck and moved up toward the station.

Slade stepped out the door. "Welcome to Horseshoe Station. May I help you?" he said courteously. At first I thought he was just a polite, neatly dressed worker, the type one normally doesn't see at a station on a wagon route. It was then that I noticed his eyes.

"Hello," I said, trying hard to look as if I wanted to be friends. "I'm Hickok. The company sent me up from Santa Fe to learn the route." I turned, looking around the station at the prairie. "Nice place."

"It is that," he said quietly, gently. "I am Slade. Joseph Slade. Most people call me 'Jack.'"

I felt a tingle run through me when he said his name, although I had known in advance that I was going to report to him. I suppose I had been apprehensive the long way up the road from Santa Fe, knowing that I was going to work briefly under one of the most deadly killers in the West. I glanced down at his vest and his watch chain. I had heard—as who hadn't?—how Jules Reni, the founder of Julesburg at the California Crossing on the South Platte, once had stolen some horses from the company. Slade went to get them back and Jules shot him with a double-barreled shotgun and emptied six shots into him with his pistol, leaving him for dead. Jules should have made certain that Slade was dead before he left, but I suppose he had been confident that Slade would not survive his wounds. Most men wouldn't have, but Slade had recovered and found Jules at Pacific Springs, where he brought him down by placing a deliberate ball in his thigh. Then Slade tied Jules up at a fence post and demonstrated his marksmanship with his pistol, breaking his knees and elbows with pistol balls, pausing to reload deliberately, then resuming his target practice, taking care not to kill him. At last, when Jules was barely conscious and coherent, Slade walked up to him, drew his knife, and slowly cut off his ears while Jules screamed and whimpered. Then Slade cut his throat. He wore Jules's ears as a watch fob.

I glanced up at him. A faint smile crossed his face. I sensed that he knew what I was looking for when my eyes dropped involuntarily to his vest. I felt my face grow warm.

"Well, come on in," he said softly, stepping back and motioning toward the station.

"Thanks," I managed through the wary thickness in my throat. He fell in beside me as I walked toward the door. I noticed the sign over the door, the letters burnt black with a hot iron: VIRGINIA DALE. I paused, looking at him.

"Virginia Dale?" I asked, puzzled. "I thought this was Horseshoe Station."

"It is," he explained. "But the house is Virginia Dale. My wife," he added. "The company owns the station, but I own the house." He nodded at the corral and barn fifty yards away. "That's actually the station over there. You can use it to stay in, if you wish. We don't use the rooms set aside for a manager. Instead, we had this built for ourselves."

I stepped in through the door and paused, my eyes taking in the clean white walls, the framed pictures hanging on them, the comfortable chairs—Belter furniture, I guessed, noticing the carved rosewood—and a circular sofa in the center of the room not that far from a stone fireplace. Deep carpets covered the puncheon floor that had been stained and waxed until it glowed like soft golden butter around the edges of the carpets. Crystal glasses had been arranged neatly around a crystal decanter filled with amber liquid—whiskey or brandy, I thought—on a small table beside one of the chairs. A bookcase filled with books stood against one wall. Starched lace curtains had been pulled back to let in sunlight from the large window looking out onto the wagon yard.

"Nice," I managed, dumbfounded at the unexpected luxury. A smile broke from his thin lips.

"Yes," he said. "Virginia and I are quite fond of our comfort." He raised his voice, calling her.

A handsome woman, voluptuous, pigeon-breasted, with wide, generous hips, came out of the back room. She wiped her hands on a dish towel she was carrying, eyeing me speculatively. I felt the force of her presence deep in my stomach and wondered just how long I was going to have to stay.

I swallowed. "Pleased to meet you, ma'am," I said. I waited for her to stretch out her hand and breathed a silent sigh of relief when she didn't.

"And what do you want here?" she asked suspiciously.

I was taken aback by her directness and looked down at Slade for help. He smiled.

"Now, Virginia, he will be our guest for a couple of days while he learns the route," he said. "I told you about his coming a week ago. Remember?"

"Are you here to replace Jack?" she asked brusquely, her eyes narrowing, making her look as if she'd bitten into a sour lemon. "If so, why, you can just climb back on your horse and get out of here. I'll give you a head start before—"

"Virginia," Slade said again. His voice stayed unchanged, but there was something about the way he uttered the word that caused her to draw up and take a half step back away from us. "Mr. Hickok is here to learn the route. That is all. Now, would you be kind enough to fix a little lunch for us? It is nearly noon and I believe Mr. Hickok might like a little repast after his long ride."

She nodded and, turning, walked away from us. I watched her buttocks swing and knew there was no corset or bustle under that dress. Not, I remember thinking, that she would need one. For a moment I had a crazy picture of the thin Slade locked between her meaty thighs; then I drove the picture from my mind.

"You must forgive Virginia," he said softly, crossing to the decanter. "She is very protective and suspicious of company men who are sent here. Not," he added, pouring two glasses full with the liquid, "that we have all that many visitors other than a few overnighters on their way across the trail. We are left pretty much alone out here. That's one of the reasons we prefer to live like this. Drink?"

He held out one glass, waiting as I crossed to take it. It was a bit early in the day, but I figured I had never needed one before to calm the nervous flutter in my stomach. I sipped cautiously. Brandy. And expensive. I took a large swallow as Slade watched approvingly.

"I expected whiskey," I said, lowering the glass.

He laughed, delighted. "I appreciate your candor, sir," he said. He motioned toward a chair. I glanced down at the spurs on my boots. "Oh, don't worry," he said. "It is a risk one takes when one tries for comfort out here."

I sat down gingerly and, placing my glass on the small table covered with a neat pile of magazines at my elbow, took my spurs off and tucked them beside the leg of the chair out of the way.

"Now then," Slade said, making himself comfortable in the other chair opposite. He sipped from his glass. "Tell me the news in Denver."

And so began a nervous week with Slade. But by the end of the time, I had become friends with him and his wife had come to accept me, even graciously offering to do laundry for me before I left. Slade may have been a hard man when he was drunk, but he maintained a rigid control over his drinking while I was a guest with him. I later discovered that he went on sporadic drunks and when he did he was totally unpredictable, as dangerous as a blind rattlesnake in a tight room.

One night, a horse whinnied, awakening me. I caught up a pistol and slid to the door of the barn and peered out. Indians had let down the bars to the corral and were quietly moving the horses and mules out. I brought up my pistol and aimed at the Indian nearest the corral. I squeezed the trigger. He yelped and threw up his arms, crumbling to the dirt.

At once wild cries filled the night and the horses bunched, then wildly galloped through the opening in the corral. I fired again and missed, then took a step away from the doorway, trying to see through the dust billowing up from the hooves of the animals. Shots slammed into the wood where I had been standing and I dived flat behind a water trough. I peered cautiously up over the edge and saw the Indians galloping away, leaning low over their horses' necks. I snapped a shot at one but missed.

Then they were gone.

I heard someone running and dropped to a knee, bringing the pistol up.

"Hold it!" Slade said, skidding to a stop. He waited until I lowered the pistol, then came up to me.

His eyes glittered like black diamonds in the moonlight. He held a shotgun in his hands, but I could see his pistol belted around his waist. I smelled brandy on his breath as he took a quick look around. His eyebrows went up as he frowned.

"Indians?" he asked.

I nodded. "I got one," I said, gesturing at the corral.

Slade grunted and hurried forward. I followed him, stepping to the side warily to keep the Indian in sight. I had heard stories about how they suddenly seemed to come to life, and I didn't want to find a knife in my stomach. I didn't have to worry. My bullet had caught him between the shoulders.

Slade rolled him over, kneeling to study the figure carefully. He nodded and rose.

"Kiowa," he said. "A long way away from their land. But who knows where their land is anymore?"

"How can you tell?" I asked.

He pointed at the scalp and the moccasins. "They club their hair like that when they're on a raid," he said. "See how the leather is stitched with one layer overlying the other? Only the Kiowa sew like that. It's something you pick up after a while," he said as he caught my frown. "Just be patient." He clapped me gently on the shoulder. "You did pretty good, catching one like that in the dark with a pistol." He glanced down at the Dragoon in my hand. "Especially a heavy load like that."

"Should we saddle up and go after them?" I asked.

He shook his head. "No. Indians usually leave a couple back to catch white men foolish enough to go galloping after them at night. We'll wait until morning and pick up a couple of men from the Pony Express station and anyone else we can find. It'll be safer that way. We'll be able to move faster than they will. Those horses will be pretty spooked and it'll take all they have to keep them from scattering over the land."

The next morning, though, we were in the saddle before light and at the Pony Express station, where we found three others. I was surprised to see Cody.

"Howdy." He grinned, coming up, his hand outstretched.

I was surprised at him. He had grown quite a bit and his shoulders were heavier with muscle. He was clean-shaven, with tired rings around his eyes.

"Well, I'll be damned!" I said, shaking his hand. "How've you been?"

The guarded look slipped from his eyes and I knew then that he was worried I would let slip how we had met, but that was in the past and, as far as I was concerned, over. I never have thought that we built up debts in the world. There just is too much of the world to worry about who was one up on the other.

"Fair to middlin'," he said. He jerked a thumb over his shoulder. "I've been riding for the Pony lately."

"It's good you boys know each other," Slade said. He nodded at the others who came out of the station. "Indians drove our stock off last night and we could use a bit of help getting them back."

"What's it pay?" a burly one growled.

Slade's eyes narrowed. "My gratitude," he said softly.

The man shook his head. "That and a dollar would buy a shot of whiskey," he said.

A dull red began to move up Slade's neck, but he held his tongue and shrugged and turned to the rest of us.

"Well, whoever's going with Bill"—he nodded at me— "and myself, saddle up. We have to get on the trail or they'll get too far ahead of us."

The burly one shook his head and turned back to the station. "You all go on without me, you want," he said. "But ain't no way I'm putting my scalp lock out for a reddie to grab without something coming back in my poke for it."

Slade's eyes narrowed as he watched the burly one disappear into the station; then he sensed my stare and turned. A cold chill washed over me and I went to my horse, covering my discomfort by fumbling at my cinch. The blackness of hell laced with leaping fires had just opened up before me.

"Mount up," Slade said softly, and we all swung into our saddles and followed him as we cantered out of the yard.

We crossed the trail five miles out. A blind man couldn't have missed it or failed to follow it. Slade sent me ahead to scout to keep the party from running into an ambush, but the Indians were more intent on putting distance between the stage station and them and pushed ahead hard. We were smaller and could move faster.

The trail led straight to Powder River and up to Crazy Woman's Fort and to Clear Creek. I found their camp by midafternoon and rode back to wait about five miles from them for Slade and the others to come up to us.

"Well?" Slade demanded as he reined in his lathered horse beside mine. Dust caked his face, and his eyes burned from the mask into mine. I remembered what I had glimpsed hours before and suppressed a shudder.

"They're camped about five, maybe six miles east of here," I said. "It's a dry camp and will be hard to come up on them. But we can if we wait until dark, I think. There's a shallow vale that comes down to them from the north. That'll keep us from being highlighted if we're careful."

He nodded with satisfaction. "Good job, Bill," he said. "You've done well." He turned to the others. "We'll wait here until dark. Sit and loosen your girths and let your horses breathe. We'll have a bit of hard riding tonight."

Cody looked around, frowning. "Mr. Slade?"

Slade turned to him, sitting back in his saddle, an eyebrow raised.

"Uh, aren't we a bit exposed out here?" Cody asked. "I mean, sir, that maybe one of the Indians will send someone out to check their back trail?"

Slade glanced at me.

I shook my head. "No, I don't think so," I said. "They've been pushing fairly hard and there isn't that many of them. They'll keep their guards close to the horses to keep them from straying. We should be all right."

Cody nodded, but his face still clouded with misgivings. He swung down and loosened the cinch on his horse, then sat on the ground, looping his reins around one wrist to wait.

"You're learning," Slade murmured to me. "How'd you know that?"

I shrugged. "Common sense," I said. "It's what I'd do. I can't figure an Indian would do more than that."

"Maybe," he said. "But always remember that you need to also think what the Indian *shouldn't* do as well. Just when you think you've got them figured out, they'll do the opposite. Common sense doesn't mean a damn thing to an Indian. That's a mark of a civilized man. I think you're right, though. What do you have up there? About six?"

"Five," I said. "And one looks hurt. I might have winged one last night. I figure that he'll stay back, and one to care for him, while the other three split a guard among them. They've been pushing hard and they'll be tired as well. Even Indians have to sleep sometime." I shrugged. "I don't know. I could be all wrong. But it just *feels* right to me."

"And that's what you need to go by," he said. "Go by your feelings."

We waited until the moon began to rise; then we tightened our cinches and the others fell in behind me as I rode in a wide detour to bring them down from the north upon the Indian encampment.

I was right; there was only one guard, and he rode slowly around the horses to keep them from straying too far. I didn't see Slade slide from his horse, but suddenly the Indian jerked upright and slipped from his horse. I hurried forward in time to see Slade rise from the ground, a long-bladed knife gleaming wet-black in the moonlight. He smiled.

"One," he said softly.

He slipped the knife into its scabbard and circled his hand over his head. We mounted and rode forward. When we were within fifty yards of the camp, Slade suddenly slapped his heels hard against the sides of his horse. It squealed in pain as Slade's rowels drove into its sides, and leaped forward.

Then we all were galloping hard behind Slade, riding down upon the camp. The Indians leaped to their feet, but a barrage of gunfire seemed to slam them back onto the ground. As quickly as it began, it was over. I became aware I was holding my pistol in my hand, but I hadn't fired it. I slipped it into its holster and turned away from the others beginning to dismount.

"Cody," Slade said, "you go with Bill and see if you can gather those horses. I'll want to move out as soon as we can. There's no telling how close we might be to other Kiowa. No sense in taking any chances."

It took Cody and me most of the night to gather the horses and mules. A couple of the others came out to help us, and by gray light we had all our horses and mules and the Indian horses as well in a tight herd. Slade grinned and waved to us, and we began to drive them back to the station.

We arrived near sundown, weary and worn, and Cody and I put the animals into the corral. They bunched up at the water trough. Cody looked over at Slade as the station manager rode up to the house and dismounted.

"I don't think I'd want to cross that man," he said thoughtfully.

"You'd be wise not to," I said. "He's killed quite a few who have tried to run his trail. And he isn't fussy how he does it, either."

Cody's eyes settled on mine. I shook my head. "Let's put up our horses and get cleaned up. I'm hungry."

Obediently he followed me into the barn.

I have to give Slade credit for taking care of those who had helped him. By the time Cody and I had cleaned up and put in our appearances up at the house, Virginia and the cook had readied a supper for us and Slade had set out bottles of whiskey. By the time the dark had gathered, we were all pretty mellow and Cody was nodding sleepily in his chair. We heard a horse coming and I stepped out into the shadows under the porch to wait for the rider to show himself.

It was the burly man who had refused to go with us. He reined in and sat on his horse, staring at me.

"Cody here?" he asked.

"He's here," I answered.

"You tell that little bastard to get his ass back to the Pony station. He's supposed to be riding the next shift due in a couple of hours."

I shook my head. "You'll have to get someone else to ride it," I said. "He's been in the saddle all day helping us bring the stock back."

"I don't give a shit what he's been doing," the man said. "It's what he's going to do that interests me."

I felt someone beside me and turned to find Slade staring out at the man. His eyes were flat and cold and I could smell bay rum on him.

"I think Mr. Hickok has told you what needs to be done," he said softly. "Now I'd be obliged if you'd ride on back and see to it. That Cody boy has been wearing himself out in the saddle and needs to get caught up on his sleep. Boys grow while sleeping, you know. But you're a full-grown man and surely know that."

The man shook his head and spit a black stream of tobacco juice on the steps leading up to the porch. "I just said my words," he said stubbornly. "You get that kid back there or he can find hisself another job come morning."

Slade stepped down off the porch and to the side. "And you, sir," he said harshly, "can climb down off that horse and scrub your spittle from my step."

"Be damned if I will!" the man said.

I don't know if he moved toward his pistol or not, but Slade's appeared as if by magic in his hand and I saw the flare from the barrel and heard the *splat!* as the bullet struck the other man in the chest. He hunched forward, then fell backward as his horse reared in fright. Slade slipped forward and seized the bridle, speaking soothingly to quiet the nervous mount.

I sighed and craned my head, looking at the leaden sky and trying to gauge the daylight left. It would be close to dark before we finished, I reflected sourly, and that would be pushing the mules up and over the pass and hoping a lead one didn't become stubborn and stop. They did that on occasion and wouldn't take another step until they were damn good and ready, never minding the whip you laid across their backs. Fact was, you'd be better coaxing them like you would a woman.

I smiled as I thought of Rose waiting for me back in Santa Fe. I had no illusions; I knew there were others in her bed when I was on the trail—she had too large an appetite for waiting faithfulness—but when I returned, there was no one. Although, I reflected as the gelding picked his way over the rocks, some of the men didn't understand or *want* to understand why she dropped everything when I came back and spent her time with me instead of spreading her favors around.

I shivered from the cold and hunched deeper into my coat.

I slipped into a remembrance of the last time I had seen Rose.

She had long, thin white hands with long nails, cool against my skin. Like ivory, only soft. Below I could hear the out-of-tune piano jangling merrily and the susurring murmur of voices, indistinct but there. Her golden hair lay long down her naked back and I lifted it away to walk my fingers over the bumps in her spine. She moaned, and her heavy breasts moved back and forth across my chest. Across the room I could see the old drawing of an old bearded man in priestly robes, holding a cross high from whose center a red heart appeared, lights radiating from its center, and and she moaned and her mouth came hard upon mine feeling fire flaming through it into mine setting a blaze going going and I thought about the day when I had to leave for St. Louis to bring the other freight train back and I thought about the road and how it curved gently across the prairie as golden as her hair waving like golden waves in the golden light when the sun was near dawn and streaks of red came like carmine blush across the blue blue sky and and and

The gelding shied and drew me from my daydream. I dropped my hand down along his neck, patting it gently, soothing him, instantly alert. "Easy, boy," I whispered. "What is it?"

And then I smelled it: rank, musky, thick in the throat. I looked around for the source, my eyes probing the darkness between the deep green of the jack pines. Then I heard a low growl and took my hand away from the gelding's neck, feeling for the pistol at my belt. Two cubs scampered back into the shadows, and at the same moment an old sow grizzly bear lumbered out of the deep pines, gathering speed as she came toward us.

The gelding screamed with fright and reared suddenly. Caught unaware, I tumbled backward off him, landing hard on the ground, my head striking a stone. Stunned, I heard the gelding's hooves hammering the trail back down the way we had climbed.

I rolled over and saw the bear still coming, faster. I clawed my pistol from my belt and, rising to my knees, fired as rapidly as I could. I saw the bullets strike, her flesh flinch, but she only groaned and never slackened her pace. The hammer of my pistol clicked on a spent cap. I dropped it and rose to my feet, backing away from her as I drew the bowie knife. Then, she was on me. I felt her hot breath, fetid from rotten meat; her tiny eyes rolled wickedly. I threw up an arm and felt her long claws rake through my coat and down my arm. I felt the scream bubbling up in my throat as another paw crashed down on top of my head, clawing my scalp away. I fell and tried to roll away. Her claws ripped through my pants and legs. Black smoke drifted across my vision. I swung wildly with the knife and felt the jar as the blade bit deep into her, striking bone. My hair hung down over my eyes, and I stabbed blindly, felt the blade sink in, and twisted my wrist, ripping up. She roared with pain and picked me up, wrapping her thick arms around me, claws digging into my back. Her mouth gaped wide and came down around my head. I felt her teeth grating on my skull and stabbed again and again, ripping the blade up as fast and hard and deep as I could drive it, ripping, ripping—

And suddenly she went slack. I felt her guts roll hotly out of her belly onto my legs and boots; then we fell, she pinning me beneath her. The air exploded from my body and the black smoke came again, but this time, it stayed—

CHAPTER

29

I SAT in the sun's rays, feeling the warmth seep in and relax my muscles, listening to Sarah Shull's husky voice singing the old ballad. She couldn't have carried a tune in an oaken bucket, but there was a sensuality to her voice that hammered away at a man's innards. A dove called mournfully from down at the creek. Lazily I opened my eyes and rolled my head against the rough logs of Sarah Shull's cabin across from the Rock Creek Station, searching for the dove in the sun-dappled cottonwood trees towering over the little creek. I heard the music of water running over rocks and a couple of logs that had been placed to make a small dam for swimming and fishing just above the deep ruts scored in the earth by iron-cased wagon wheels making their way over the Oregon Trail.

I had the smell of the earth in my nostrils, warm and dank. I heard Fritz lapping water from an old bucket near me and reached down automatically to scratch his ears. I smiled as he walked slowly away so that I was scratching close by his tail. Fritz was a mongrel who had discovered the Muddles' bitch about three miles away. I figured it must have been his first encounter, for he seemed to be in an extremely agitated state the past four days. I glanced down at him. He turned brown eyes up at me.

"You old phony," I said affectionately. He grunted with pleasure, then moved down the cabin wall and plopped down in the shade, one ear falling over an eye. I watched his brown and white body pant in the heat, then slow as he dozed. A bee bumbled its way around us for a moment, then streaked off to the side of the cabin where Sarah Shull had planted hollyhocks. I shifted position and grimaced as scar tissue tried to stretch. I sat up and gently massaged my left arm to ease the ache. I glanced across the creek to where the Rock Creek Station stood. Jane Holmes—I called her Mrs. Wellman, as she was the common-law wife of Horace Wellman—was out hanging up laundry on cords stretched between two wooden Ts tamped into the earth about fifty feet from each other.

I frowned, remembering how the company had sent me to Kansas City for a doctor to take care of me and then moved me to the station, where I could work as a hostler while I healed. I was weak then, terribly weak, and could barely shuffle around the yard, let alone pitch hay. But Doc Brink, a sometime hired hand, was always willing to help out, laughing and joking good-naturedly to help me forget the pain. He rode occasionally for the Pony Express, which also shared the station with the Central Overland California and Pike's Peak Express Company owned by Russell, Majors & Waddell. Dave McCanles, who had built the station before selling it to the company and moving to a new ranch along the Little Blue River, had been swaggering arrogantly around the station lately, demanding that Horace Wellman, the new superintendent for the company, pay him the rest of the money the company owed him for the station. Unfortunately, the company was teetering on bankruptcy and there was nothing that Horace could do.

I knew what McCanles was capable of. He was a bully of the first sort and had taken to grabbing me and throwing me to the ground whenever he came upon me, then standing, laughing, over me as I tried to struggle with one arm to my feet. There wasn't much I could do, though, except try to stay out of his way. I was barely strong enough to use a hay rake, let alone my pistols that I kept in a satchel beneath my bunk in a small room at the back of the large barn where the horses were stabled during foul weather. Wellman kept a fringe-topped surrey there, too, for the Sunday outings whenever they could get away—which was practically never.

I sighed and cautiously stretched. No, nothing good was going to come of McCanles and his nearly daily visit to the station these days. It didn't help that McCanles favored the South while I had foolishly made my feelings regarding slavery known in a lax moment with a bottle of whiskey and a few hardcases I had mistakenly earmarked for friendship down at the juncture where Rock Creek flowed into the Little Blue River, where catfish and bass lived lazily in back pools, ready to snap at a grub or manure bug impaled upon a hook. Foolish! Foolish! McCanles knew my place in the gathering of sides within a day or two of ill-fated afternoon fishing.

McCanles had a number of "wannabes" hanging around him at the time, playing to his pompous preening and posing. The number varied, as many became disgusted with his bullying and left the euphoric inner sanctum where he admitted those who placated his favor. He was a burly man, strong as an ox, with curling black locks that he painstakingly combed over his collar. Unfortunately, although he was usually closely shaved, he had a disdainful appreciation of soap and water, and when he stood upwind and close to me I nearly gagged from the sour stench reeking from his clothes.

He had been a sheriff of Watauga County in North Carolina—or so he claimed; I have my doubts—and came to Rock Creek with Sarah, his lover, after his wife discovered that their marriage did not reside in the Garden of Eden but rather on the slopes of Mount Purgatory. Perhaps I should say he "fled" North Carolina, for had he stayed, the courts would have stripped him naked of his mercenary belongings and awarded everything to his legal wife and children. North Carolina took a dim view of philandering—when the event was brought to the law's attention. I think it was the narrow view of the Baptist convention that had a throttlehold upon the political machine of the state. The Baptist crowd finds sin in everything except the making of jelly—provided that is not done upon the Sabbath.

When McCanles came to Rock Creek, he established a station on one side of the waters and on the other a ranch where he placed Sarah and against whose log cabin I lazed away the day while I mused wonderingly on what prompted him to send for his wife and children after he had settled in. If a man was looking to live in a hornet's nest, that was one way to do it.

Jane looked across the creek, noticed me lounging about, and waved. I waved back, admiring her beauty and natural figure that needed no corset to set an hourglass figure upon her womanly frame. She was far better-looking than Sarah Shull, but Jane was dedicated to her husband and such dedication put a damper upon other men's thoughts. *Or would have*, I thought suddenly, *if that man wasn't Dave McCanles. Could that be the reason for his hard-nosed attitude toward Horace?*

I frowned, musing at a couple of dragonflies darting around each other a few feet from the hollyhocks. When Russell, Majors & Waddell organized their Pony Express, they had thought to lease the Rock Creek Station, but Mc-Canles had convinced them that they would be better off buying it from him at one-third down and the rest in three-month payments.

I suppose that was a good arrangement, but setting up a new enterprise on a shoestring budget doesn't allow much leeway for unseen expenses, and Russell, Majors & Waddell had been plagued by several—Indian raids upon outlying stations, the sudden disappearance of stock, exorbitant expense accounts turned in by station managers for supplies, equipment, wages: The list went on and on, and before long, the firm found black ink becoming a scarce item in their ledger books.

McCanles let the first month's payment ride, but when the second month rolled around he began to get ugly, hovering over Horace, who was half his size, his apelike arms threatening to encompass the smaller man in a death hug, sausagelike fingers jabbing his point home in Horace's skinny chest as the Roman legionnaire's hammer had driven forth the heretical nails into the sacred hands and feet, demanding payment. But Horace could do nothing and finally agreed to accompany McCanles to Brownsville to ask Benjamin Ficklin, the line superintendent, to make good the account.

That had been three weeks ago and the party had yet to return. That didn't bode well, although there were numerous possible explanations for their tardiness. Unfortunately, I could think of only one, since I had not been paid myself during the same period that McCanles had been waiting for his money.

Soft arms crept around my neck, startling me. I smelled her sweet breath as she breathed gently upon my ear.

"Jim, you've been sitting here for hours now. Can't you think of something better to do with your time?"

I turned my head to Sarah and found her rosebud lips a scant inch away. I kissed her and felt the giggle rise up from her breast, shaking her. I leaned back, staring sternly at her.

"Woman, is this such a laughing matter to you?"

"No," Sarah said, freeing one hand to brush a stray tendril of honey blond hair off her fine forehead. Her cornflower blue eyes stared merrily into mine. "But you forget that Jane can see what you are doing."

"What *we* are doing," I corrected, slipping my hand over her generous haunch. Her eyes turned smoky gray, and her nostrils widened as she breathed deeply, her large breasts moving against my arm. "You forget," I added slyly, "that it takes two to play this tune."

"Ah, Bill," she said.

"Jim," I corrected, but she ignored me and turned, plopping herself onto my lap. She squirmed slowly and I felt myself responding to the movement of her buttocks. She looked half-lidded at me. A trickle of perspiration ran down from her temples along the line of her jaw, down her thin neck, past the quickening pulse-beat in her throat, to disappear under the collar of her calico dress.

"Whatever," she sighed indifferently.

I smelled fresh-baked bread on her and a hint of Pears Soap from the bath she had taken earlier and the earthy smell of her want. I grinned at her and pressed my hand harder against her hip. I could almost feel her blood humming through her veins as she slumped against me.

"Let's go inside," she whispered hoarsely. Her teeth bit my earlobe none too gently and the wild recklessness exploded within me.

"Now why would we do that on such a sunshiny day?" I asked, teasing.

She began breathing heavily, swearing gently. Her arm slipped from around my neck and I felt her groping, trying to push her fingers behind my belt. I laughed and her eyes widened.

"Dammit, it's not funny!" she said furiously.

"Of course it is," I said, and rose. She slid off my lap, catching herself unsteadily upon her feet. I wrapped an arm around her waist and led her into the cabin.

CHAPTER

30

I WAS at the station with Mrs. Wellman when McCanles rode up with three others, demanding that we vacate the premises immediately. Mrs. Wellman stepped out of the cabin to try to talk with him, but McCanles refused to listen to her.

"You send your man out," he said. "I want to settle with your husband. One way or the other." He laughed, rolling his big shoulders, confident that he would win whatever battle Wellman tried to put up to keep control of the station.

"He won't come out," Mrs. Wellman said, a bit embarrassed.

I glanced over at her husband, crawling under a bed at the far end of the cabin, and felt a surge of disgust go through me at a man hiding behind a woman's apron strings, but I knew that he was no match for McCanles any more than I was in my weakened condition. I sighed and stepped into the doorway. McCanles saw me and his eyes narrowed.

"Well, well," he said. "Hickok. I got a bone to pick with you, too, Dutch Bill."

"James," I said softly. "My name's James."

"I don't rightly care one way or the other what your name is," he said boldly. "You want to take a hand in this, come on out and we'll settle it like men."

I shook my head. "You just go on about your business, McCanles," I said. "You're not wanted around here. In fact, you're trespassing."

"Trespassing!" His eyes bulged with fury. "Why, you, you—I own this place until I'm paid in full. And that's been a damn long time coming! Now I want all of you to get off this here property right now!"

"Nope," I said softly. I touched the handle of my pistol at my belt. McCanles caught my gesture and settled back in his saddle, eyeing me narrowly.

"Very well. Then send Wellman out or I'll come in after him," he said. He touched a long blacksnake draped over his saddle horn and I knew full well what he had planned for Wellman.

I shrugged and stepped back inside, but I drew my pistol and held it ready at my side. McCanles kneed his horse around to the front door of the station, where he had a clear view of the inside of the station except for a calico curtain that partitioned the front room into two bedrooms. I stepped up against the edge of the curtain so I could keep him in sight. McCanles saw me and yelled, "Come on out and fight fair!"

"What kind of fair fight you planning on, McCanles?" I said loudly. "A cripple and an old man. That the type of odds you favor?"

"You sumbitch," McCanles said, and swung down from his horse. He pulled his pistol from his holster as he stepped inside the cabin. He saw me and grinned, raising his pistol to take aim. I knew in that instant that he had not come for Wellman or to take possession of the station. That was his excuse. He had come for me. I could see it in the excitement in his eyes and then I felt my pistol leap in my hand. Gray smoke separated us for an instant, but I heard the heavy, meaty *thuwunk!* and knew my bullet had struck him in the chest. I stepped around the side of the curtain and saw Mc-Canles sprawl across the threshold.

At the same instant, the three with him leaped from their horses and ran toward the house. One of them, Jim Woods, I later discovered, started in through the kitchen door with pistol drawn. I fired twice, wounding him. He reeled away as Jim Gordon, McCanles's foreman, tried to come in the front door. I winged him with a quick shot from the hip. He staggered out the door.

"Let's get out of here!" Woods hollered, and he and Gordon ran for the trees along Rock Creek. That yell must have spiked Wellman's blood with a dose of bravery, for he climbed from beneath the bed by now and ran outside, snatching a grubbing hoe from where it leaned against the side of the house. Doc Brink, who had been working in the barn at the time, appeared with a scattergun.

"Come on! Let's get 'em!" Wellman yelled, and took off after them, whooping like an Indian on the scalping trail.

The third man wasn't a man, I noticed. It was McCanles's son, twelve years old, who gathered his father in his arms, tears spreading down his cheeks.

"Kill him! Kill him!" Mrs. Wellman screamed hysterically. She pointed a trembling finger at the boy, but I shook my head and slipped my pistol into its holster.

"There's been enough of that around here," I said quietly.

I meant the death of McCanles, but seconds later I heard the boom of Brink's shotgun. I ran toward the creek and saw where Brink had killed Gordon with a double blast, the pellets ripping a huge hole in his back.

I heard screams rising from a patch of weeds to the side of the house and raced there just in time to see Wellman finish chopping the life out of Woods with the grubbing hoe. He turned to look at me, the craziness showing in the whites around his eyes, his clothes and face spattered with blood.

I sighed heavily, knowing no good would come of this, and made my way back to the station.

I was right: The courts found all of us innocent, especially after a couple of people swore they had heard McCanles planning to whip Wellman to teach him not to welsh on a deal. But what came out of this was a story that came to be known as "The Massacre at Rock Creek Station" and I found myself the sole hero of that fight, thanks to people like George Ward Nichols, who wrote a highly warped account of the fight in *Harper's New Monthly Magazine* that came out after the war.

But it was the war that drew me next. What war doesn't do that to the young and foolish who have been named after kings and raised on the nobility of man in diversity?

CHAPTER

31

THE HEARING was held in Beatrice before T. M. Coulter, Gage County justice of the peace, but despite the charges brought against me by the McCanles faction, I was found not guilty.

Immediately afterward, I left Rock Creek and was nearly to Fort Leavenworth, where I hoped to pick up work on a wagon train heading west, when a rider came galloping past in a cloud of dust, wild-eyed and bushy-tailed, yelling at the top of his voice that we were at war. I pulled the brown mare I was riding to the shade of a cottonwood and dismounted to sort through some options. I loosened the mare's girth and leaned back against the scabrous bark in the sultry heat and watched the mare as she nuzzled a swath of brown grass with halfhearted interest. But I sensed that I had to get involved in the war; there was something more than an adventure waiting in front of me; it seemed as if I was coming toward a reckoning. The idea of being a soldier didn't appeal to me, and my still-weakened condition would have kept me from enlisting anyway. But I could be a scout or a wagon master. I sighed and scrunched down against the side of the tree, tilting my broad-brimmed hat over my eyes. Within moments, I was asleep.

I awoke with a start, feeling a certain tension in the air. A small runnel of perspiration trickled slowly down my back. Tiny hairs prickled along my arms like I was in an electric storm. I took a long, slow breath. A sour smell seemed to wash over me, and I knew I wasn't alone. Then I heard a small sound like leather scraping softly over small pebbles and rolled quickly to my right, palming my pistol as I came up on my knees.

Two men, filthy and bearded, gaped at me. Their clothes looked caked with old dirt and grease and smoke from a thousand fires. One held a long-bladed dagger. I dropped the barrel on him, rocking the hammer back on my Navy Colt. I swept my second pistol from my belt and leveled it at the other as he tried to bring his Sharps rifle around.

"Hold it, boys," I said, although each was at least twenty years my senior. They froze and I used the moment to look around; my mare's bridle was tied to an old, spavined mule standing with drooping head in the sun. The mare shuffled her feet nervously. I couldn't blame her; the mule looked as tattertatted as the men.

"You know," I said conversationally, "there isn't a court in the land wouldn't hang you in a minute for what you boys are trying to do."

"A-huh," the one with the rifle grunted. He spit a long stream of tobacco juice at a rock, missed. "Wal, ther's many slip twixt here and there. An' yuh ain't out of heah yet." His rheumy eyes shrewdly considered me. He glanced at the one with the knife. "Ah don' think you can make both of us."

"Like you said," I answered, "there's many a slip between fact and expectation."

His rheumy eyes shrewdly gauged me, trying to decide if I was the trouble I was promising. He glanced over at his partner and shook his head. "Yuh could be good enough to put the move on both of us, but Ah don' think so," he said slowly.

"Like you said," I answered, "there's a lot of slip between doing and expectation. I guess it amounts to one thing: Do you feel lucky?" I waved both pistols. "It seems to me I have enough for both of you."

Broken yellow teeth peeked from his tobacco-stained lips. He nodded. "As Ah 'spected, boy. Yuh ain't got enough salt on yuh or yuh wouldn't be puttin' that much faith into luck."

I smiled faintly and rose to my feet, taking a step backward and to the side, narrowing the gap between them. "Oh, I wasn't counting on luck," I said. "I thought *you* were."

"Boy, yuh sure have sand. Ah'll give you that," he said. "Wal, guess we'd better know yer name so's we know what name to bury yuh under."

"Hickok," I said. "James Butler Hickok."

I watched as the dagger man's eyes widened. "Lem," he said urgently. "That's the one who did for those folks up at Rock Creek Station. Yuh 'member that drummer telling us 'bout it over that jug last week?" His eyes flicked back to mine. "Yuh that one, boy?" I nodded. Slowly he replaced the dagger into the top of his calf-high boot. Twine had been wrapped around the arch to hold the boot together.

"They say he kilt six there faster'n a man could blink," he said. He held dirty palms up. The lines were ridged with caked dirt. "Ah don' want no hand in a game like that."

Lem gave me a hard look. His eyes traced me slowly, noting the pallor in my color, the hollowed cheeks, and he shook his head.

"Yuh talkin' hell on wheels, Seth," he said. "Yuh take a look at this feller? Harsh wind blow him clear to Alabama."

Seth shook his head and turned away, deliberately leaving me his back as he walked to the mule. "Yuh 'cide for y'self, Lem. Me, Ah don' cotton to no hastened grave. This heah world's harsh 'nough for gettin' by. But Ah ain't in no hurry to step inta the other on a chance it'd be better. Leastways Ah know what to 'spect heah."

He reached the mule and deliberately untied the mare and

dropped the reins upon the ground. The mare took a couple of skittish steps away from the mule and stood, ears pricked, watching nervously. Seth pulled himself upon the mule's back and drummed his heels against the mule's ribs, gigging him forward. The mule took a couple of steps, then stopped, dropped a loose pile on the dust, and moved forward reluctantly.

"Seth!" Lem yelled. "Gawd dum yuh! That's my mule!"

"Then cum with him," Seth said without looking back.

"Seth!"

But this time Seth ignored him, kicking the mule as hard as he could, but the mule ignored him and continued his steady plodding down the road. Lem sighed and shook his head in despair and looked again at me. I thought for a moment I saw resignation in his eyes, but then his features hardened.

"Yuh see how 'tis," he said, but I heard no regret in his voice. A lone dove called, and down by the creek a jay answered.

"It'll be a mistake," I said warningly. "You can just walk away from it all. You'll have to leave that Sharps behind, though."

He glanced down at the rifle in his hands and slowly shook his head. "No, reckon Ah couldn't do that." He raised his eyes and I could see the uncertainty gnawing at him and knew then he was going to try to swing the barrel of that Sharps. Even as I spoke I could see the decision take hold and squeezed the Navy's trigger.

The ball took him square in the chest, punching him back into the sunlight. He gasped twice and lay still. I took a long deep breath and let it out slowly.

"Wasn't much of a choice," I said. I picked up the rifle and checked it. The rifle was far cleaner than him. I was surprised. A man normally keeps his weapons as he keeps himself. I heard a wagon coming and dropped the Sharps on top of him before walking out and gathering the mare. I stepped in the stirrup and swung up, settling in the saddle as a farm wagon hoved into view, a gaunt and bearded fellow in clean overalls sitting in the spring seat. He reined in his team and stared from me to the dead man on the ground. I nodded at him.

"That man's name is Lem," I said. "That's all I know. He tried to steal my horse."

"Don't look like he made it," the man drawled.

I pointed at the Sharps. "That rifle's got the cost of a burial in it."

"Then why don't you take it?" the man said in a reedy voice. "He sure ain't gonna know the difference."

"I don't need a rifle," I said. I touched mine in its scabbard beneath my leg. "I have one."

"Saw that," he said. "That's why I figure it's as you say. Even if it wasn't"—he shrugged—"don't matter none to me. But what's to keep me from just taking the rifle and leaving him?"

"Depends on you," I said, and nudged the mare with my heels. "Reckon nothing would stop you as long as you don't mind listening to yourself each day."

I lifted the mare into a canter and rode after Seth. I caught up to him in a few miles. He glanced up at me, alarm in his face. I paused long enough to tell him about Lem and the farmer, then rode away toward Fort Leavenworth.

CHAPTER

32

AT FIRST I joined Lorenzo, who was working as a wagon master, but I soon took on a job as a special policeman under Lieutenant N. A. Burns, who was the provost marshal at Springfield. That didn't last long, either, however, as I quit when they shorted me pay and, not long after, Brigadier General John B. Sanborn hired me as a scout. That was, in a way, the beginning of the legend of Wild Bill—although the McCanles incident at Rock Creek was beginning to make the rounds as well—and I spent most of the war either scouting for the Union or else behind enemy lines, trying to find out Confederate plans.

A pearl gray mist sifted over the trees and road down through Arkansas as I rode a mule above the road through the tree line, looking in vain for the Confederate soldiers that were supposedly in the area. I knew I was close to Pea Ridge, but in the mist I found the road appearing and disappearing and then it was gone for good and I was lost. Not a very good position to find oneself in when he doesn't know where the enemy might be.

"All right now, y'all just rein in that mule and sit tight."

The voice startled me, coming from the mist as it did. I reached automatically for my pistols, but a shot *popped!* by my ear and I froze. "Raise 'em," the voice said again, patient and amused.

Slowly I raised my hands. A couple of gray-clad men suddenly appeared beside my stirrups. One of them, the speaker, moved a wad of tobacco around in his cheek and spit on the ground, staring up at me, bemused at my appearance. I wore heavy boots, canvas pants, a butternut shirt—not embroidered; I didn't want to be shot as a bushwhacker by one of my own—and a slouch hat with a broken brim. I carried a pair of Dragoon pistols, .44 caliber, so heavy that they would have pulled my britches down if I hadn't helped my belt along with a pair of leather suspenders.

"Take his pistols, Jed," the man said. He laughed as he watched the Dragoons be taken from my belt. "Son, y'all should put wheels on them things and pull 'em around as cannons. Now, who are yuh and whar you headed?"

"Butler," I managed around the sudden dryness in my mouth. "Jim Butler. I'm just headin' away from those folks behind me. Bunch of fellows in blue coats. They burnt Daddy's cabin and shot his pigs and—"

He held up his hand, near choking on his plug from laughter. "Son," he gulped and spit. "Now Ah ain't no such fool as y'all seem to think. Nor is Jed there. There ain't a damn pig around here for fifty mile or we'da found 'em instead of livin' on coon and possum and drinkin' acorn coffee like we been for the past couple of weeks. Hell, boy, get y'all's story down 'fore y'all spit it out at a man and try to make 'im y'all's fool. All right. Ah reckon Ah know what y'all is." He nodded at Jed. "Take 'im back to camp and give 'im to the captain. Mayhap the boy'll come to his senses and tell the truth when he's standing 'fore a firin' squad for being a spy."

"Spy?" I shook my head and spoke as anxiously as I could manage. "Mister, I don't know what you're talking about.

I'm just what I told you and I know there ain't no pig around behind me. I'm from Missouri and this here's Arkansas, near as I can figure. I'm looking to join up."

He shook his head, beaming merrily at me. "Boy, y'all just ain't got quit in your words, do yuh? Well, take him back to camp and let the officers sort 'im out. Mayhap he's tellin' the truth; mayhap he's lyin'. One means he could be good for us, and t'other, well, hell, a bullet will take care of that."

Silently the other man nudged me with his rifle. I climbed down off the mule and waited while he tied my hands behind my back; then I stumbled through the mist in the direction he pointed. He followed, leading my mule behind him.

We must have walked a mile or two; then suddenly the mist lifted from a hollow and I saw what I had been looking for camped down around a tiny brook under a bunch of trees. I don't know how many there were, but I could see groups of men huddled around tiny fires all down through the hollow and around a bend of the creek.

We made our way down the slope and were stopped by a young lieutenant and a couple of whiskered soldiers who lacked the humor of the one we'd left behind. The lieutenant eyed me carefully, then looked at the soldier behind me.

"Well, Allen, where did you find this one?"

Jed spit and jerked his head back the way we had come. "Back there," he said quietly. "Me and Ben found 'im riding this here mule above the road. Looked kinda suspicious and all, what with the road being just a hill away and all. Mean, why would he be ridin' there instead of in comfort on the road if he weren't looking for us?"

"Because I didn't know the damn road was there," I said. "Hell, I been trying to stay out of Yankee hands for the past two weeks. Why would I want to take a chance on a road anyway, not knowing friend from foe in this damn fog?"

"Uh-huh," the lieutenant said. His eyes looked unfriendly and I knew at once he didn't believe me. "Well, we'll just take him on up to the captain and let him decide."

But he couldn't decide, either, and I was led right up the ranks until I was before General Sterling Price. I reckoned I was in deep water that was getting hotter and hotter as we went deeper and deeper into that camp. Every time we passed a campfire the men would rise and step forward to study me carefully. I kept getting more and more edgy as we went along, fearing that sooner or later someone was bound to recognize me. The Union wasn't the only one with scouts out; the Rebels had them out, too, and whether they knew it or not, I knew that the Union army wasn't that far behind me. I hadn't been on the trail more than a day. The Union and the Rebels were closer than anyone thought.

"General?"

Price turned around, staring at me. His uniform was neat and clean. He wore a beard that looked like it was trimmed daily.

"The guards found this man wandering around out along the line. Thought he might be a spy."

Price pursed his lips, studying me. His black eyes remained expressionless. I knew instinctively that bluster wouldn't win him over, so I stared back at him, waiting, somehow feeling that silence was my best defense at the moment. At last he nodded and said, "Well? What were you doing out there?"

"Looking for you," I said. It was the truth and I felt he would hear that in my voice and maybe, just maybe, I could fool him after with a lie.

He smiled faintly. "And how did you know I was in the area?"

I shook my head. "Not *you* precisely. I don't know you from Adam. I was looking for a camp of any Southern soldiers."

"Why?"

So I spun my story again, watching him watch me, listening to my words. I forced myself to remain calm and tried to speak over the fluttering in my stomach and hoped that my bladder, threatening to burst at the time, would not betray me.

When I finished, he nodded and said, "Well, I know that there are Union soldiers around here somewhere. There has to be. Where I don't know." He nodded again at me. "You've had some education; I can see that. But you're young. . . ." He paused, furrowing his brow. "All right. I'll give you the benefit of the doubt." He nodded at the captain behind me. "Untie him and swear him in. We can't give you a uniform, because we have none to spare. You stay here with me as a runner, though. We'll put you to use there."

I didn't have any reservations about that. I knew why he was keeping me close at hand. He did mean to give me the benefit of the doubt—Price had a good reputation for being fair that he had earned while serving in the Missouri General Assembly and even in Congress. He had even been Missouri's governor for a term or two. But I didn't have any illusions; I knew he would have me shot in a minute if he thought I was a spy—I couldn't be anything more, as I wasn't in uniform.

And so I went to work for Price, watching, learning, memorizing, waiting for my chance to get away. Two weeks passed and I knew that I had to be making a move soon or else I would be listed as a deserter—if I wasn't listed so already.

Then one day Price told me to take a message to Archibald S. Dobbin north of Pea Ridge. I borrowed a chestnut—a fine mare with a white blaze down her face—that I knew had bottom and rode to find Dobbin. I wasn't exactly sure where Dobbin and his men were, but I did have a rough idea of Pea Ridge. I found them about a hundred yards from the river and delivered my message that he was to engage the Union army under Curtis only if they came across the river. He laughed and said he had no intention of trying to cross the river with the Union boys dug in the way they were but to wait a bit and he'd write a note for me to take back to Price.

I rode down toward the river where a group of men were sitting around a fire, having a cup of coffee—not the acorn mash Price's men were drinking, either, but real coffee, which set my mouth to watering. One of the men looked up and saw me sitting on the chestnut and asked if I would like to join them.

"Hell," a sergeant said. "Y'all gonna give coffee to every

young'un wet behind the ears that comes this way won't be none left a-tall for the men."

I stared at him for a second while the man who had spoken to me stood uncertainly half between the sergeant and me. I stayed on the chestnut and laughed at the sergeant. I nudged the horse forward and took the cup of coffee from the man. The tin cup burned my fingers, but I took a swallow and sighed as it burned its way down, then sighed again as I felt its magic work through my stomach.

The sergeant was annoyed at the man for letting me have the coffee and started to complain when I spoke up.

"Hey," I said softly. He looked up at me, his brown eyes challenging me brazenly. "I'll bet you a dollar I can ride closer to the river than you."

His eyes widened at that. The man who gave me the coffee turned away, hiding his grin behind a cough.

"Well? What's it going to be?" I continued. "You been sitting there flapping your lip about being so damn brave and all, how about it? You game for a buck?"

He looked uncertainly from me to the river about a mile distant. He rubbed the palm of his hand over his lip, staring at the Union line on the other side, trying to gauge just how close he could get to the river without being shot.

"Hell," I said, tossing the empty cup to him. He fumbled before catching it and swore when the dregs splattered his tunic. The others laughed. "Tell you what I'll do. I'll give you a mark and you see if you got the nerve to follow."

I reached down and pulled their guidon from the ground where it was stuck.

"Hey!" he said, raising a hand to snatch it back, but I kneed the chestnut away from him. I laughed, feeling a certain craziness swing giddily through me.

"You want it, come and get it!" I shouted, and kicked my heels against the sides of the chestnut.

She leaped forward, reaching full gallop quickly, her hooves kicking large gouts of the wet earth behind her. I heard the sergeant swear and call for his horse, and bent low over the chestnut's neck, urging her on.

A shot snapped by us from the Union lines and I stuck her reins between my teeth and whipped my hat off and waved it back and forth. Another shot came and I swore and waved the hat harder, then leaned over the chestnut as we neared the river. I dropped the guidon as the chestnut didn't pause but leaped into the river and began swimming for the other side. I slipped out of the saddle, placing her between myself and the Confederate shore. Bullets from behind us began to kick up the water as it dawned on the Rebels that they had been played for fools and a barrage from the Union side answered them. I glanced back over the top of the chestnut and watched as the sergeant and a small party turned their horses to gallop back from the river. Then the sergeant threw up his hands and tumbled from his horse. The others lay low over the backs of their horses and put the spurs to their sides, galloping away.

The chestnut climbed the bank, dragging me with her, as a squad of soldiers hurried over, their rifles covering me cautiously. I shook the water from my hair and grinned at them.

"Thanks for the help, boys," I said. "My name's Hickok. Who's in charge here?"

That was what happened, although by the time Nichols got done with the story I had raced the sergeant to the river, then leaped over it, turning in midair and firing with my pistols, killing half a dozen or so Rebs before my horse's hooves touched the ground on the other side. I think Nichols had me killing that sergeant, too, but I didn't. Fact is, I barely got away with my life and my grinning at the end was more relief than anything—relief that I wasn't shot by either the Confederate or Union soldiers.

There were other adventures as well, including one where Quantrill damned near killed me and another one where I almost killed Bloody Bill, but somehow the truth of those got lost in the stories and the stories got lost in the truth and over the past years all that got mixed up with whiskey and rye and each other, and I doubt if I can even remember everything about what happened during the war. I do remember one time, though, because I still can't explain it and never did tell anyone else about it for fear they would think I was a fool and a liar. I don't mind the latter, but the former is valuable only insofar as everyone knows you've been joking around with them at the end. Somehow, though, what happened in those Arkansas woods never seemed like a joke to me.

The day came slowly in a gray swirling mist settling in for a long stay over Wilson's Creek. Those weeks earlier, I had signed on as civilian scout with the Union army at Fort Leavenworth and was taken by General Niles Becker, a vain and arrogant man with well-oiled black hair swept back from a fine high forehead. But he was a bit too cautious and reluctant to move forward until the entire terrain was well scouted. Yet he put limits on the distance for the scouts, preferring to keep them close at hand in case the troops had to suddenly move elsewhere. It seemed like he wanted to know but yet he didn't want to know—which left his scouts scratching their heads more than once, trying to figure out what to do next.

Report after report came back negative from scouting trips over Missouri's rough terrain, and I began to get a strange feeling that something wasn't right. I knew that Rebels were around because I never found a single head of livestock in all the forays I made through those hills. Yet I found no one, even though I worked myself deeper and deeper into the hills and woods.

"You boys stay close," General Becker said when I requested permission to make a deep scout into southern Missouri. "If we get orders to move out, I don't want to have to send someone looking for you."

"But, General," I said, feeling frustration building up inside. "General, I'll always be able to catch up. You can't move that fast that I won't be able to find you. An army this size leaves a mighty big trail."

"Sir," he said, suppressing his irritation. "We are training for rapid deployment."

And I knew by the note of finality in his voice that the

subject was closed. I could have suggested that I might find the golden goose or Boru's Harp by going over the next ridge and gotten nowhere.

"Besides," he said disdainfully, "we have over five thousand soldiers here. If a Rebel force large enough to launch an attack against us was anywhere near, we would have known about it by now."

"Nice to be certain," I muttered, and left.

The woods seemed still, dark, and deep under the low gray falling slowly over Wilson's Creek. A damp cloying smell like swamp gas and mold seemed to wrap around us. I couldn't shake the feeling that everything was all wrong as I squatted on my heels over a cup of coffee, huddling as close around the small scouts' fire as I could to keep the swarms of mosquitoes away. Voices became soft murmurs and all of us threw uneasy looks out at the gray bank rolling in toward us.

At last I tossed the dregs of my cup on the fire and made my way to the picket line to get my horse. Perhaps I would feel better if I rode around the ridgeline and made certain that we really were alone. The quiet pressed down upon us and I heard the edgy but quiet arguments of the men who felt it, too, as I rode through the camp.

Then I was among the wet trees, slowly making my way across the creek and into the trees. I heard a *clunk!* and instantly thought of a rifle barrel accidentally striking against a cannon. A muttered curse followed. I reined in and froze, trying to find the direction of the noise, straining to hear. My mare's head suddenly jerked up and her ears pricked and twitched. I nudged her and she moved forward. A swirling mist coiled slowly around us like a Hydra's breath. Suddenly a little breeze swept a hole in the cloud and I saw a small battery of cannon being pulled into position by Rebel soldiers. At the same time, a lieutenant in a plumed hat turned and saw me and froze in astonishment, his jaw dropping down to his gray tunic.

I whirled the mare around and clapped my heels hard against her ribs. She grunted in surprise but sprang forward, her tiny hooves flashing as she flew back toward our camp. I heard the lieutenant's warning shout. Then the roar of the cannon and whistle of shot as it rose out of the trees. The ground trembled when the shells landed ahead of me, and then the screaming began. Tiny pops sounded, then the buzz of angry bees as balls zipped past my head from the wild firing of our troops shooting madly into their own fear.

"Goddamnit! I'm coming in!" I bawled, and bent forward over the mare's neck as we splashed into and across the creek. I reined in in front of Becker's tent and slid quickly out of the saddle. I burst into the tent and encountered Becker pulling on his boots, eyes wild.

"What's going on?" he demanded, rising and stamping his feet to settle them in his boots.

"You're under attack, you damn fool!" I snapped. "A force of ghosts suddenly materialized along with phantom cannon"—another shell burst nearby, followed by the screams of injured men—"and is blowing the hell out of your troops who don't know they aren't supposed to be hurt!"

"That's enough, Mr. Hickok!" he said. "When one can keep his head—"

Another explosion came, nearer than the last, drowning out his words. Suddenly it dawned on me that the Rebels probably had placed spotters in the trees around the camp days before to mark out targets.

"Damn!" I said. The commanding general's tent would have been one of the first marked. I turned and ran out of the tent.

"Mr. Hickok! Come back! I haven't finished—"

A loud *whoosh!* came overhead and I dived headfirst behind a fallen tree as Becker's tent disappeared under a direct hit, cutting off his indignant yell. My ears filled with the roar of exploding shells, and shrapnel rattled through the trees above me. Leaves and sticks and bark rained upon me, followed by a cloud of black dirt and dust.

"General Becker! General Becker!" screamed a captain. "What'll we do? What'll we do?" I sat up and spit dirt from my mouth and wiggled my little fingers in my ears in a vain attempt to clear the ringing. The captain saw me and ran toward me.

"Where's the general?" he cried.

"Dead, I think," I said, and pointed at the hole where his tent once stood.

The captain turned and looked, stunned, at the hole. "But," he stammered, "where's the general?"

"In heaven or hell, and right now I don't care which!" I shouted. Then I heard that wild ululating Rebel yell and swore. We were being attacked in force by Confederate cavalry. It was too late to form a line or redoubt or whatever plans Lyon had drawn up in the past weeks to cover what he calls "contingencies."

"Tell the men to fall back away from the creek!" I shouted. "If we can get some distance between us, we can make a stand. Maybe," I added.

But we couldn't. The men were already running with wild abandon through the woods. Some of the other scouts found me, and together we fought our way clear, slicing our way through the Rebel cavalry toward the east, hoping to beat a flanking movement. We didn't bother with trying to rally our soldiers; that would have been a mark of vanity to expect that we could. I had no doubts that this day would be a momentous day for the Confederate forces. My first experience in war had ended in complete disaster.

CHAPTER

33

ISRAEL PUTNAM and I rode across the bridge spanning Wilson's Creek and immediately turned south into the shadowed woods of bare trees reaching black arms toward the leaden sky. Spring was late in coming, and although it was April, it was colder than a witch's behind. I huddled inside my deep-pocketed canvas coat, shivering as we made our way cautiously through the damp trees and bushes. Silence covered us like a thick blanket. No squirrels chattered angrily at jays coming too close to their nests, no birds sang warnings to others, as we plodded along a bare deer trail that wove its way around trees, down to the bank of the river, and back into the middle of the woods. Israel rode in front of me, the back of his beefy neck wrinkling as he swung his gaze from left to right and back again, his gloved right hand resting lightly on his pommel near a holstered Dragoon Colt revolver. Automatically I touched my own Colt .44 caliber Dragoons hanging on either side of my saddle horn, loosening them in their holsters.

We rode down a hill and into the boundary of a valley,

damp fog wrapping itself around us as we descended. I ached
with weariness and I was cold, my nose red and snot dripping
into my mustache, freezing almost immediately, and I felt
uneasy, that feeling I always got when I knew someone was
watching us and I couldn't see him. I cast back to the night
before when Tan Jenkins, shot to holes, rode in on a lathered
horse and reported a guerrilla force moving south to link up
with Confederate forces near Pea Ridge. After the Becker
debacle, General Nat Lyon had lost no time in ordering Israel
and me to saddle up and go find them. Lyon was a fire dragon
for certain, constantly looking for a war even if he lost a third
of his men or so. He had his eye on politics after the war and
knew a good war record would bring in lots of votes from the
zealous New Englanders who eagerly read his daily reports
back to the home newspapers with the eagerness of a sinner
looking for a Messiah to follow. I didn't much care for Lyon,
although I had to admire the results of his recklessness.

"Boys," he said once as we were having a cup of coffee
before heading into our blankets for the night, "victory
comes only to those who don't flinch away from gunfire."
He had pointed into the darkness. "Back east there's a young
man called Custer who said he always rode to the sound of
the guns, and he's right. You don't win battles sitting around
campfires, telling everyone how good you are while running
a cleaning rod through the bore of an unfired rifle. You have
to get up and take the fight to the enemy to keep him off-
balance. Like a fighter." He rose to his feet and danced a bit
on the balls of his booted feet, throwing lefts into the darkness, hooking with his right. "Don't let him get set and
choose the ground upon which to fight you."

A loud *awk!* brought me from my dreaming, my hand
half-drawing one of the Colts from its holster while I looked
around quickly for the source of the noise.

"Crows," Israel said sourly, pointing upward.

I glanced at the gray sky showing through the nude black
limbs. A flock of crows circled in slow, lazy gyres, climbing
and dropping down nearly to the highest branches of the
trees before swinging back up, ever in a circle.

"They see something," I said softly.

"Ay-uh," Israel grunted. He reined in his horse and stood in his stirrups, trying to see ahead on the deer trail. "I don't like this, Bill. The back of my neck's just a-crawling. I got a hunch we're being injuned."

A gray shadow moved at the edge of my vision. I slipped one of the heavy Colts from its holster, cocking it as I turned toward the movement. A she-wolf, bags heavy with milk for her pups, melted like twilight into the darkness of the brush. My skin prickled. I took a deep breath, smelling the damp and mold from the moss in the scaborous bark of the trees. She turned to look back at me just before she disappeared, her yellow eyes gleaming at me like the devil's lanterns.

"Don't think nothing's worse than a she-wolf with pups," Israel said softly. I glanced at him, his jaw bunching as he worked a wad of tobacco he'd stuffed into his cheek. His brown eyes looked nervous, darting around the woods. "And something's got her up and moving to draw it away from her litter. Otherwise, she'd a-held tight to her pups, waiting us out as we rode past."

"You ever get tired of being right?" I asked anxiously. My pulse seemed to shudder as blood pounded in my temples.

"She's crossed our path," he said solemnly, his head turning to his left.

I leaned away in my saddle to look around him and heard the snap of a rifle ball passing where my head had been only a moment before. Then guns roared from the bushes and half a dozen balls slammed into Israel, blowing him backward off his saddle. His horse screamed, reared, and galloped away. I dropped the knotted reins over the neck of my horse and drew the second Dragoon from its holster and blazed away at the bushes. My horse gave one leap, then grunted and hunched down and seemed to draw in upon herself. I kicked free from the stirrups and dived out of the saddle as she crumbled to the earth. I landed hard in a pile of dead leaves next to Israel. His eyes looked wildly at me, his mouth open and gasping for air. I glanced down at his chest and saw the blood bubbling out.

Lung-shot, I thought automatically. I snapped a couple of

shots at a quivering bush and heard a yell of pain. The firing eased for a second and I stuffed one of the pistols under my belt and rose, seizing Israel by the collar and dragging him around behind the thick bole of an oak. Bark flew off the side of the tree, stinging my cheek.

"Bill!" Israel gasped, clutching at my coat, pulling me down. The tree shivered as bullets pounded into its trunk. "I'm finished. End it and get away."

I ignored him and leaned around the tree and fired at a figure that broke from the brush, running toward us. The heavy ball took him in the belly, doubling him over and knocking him off his feet. He yelled, his hands flying up in the air, a pair of pistols slipping from them as he rolled on the ground, clutching the big hole in his belly, trying to push away the pain. He screamed and screamed again; then a bullet came out of the brush and blew the top of his head away, silencing him.

"Tan was right," I said. "Guerrillas are here. They're the only ones who kill their wounded rather than leave them behind. No soldier would do that."

"Joe Shelby, I reckon," he gasped, his face white beneath his scraggly beard. "Get the hell out of here, Bill!"

"I ever tell you my name's James?" I said. I slipped the cylinder out of a Dragoon and dropped it into my pocket, taking a loaded one out of the other pocket and snapping it into place. I laid it on the ground and placed a fresh cylinder into the other Army, then checked the Navies in their holsters at my waist. Both seemed all right and I replaced them, slipping a thong over the hammers to secure them. I cocked the two heavy Dragoon Colts and peeked cautiously around the trunk. White smoke seemed to hover beneath the layer of fog above us, slipping slowly over the deer trail, disappearing into the bushes. I yawned, trying to clear the ringing in my ears.

"You think I give a rat's ass about that now?" he gasped. His head jerked back from a sudden stab of pain, banging into the ground. "Ah, Jesus!" He pulled his hands away from his chest and looked at them, bright red. "Lung-shot."

It wasn't a question, but I treated it as one. "Yep," I said. "Reckon so."

"That finishes it," he said. He wiped his hand on his pants, then hawked and spit into his hand and stared at the bright red-spotted spittle. "Ay-uh. Well, I'm between shit and sweat." He moved, rolling over, gasping with pain at the movement. His hands clawed his pistols from his belt. "I reckon you'd better get back to Lyon and tell Old Dragon Breath that we found his Rebels for him."

"Israel," I began, but he cut me off.

"Git," he said firmly. He looked at me, his eyes clear from pain for a moment, but I knew he hadn't long. It was that look of calm resignation one gets just before death washes over him. "I can hold them for a few minutes." He lifted his pistols, wincing from the effort. "Barely feel any pain now at all. That's pretty bad. Well, I got twelve shots and I'll get at least one of them with it. Promise you that. Now clear out of here. I'll cover while I can."

I reached out and squeezed his arm. "You want me to tell anyone?"

He shook his head. "Nope. Don't have no one 'cept a brother back in Springfield. He's a shopkeeper back there. Don't put up much with guns and such. Flour and sugar man. A made Quaker, I think. You might tell him if you get back there."

"I'll tell him," I promised.

He jerked and fired and I heard someone scream. "Well," he said with satisfaction. "I got the one I promised you. Now you don't haul ass, you ain't gonna be tellin' no one nothing."

"Been good knowing you, Israel," I said. I rose to my knees and blasted away at the bushes, then leaped to my feet and sprinted away from the oak, trying to keep between it and the bushes.

"Get going, Wild Bill!" he yelled. "Come on, you butternut-shirted sonsabitches!"

I glanced back and saw him firing away at the bushes, then slipped bchind a close stand of hickories and lost him. I jammed one Colt into my belt and used my free hand to push branches out of my way, keeping the other Dragoon up and cocked, ready for anyone who tried to stop me.

Then the firing stopped behind me, and I knew Israel was finished and the guerrillas would be along behind me soon, if not now.

I suddenly found myself beside the river and paused, looking for a hiding place. Behind me, the guerrillas came closer, moving cautiously now, as they sensed that I had been cornered. I saw a dead log washed up from the last spring flood and made my way to it, reckoning that it would give me a little cover and if I could hold them off until dark, I might have a chance of slipping away through the brush.

Little hope, I thought sourly as I settled behind the log, facing back the way I had come. It wouldn't take a Grant to figure out that I could be flanked by someone willing to get a bit wet.

A bit wet.

I crawled to the edge of the bank and looked up and downriver. I saw what I was searching for about a hundred yards downstream where the river cut back into the bank, then swung away in a tight oxbow, looping around almost upon itself before turning and heading south again. A natural overhang stood at the top of the river's curve, with a tangle of willow roots and swamp grass forming a kind of curtain over whatever lay behind. It wasn't much, but if it was deep enough—I glanced over the bank to where a young alder had washed, bobbing gently in the undulating waves that came from the current.

I rolled over and looked quickly back over the dead log. No one had yet to break out of the tree line, but that didn't mean they weren't in there watching and waiting for me to make the first move.

I chewed the end of my mustache thoughtfully. It was risky, but options weren't presenting themselves at the moment. I sighed and rolled back to the edge of the bank and slipped off into the water, trying desperately to hold my pistols in one hand above the water to keep the powder dry. Whatever was in my coat pockets was immediately soaked and useless. If I was cornered, I had twelve shots and then my heels if I was lucky. But I knew the chances of outrunning a guerrilla were slim and none. Those folks in their embroidered butternut shirts were far more used to these woods than I was. I had to try to think my way out.

The air exploded in a gasp as the cold water seeped through my clothes. My legs went numb almost immediately and I gritted my teeth tightly to keep from crying out. Gently I edged the alder free from its mud anchor so the water wouldn't muddy itself. Then a good tracker would know instantly what had happened. I took a deep breath and worked the tree out into deeper water, into the current, and let myself sink down to my neck behind the trunk of the tree, trying to hide the hand holding the pistols in its branches.

The tree swung gently in the current, floating tantalizingly slowly downriver. I resisted trying to speed it up, knowing that everything had to look as natural as an apple hanging on the tree. Then I saw a small group of figures edge out of the shadows and make their way cautiously toward the dead log. Had I not been watching for them, I would have thought them to be the very shadows themselves forming a thicket of the imagination, the way the guerrillas blended with the trees and bushes at the edge of the woods. Their leader straightened and cast a quick look around. He pointed toward the alder tree and the others turned, bringing their rifles up. I gave up on keeping my powder dry, jammed my pistols back behind my belt, touched the Navies to ensure they were secure in their holsters, and took a deep breath and went under the water as a fusillade struck the trunk of the tree and the water on the other side.

I felt the tree press against me as the current turned it slightly to make the bend. I took a chance and slipped up to grab a quick lungful of air. The cutback was just in front. I ducked under the water again and opened my eyes, peering through the silt. My lungs burned as I tried to work my way through the web of roots, hoping that there was a little space behind where I'd be screened from the river and the other side of the bank. Finally, I had to force my way up or drown.

I found myself against the wall of the bank, the grass overhang nearly touching the water. In front of me were roots and root tendrils forming a thick screen. I edged the heels of my boots against the bank to form a small grip and dug my fingers deep into the clay to hold myself still and keep ripples from working out of the cut into the open water. By now I couldn't feel much of anything and fought to keep myself from shivering, gritting my teeth tightly to keep them from chattering.

The thump of horses' hooves came through the small cut from overhead. I breathed shallowly, hoping that they hadn't noticed how the river had taken a large dig out of the bank before looping its way around the oxbow. Voices murmured, but I couldn't make out the words. Then the horses began moving away, but I remained where I was, as someone might have been trailing behind to catch the odd fellow trying to double back on a trail. It was a favorite trick of the Southern boys to leave a couple riding drag. A lot of good men went under because of that trick.

I waited for an hour or so more and had started to work my way out through the veil of willow roots when a king-fisher swooped toward the bank, then turned abruptly and darted away. I sank back to where I had been and gritted my teeth against the cold that seemed to seep into my very bones. Even my teeth ached from the chill when twilight began to fall. When I could no longer see through the veil, I decided to take my chances and cautiously crawled and pawed my way through. I swam downstream and around the bend to where a small cove tucked back up among the trees. I made my way into the cove, then hauled myself, dripping wet, out of the river. I touched my pistols automatically. The Navies were still in their holsters, but I had lost the Dragoons somewhere during my time in the water. I was so cold that I hadn't even felt them slip from my belt.

A cold breeze slipped down from the north, and despite my attempts to keep my teeth from chattering, my body seemed to be consumed by Saint Vitus' dance. I stood on the bank and swung my arms and tried to run in place to warm myself, but my feet thudded upon the ground like blocks of ice. Dizziness washed over me, followed by waves of cold and hot. I gave up and started to make my way around the cove, hoping that I was upstream from the bridge.

I traveled for hours; then night fell without warning, and I knew that I was hopelessly lost in the dark woods. I stumbled and fell over twisted roots that seemed to throw themselves up in my path. Brambles clawed at my clothes and ripped into the flesh of my hands when I tried to push them away. A strange savageness came out of the darkness, wrapping itself in thickly muscled arms around me. Bitter death seemed to breathe upon my collar.

Somehow I blundered off the one true path that seemed to be looping its way through those woods. I felt warm, then hot, then cold, then hot again, and a cold perspiration began to bead and flow down my face, chest, and back. I panted from the exertion of my efforts. I knew I was going downhill only because one foot always planted itself lower and lower. Then I saw a light in the trees and made my way toward it, hoping that luck was still with me.

I found a small tavern in a clearing back from a small trail. A weathered sign swung, creaking on an ancient hook. I could just make out ARIAL'S KEEP. Strange name for these parts, I thought, and cautiously worked my way around to the front, coming in from the south out of the way of the north breeze. I wanted to be downwind of any horses that might be hitched out front.

I peeked around the corner of the tavern. No horses. Cautiously I approached the door and gingerly leaned my ear against it, trying to hear inside. Silence. I pulled a pistol from its holster—whoever was inside wouldn't know the powder was wet and useless and, I hoped, wouldn't be bold enough to challenge a man already holding a pistol—took a deep breath, and cracked open the door. I peeked inside but saw no one. A fire blazed cheerfully in the cobblestoned fireplace. A pot of stew bubbled merrily, its rich odor floating out upon a slight draft through the open door, making my mouth water. My eyes blurred. I rubbed them with the heel of my hand. The door jerked open and I staggered inside. I tried to turn, but my balance was gone and I sprawled on the floor, my pistol skittering away into a corner of the room.

I heard the door slam shut and tried to rise, but my arms were weaker than my resolution and I thumped back to the floor again, staring up at the log trusses of the ceiling as they swam around as if a swing in a breeze. I heard a rustle like lone bat wings on a hot summer night—but it wasn't summer, I told myself, barely spring. Remember that: barely spring.

A pair of bare feet beside me. I noticed the thickly ridged yellow-casted toenails and caught a glimpse of the heavy yellow pads of callus under the balls of the feet. The ankles were trim and went up into sturdy calves, but the rest of her legs flitted in and out of the darkness folded under her green and white calico dress—green and white? I frowned, trying to remember if there were such colors in calico. The dress swam and disappeared and I realized what I had thought to be green and white was soft gray, a plain gray dress, clean and hard-ironed, that spread around generous breasts, tucked in at a narrow waist, and ambled down over ample hips. The dress rustled and her face swam down to me, lantern-jawed, with luminous black eyes and premature silver hair. Her face was smooth and deeply tanned, so one might take her for an Indian except for the golden sheen of her flesh that could have only been given her by the sun. Her heavy breasts pushed against her dress as she leaned over me like a forest mother, her generous eyebrows furrowed in concern.

Lightning flickered through the windows, flashing across her face like a burning brand. Thunder boomed hard on its heels—*boooooo-arrrrr-maaaccccchhhhhaaaaa-aaa-aaa-*

aaa—and the fire flickered and ducked and danced in answer. Tallow candles dimmed—had I seen them before? I no longer knew as memory began to shatter and separate into tiny pictures: Israel jerked and fell from his horse; tiny spurts of red fire like animal eyes flickered from the bushes; Father stepped from the grave with the grave still clinging gravely to him, flesh hanging in gray strips, hair in gray tangled knots, eyes hollow and accusing, a strange, earthy smell wafting from his decaying flesh to me. . . .

"Y'burning up, mister," she said, her voice soft and musical, rolling over me like warm water. Her hand pressed against my forehead, wiping away the cold sweat. "Y'all been out there long? Must've been," she said, answering her own question. "This heah's Ah-real's Keep. Y'all welcome heah. Don't matter at all to me what y'are. Not many find their way heah through those dark woods."

"Water," I croaked.

She nodded, then rose. I closed my eyes, trying to still the red-crazy images darting and dashing around in my mind. A dipper of cold water pressed against my lips. I drank thirstily, but somewhere between my fevered gulps I drifted away into darkness and

a fiery wheel came spinning out of the darkness pulled by rearing black horses with flying manes and fierce eyes blazing leaping over flaming ditches gullets where every flame strives against another flaring blue then a yellow-red hurtful to the eyes and the flames reached over hungrily trying to seize me as I stepped into the chariot and met a man with long flowing black locks and burning eyes and shoulders bursting his tunic and I knew this was the one who wrestled with the gods and angels and he said I was among the captives by the Chebar River when a whirlwind came out of the north bringing with it a great cloud and a fire that folded and unfolded upon itself and within that fire I saw four men with four faces and four wings and they glowed like burnished brass as bright as burning coals and a spirit entered me and I felt words pressing against my brain saying Son of

man I send thee to the children of Israel to a rebellious na-
tion that hath rebelled against me and sinned against me like
impudent children and I have chosen you to go among them
as a watchman and say unto the wicked that they will die and
his blood will I require at thine hand and then Father came
toward me dripping the grave around him and said I was an-
other Jacob who deceived his father's trust by wearing goat
sleeves so he would be as hairy as Esau and I protested but
knew of my betrayal of his death and his life with Josephine
as he lay dying and suddenly I saw Hannah staring at me
with accusing eyes and then she moved away from me falling
rapidly away as if someone was pulling her backward into
darkness and

I awoke in a strange room, my throat raw and my mouth
dry. I seemed to be floating, light-headed, around the timber-
walled room. I smelled lavender and tried to lick my lips
from feeling like parchment. My tongue felt bristles and I
rubbed my hand over my chin, expecting to feel my chin
smooth, and felt, instead, a nascent beard. Wonderingly, I
tried to remember when last I had shaved, and could not.
"Yesterday?" I said the word aloud.

"Longer, I'd say."

The soft voice twanged at my memory. I rolled my head
and saw the forest maiden sitting in a straight-backed
wooden rocker, watching me carefully.

"Y'all been heah a long time."

I remembered suddenly Israel and our assignment. "Gotta
get back," I murmured. The words made my throat hurt. My
gun belt hung on the bedpost next to my pillow. She caught
my glance and nodded.

"They're loaded. Ah thought you'd want that," she said.

I nodded and tried to sit up, but I was too weak and fell
back against the bed.

"Gotta . . . gotta . . ."

"Uh-huh. Thought you'd think that way, too," she said. The
chair creaked as she stood. "But a man's gotta find such things
out for himself. Won't do no good at all trying to tell him."

She walked to the bed and rested her hand on my forehead. I felt the thick callus on the palm but the gentleness, too, and it felt cool and good lying there. She frowned for a moment, then nodded, and her eyes smiled down at me.

"Y'all still got a bit of the fever, but it's passing by right good now, Ah'd say." She pursed her lips *like twin rosebuds* and her thoughts seemed to nudge into mine.

Won't do no good at all to be gettin' up and goin' now y'all safe here and won't take long at all for y'all to fall sick out in the wet woods and then the bushwhackers will find y'all for certain and it'll be all up with y'all then swinging from a white oak tree and your body burning—

I shook my head weakly. "Where am I?"

"Y'all know that," she said calmly. "Think back."

Memory came flooding back in a mad cycle of shadows. I saw myself riding behind Israel, saw the winking flash of red gunfire, the bright spurt of blood from Israel where the bullets struck him, heard the *ka-rrracck!* of the bullets passing, the sound of Israel's last stand, felt the thorns as I crept through the bushes, the cold river, the sound of bullets ricocheting off the water, the deep dark woods, rain—I shivered—and the sign, but I couldn't read it in the misty darkness

ARIAL'S KEEP

whispers whispering

I said the words aloud: "Arial's Keep."

She smiled and nodded and patted my shoulder gently. "Ah'll get y'some broth," she said.

"I need to go—"

She spoke without turning. "Y'all goin' to go through that again? Being foolish just like a man."

"No. Sorry. You're right," I stammered. "Wait." She paused and glanced over my shoulder. "How did you know I wanted my pistols?"

She shook her head, smiling with irony. "Why else would y'carry them like that? A man'd be a foolish one indeed if'n he went walking around these woods heah with unloaded pistols."

"But the powder—"

"Common sense. Y'all were soakin' when y'came in heah. Stands to reason the powder would be damp."

"Of course," I murmured, feeling foolish for the asking.

"Yes," she said.

"What is your name? Sorry." I blushed. "I'm forgetting my manners—I should have asked that before."

"Helen Caroline Ernst," she said. "And I'm not married." She smiled faintly as I blinked in surprise.

"Then, Arial?"

"It's always been named that."

"How long?"

"Always," she repeated, and nodded at me and went outside.

I sighed deeply, trying to focus my thoughts, but they seemed to dart and slide around like swallows on the wing, here, there, everywhere, slipping easily away when I tried to grasp them. Then I frowned, remembering words that had not been spoken. Where had they come from?

The door opened and she came back in, carrying a bowl of broth with a horn spoon lying out upon the lip. Steam rose from the bowl. She heeled the door shut behind her and came to my bed, sitting on the side next to me. A tiny smile flickered at her lips as she spooned the broth from the bowl, blew gently upon it, then carried it to my mouth. I opened my mouth automatically and felt the hot beefy broth slide over my tongue and down my throat. I coughed, a hard, racking cough, and felt something break loose in my chest and flood up into my mouth. She held out her hand.

"Spit," she commanded.

I hesitated for a moment, then meekly complied. She wiped her hand upon the apron she had tied around her gray dress, then took another spoonful of the broth. Like a baby bird I opened my mouth, this time tasting a bit of honey. I frowned.

"What's the matter?" she asked.

"I—" But I couldn't answer. How could I explain the differences in taste to her without sounding ungrateful? *Best,* I thought, *to keep silent about what you don't know and what might hurt her.*

"Wise idea," she said, and held another spoonful to my mouth. I swallowed obediently before registering that she had spoken to my thoughts and not my words.

"How did you know? What I was thinking, I mean?"

"Some things a man is not given to know," she said calmly. "Heah." She placed another spoonful next to my lips. I swallowed, tasting something strong, like horsemint with something behind it—tag alder bark? I didn't know, but I knew there was meadow cabbage in it, maybe some lobelia—Indian turnip?

"Yes," she said.

I started to speak, but a warm drowsiness came over me. *Drugged*—I fought against the approaching twilight, then felt her cool palm again upon my forehead.

"Y'all still feverish a bit," she said softly. "But sleep now. When y'awake—*everything will be all right and y'all will be able to walk some, but y'all will still be weak, but sleep now, sleep*

a strange humming came to me, softly at first, then building into a lullaby, and I clung to the melody, feeling it work its magical way into my senses, numbing them gently, gently taking them into slumber—

the sedge had withered from the lake and no birds sang in the warm still of the air then she came my forest maiden walking across the meadowland to me and knelt by my side and her gray dress slipped from her shoulders and gathered softly in folds at her waist before sliding down her shapely thighs and she stood naked before me gloriously naked her breasts falling gently to the side large nipples like ripe plums and the soft fold of her stomach folding gently into the tangled weave between her legs and she knelt beside me and slid into my arms and her lips fastened gently to mine for a moment for a moment only and then pale kings and princes drifted slowly by smiling sadly but knowingly at me and I felt myself a prisoner but a willing prisoner and—

I awoke rapidly, the dream remaining with me for a moment before slipping away into the tattered darkness momentarily in my mind. I looked around the room; I was alone, my clothes washed and neatly ironed, hanging over the straight-backed rocker close beside my bed. My Navies still hung in their holsters beside the bedpost, but the thong had been slipped away from their hammers. I lifted one from the holster, feeling the familiar curve of the butt settle handsomely into my palm. I slipped the cylinder from the pistol and checked it: fully loaded, the caps seated firmly upon the nipples. I replaced the cylinder and slid the pistol back into its holster.

I rose, steadying myself by gripping the bedpost until the soft blackness disappeared from my eyes. I crossed to the chair and began to dress, smelling something faintly like clover wafting from my clothes. I took a deep breath and tried to lift my gun belt from the bedpost, but although I had checked one of the revolvers only moments before, I now found the weight too much for me and was forced to leave them hanging from the bedpost. I frowned, moving my fingers, trying to work the stiffness from them, feeling supple energy flowing into them. I tried to lift the pistols again, but this time they seemed to be nailed to the bedpost. I couldn't lift them a quarter inch.

I gave up and walked to the window and looked out; pandemonium reigned among the birds, suggesting great events to take place. The day seemed different, almost as if the light had shifted and a shadow had swept over the trees and left something behind it, a darkening, a chill. Then I saw her moving through the line of the woods, grubbing among the dead leaves, among the wood scruf, looking for something that would give moment to time, meaning to a meaningless remembrance, looking for reality under the camouflage of the accidental.

I tried to open the window to call to her, but I couldn't budge it and the effort made me weary. I crossed back to the bed and sat, then fell back onto the pillow, telling myself that I would only rest another minute.

I awoke on a bare hillside above a small lake from which the sedge had withered. Coming toward me was a young woman with a garland of flowers in her hair. She bent and kissed me and a lily appeared on her brow and a decided dreadfulness entered me. Her foot was light as she approached, her eyes wild, and when she fell in my arms I heard a sweet moan rise from her lips. Quick pictures of pale kings and princes swept in front of my eyes. I closed them and gathered her into my arms. Her filmy gown fluttered over us like an opaque cloud, and when the cloud lifted she was gone and I stood clad in strange armor not far from a saddled gray horse grazing.

"Orlando!"

I turned, feeling the heaviness of my armor upon me. I opened my mouth to ask who was Orlando, but instead strange words came forth, strange but familiar: "Yes, milord?"

A man dressed in mail sat upon his horse, a magnificent black stallion. A golden circlet crowned his head.

Charlemagne.

The name whispered out of the shadows to me. It felt familiar and *I knew him*!

"You will be the rear guard as we make our way through the pass at Roncesvalles. Select your men." He smiled at me and a warm feeling swept over me. "I don't think you will need many. There has been no trace of the Saracens since we left Pamplona."

A man all in black rode up beside him. His face looked like a somber cloud had rested upon it until it melted permanently into the flesh.

"Ganelon," I said with distaste. My hand dropped down to my pistol and found the hilt of a great sword. My fingers closed comfortably, familiarly, around it. My other hand found an odd horn at my waist.

He smiled faintly at me; his black eyes, the type that some women called sad, stared savagely, glittering, at me. His hand went to his own sword strapped on his saddle.

Charlemagne nudged his horse between us, his eyes flashing angrily.

"Hold, you war hounds!" he snapped, annoyed at the animosity between us.

Ganelon's lips lifted in a snide smile. "Again you are lucky, Orlando," he said contemptuously.

My blood raced hotly through me. I stepped around the king's horse. I slipped my sword from its sheath and slapped Ganelon smartly upon his thigh.

"Come down with your blade, Ganelon!" I challenged. "Come down to your death! 'Tis been well earned."

"Enough!" Charlemagne roared. "Put up your sword, Orlando!" I hesitated and glanced up at him. His black eyes were flat and hard. "It's not a request, Orlando! It is my command!"

I stepped back, unwillingly sliding my sword into its sheath.

"What is it, Ganelon?" Charlemagne demanded, his eyes holding me in place.

"The army is ready to march, my liege," he said, his voice undergoing a fawning change that brought a hot flush to my cheeks.

"Very well," Charlemagne said. "Return to them. I shall be along shortly." Ganelon tapped his breast in an almost insolent salute and rode away. Charlemagne glanced over his shoulder at him, then back to me.

"You must learn to control your anger, Orlando," he said harshly.

"He is a traitor! I know this, my king!" I replied hotly.

"And how do you know this? No," he said, holding up his hand as I made to answer. "No, I do not want to know this now. But when we return to our home, you will prepare and present your charge formally as should be done. I cannot have such malevolence between my paladins. There must be peace and harmony between them or else they will lose the strength that makes them worthy of helping those who are oppressed." His lips pressed into a hard line beneath his beard; then his eyes softened.

"You are my favorite, Orlando. You are destined for greatness. Men will sing about your bravery and deeds long after we are all dust. Ganelon will be forgotten. But for now"—a hard edge came into his voice—"I have a need for all my paladins. *All* of them," he repeated slowly for emphasis. "Am I understood?"

I bowed my head. "Yes, my king."

"Then choose your men. We leave immediately after."

He wheeled the mighty black and rode away toward the waiting army.

I sighed and walked to my horse. He raised his head at my approach and nickered in greeting. I patted his neck affectionately. "Well, my friend," I said softly, "I think that no good will come of this. But we have to make do. We have to make do."

A dread seeped uneasily into my veins as I mounted and rode toward the waiting men to make my choices, feeling hollow and cold inside.

I made my decision and stood aside while Charlemagne rode past at the head of his army in the company with Ganelon as his companion. Several Saracen heads topped the lances of the army as it passed.

I sighed and turned, studying the small troop that I had chosen to remain behind with me. We had driven the Saracens away, but they had also been weaker than they should have been, and I thought that they had been bringing Charlemagne's forces ever southward over the mountains and to the sea. Yet Ganelon assured the king that nothing was amiss, everything was proceeding according to plan. I didn't trust him.

A shadow seemed to fall over me as the last of Charlemagne's army passed, leaving me alone with my small force of men.

"Well," Oliver said from beside me. "What now?"

I shrugged. "Obey the king's wishes. That worthless King Marsilius is supposed to meet us at the pass of Roncesvalles to pay tribute to Charlemagne. We are to collect it and bring it with us."

Oliver made a face and stared around at the rugged country. "A good place for an ambush, you ask me, though no one ever does, so I do not know why I waste words and breath."

"Because you like to hear yourself talk," Eggihard said teasingly. "You would rather sit on the silks and satins of the king's court than upon an honest man's leather. Right, Anselm?"

Anselm grinned. "True enough in Oliver's case. He was always one for the ladies."

"Stuff that nonsense," Oliver said gruffly.

"Enough," I said, laughing. "We may have need of Oliver's gift of gab before we are home. Meanwhile, we have need of his eyes." I stood in my stirrups and noted a large cloud of dust to the southwest. I pointed to it. "And here comes Marsilius with his tribute for Charlemagne's coffers, or I miss my guess."

Anselm frowned as he studied the approaching cloud.

"Perhaps it isn't my place to say, Orlando, but that seems to be a lot of dust for someone bringing tribute. 'Tis an army's dust, I'm thinking."

"Uh-huh," Oliver said, suddenly sober. He set his spurs to his horse and rode away. "I'll check it!" he called back over his shoulder.

"Eager, isn't he?" Eggihard said. He grinned. "I happen to know that a fine barrel of wine will have been delivered by the time we get back." He put a finger alongside his nose conspiratorily. "As seneschal, I distribute the wine—"

"Something's wrong!" Anselm interjected.

We turned as one, watching Oliver gallop back faster than the canter he would have assumed if all had been right. He reined in beside us in a cloud of dust. I suddenly became aware of the barren landscape, the harsh rocks rolling up against the hills.

"Well? What news?" I asked.

"It's as you suspected," he reported grimly. "That bastard Gamelon—"

"Well?"

"I wish this was yesterday. Then we would have the full army here. Marsilius is coming! Oh yes, he is coming! But bearing arms as his tribute, and the whole world is with him!"

The others gathered around me. "Better blow your horn to warn Charlemagne," Anselm suggested.

"Let's wait a moment," I said.

The others exchanged glances as Archbishop Turpin rode up.

"What's wrong?" he asked.

"Betrayal of the highest order," Anselm said. "Marsilius, being the good king that he is, has decided to give cold steel in lieu of the promised gold for his tribute."

"You had better warn Charlemagne," Turpin said to me.

"That's what we have been telling him, but he wants to wait!" Anselm said in exasperation.

I ignored them and galloped to the top of the Roncesvalles Pass. I reined in and studied carefully the sea of men marching toward the pass. Death's wings fluttered past me and I felt the old restlessness returning. I looked down in the valley to where the trail through the pass began.

"You miserable little valley!" I murmured. "The blood shed here today will be your shame forever."

I turned and rode furiously back to my little group. I nodded at Oliver. "You were right, my friend. Marsilius the traitor is coming."

"Then hadn't you better signal for Charlemagne to rejoin us?" Anselm asked nervously.

I shook my head. "And fall into the trap? No. Only as a last resort."

"I don't think it gets any more final than this," Oliver muttered, drawing his sword.

"Even if I did sound the horn," I said, "I do not think Charlemagne would return in time." I turned, studying the rocky terrain around us, and nodded.

"If we had to meet them, this is a better place than most. Marsilius will have to come up to us, and only a part of his men at a time."

"The sea only throws one wave at a time against the land, but eventually it works its way," Eggihard said. "Even granite cliffs give way to it."

"But for a while, the cliffs are triumphant," I cried. "Where is it written that man will escape death?"

"I just wanted to put it off a little longer," Anselm said,

drawing his sword. He settled his helmet firmly on his head. "If that be the way of it, though, then let's get on with it!" His teeth flashed whitely in an eager grin.

I drew Durindana, the sword that had been Hector's at Troy, and roared, "Away to the Saracens!"

As we rode down upon them, I prayed that the Virgin Mary would take pity upon my men. As we neared the front line, I looked back at my comrades and said, "All for himself and Saint Michael for us all! We are all perfect knights!"

"Perfect fools maybe!" Oliver said, but a grin spread his lips and his eyes shone with the promise of battle before him.

And then we fell upon the Saracens, and such was the deceptiveness of our charge that great confusion reigned. We took advantage of them, slicing through their ranks like the Lord's flail. The air filled quickly with dust and the cloying odor of blood. A large din rose from the floor of the pass of Roncesvalles until I thought the whole world would know what was happening. Men and horses screamed their death song; others cursed. Heads flew from shoulders to be trampled under the feet of heavy chargers.

But there were too many, and one by one the paladins fell from Saracen blade and spear. My blood trickled from a hundred wounds. Then I saw Oliver standing alone in the midst of fallen warriors. His face was a mask of blood flowing from his terrible wounds. I cut my way through the Saracens separating us. Oliver heard me but could not see me through a veil of thick blood over his face. He struck hard, but I blocked the blow with Durindana, the only blade that could have withstood such a blow without shattering.

"What, Cousin? Do you fight for the Saracens now?" I asked.

Oliver laughed and wearily lowered his blade. "I beg your pardon, but I can see nothing. The curtain of death has drawn close around me."

"'Tis only blood," I objected.

"Aye, mine," he said. "I die. Some traitor has dealt me a death blow in the back."

"I shall take you someplace safe," I said, bringing his horse to him. He mounted and sat determinedly.

"No," he said. "Lead my horse into the thick of them so I may avenge my own death."

I led him through the heart of the Saracens, our swords hewing a street out of flesh. By the time we reached the other side, blood poured from another fifty wounds hacked upon me.

"Rest here," I panted, helping Oliver from his horse. "I will ride to the hill and sound my horn. It is time to let Charlemagne know what has happened to his rear guard."

Oliver laughed painfully. "*Now* you decide to toot that damn thing. But when you return here, you will find only the grave man."

He sat down with his back against a rock, drew two last deep breaths, raised his sword, then died, frozen in defiance.

I sighed and rode to the top of the hill and raised the great horn to my lips. Twice I blew it, the second time louder than the first, blood bursting from my lungs. I blew the horn again, the dark gray mist creeping ever closer toward me as my blood flowed freely from my wounds. The horn burst and blood poured from my mouth and nose—

The door flew open and armored soldiers rushed in followed by Agravaine, who swaggered, sneering, toward me. I heard a sharp, indignant gasp and a naked body rose from me, clasping a coverlet to her breasts. Her golden hair lay tousled on her bare shoulders and her sea green eyes flashed angrily.

"How dare you enter my chambers in this manner?" she demanded.

"To arrest traitors, my queen," Agravaine said mockingly. "On the king's orders."

She slumped forward, the coverlet nearly slipping from her hands.

"Lancelot," she whispered.

I pushed her back and rose, naked, from the bed. Agravaine laughed.

"Well, Lancelot," he said. "And how fares it tonight? I see your sword is at ready use!"

A great loathing surged through me. "You go too far, Agravaine," I said.

He drew his sword and touched me lightly upon the left nipple, pressing the skin to near breaking.

"I go too far? And what about you, Lancelot?" A mad grin stretched across his face. "This will bring the king's favor to me instead of you, Lancelot. You and"——he looked deliberately at—

Guinevere.

Again the whisper of a name flitted across my mind, lifting images of our love—naked bodies in the flickering firelight, clutching each other furiously as we pressed closer, trying to merge our flesh and souls into one—from the depths. How long? I couldn't remember. It didn't matter. She was the world to me. But Arthur—

"—and your trollop burn at the stake for treason!" he finished with a satisfied licking of his lips.

Blood pounded through my veins. My muscles swelled, and I slapped his sword away with my left hand. I stepped forward, grasping his shoulder and pulling him to me. His breath, reeking of onions, exploded in my face. I spun him around, grasping his sword arm by the wrist with my right, twisting it behind him. I levered it up hard between his shoulder blades, hearing and feeling the tendons snap in his shoulder just before he screamed in pain.

We stood for a moment in grotesque meeting, shaking hands—dear long-lost brother, kinsman, lord, thane—then I took the sword from his hand and slipped my arm around his neck, bringing his head sharply into my shoulder. I heaved upward and felt his neck crack and dropped his suddenly lifeless body to the floor.

"Look out!" someone—Gareth, I thought dimly—cried out just before I swung the sword, beheading him. His headless body stood stock-still for a moment; then the nerves in its legs jerked spasmodically, making two backward steps, the fountaining blood spattering those behind, briefly blinding them.

The blade danced in a blur of its own devising as I stepped

forward among them, felling them as a scythe would stalks of wheat.

I watched coldly, dispassionately, as they fell away from me, feeling the invincible, familiar power surging through me. My strength grew, seeming to sap theirs from them. Panic came upon them, and they fled screaming toward the fireplace at the far end of the room, pushing and shoving, each trying to get behind the other. A mad laugh leaped from my throat and I felt my lips spreading in a smile I saw reflected in the terror in their eyes. I started forward, the blade singing in my hands as all do when I heft them—

"Lancelot! Save yourself!"

I turned toward her. She pointed toward the door, the coverlet slipping away from a white cone-shaped breast whose ruby tip I had kissed—was it only minutes before?

"Go!"

"My lady," I began.

"It is my order!" she shouted. Her eyes widened fearfully. "Look out!"

Without thinking, I swung the blade over my head, blocking a sword stroke from Garse, who tried to take advantage of my brief unguarded moment. I spun, sliding the blade down his blade, then reversed the stroke and ripped sideways, gutting him.

He screamed and fell to his knees as he tried to press the thick, bloody worms back into his bowels. I spun away from him on the balls of my feet, swinging the sword in a tight arc. I severed one man's arm at the shoulder. He spun away from me, the stump spurting blood around the room, upon others who stepped back reflexively from him.

I took the moment to dash from the room. I glanced down the hall. Armed men came up the stairs toward me. I turned and ran down the hall into the chapel, slamming the door tightly behind me. I drove the blade deep into the wood beneath the door lever, jamming it. Then I ran to the stained-glass window. A candle flickered bravely in a red glass chimney on the altar. I paused and looked up at the crucified figure on the cross above the altar.

"Keep her safe until I can return for her," I begged.

I seized a candelabra from the altar and raced to the window, shattering the glass and breaking it free from its frame with three blows. I dropped the candelabra to the floor and stepped gingerly out onto the stone sill.

A great banging came from the iron-strapped door behind me. I glanced down at the waves of the moat lapping softly in the pale moonlight far below me.

A hundred feet? I pushed the thought away and, taking a deep breath, leaped up and away into the dark, praying— *"Guinevere, Guinevere, Guinevere"*—softly as I fell into the inky blackness of the waters. . . .

Guinevere . . .

. . . standing tied to the stake, wood piled around her, the flames beginning to leap toward her as I charged through the gate into the courtyard, my sword slashing and hewing a path open to her. Her lips formed my name and I heard the din of battle behind me as those knights still loyal to the two of us protected my back. I rode up behind her, my horse dancing, wild-eyed, squealing in terror from the flickering fire. I swung the blade down, severing the ropes binding Guinevere to the stake. I seized her arm and pulled her up behind me, then let my charger race away from the fire. Men fled from his hooves, but still he trampled some.

"Away! Away! The queen is safe!" I cried. Obediently the others fought their way back to the gate, then turned and galloped after us, away from Camelot—

> *A gentle knight was pricking on the plaine,*
> *Ycladd in mightie armes and silver shielde,*
> *Wherein old dints of deepe woundes did remaine,*
> *The cruell markes of many' a bloody fielde;*
> *Yet armes till that time did he never wield.*
> *His angry steede did chide his foaming bitt,*
> *As much disdayning to the curbe to yield:*
> *Full-jolly knight he seemd, and faire did sitt,*
> *As one for knightly giusts and fierce encounters fitt.*

I awoke bathed in sweat and glanced around the room. I was alone. I sighed and closed my eyes again

and then a mythic ancestor came out of the forest old and bent with grief his hand trembling upon a cane that he leaned on to shuffle forward hesitantly one step at a time his shaggy head covered with wild white hair shaking from side to side as if he could see into the depths of the woods around with his ash gray eyes in the dark hollow sockets of his head and he said do you hear the pain carried on the wind it is the cry of wasted lives and he laughed when I did not answer and asked if I dared to drain the world of its light and smiled and beckoned to me to join him among the trees but I was afraid and remained frozen where I was and he called to me on the wind saying come journey with me through the centuries and learn to walk decades with your steps I took a willing step

Her hand gripped my shoulder, shaking me awake. She smiled down at me.

"Y'all been sleeping for a long time," she said. "I see that y'got up and did a little moving around. That's good. Y'all need to get your strength back, and that ain't gonna happen lyin' around in a bed for me to wait on yuh."

"Thank you," I said. "If you will just give me a hand—"

I tried to sit up, but she pushed me back against the pillow. "Ain't no reason to be pushin' it, though. It takes more'n a day to get over the hackin' and coughin' y'all been doin' since I tucked y'into that bed."

"I'm grateful," I said, trying to push against her hand. I felt a fine sheen of perspiration begin to form from my efforts. "But I have to get back across the river."

"Uh-huh," she said, and laughed. "Y'all may have to get back across the river, but it'll take y' a while. There's many a bushwacker between here and there. I'd wait awhile. Another day or two won't make any matter."

"You don't understand—" I began, but her eyes began to glow and I found myself drawn into their depths

Better than you think. But you still ain't going anywhere

until you're ready. Won't make another bit of difference at all despite what you think. The pattern's been cut and the fabric sewn and there ain't a way that you can change that. Not a way. 'Sides, you ain't got a horse

"I need one," I mumbled. "I can buy one—"

Not here you can't. But good things come to him who waits. And you need to wait.

Look.

"Gotta get back—"

and she slipped her hand behind her back and her dress fell again from her and naked she climbed in beside me naked and her lips caught hold of mine and I felt my soul lift up from inside me and go winging away into the dark and I begged for it again and felt her lips again hotly upon mine and her legs wrapping themselves lithely around me and I tasted hell or heaven in her lips and then I heard her laugh and felt—was it scorn not love—

Again I awoke and found myself naked and wary. Then memory came back to me and I threw the covers back from me. Wonderingly I gazed down at my naked self and frowned to find my clothes neatly gathered upon the rocker. Had I dreamed everything? No, I decided, I could not have dreamed it. Not all. Not everything.

The door opened and she came in again, smiling at me. Embarrassed, I fought to bring the covers quickly over me, much to her amusement.

"Do y'remember?" she asked. I gave her a startled look and this time she laughed, the notes of her laughter tinkling like silver bells. "Don't tell y'all have forgotten!"

I shook my head, managing a weak smile. "No, I haven't forgotten. I'm not certain that I will forget anything."

She laughed again, amused at my youthful gallantry. "Perhaps not," she said graciously. "I hope not. Y'll have to remember everything at all times if y'all are going to succeed."

"Succeed?" I frowned. "At what?"

"At what y'all have been chosen for," she answered calmly.

I shook my head. All this was becoming too obscure for

me to grasp. A sound came as if a painter was falling down his ladder *rumpabababababababagalharaghtakammminarronkonnbrontonnertoohoohordenenthurnu!* and I jerked upward, turning quickly toward the window, one of my pistols slipping into my hand before I thought of it as if by magic. I glanced down at it, then at her.

"Yes," she said in reply to my unspoken anxious expectancy. "There is a bit of magic to it. There is always magic."

"Magic." I felt a laugh bubbling up inside me but fought to keep it away.

A wry smile twisted her lips, her eyes hooded, and she shook her head slightly, recognizing my disbelief in the single word. "Y'all don't know the wind, but it is there when y'least expect it. There's no reason to think other things cannot exist as well in a like manner, is there?"

"I suppose not," I said. "But what magic would you be talking about?"

"Y'all'll know before you leave," she said cryptically. I tried to ask her more questions, but she held up her hand, staying my tongue. "Enough for now. Y'all be ready to leave in two days. *In two days,*" she emphasized when I started to object. I sighed and looked down at the pistol.

"No, y'all can't do that," she said, intercepting my thought a moment before it came to me.

I looked wonderingly at her, thinking the thought at the time: *I could force you*—and knowing instinctively that I couldn't. I let my hand with the pistol drop to my side and then and only then realized again that I was naked and felt the burn of embarrassment flush over me. She placed her hands on her hips and laughed merrily at my discomfort as I tried to cover myself with my hands.

"All right," she said, bemused. "Come on down when y'are ready. But leave your pistols behind. Except that one," she said roguishly, glancing at my hands. "Y'all won't be needing the Colts tonight. As to the other, well, we'll see."

She turned and left the room, closing the door gently behind her. I crossed to my clothes, pausing to slip the Colt back into its holster, and again dressed. It seemed as if only minutes before I had stepped into my clothes and felt them softly warm me against the chill of the room. I tried to lift the gun belt again from the bedpost, but it seemed again as if it had been nailed in place. I could take the pistols from their holsters, but when I tried to turn with them toward the door they seemed to weigh my arms down, impossibly heavy, and I replaced them in their holsters.

I crossed to the door and gently lifted the latch. The door swung smoothly open, revealing the hallway leading to the flight of stairs downward. Firelight danced its shadows on the timbers of the wall opposite the banistered railing across from me. The wood looked hand-rubbed with molten candle wax, shining dully, richly, in the dim light. I walked cautiously to the stairs and looked down. The planked table had been richly set with a white linen cloth. The dishes glittered silvery and candles burned steadily in tall silver candlesticks in the center of the table. I noticed that four places had been laid for dinner and frowned, wondering who the other two would be, then catching my thoughts warily before they could escape into the magic—if there *was* such a thing—and betray me. Candles flickered in the wooden sconces pegged into the wall, casting a dancing light over the room.

"Come on down," she called.

I looked quickly for her, and for a moment I wondered if the words had been spoken or if they had been thoughts slipped into my mind. Then I saw her beside a spinning wheel, wearing a white dress with a low neckline and what looked like green ivy embroidered around the neck and hem. The sleeves were long and wide and edged in ivy, too. Her feet were bare and her silver hair glinted in the light as if it had been freshly washed and brush-dried. It fell softly over her shoulders. A wreath of tiny red rosebuds had been woven and circled her forehead. Her black eyes danced merrily, tiny lights like shooting stars coming toward me. She gestured, and I obeyed, walking slowly down the stairs.

I glanced at the spindle on her wheel and frowned, trying

to put a name to the color she was spinning, but it seemed to change color as I watched, shining, then darkening, then exploding into a series of ripe colors—blue, green, yellow, orange—before fading softly to shades becoming darker and darker until a single black thread was drawn. I blinked and the spool seemed to leap up shimmering in sunlight and then disappeared.

"What—"

"Does it matter?" she said. She frowned, tilting her head to the side.

"I remember your spinning."

She shook her head. "But it isn't wise to tell man everything." She smiled to take the sting from her words. "Y'all been born for violence, James. But y'all are needed." She shrugged. "Ah 'spect y'all know that, though. Or have an inkling. There's good and bad in all people and all people taste the side of each a time or two. But Ah have a feeling y'all going to eat more from the right side of the platter. At least, that's why you were woven."

I shook my head, frowning, and started to speak to ask her to explain her strange words, but then I felt a cold breeze caress my neck.

I turned quickly. Two men stood behind me. My hands instinctively went to my waist, clawing for pistol butts that were not there. I swallowed and backed warily away from them until I bumped into the table. They watched me soberly, without speaking. She came forward and put her hand on my arm.

"Don't be frightened," she said lowly. "They are not here to harm you."

I looked at them carefully and saw that they were weaponless—or at least, I could see no weapons on them. Each was dressed in a Prince Albert coat with checkered trousers, a red sash around his waist. They wore white ruffled shirts with a white scarf tied around their throats. Their boots were highly polished and reflected the light of the room back into it. Their long blond hair had been carefully combed and fell to their shoulders. For a moment I thought I was staring into a coming reflection of myself, but they moved into the room and the thought slipped away from me on swallow's wings. Each took a seat at the table and waited as she pulled me to a place at the foot of the table, then seated herself at the head.

She smiled down at me. "Drink your wine," she said gently. Automatically I lifted the wine to my lips and tasted it. Like honey. And I drank deeply before I knew I was drinking it. I placed it back on the table and looked from one man to the other, trying to understand the unearthly aura that exuded from them, a negative radiance like dark light.

"There is a need for you," the one on my right said gently. "A great need. Now and in the future."

"By whom?" I asked. My tongue felt thick and I looked suspiciously at my wineglass. It was full again, but by whose hand I did not know.

"You will know," the other said. He turned to the first speaker. "Like Achilles?"

It was a question before I knew it was a question and the other shook his head, saying something, but I was not listening to his voice

a short life and not always a happy life and you will be alone until the end but you will never know family for a man like you there is no family and the happiness of children is a myth for others who will envy you and hate you and you shall know both by their envy and hatred and although there will be some who will become close to you do not expect to find your salvation in them for that will be only through your deeds and your responsibilities

I heard a noise at the door. She raised her eyebrows, looking at me, and nodded slightly. I rose and crossed over the tightly pegged floorboards and opened the door. A marvelous black stallion stood there, saddled. He was alone. I walked out, speaking softly to him.

"Whoa, boy. Where's your master? Easy now," I crooned as I placed my hand gently upon his neck. He turned his head toward me and I saw that he was blind in one eye, a film covering it like a sheet. I glanced at the saddle and started, noticing the saddle was mine and the Army pistols in holsters on either side of the pommel were mine as well.

"What?—"

I turned toward the tavern—

And saw nothing. A twilight gloaming was coming over the woods and I heard the cawing of crows in the distance. My hands went to my waist and I felt the familiar weight of my pistols, snugged in their holsters. I glanced down at the heavy canvas coat over which they had been buckled. My pants were fresh and clean and warm against my legs. I moved my toes inside my boots and felt the heavy woolen socks in which they had been encased.

The horse snorted behind me, and I turned, suddenly aware that I held the reins in my hand. I looked at him wonderingly.

Black.

Where did that word come from? I said it aloud and the horse nodded his head.

"Black. Your name is Black," I said automatically.

He grumbled deep within his chest and twisted his head from side to side, hearing or seeing something; I couldn't be certain.

"What is it, boy?" I asked.

I glanced around at the woods; we were alone all right. As alone as anyone could get in a late spring woods.

Where is Arial's Keep? And where is the woman? Where is Helen Caroline Ernst? Where is—

A jay chattered angrily near us. I glanced around, half-fearfully, expecting—anything. I drew one of the Navy Colts from my waist and cocked the hammer, trying to penetrate the gloom beginning to deepen around me like a pearl mist.

you are disappointing me James you men are all tragedians looking for the romance of atonement but you won't find it here and you won't find it in the war although that is where the story of Bill will begin to find its ending now go to your beginning for you know what is expected what is needed of you

Swiftly a picture flashed upon my memory and I held it

tightly for one crystal clear moment. Helen coming toward
me in a filmy gown, her beauty radiating through the gar-
ment, nearly blinding me. There was a terrifying earnestness
in her face and I knew that I had become her lover and she
my guardian, a figure more deeply felt than motherhood.
Then everything seemed to confront me at once: Father's
death, Josephine, Mary, another Mary, a couple of women
whose names I no longer knew if I ever did, Kansas, and,
briefly, a glimpse of the last call of fate in a blurred image of
dead branches, twisted, bone white, stripped of bark, nude,
and then the picture was gone and I stood alone in the clearing, clean and alone, my pistols freshly armed, a black horse
moving restlessly beside me.

I turned and mounted. I pulled on the reins, trying to turn
him to the left, but he shook his head. *Annoyed.* I loosened
the reins, dropping my hand to the pommel, comfortingly
near the Army pistols. Black turned to the right and moved
confidently off through the woods, his hooves finding a trail
where none existed. I crouched low over his neck, watching
the growing dark in the bushes half-fearfully, but Black gave
no evidence of others being in the woods with us as he made
his way through them as sure-footed as if he was on a graded
highway.

For an hour or better we rode like this, and then we
emerged into the twilight of a turned field and I smelled the
earth, musty and dank beneath his hooves as he picked his
way across the furrows to the road. He paused, flicking his
mane, then turned decidedly toward what I took to be the
west, although there were no stars to guide me, only a
crescent-shaped moon beginning to appear, a milk white
outline at first, slowly deepening into yellow, then bloodred.

I heard the hollow *clud-clud-clud-clud* of his hooves as
we crossed a wooden bridge. A burned-out schoolhouse
loomed on our left; then a small graveyard appeared on our
right, the white-pine planks used as tombstones stretching
up from the black ground like bones. We passed under a
leafless gnarled oak tree and then I saw the flickering of
campfires on a broad hillside and wondered if I was seeing

Union or Confederate fires, but it didn't seem to matter at the moment, for I felt as if I was riding through a vision—not a dream, for a dream lacks sustenance and I could smell and hear and feel the night around us and the bunching and releasing of the black's muscles as he lifted into an easy, ground-gaining lope toward the fires.

I didn't touch my pistols but left the path to the horse, trusting in him to find the way for me.

An hour later, we were among the tents of a Union regiment and the men were shouting and calling me by name as they rushed toward us:

"Wild Bill. Wild Bill. Wild Bill—"

CHAPTER

34

THE SUN came up as red as Sally's bloomers: a fiery red that seemed to rise and expand until the red covered the whole of the horizon. It began to bleed over the rest of the sky, and with it came the breath of brimstone, harsh and biting upon the nostrils. A sulfuric yellow haze began to roil by the treetops.

"Damn," Peter Pelican breathed silently from beside me.

I rolled to my side and looked at the youth. He was looking with awe at the sky, shaking his head. "What's the matter?" I asked.

He jerked his head, indicating the sun. "Pa was a preacher," he began. "He see a sky like that, we'd be hearing the words of Revelation being shouted at us from the time he first saw it. That's the sign of the apocalypse, Jim. Sure as I'm sitting here, that's what the world's gonna look like when the four horsemen come ridin' out of it."

"You believe that?" I asked.

He shrugged. "Reckon it don't mean a thing if'n I believe

it or not. Can't stop the sun from rising; can't stop the horse-men from ridin'. Might as well make the best of it we can."

I nodded and rolled back over, peering cautiously over the bluff down into the Rebel camp. I put a glass to my eye and sorted out the colors flying near General Ben McCulloch's tent. I remembered the words I had had with Curtis, who had insisted that we try to pick McCulloch off with some of his staff after I came back with a report of the camp. I didn't think that Curtis would have gone for this, but he had and here I was, again behind the lines with young Pelican, who was the best shot in camp with a rifle. I looked down at the Springfields on the ground beside us. Both had been fitted with telescopes as long as the barrels, and the bullets had been carefully loaded by Pelican. I looked back at the camp and saw the general's striker go into his tent.

"Get ready," I said, and picked up my rifle, settling myself comfortably. Out of the corner of my eye I watched Pelican carefully wipe the barrel of his Springfield and squirm into position.

"You get the first shot," I said. "Make it a good one." I re-called my words with Curtis as I began to breathe deeply, slowly.

That isn't the way I fight, Curtis.

War is war, Hickok. People die in war. It doesn't make a difference if it's in battle or not. You know that. You've done it before.

Doesn't mean I have to like it. When it comes my turn, I sure as hell hope I see the man who does it. I want it to be a man with sand, not someone with a good eye.

"Here he comes," Pelican breathed.

I looked through the scope and watched as McCulloch came out, holding a cup of coffee. He slapped his chest with the other hand and took a long, slow breath, reveling in the morning. He was as predictable as running water. We had been watching him for four days and his routine never var-ied. Now he would take a long sip from his coffee.

"Take him," I said softly.

Pelican grunted. I heard his breath slip slowly from his lips and then a loud *crack!* as he squeezed off the shot. I watched and saw the tent flap jerk beside McCulloch.

"Damn!" he said.

Without thinking, I held a half foot above McCulloch's head and squeezed the trigger. The rifle lurched back hard against my shoulder, the telescope jamming me under the eye. For a moment I was blinded; then I heard Pelican's gleeful shout, "You got 'im, Jim! You got 'im!"

I blinked the fog out of my eye and looked through the glass to where McCulloch lay motionless on the ground, soldiers swarming around him.

"Take as many as you can," I said, and slid a cartridge into the Springfield.

Pelican's rifle sounded. A major threw up his arms and slumped to the ground. I fired randomly and watched as somehow I managed to hit another soldier. The shot hadn't been well aimed, but somehow I had managed to hit another. Pelican began to shoot deliberately and every shot seemed to strike home. I fired another couple of shots, then noticed a mounted patrol sweep out of the camp to our right.

"Time to go," I said, and squirmed back from the edge of the ridge. I ran low to where Black stood, trembling anxiously from the gunfire. I mounted and watched as Pelican swung up on his mule.

Together we turned and rode hard, heading back toward our lines. The day had been good for the Union, but it still left a bad taste in my mouth. There wasn't anything honorable in doing what we had done. Perhaps we had shortened the war by a few days; perhaps not. But man was meant to live and die honorably. McCulloch had just died.

I turned in my report and gave Pelican credit for the kill. But Pelican was a product of his daddy's preaching and lying just wasn't in him. He had already told the others around the camp how he had missed and I had shot McCulloch.

Curtis, however, believed me and not the rumor running like wildfire through the camp. He granted my request to be transferred to Captain John Kelso's command as a scout. I didn't care much for Kelso—he was wild and careless with his men but extremely lucky, and I had learned by now that luck was better to have than all the careful planners who wouldn't make a move unless they had a dozen confirmed scouting reports.

CHAPTER

35

SOMEONE KEPT kicking the sole of my boot. I opened an eye and saw John McKoan grinning in the gray light of morn. I sighed and rolled away, wrapping myself deeper into my blankets.

"G'way," I mumbled. "I was up all night."

"I know," McKoan said. He squatted and placed a cup of coffee near my head. "But Kelso has an idea that we can make a raid down through Elkhorn Tavern and Van Buren."

"What?" I sat up, kicking my blankets away. I sat up and reached for the cup of coffee, swearing as I burnt my fingers. "But that's—that's—"

"Yeah, we told 'im," McKoan said. "But he thinks a small group can do a bit of damage and take the Rebs' attention away from the front. Sort of a"—he motioned with his hand as if sliding butter across a table—"detraction action."

I stared at him in disbelief. "Detraction action? What the hell?"

He laughed and turned his head, spitting a long stream of tobacco juice that narrowly missed my blankets. "Wal, that's what he calls it. Don't know what he's thinking, but it's enough for him to get antsy, and you know what he's like when he gets that way."

I sighed and stood up, sipping cautiously on the coffee. "Yeah, I know," I said disgustedly. "Well, if this don't make the cat piss milk!"

But Kelso had made up his mind and there was no changing it. We rode out of camp that night, which made me even more nervous, since we didn't know where our patrols were and at night all uniforms and men look alike. The Kelso luck held, though, and we crossed the river and into the trees and made a mad race down through Rolla and Springfield and back across Wilson's Creek to Elkhorn Tavern.

We came down hard on a couple of camps, surprising the sentries and riding through, shooting wantonly into the tents and sleeping forms around the fires. We didn't wait to see the damage that we did but continued on our wide detour, riding recklessly and with wild abandon deeper into the Confederate territory. I thought about the Fatal Sister and wondered if we would pass Arial's Keep, but we didn't and I'm not certain what I would have done if we had. But then I wasn't certain anymore if that had indeed happened. But I didn't have time to dwell upon such thoughts, as Kelso kept us moving at a lathered pace throughout the night.

We pulled up for the night in a hickory grove and kept a sharp watch, but no Confederate patrols came near us. That night we rode on toward Elkhorn Tavern, and that is where we ran across a small Rebel patrol accompanying a couple of young women in a carriage toward General Buford Hacker's camp. I pulled up in a thicket and watched as they went by and frowned as I saw the two women sitting primly in a carriage with riders flanking them on either side.

I waited until they disappeared around a bend in the road, then nudged Black with my heels and rode down a ravine to where Kelso and the others waited. He was on his feet by the time I drew Black in. McKoan and John Allen and Zeke Stone rose, Stone groaning and complaining about his lumbago but still moving as spryly as a man half his age.

"Yes, Mr. Hickok?" Kelso said. "You have found something, I take it."

His eyes gleamed with a fanaticism that made them burn with green fire. He rubbed his gauntleted hands together anxiously.

"Don't know," I said, taking a canteen of water from McKoan and drinking thirstily. I lowered the canteen. My teeth ached from the cold water, but I still felt a sheen of perspiration on my face and scrubbed my hands over the stubble on my chin. I felt dirty and hated that more than anything.

"Well?" Kelso said impatiently.

"A small patrol went by escorting two young women in a carriage," I said.

"Whores for the camp," Zeke said with satisfaction.

"No," I said, shaking my head. "I don't think that's right. They seemed to be under guard. Riders flanked them. I don't know." I took my hat off and wiped my head, scrubbing my hands through my hair. "It just didn't 'feel' right, you know, Captain?"

Kelso pursed his lips and stared thoughtfully back at me. Allen shook his head. "Don't mean a damn thing," he said. "For all we know, Zeke could be right. Be the first time, I know, but he's gotta be right oncet."

"That's what I call confidence," McKoan said, spitting.

"What do you say, Mr. Hickok?" Kelso asked, his eyes burning into mine. I felt the heat of his desire and knew he was willing to go after them.

I took a deep breath and shook my head. "Well, it just didn't look right to me. I think those ladies were prisoners." I shrugged. "And hell, if I'm wrong, we can't be any worse off than we are now, can we?"

Zeke laughed and said, "Damn if you ain't right, Bill. Ain't one of us coming out of this alive, so might as well be shot for a fish as a carp."

"Now what the hell does that mean?" Allen demanded. "Hell, you don't make no sense at all. Captain, that ain't—"

Kelso shook his head. "Doesn't matter. I know what he

was trying to say." A reckless grin plastered across his face. "Mount up, men!"

"Oh shit," Allen sighed, and went to his horse, a mean bay that tried to take a chunk out of his leg each time he stepped into the stirrup. He kicked it automatically and the horse screamed in fury. "Well, dammit, if we're gonna get killed, let's get on with it!"

Kelso clapped his hands with satisfaction and leaped onto his sorrel and motioned for me to ride ahead. I led them down the ravine. Black moved anxiously under me, sensing the battle coming, heading toward the patrol. I took a hard hand on the reins. He threw his head angrily, mouthing the bit as if he could chew through the metal. His neck arched; his mane flew back and forth as he snorted in disgust.

I led the patrol through the woods and across a pasture on a wide detour, guessing where the road would loop back again, keeping a creek on my left as I rode. We came out of the trees just as the patrol came into view. The lieutenant in the lead pulled up, startled at our sudden appearance. I dropped the loop of the reins on Black's neck and slammed my heels hard against his sides. Black squealed with fury and leaped forward. I lifted the Army Colts from their holsters and thumbed back the hammers as I rode down upon the lieutenant. He opened his mouth to yell, but I snapped a shot off that struck him in the chest, somersaulting him backward off his horse. Then I rode into the patrol, gripping Black's sides hard with my legs as he drove into the side of a horse, his yellow teeth snapping, tearing a chunk out of the horse's neck. I shot his rider, then shot another and turned in the saddle to snap a shot at a third as Black wheeled and charged the trail rider. I raised my pistol, then saw shock cross his face and a bright scarlet flash explode from his chest. He fell from his saddle and his horse turned and galloped away. I pulled Black up and turned, raising my pistols, but it was over; all were dead.

I looked back down at Kelso and the others, staring open-mouthed at me. Zeke grinned and waved his long rifle.

"Well, you didn't git 'em all, Wild Bill!" he chortled.

"Damnedest thing I ever saw," Kelso said as Black cantered back to him. "And folks call me crazy."

I reined in and looked down at the ladies. One of them, blond-haired with flashing blue eyes, laughed, her full lips spreading generously over her face, lifting into dimples in her cheeks.

"Yes, I'd say you are one wild man," she said.

"We thought you might be in difficulty, ma'am," Kelso said, gallantly tipping his hat at her.

"And we were," she laughed. "Mary Ladd and I have been accused of spying for the Union." She shrugged. "But now it seems that our accusers aren't around anymore. I'm Susannah Moore." She smiled archly at me. "And I'm eternally grateful, sir, for your gallantry."

I grinned down at her as Zeke spit disgustedly. "Hell," he grunted, "you'd think Wild Bill was winning the war all by hisself!"

PART THREE

Paladin

He snatched the lightning shaft from heaven

CHAPTER

36

PERHAPS WHAT began it all ends it all. I don't know—
that is one of the mysteries I haven't been able to solve and
know, now, that I never will. I know the mystery—the cruelty
within people that cannot be excised with a burning brand
despite all the assurances of our priests and preachers—

The war ended and for a while I cast around like others who
had fought in it, trying to decide what to do next. For a while
I hauled freight, working as a teamster for McFadden & Co.,
but I quickly became bored with the slow-moving wagons
rolling over the brown plains. I hunted a bit and thought
fleetingly about going up into the mountains and becoming a
mountain man, but I knew that was only a maudlin dream
held over from the youth that I no longer was. I went home
to visit Mother, but I had been gone too long to belong there
anymore and I soon made my way to Springfield, looking
halfheartedly for a job but not knowing what it was I wanted
to do. Springfield wasn't much to shine a lantern at, but it

was the largest excuse for one in that part of the state. An uneasy pall seemed to hang over the town even on the sunniest days as former Rebels and Yankees moved nervously through the streets together. Most, however, seemed to be looking for the same elusive moment to present itself and tuck them beneath a blanket of success. But moments like that have to be made to happen, and few showed any inclination to become that involved in the day.

I was infected, too. A restlessness had seemed to enter my soul and I soon found myself irritated and angry at others who meant to do me no wrong but still somehow managed to easily offend me all the same.

I began to gamble recklessly and for a while Lady Luck smiled favorably upon me as coins and chips seemed to flow steadily over green felt and scarred pine tabletops toward me. But I took little satisfaction in my growing finances, boredom quickly following upon the heels of the brief exhilaration of winning.

I met Dave Tutt at one of the tables in one of the saloons and took an instant dislike to the man. It's strange how sometimes a man can meet another and find the hackles rising upon his neck. But that was the way with Tutt. I knew he had been a Rebel and probably a bushwhacker—he had that look about him: arrogant, lip-curling, and a chip on his shoulder large enough to be a loblolly pine. But the real reason we rubbed each other raw was Susannah Moore.

Susannah—long blond hair, breasts that moved beneath her dress when she walked despite all she tried to do to hold them still, and, in the dark, soft white skin that seemed to glow beneath my hand. Any male who stood around her breathed deeply and I knew what they were smelling, for I smelled it as much as they—the salt of the woman who wants a man. Susannah wasn't particular about any man, although when she stayed with one she was true to him until she left and then she never went back. That was her own strange code of honor. In her mind, I suppose, it kept her from seeing herself as "loose" or a "soiled dove" or an "adultress," which were the terms most often flung the way of women like her.

Susannah was none of those; she was just a woman who met men on their own terms and hers. Nothing more.

But Tutt, well, Tutt was different. He had a cruel streak in him that others sensed whenever he was near and stepped wide of him—all of which fed his arrogance and made him strut more, the cock of the boardwalk in Springfield.

I wouldn't play cards with him, because he was a poor gambler—he always lost, and when he lost he drank, and when he drank he became ugly and unreasonable and as certain as the rising of the sun that he was immortal. Father would have called it the bravery of Achilles, which wasn't bravery so much as it was an arrogant assurance of his own moment in time.

Tutt had come upon the game in The Lyon House and tried to sit in, but as I had started the game, I refused to let him play. He turned red with rage; then his face went strangely white and he smiled and picked up my watch, saying, "I reckon you owe me this much from the last time we played."

I laid my cards on the table and looked up at him. "I've never played with you, Tutt," I said quietly. "And I never will."

"You think you're too good for me, don't you?" he challenged, a wild recklessness coming into his eyes.

"No," I said carefully. "I *know* I'm too good for you."

The room became silent as all eyes turned toward us. Tutt hesitated, an uncertainty flashing momentarily in his eyes; then he, too, felt the eyes of the room and knew he had gone too far to simply replace my watch and walk from the room.

He forced a laugh and dropped the watch in his shirt pocket, then said, "You can have it back when you bring my money to me. I'll be in the square tomorrow at noon." And he walked from the room.

I excused myself from the table and rose and left quickly to reclaim my watch, but by the time I made it to the doorway he had gone. I knew, however, that he would be in the town square in the morning with my watch: He had already said that, and if he did not show up at the appointed time he would be laughed out of Springfield, and a man like Tutt can take no laughter directed his way.

The next day at noon, I was waiting in the square when I saw him take my watch from his pocket, pretend to consult it, then step out into the sunlight, holding the watch in his left hand.

"That's enough, Tutt," I called warningly. "You've taken this too far."

"Too late for that!" he said. "Come and get it."

I started across the square and he pulled his pistol from its holster and let it dangle at his side. I placed my hands on the butts of my Navy Colts and continued across the square until only ten feet separated us. His eyes glittered black hate at me from beneath the brim of his hat. He laughed again, but it was a nervous laugh, and then he was caught up in the moment.

"You know I don't give a damn about this watch," he said softly.

"I know," I answered. "But it's her choice to make. Not yours. Not mine."

"With you gone, there won't be much of a choice left!" he said. Something moved in his eyes, and I knew he was finished talking. I twisted my wrists, flipping the pistols from their holsters. I fired as I leveled it, and saw the bullet strike him in the middle of his belly, knocking him down. His pistol flew from his hand. I stepped forward and took my watch out of his hand.

"You were a stupid man, Tutt," I said softly. "Is anything worth the dark?"

His eyes looked frightened for a moment; then the tendons of his neck stretched hard as he tried to jerk himself away from approaching death. He moaned and I knew it would have been a scream had not his throat contracted suddenly, shutting off all sound, shutting off life. A glaze came over his features, and his muscles relaxed into the dirt.

I sighed and turned back to the crowd, holding the watch in one hand, one of the Navy Colts in the other. I saw metal flash and said sharply, "I hope there's not another stupid person here. It was a fair fight."

My friends Jim and Art appeared then, each holding a shotgun. The hostility of the crowd immediately vanished and they turned away, dispersing. A couple came forward to carry Tutt to the undertaker's house and I walked toward the nearest saloon to wash the brassy taste out of my mouth.

I was arrested shortly after the Greene County coroner returned his report and had a bench warrant issued for me for killing Tutt. But two days later the charge was reduced to manslaughter, and some friends put up a two-thousand-dollar bond to bail me out of jail. Captain R. B. Owen then pulled a few strings and talked John S. Phelps, one of the leading attorneys of the time, into taking my case. Phelps made short work of the charges against me, rounding up witnesses who swore Tutt had fired first—that didn't take long, as almost the entire town had witnessed the battle—and I was acquitted.

I thought that was the last of that affair, but I couldn't have been more mistaken. The local newspaper, the *Missouri Weekly Patriot,* tried to scrape my hide away with a series of articles, lashing not only me but the jury as well within the sanctified safety of its editorial columns. But I refused to rise up against the writer, recognizing instinctively that I wouldn't win in a war of words and knowing full well that nothing would be gained by hauling him out into the street and thumping him. But I didn't know how such a controversy appealed to others. People always want to know the dirt upon a fellow even if he's cast as a hero. Fact is, I think if a fellow is a hero to some, there's others who don't rest until they've dug something up to tarnish his reputation. Most men aren't happy unless they can make others more miserable than themselves. Then they're happy. I suppose, however, that it was the idea of finding a hero in peacetime to take the place of those lost with the end of the war that brought Colonel George Ward Nichols to Springfield in search of me.

I was playing cards in Springfield with a couple of friends when Clark came into the saloon, saying, "Jim, there's a Colonel Nichols asking for you over at the hotel." He grinned. "Says he wants to talk to the great hero Wild Bill Hickok."

I swore softly as the others around the table grinned at me.

"Hero, eh, boys?" Wallace said, chuckling. "Maybe we ought to just give up while we can on this here game and give him our money."

"I'll get it anyway," I said, spreading my cards out. "Three queens."

Wallace laughed and tossed his cards in. "Thought you were bluffing, Bill," he said congenially.

"I didn't," Art said. "Figured you for the queens, Bill, and knew you didn't have the fourth 'cause I buried it in the deadwood. Three kings." He laid them gently in front of him, smiling gleefully. I shook my head in irony as the others broke into laughter.

"So what do you want to do about the colonel, Bill?"

I nibbled on the edge of my lip as I thought for a second. "He really a colonel?" I asked.

Clark shrugged. "Claims he is. Fact is, ask him once and you'll understand how he won the war single-handedly, thanks to his genius. But I guess all those writers are that way."

"I beg your pardon," Bob White said stiffly, leaning back in his chair. Bob had been a correspondent for some eastern paper during the war and took slurs upon his former occupation as a personal insult. "That is a gross generalization made by a fool."

"No offense," Clark said easily. "Present company excepted."

"Yes, I imagine," Bob said. He looked owlishly at me. "Well, why not have a bit of fun with him? Let's give him a hero."

"I don't know," I started doubtfully.

"Oh, come on!" Art said gaily. "Don't be such a stuffed shirt."

The others grinned at me. I threw up my hands, surrendering. "All right. Let's see what we can come up with."

Eagerly they tossed their cards aside. Bob brought glasses and a bottle of Monongahela from the bar. We all took a glass. I leaned back resignedly as the others put their elbows on the table and began to talk animatedly, arguing gleefully as they built a proper hero's life for Wild Bill Hickok.

Colonel Nichols looked eagerly around the lobby as he tripped down the stairs of his hotel. He spied me sitting on a medallion-back sofa next to a Hepplewhite chair near the corner. He made a beeline toward me, his eyes shifting nervously around the room, sizing up the "color" for the article I suspected he had already written and was looking for a few details to plug in and give it the ring of reality. A grin tugged at my lips. Everyone in the lobby was from the poker game and dressed in the dime novel's idea of what a westerner should wear, after an hour spent in Martin's Mercantile choosing their costumes. Even Bob had dressed up in a pin-striped collarless shirt with a huge yellow bandanna spread over it. He wore a broad-brimmed hat with a crown tall enough to hide a pony keg of beer in it and sheepskin chaps with an old revolver tucked awkwardly in his belt. I hoped it wasn't loaded or he'd probably shoot his nuts off pulling it out, as the blamed fool had cocked it before jamming it under his belt.

Deke wore a fire-engine red shirt and blue bandanna under a rawhide vest, a wad of tobacco bulging one cheek like a foraging chipmunk.

The others sprawled in rainbow colors around the room, affecting the bored look of fresh-washed cowboys the fourth day off the trail.

"Mr. Hickok?" Colonel Nichols said, halting in front of me. I rose and stretched out my hand. "Call me James," I said.

"You are 'Wild Bill' Hickok?" he said anxiously.

I thought I heard a giggle and looked toward Bob. I could tell from his bright eyes he was having a hard time holding his laughter in. I glared at him. He made a strangled noise and looked away.

"I don't really care for that," I said uncomfortably. "That's just something the folks hung on me."

No mistake about it; Bob stuck his knuckles in his mouth, trying to stifle the giggles.

"Wild Bill," Nichols breathed with relish, pumping my hand like he was trying to draw water. "You don't know how long I've been looking to meet with you! Ever since I heard about the McCanles massacre—"

"Yeah, well, you know," I said, uncomfortable with his beaming presence and his reference to the fight at Rock Creek Station that I had been trying to put in history ever since the courts had found me not guilty of murder.

He beamed. Positively beamed. I felt myself growing red with embarrassment. "I'm Colonel Nichols," he said, drawing out his title so I had a half hunch it was self-awarded. Fakes make a ceremony out of what they pretend to be while those who have brought themselves up by their bootstraps don't feel the need to lay their rank out on the table in front of anyone. But for the next quarter hour he oiled my ears with his gab and stories about the glory he'd earned, looping his way up and around just about every major battle I'd ever heard about—except the Trojan War; somehow he missed that one—and, as near as I could tell, the North owed him a debt of gratitude for having saved it from a terrible fate at Gettysburg.

Toward the tail end of his tale, I gave Bob a dirty look and tapped the handle of one of the Colts holstered, butts forward, at my waist. Bob laughed and looked deliberately away, pretending he hadn't noticed me. I sighed and turned my attention back to the colonel, who hadn't noticed my attention lapse, just as he wound up his lecturing.

"But enough about me," he said modestly, his lips spreading in another smile that would have blinded an Indian a mile away with its brightness. "Tell me about yourself, Wild Bill."

He leaned back in his chair, looking with high expectations at me. I nodded, staring back at him for a minute, until a tiny frown began to appear between his brows and his eyes began flickering nervously away from mine.

"Something wrong?" he asked uneasily.

I shook my head and leaned forward conspiratorially. He leaned back away from me for a second, but I motioned for him to lean forward. He hesitated, then slowly bent forward, his eyebrows jerking up and down in question.

"I don't know," I said, frowning and nodding toward Bob. "But that fellow over there looks just like a face on a wanted poster I've seen hanging around the sheriff's office. No, don't look!" I said sharply as he started to turn automatically in the direction of my nod. "You might give us away."

"Us?" He swallowed and his eyes started their wild dance again. "Why. Yes. Yes. Of course."

I nodded and gave him a grim look. "And if I don't miss my guess, he's got his gang with him, too."

Nichols's face became grim, but a welcome joy seemed to creep into his eyes. His tongue crept out and wet his lips nervously. "Ah, gang?"

I pursed my lips and shook my head. "Some of the most bloodthirsty rascals who ever came down the wood," I said. "Robbed a bank over in White River and killed eighteen people before riding out. Then they rode back in for pure orneriness and killed another six or seven before they rode away. Three of the dead were women."

"Women?" he replied with relish, and I could read the headlines of his stories gleaming in his eyes. A fine sheen of perspiration appeared on his forehead.

"Yes," I said, lowering my voice. "One a grandmother."

"Grandmother," he repeated. His cheeks began to look a little flushed with anxiousness. Again he licked his lips. "Ah, maybe we should get some help."

"No time for that," I said. I took an old Manhattan from beneath my coat and pressed it into Nichols's hands. He looked like he might faint from glee in his chair.

Bob caught the motion and gave a thumbs-up to the others. "Look out, boys!" he roared. "It's Wild Bill Hickok!"

He drew the pistol, accidentally nudging the trigger as it came out of his pants. Most of us had loaded our guns with blanks before starting off with the joke, but Bob had put a full load in the revolver and a streak of flame shot out a foot long from the barrel, setting his trousers on fire. He yelped and dropped the pistol and began slapping at his groin with his palms to put out the fire. The others stared openmouthed at his wild dance, forgetting their roles.

I swore and leaped to my feet, drawing my pistols as I came out of the chair. "You boys have been terrorizing folks long enough! Now you've got"—*aw, hell*, I thought, and swallowed gamely—"Wild Bill to deal with!"

I almost threw up as I said those lines and decided the hell with the rest of the speech the boys had written. I started shooting, and the others snapped out of their trance, drew their pistols, and began firing back. Out of the corner of my eye, I saw Nichols dive out of his chair and fall flat on the floor behind me. I emptied one pistol as Nichols rose to a crouch and stretched his pistol over the arm of the sofa, shooting with grim satisfaction in Bob's general direction. The fire crept up Bob's pants, and he howled and slapped wildly at his groin. The others began grabbing their bellies and falling to the floor, dying dramatically, caught up in their finest hour. All of them discreetly spilled flat bottles of snake oil mixed with chicken blood we had gotten from the butcher on their shirts, then stuffed the bottles back under their shirts and sprawled grotesquely on the wood floor.

All save Bob, that is, who jerked spasmodically out the door, britches flaring, and jumped into the horse trough. A small cloud of steam rose up. His shoulders slumped in relief for a second; then he climbed out of the trough, water streaming from his clothes, and limped painfully, spraddle-legged, down the alley.

A white fog filled the lobby. I peered through the smoke and nodded satisfactorily. "Well, Colonel, reckon we got them all." I stumbled for a second, trying to remember the name Bob had given himself, then gave up and invented one. "Short-armed Bob's heading for Hades even now as we speak!"

Nichols rose from behind the arm of a heavy chair, waving his pistol. He saw the "dead" bodies and his face broke into a wide smile and he dusted off his suit.

"We did?" he said, then added, "Well, by God, so we did!"

He handed the pistol to me and started toward the "bodies," but I caught his arm. He gave me a puzzled look.

"What?"

"One of them might be playing possum," I said solemnly.

"What?" he asked, looking blankly at me.

"One of them might be waiting for us," I said loudly. "Faking, you know?" I roared. I knew what the problem was—their ears were ringing from the pistol shots made louder in the room than they would have been out in the open.

Art finally heard me and jumped up, leveling his pistol at us. Nichols roared angrily as I pulled a double-barreled shotgun, sawed off six inches in front of the chambers, from beneath my coat, rocked back the hammers, and tripped the triggers. It sounded like a cannon in that narrow lobby. The recoil damn near knocked me back on my ass, but I caught the back of Nichols's chair and managed to remain upright. Clark threw himself backward as Nichols charged toward him, windmilling his arms furiously. His foot stepped on one of the pistols and rolled out from under him.

"Ark!" Nichols yelled, stumbling, trying to catch his balance. He failed and fell forward, his head smacking into the walnut leg of a table. His eyes rolled up in their sockets. He tried gamely to rise but fell, unconscious, to the floor.

"I'll be damned!" I said.

Art opened an eye and, not seeing Nichols standing beside me, rose cautiously. "What's wrong?"

"I think he knocked what little brains he had out," I said, kneeling beside Nichols. I pressed my fingers against the side of his throat and felt his pulse beating. "No, the hero of the War Between the States is still alive."

"You sure?" Art asked, coming forward. He squatted, looking at the bump rising like a mountain on Nichols's forehead.

"I think I know a dead man from a living one," I said dryly. "Help me get him into the chair."

Art helped me raise Nichols and sit him upright in the chair. Deke, sensing something was wrong, rolled his head around. He saw the two of us standing beside the chair. "What're you doing?" he asked.

"He knocked himself out," Art said disgustedly.

"What?" Deke climbed up, giving us a disbelieving look. He nudged the others with the toe of his boot.

"I didn't stammer," Art said sourly. "Shit. It all went beautifully."

"What? What?" Jim asked, rising. "That damn cannon's got my ears ringing like a blacksmith's anvil," he said reproachfully, glaring at me.

"It was your idea," I said, lifting the shotgun and looking at it disapprovingly. "If I had shot loaded in this, I would have wiped out half the town with its spread. Here." I tossed it to him. He wasn't expecting it and it struck him on the forehead. His eyes crossed; he wavered for a second, then collapsed to the floor unconscious.

Art threw his hands up in the air disgustedly. Then he noticed Bob was gone. "Where's Bob?" he asked.

I explained quickly. He shook his head. "Damn, this thing's turned to horse poop real fast."

"Shit," Deke said automatically.

"That's what I said," Art said.

"You said 'poop.' There's a difference," Deke said defensively.

Nichols moaned in his chair, moving his head slightly back and forth on the tatted throw over the back of the chair.

"He's coming around," I said.

Without thinking, Art whipped out his pistol and whacked Nichols on the head. Nichols slumped deeper into his chair, a second lump already forming on his forehead.

"Now why did you do that?" I asked, feeling frustration climbing up through me like a raccoon scaling a tree.

"He would've seen us," Art said.

I shook my head. "You boys grab Jim and get him out of here."

"What are you going to tell him?" Art said.

"I'll think of something. Maybe I'll tell him he got creased."

Art motioned at his forehead. "That don't look like no bullet to me."

"Maybe he won't know the difference," I said.

"If he really was—is—was a colonel, he will," Deke said mournfully.

"Bullets can do the damnedest things, though," Art said philosophically. "Come on, Deke. Let's get Jim and go find Bob."

"You might try the widow's place," I called as they hoisted the unconscious Jim between them and made their way awkwardly out the door.

The hotel clerk came forward, holding a couple of glasses and a bottle of whiskey. He shook his head as he handed them to me. "Pour a little of this in him," he said.

"Let's get him up to his room first," I said.

The clerk helped me raise the colonel to my shoulder, then followed me with the whiskey and glasses as I carried Nichols up the stairs. We laid him on top of his bed after removing his coat and tie. I unfastened his celluloid collar as the clerk wet a towel in the hand basin, wrung it out, and brought it to me.

"All right," I said. "I'll take it from here."

He left as I folded the towel and placed it over Nichols's forehead. I sighed, poured myself a drink, and pulled a chair up next to the bed and sat, waiting for him to awaken.

The next day, I put a shaken but swaggering Nichols on the noon train heading east. His head was swathed in bandages, giving him a piratical look. He pumped my hand enthusiastically and promised he would, by God!, write the truth about Wild Bill Hickok. He climbed aboard and waved his broad-brimmed hat with a grandiose gesture as the train pulled out from the station.

I thought that was the last I would hear about Colonel Nichols, but six months later Bob came into The Lyon House holding a copy of *Harper's* in the air.

"Here it is, gentlemen!" he crowed. "The true story, part one, of Wild Bill Hickok!"

"You sorry-assed son of a bitch," I said accusingly. "And after all I've done for you."

He ignored me as the others clamored for him to read it aloud. He cleared his throat, made certain that a glass of whiskey stood at his elbow to lubricate his speaking facilities, and began:

WILD BILL

Several months after the ending of the Civil War, I visited the city of Springfield in Southwest Missouri. Springfield is not a burgh of extensive dimensions, yet it is one reason why it was the *point d'apari* as well as the base of operations for all military movements during the war.

On a warm summer day, I sat watching from the shadow of a broad awning the coming and going of the strange, half-civilized people who, from all the country round, make this a place for barter and trade. Men and women dressed in queer costumes; men with coats and trowsers made of skin, but so thickly covered with dirt and grease as to have defied the identity of the animal when walking in the flesh. Others wore homespun gear, which oftentimes appeared to have seen lengthy service. Many of those people were mounted on horseback or muleback, while others urged forward the unwilling cattle attached to creaking, heavily laden wagons, their drivers snapping their long whips with a report like that of a pistol-shot.

In front of the shops that lined both sides of the main business street, and about the public square, were groups of men lolling against posts, lying upon the wooden sidewalks, or sitting in chairs. These men were temporary or permanent denizens of the city, and were lazily occupied in doing nothing. The most marked characteristic of the inhabitants seemed to be an indisposition to move, and their highest ambition to let their hair and beards grow.

Here and there upon the street the appearance of the army blue betokened the presence of a returned Union soldier, and the jaunty, confident air with which they carried themselves was all the more striking in its contrast with the indolence which appeared to belong to the place. The only indication of action was the inevitable revolver which every body, excepting, perhaps, the women, wore about their persons. When people moved in this lazy city they did so slowly and without method. No one seemed in haste. A huge hog wallowed in luxurious ease in a nice bed of mud on the other side of the way, giving vent to gentle grunts of satisfaction. On the platform at my feet lay a large wolf-dog literally asleep with one eye open. He, too, seemed contented to let the world wag idly on.

The loose, lazy spirit of the occasion finally took possession of me, and I sat and gazed and smoked, and it is possible that I might have fallen into a Rip Van Winkle sleep to have been aroused ten years hence by the cry, "Passengers for the flying machine to New York, all aboard!" when I and the drowsing city were roused into life by the clatter and crash of the hoofs of a horse which dashed furiously across the square and down the street. The rider sat perfectly erect, yet following with a grace of motion seen only in the horsemen of the plains, the rise and fall of the galloping steed. There was only a moment to observe this, for they halted suddenly, while the rider springing to the ground approached the party which the noise had gathered near me.

"This yere is Wild Bill, Colonel," said Captain Honesty, an army officer addressing me. He continued:

"How are yere Bill? This yere is Colonel N——, who wants ter know ycr."

Let me at once describe the personal appearance of the famous Scout of the Plains, William Hickok, called "Wild Bill," who now advanced toward me, fixing his clear gray eyes on mine in a quick, interrogative way, as if to take "my measure."

The result seemed favorable, for he held forth a small muscular hand in a frank, open manner. As I looked at him I thought his the handsomest *physique* I had ever seen. In its exquisite manly proportions it recalled the antique. It was a figure Ward would delight to model as a companion to his "Indian."

Bill stood six feet and an inch in his bright yellow moccasins. A deer-skin shirt or frock, it might be called, hung jauntily over his shoulders and revealed a chest whose breadth and depth were remarkable. These lungs had had growth in some twenty years of the free air of the Rocky Mountains. His small, round waist was girthed by a belt which held two of Colt's Navy revolvers. His legs sloped gradually from the compact thigh to the feet, which were small and turned inward as he walked. There was a singular grace and dignity of carriage about that figure which would have called your attention meet it where you would. The head which crowned it was now covered by a large sombrero, underneath which there shone out a quiet manly face; so gentle is its expression as he greets you as utterly to belie the history of its owner; yet it is not a face to be trifled with. The lips thin and sensitive, the jaw not too square, the cheek bones slightly prominent, a mass of fine dark hair falls below the neck to the shoulders. The eyes, now that you are in friendly intercourse, are as gentle as a woman's. In truth, the woman nature seems prominent throughout, and you would not believe that you were looking into eyes that have pointed the way to death to hundreds of men. Yes, Wild Bill with his own hands has killed hundreds of men. Of that I have not a doubt. "He shoots to kill," as they say on the border.

In vain did I examine the scout's face for some evidence of murderous propensity. It was a gentle face, and singular only in the sharp angle of the eye, and without any physiognomical reason for the opinion, I have thought his wonderful accuracy of aim was indicated by this peculiarity. He told me, however, to use his own words:

"I allers shot well; but I come ter be perfect in the mountains by shootin at a dime for a mark, at best of half a dollar a shot. And then until the war I never drank liquor nor smoked," he continued, with a melancholy expression; "war is demoralizing it is." Captain Honesty was right. I was very curious to see "Wild Bill, the Scout," who, a few days before my arrival in Springfield, in a duel at noonday in the public square, at fifty paces, had sent one of Colt's pistol-balls through the heart of a returned Confederate soldier.

Whenever I had met an officer or soldier who had served in the Southwest I heard of Wild Bill and his exploits, until these stories became so frequent and of such an extraordinary character as quite to outstrip personal knowledge of adventure by camp and field; and the hero of these strange tales took shape in my mind as did Jack the Giant Killer or Sinbad the Sailor in childhood's days. As then, I now had the most implicit faith in the existence of the individual; but how one man could accomplish such prodigies of strength and feats of daring was a continued wonder.

In order to give the reader a clearer understanding of the condition of this neighborhood, which could have permitted the duel mentioned above, and whose history will be given hereafter in detail, I will describe the situation at the time of which I am writing, which was late in the summer of 1865, premising that this section of country would not to-day be selected as a model example of modern civilization.

At that time peace and comparative quiet had succeeded the perils and tumult of war in all the more southern States. The people of Georgia and the Carolinas were glad to enforce order in their midst; and it would have been safe for a Union officer to have ridden unattended through the land.

In Southwest Missouri there were old scores to be settled up. During the three days occupied by General Smith—who commanded the Department and was on a tour of inspection—in crossing the country between Rolla and Springfield, a distance of one hundred and twenty miles, five men were killed or wounded on the public road. Two were murdered a short distance from Rolla—by whom we could not ascertain. Another was instantly killed and two were wounded at a meeting of a band of "Regulators," who were in the service of the State, but were paid by the United States Government. It should be said here that their method of "regulation" was slightly informal, their war-cry was, "A swift bullet and a short rope for returned rebels!"

I was informed by General Smith that during the six months preceding not less than four thousand returned Confederates had been summarily disposed of by shooting or hanging. This statement seems incredible; but there is the record, and I have no doubt of its truth. History shows few parallels to this relentless destruction of human life in time of peace. It can be explained only upon the ground that before the war, this region was inhabited by lawless people. In the outset of the rebellion the merest suspicion of loyalty to the Union cost the patriot his life; and thus large numbers fled the land, giving up home and every material interest. As soon as the Federal armies occupied the country these refugees returned. Once securely fixed in their old homes they resolved that their former persecutors should not live in their midst. Revenge for the past and security for the future knotted many a nerve and sped many a deadly bullet.

Wild Bill did not belong to the Regulators. Indeed, he was one of the law and order party. He said:

"When the war closed I buried the hatchet, and I won't fight now unless I'm put upon."

Bill was born of Northern parents in the State of Illinois. He ran away from home when a boy, and wandered out upon the plains and into the mountains. For fifteen years he lived with the trappers, hunting and fishing. When the war broke out he returned to the States and entered the Union service. No man probably was ever better fitted for scouting than he. Joined to his tremendous strength he was an unequalled horseman; he was a perfect marksman; he had a keen sight, and a constitution which had no limit of endurance. He was cool to audacity, brave to rashness, always possessed of himself under the most critical circumstances; and above all, was such a master in the knowledge of woodcraft that it might have been termed a science with him—a knowledge which, with the soldier, is priceless beyond description. Some of Bill's adventures during the war will be related hereafter.

The main feature of the story of the duel was told me by Captain Honesty, who was unprejudiced, if it is possible to find an unbiased mind in a town of three thousand people after a fight has taken place. I will give the story in his words:

"They say Bill's wild. Now he isn't any sich thing. I've known him going on ter ten year, and he's as civil a disposed person as you'll find hereabouts. But he won't be put upon.

"I'll tell yer how it happened. But come inter the office; thar's a good many round hy'ar as sides with Tutt—the man that's shot. But I tell yer 'twas a fair fight. Take some whisky? No! Well, I will, if yer'l excuse me.

"You see," continued the Captain, setting the empty glass on the table in an emphatic way, "Bill was up in his room a-playing seven-up, or four-hand, or some of them pesky games. Bill refused ter play with Tutt, who was a professional gambler. Yer see, Bill was a scout on our side durin the war, and Tutt was a reb scout. Bill had killed Dave Tutt's mate, and, atween one thing and other, there war an onusual hard feelin atwixt 'em.

"Ever sin (*sic*) Dave come back he had tried to pick a row with Bill; so Bill wouldn't play cards with him any more. But Dave stood over the man who was gambling with Bill and lent the feller money. Bill won bout two hundred dollars, which made Tutt spiteful mad. Bime-by he says to Bill:

" 'Bill, you've got plenty of money—pay me that forty dollars yer owe me in that horse trade.'

"And Bill paid him. Then he said:

" 'Yer owe me thirty-five dollars more; yer lost it playing with me t'other night.'

"Dave's style was right provoking; but Bill answered him perfectly gentlemanly: "I think yer wrong, Dave. It's only twenty-five dollars. I have a memorandum of it in my pocket down stairs. Ef it's thirty-five dollars I'll give it yer.'

"Now Bill's watch was lying on the table. Dave took up the watch, put it in his pocket, and said: 'I'll keep this yere watch till yer pay me that thirty-five dollars.'

"This made Bill shooting mad; fur, don't yer see, Colonel, it was a-doubting his honor like, so he got up and looked Dave in the eyes, and said to him: 'I don't want ter make a row in this house. It's a decent house, and I don't want ter injure the keeper. You'd better put that watch back on the table.'

"But Dave grinned at Bill mighty ugly, and walked off with the watch, and kept it several days. All this time Dave's friends were spurring Bill on ter fight; there was no end ter the talk. They blackguarded him in an underhand sort of way, and tried ter get up a scrimmage, and then they thought they could lay him out. Yer see Bill has enemies all about. He's settled the accounts of a heap of men who lived round here. This is about the only place in Missouri whar a reb can come back and live, and ter tell yer the truth, Colonel—" and the Captain, with an involuntary movement, hitched up his revolver- belt, as he said, with expressive significance, "they don't stay long round here!

"Well, as I was saying, these rebs don't like ter see a man walking round town who they knew in the reb army as one of their men who they now know was on our side, all the time he was sending us information, sometimes from Pap Price's own headquarters. But they couldn't provoke Bill inter a row, for he's afeared of hissel when he gits *awful* mad; and he allers left these shootin irons in his room when he went out. One day these cusses drew their pistols on him and dared him to fight and they told him that Tutt was a-goin ter pack that watch across the squar (*sic*) next day ast noon.

"I heard of this, for every body was talking about it on the street, and so I went after Bill and found him in his room cleaning and greasing and loading his revolvers.

" 'Now, Bill,' says I, 'you're goin to get inter a fight.'

" 'Don't you bother yerself, Captain,' says he. 'It's not the first time I have been in a fight; and these d——d hounds have put on me long enough. You don't want me ter give up my honor, do yer?'

" 'No, Bill,' says I, 'yer must keep yer honor.'

"Next day, about noon, Bill went down on the squar. He had said that Dave Tutt shouldn't pack that watch across the squar unless dead men could walk.

"When Bill got onter the squar he found a crowd stanin in the corner of the street by which he entered the squar, which is from the south, yer know. In this crowd he saw a lot of Tutt's friends; some were cousins of his'n, just back from the reb army; and they jeered him, and boasted that Dave was a-goin to pack that watch across the squar as he promised.

"Then Bill saw Tutt standing near the court-house, which yer remember is on the west side, so that the crowd war behind Bill.

"Just then Tutt, who war alone, started from the court-house and walked out onto the squar, and Bill moved away from the crowd toward west side of the squar. Bout fif-

teen paces brought them opposite to each other and about
fifty yards apart. Tutt then showed his pistol. Bill had kept a
sharp eye on him, and before Tutt could pint it Bill had
hi'sn out.

"At that moment you could have heard a pin drop in that
squar. Both Tutt and Bill fired, but one discharge follwed the
other so quick that's hard to say which went off first. Tutt was
a famous shot, but he missed this time; the ball from his pistol
went over Bill's head. The instant Bill fired, without waitin ter
see ef he had hit Tutt, he wheeled on his heels and pointed his
pistol at Tutt's friends, who had already drawn their weapons.
" 'Arent' yer satisfied, gentlemen?' cried Bill, as cool as an al-
ligator. 'Put up your shootin-irons or there'll be more dead
men here.' And they put 'em up and said it war a far fight.

"What became of Tutt?" I asked of the Captain, who had
stopped at this point of his story and was very deliberately en-
gaged in refilling his empty glass.

"Oh! Dave? He was as plucky a feller as ever drew trigger;
but Lord bless yer! It was no use. Bill never shoots twice at
the same man, and his ball went through Dave's heart. He
stood stock-still for a second or two, then raised his arm as if
to fire again, then he swayed a little, staggered three or four
steps, and then fell dead.

"Bill and his friends wanted ter have the thing done regular, so we went up ter the justice, and Bill delivered him self
up. A jury was drawn; Bill was tried and cleared the next day.
It was proved that it was a case of self-defense. Don't yer see,
Colonel?"

I answered that I was afraid that I did not see that point
very clearly.

"Well, well!" he replied, with an air of compassion, "you
haven't drunk any whisky, that's what's the matter with yer."
And then, putting his hand on my shoulder with a half-
mysterious half-conscious look in his face, he muttered, in a
whisper: *"The fact is, thar was an undercurrent of a woman
in that fight!"*

The story of the duel was yet fresh from the lips of the
Captain when its hero appeared in the manner already de-

scribed. After a few moments' conversation Bill excused himself, saying:

"I am going out on the prarer a piece to see the sick wife of my mate. I should be glad to meet yer at the hotel this afternoon, Kernel."

"I will go there to meet you," I replied.

"Good-day, gentlemen," said the scout as he saluted the party; and mounting the black horse, who had been standing quiet, unhitched, he waved his hand over the animal's head. Responsive to the signal, she shot forward as the arrow leaves the bow, and they both disappeared up the road in a cloud of dust.

"That man is the most remarkable character I have met in four years' active service," said a lieutenant of cavalry, as the party resumed their seats. "He and his mate—the man who scouted with him—attempted the most daring feat that I ever heard of."

As there appeared to be no business on hand at the moment the party urged the lieutenant to tell the story.

"I can't tell the thing as it was," said the young officer. "It was beyond description. One could only hold their breath and feel. It happened when our regiment was attached to Curtis's command, in the expedition down into Arkansas. One day we were in the advance, and began to feel the enemy, who appeared in greater strength than at any time before. We were all rather uneasy, for there were rumors that Kirby Smith had come up from Texas with all his force; and as we were only a strong reconnoitring party a fight just then might have been bad for us. We made a big noise with a light battery and stretched our cavalry out in the open and opposite to the rebel cavalry, who were drawn up in line of battle on the slope of the prairie about a thousand yards away. There we sat for half an hour, now and then banging at each, but both parties keeping pretty well their line of battle. They waited for us to pitch in. We were waiting until more of our infantry should come.

"It was getting to be stupid work, however, and we were all hoping something would turn up, when we noticed two men ride out from the centre of their line and move towards us. At the first instant we paid little heed to them, supposing it some act of rebel bravado, when we saw quite a commotion all along the enemy's front, and then they commenced firing at the two riders, and then their line was all enveloped with smoke, out of which horsemen dashed in pursuit. The two riders kept well together, coming straight for us. Then we knew they were trying to escape, and the Colonel deployed our company as skirmishers to assist them. There wasn't time to do much, although, as I watched the pursued and their pursuers and found the two men had halted at what I could now see was a deep wide ditch, the moments seemed to be hours; and when they turned I thought they were going to give themselves up. But no; in the face of that awful fire they deliberately turned back to get space for a good run at the ditch. This gave time for two of their pursuers to get within a few yards of them, when they stopped, evidently in doubt as to the meaning of this retrograde movement. But they did not remain long in doubt, for the two men turned again, and, with a shout, rushed for the ditch, and then we were near enough to see that they were Wild Bill and his mate. Bill's companion never reached the ditch. He and his horse must have been shot at the same time, for they went down together and did not rise again.

"Bill did not get a scratch. He spoke to Black Nell, the mare you saw just now, who knew as well as her master that there was life and death in that twenty feet of ditch, and that she must jump it; and at it she went with a big rush. I never saw a more magnificent sight. Bill gave the mare her head, and turning in his saddle fired twice, killing both of his pursuers, who were within a few lengths of him. They were out of their saddles like stones, just as Black Nell flew into the air and landed safely on our side of the ditch. In a moment both the daring scout and the brave mare were in our midst, while our men cheered and yelled like mad.

"We asked Bill why he ran such a risk, when he could have stolen into our lines during the night?

"'Oh,' said he, 'mate and I wanted to show them cussed rebs what a Union soldier could do. We've been with them now for more than a month, and heard nothing but brag. We thought we'd take it out of them. But'—and Bill looked across the greensward to where his companion still lay motionless—'if they have killed my mate they shall pay a big price for it.'

"Bill must have brought valuable information," continued the lieutenant, "for he was at once sent to the General, and in an hour we had changed position, and foiled a flank movement of the rebels."

I went to the hotel during the afternoon to keep the scout's appointment. The large room of the hotel in Springfield is perhaps the central point of attraction in the city. It fronted on the street, and served in several capacities. It was a sort of exchange for those who had nothing better to do than to go there. It was reception-room, parlor, and office; but its distinguished and most fascinating characteristic was the bar, which occupied one entire end of the apartment. Technically, the "bar" is the counter upon which the polite official places his viands. Practically, the bar is represented in the long rows of bottles, and cut-glass decanters, and the glasses and goblets of all shapes and sizes suited to the various liquors to be imbibed. What a charming and artistic display it was of elongated transparent vessels containing every known drinking fluid, from native Bourbon to imported Lacryma Christi!

The room, in its way, was a temple of art. All sorts of pictures budded and blossomed and blushed from the walls. Six penny portraits of the Presidents encoffined in pine-wood frames; Mazeppa appeared in the four phases of his celebrated one-horse act; while a lithograph of "Mary Ann" smiled and simpered in spite of the stains of tobacco-juice which had been unsparingly bestowed upon her originally encarmined countenance. But the hanging committee of this undersigned academy seemed to have been prejudiced—as all hanging committees of good taste might well be—in favor of *Harper's Weekly;* for the walls of the room were covered with wood-cuts cut from that journal. Portraits of noted generals and statesmen, knaves and politicians, with bounteous illustrations of battles and skirmishes, from Bull Run number one to Dinwiddie Court House. And the simple-hearted comers and goers of Springfield looked upon, wondered, and admired these pictorial descriptions fully as much as if they had been the masterpieces of a Yvon or Vernet.

A billiard-table, old and out of use, where caroms seemed to have been made quite as often with lead as ivory balls, stood in the centre of the room. A dozen chairs, filled up the complement of the furniture. The appearance of the party of men assembled there who sat with their slovenly shod feet dangling over the arms of the chairs or hung about the porch outside, was in perfect harmony with the time and place. All of them religiously obeyed the two before-mentioned characteristics of the people of the city—their hair was long and tangled, and each man fulfilled the most exalted requirement of laziness.

I was talking a mental inventory of all this when a cry and murmur drew my attention to the outside of the house, when I saw Wild Bill riding up the street at a swift gallop. Arrived opposite the hotel, he swung his right arm around with a circular motion. Black Nell instantly stopped and dropped to the ground as if a cannon-ball had knocked life out of her. Bill left her there stretched upon the ground, and joined the group of observers on the porch.

"Black Nell hasn't forgot her old tricks," said one of them.

"No," answered the scout. "God bless her! She is wiser and truer than most men I know on. That mare will do any thing for me. Won't you, Nelly?"

The mare winked affirmatively the only eye we could see.

"Wise!" continued her master; "why, she knows more than a judge. I'll bet the drinks for the party that she'll walk up these steps and into the room and climb upon the billiard-table and lie down."

The bet was taken at once, not because any one doubted the capabilities of the mare, but there was excitement in the thing without exercise.

Bill whistled a low tone. Nell instantly scrambled to her feet, walked toward him, put her nose affectionately under his arm, followed him into the room, and to my extreme wonder-

ment climbed upon the billiard-table to the extreme astonishment of the table no doubt, for it groaned under the weight of
the four legged animal and several of those who were simply
bifurcated, and whom Nell permitted to sit upon her. When
she got down from the table, which was as graceful a performance as might be expected under the circumstances, Bill
sprang upon her back, dashed through the high wide doorway,
and at a single bound cleared the flight of steps and landed in
the middle of the street. The scout then dismounted, snapped
his riding-whip, and the noble beast bounded off down the
street, rearing and plunging to her own intense satisfaction. A
kindly- disposed individual who must have been a stranger,
supposing the mare was running away, tried to catch her,
when she stopped, and as if she resented his impertinence, let
fly her heels at him and then quietly trotted to her stable.

"Black Nell has carried me along through many a tight
place," said the scout, as we walked towards my quarters. "She
trains easier than any animal I ever saw. That trick of dropping
quick which you saw has saved my life time and again. When
I have been out scouting on the prarer or in the woods I have
come across parties of rebels, and have dropped out of sight in
the tall grass before they saw us. One day a gang of rebs who
had been hunting for me and thought they had my track, halted
for half an hour within fifty yards of us. Nell laid as close as a
rabbit, and didn't even whisk her tail to keep the flies off, until
the rebs moved off, supposing they were on the wrong scent.
The mare will come at my whistle and foller me about just like
a dog. She won't mind any one else, nor allow them to mount
her, and will kick a harness and wagon all ter pieces if you try
to hitch her in one. And she's right, Kernel," added Bill, with
the enthusiasm of a true lover of horse sparkling in his eyes.
"A hoss is too noble a beast to be degraded by such toggery.
Harness mules and oxen, but give a hoss a chance ter run."

I had a curiosity, which was not an idle one, to hear what
this man had to say about his duel with Tutt, and I asked him:

"Do you not regret killing Tutt? You surely do not like to
kill men?"

"As ter killing men," he replied, "I never thought much

about it. The most of the men I have killed it was one or t'other of us, and at sich times you don't stop to think; and what's the use after it's all over? As for Tutt, I had rather not have killed him, for I want ter settle down quiet here now. But thar's been hard feeling between us a long while. I wanted ter keep out of that fight; but he tried to degrade me, and I couldn't stand that, you know, for I am a fighting man, you know."

A cloud passed over the speaker's face for a moment as he continued: "And there was a cause of quarrel between us which people round here don't know about. One of us had to die; and the secret died with him."

"Why did you not wait to see if your ball had hit him? Why did you turn round so quickly?"

The scout fixed his gray eyes on mine, striking his leg with his riding-whip as he answered,

"I *knew* he was a dead man. I never miss a shot. I turned on the crowd because I was sure they would shoot me if they saw him fall."

"The people about here tell me you are a quiet, civil man. How is it you get into these fights?"

"D——d if I can tell," he replied with a puzzled look which at once gave place to a proud, defiant expression as he continued—"but you know a man must defend his honor."

"Yes," I admitted, with some hesitation, remembering that I was not in Boston but on the border, and that the code of honor and mode of redress differ slightly in the one place from those of the other.

One of the reasons for my desire to make the acquaintance of Wild Bill was to obtain from his own lips a true account of some of the adventures related to him. It was not an easy matter. It was hard to overcome the reticence which makes men who have lived the wild mountain life, and which was one of his valuable qualifications as a scout. Finally he said:

"I hardly know where to begin. Pretty near all these stories are true. I was at it all the war. That affair of my swimming the river took place on that long scout of mine when I was with the rebels five months, when I was sent by General Curtis to Price's army. Things had come pretty close at that time, and it wasn't safe to go straight inter their lines—"

I had heard enough and let my thoughts drift back over the stories that Nichols had embellished so much in his article—I could hardly recognize them—but he had caught a hint of the story for the duel between Dave Tutt and myself. It wasn't so much the watch as it was Susannah Moore, whom Tutt had been trying to talk into bed ever since I had known him. As to killing his "mate," I had no idea where that came from and I was certain that if Tutt was still alive, he would have wondered what mate Nichols was talking about as well.

As to the war—well, there were moments, and then there were moments, but nothing like the stories Nichols claimed he had heard. Yes, there had been nearly four weeks when I was lost in the woods and sick after Israel's death, but that was a private matter that I kept to myself. I had made the long shot on a Confederate colonel that everyone said was impossible and there was as much luck in that shot as skill as I had held high over his head and hoped the bullet would loop itself down at the right moment and it did. I remembered the battle of Wilson's Creek, running supply wagons from Rolla to Springfield with Lorenzo, fighting at Pea Ridge in Arkansas with Curtis—where I had made a lucky shot at a Confederate officer, knocking him into a ditch, but it was not General Ben McCulloch, as everyone claimed—among several other places. But there is a long way between truth and the storyteller and—

I became aware of the silence in the saloon and glanced around. The others were looking expectantly at me, grins wide on their faces. I wondered what all Bob had read to them, then knew I had to say something.

"If I ever talked like that, my father would have given me a tongue-lashing that would peel paint off a fence," I said.

The others collapsed in peals of laughter, whooping and hollering at my statement. I felt a dull red mounting to my cheeks and shook my head. "And damn the man who can't tell a stallion from a mare. Black's blind in one eye and she's a he and—"

All of which made them laugh even harder. I gave up in disgust and left, my ears burning from the lies of Nichols and promising myself that I wouldn't go through another episode with another writer as long as I lived. But once a person has such a story written about him, he is no longer the private person he wants to be; he has become a public person, and the public does not care for the truth. The lies are much more interesting to them and that article became the springboard for hundreds of others until I couldn't recognize any resemblance to me at all.

In time, I became lost in that identity, the Scout of the Plains, the killer of Indians and badmen. Charlemagne would have been proud to have me as one of his paladins, and in some of the stories I thought I recognized a vague resemblance to those stories Father used to read to us on cold wintry nights with the wind whistling outside and the fire roaring up the chimney and sending warmth back into the room. But any further chance at those days was gone forever after Nichols's story came out. The rest of my life was spent being the legend, not the man. But I had had plenty of warning about that.

CHAPTER

37

FORT RILEY stood upon the Kansas plain like a large keltoid scar while the land rolled gently in endless brown waves away from it from horizon to horizon, no beginning, no ending, just countless miles in any direction one looked.

Black's hooves kicked up a fine sifting of dust as he moved down the road toward the fort. Although it had been a long ride from the Ozark hills, he still moved effortlessly through the heavy heat that brought crinkly heat waves rising in the distance against the low hills. A thin trickle of sweat ran down my spine and my mouth felt like a wad of cotton had been stuffed in it. My eyes stung and my skin prickled beneath my blue shirt and the inside of my thighs felt chafed from rubbing so long against the saddle leather.

There had been no rush to leave Springfield, yet I felt the time had come after I lost the election for marshal. Strangely, I didn't seem to care as much as those who had supported me. They took it hard and threw dark looks at the gleeful celebrants the night the results were announced. A restlessness had come over me in the past few weeks along with a certain infamy that hung over me as I moved along the Springfield streets after Nichols's article became familiar to the people. Boys dogged my footsteps, wooden pistols tucked into waistbands in emulation of me, adopting my walk as their own. Women tilted their heads and coquettishly batted eyes at me. I picked up many scented handkerchiefs dropped "accidentally" in front of me as their owners sashayed past me, balancing parasols over their shoulders. Men either sneered in derison or teased me relentlessly in saloons and cafés. Yet there were some who cast withering glances at me and spit when they spoke my name.

A normal life was no longer an option for me. At least, not in Springfield. And the easy money flung recklessly over the gambling halls by ex-soldiers frantically searching for a taste of the excitement they had known in the war began to dry up. When an offer came for me to return to working for the government, I seized it and left for Fort Riley, taking a roundabout way to pay a strained visit to Mother. But I didn't stay as long as I had planned. Resentment still ran high within each of us despite the four long years that had passed while I was in the war. Although Mary was a distant memory—I could scarce recall her name—Mother's meddling still rankled me, while she considered my anger unwarranted and became angry herself, a defense she had used all her life, even when she knew she was in the wrong. I left with a sour taste in my mouth and my guts churning, riding Black in the general direction of Fort Riley as I thought about the wire that had found me while I was working my way through the mellow stage of a bottle of Old Hickory.

The field officers at Fort Riley were going ragged trying to bring order to the post from the chaos that had engulfed it after the end of the war. When Captain R. B. Owen was appointed the assistant quartermaster at Fort Riley, he sent a wire to me in Springfield asking me if I would come and help out as a deputy U.S. marshal. The teamsters and soldiers were often at odds with each other, and fights were frequent and often deadly. The army had fallen into a deplorable state after the war, with several recruits enlisting

for the sole purpose of being sent west, where they promptly
deserted after stealing horses and mules from the army stables and corrals. The scouts did not help matters, either, by
siding with the teamsters against the bullying of the soldiers.

I rode into the fort and noticed a teamster and soldier
rolling in the dust behind the stables, cursing and striking
wildly at each other. I paused for a moment, then shook my
head and rode on until I found Owen's office. Wearily I dismounted and tied Black to a post, made a halfhearted effort
to dust myself, then climbed the steps and entered the office,
ducking my head as I crossed under the short doorway. I
paused for a second to allow my eyes to adjust to the cool
dim light inside, then found my hand being seized and
heartily shaken by Owen.

"Bill! Damn, but if you aren't a sight for sore eyes!" he
exclaimed, beaming at me.

I returned his grip and nodded. "Got your wire in Springfield and it just seemed like too good a chance to pass up," I
declared. "You say you have a problem here?"

His face fell and he released my hand and moved behind
his desk to his chair, motioning me to another across the
desk from him. "Yes, a severe problem," he said. He gestured toward the window. "We are in danger of losing control of the fort unless something can be done quickly. We are
losing horses and mules almost every day as someone
deserts and takes them with him and I don't have enough
troops to mount a regular provost marshal patrol. In fact," he
added gloomily, "I don't know which soldiers are honest
enough to put on such a patrol even if I had enough to go
around."

"Uh-huh," I said, stretching until the kinks popped out of
my back. "And you want me to do what, exactly?"

Owen made a face. "A bit of everything, I'm afraid. I've
secured an appointment for you as a deputy U.S. marshal,
but you will not report to Tom Osborne, the United States
marshal for Kansas. For all practical purposes, you will report to me or the commander. Marshal Osborne is a bit upset
about this, but"—he shrugged—"he hasn't been able to help

us, either, being tied up with the rest of the state and all. No, we need someone for ourselves. We can also use your expertise as a scout." He grimaced. "Ours are a bit less than competent and I'm not certain if I would trust them to find water in a horse trough. Fact is, I planned on making you the chief of scouts. You will have total authority to do your job."

He slid the badge and my appointment across the table to me.

"We'll put you up in officers' quarters. That way, you'll have a bit of privacy and I think that will send a message to the others that change is coming. It might make your job a bit easier. But," he said, waggling a finger at me, "don't think that this is going to be a cakewalk. You are going to have one hard time bringing order here."

I yawned and slipped the badge and paper into my pocket. "Well, if it's all right with you, I'd like to get a bath and cleaned up a bit and Black taken care of before I start. I'd also like a meal. How about tomorrow?"

Owen shrugged and leaned back in his chair. "One more day won't make any difference. Fact is, I thought about sending you out after a couple of deserters who left sometime last night. They took nine good Arkansas mules with them as well."

"All right," I said, yawning again. My eyes felt sandy and at the moment all I really wanted was a bath and bed. "I'll get after them first thing in the morning. Black could use a rest, though. Okay if I take another mount?"

"Take what you want," he said magnanimously. "I'll have a pack ready for you by sunup."

"Sounds good," I said, standing. I shook his hand. "I'll help myself to a mount once I see your stock."

I left and winced as the hot sun blinded me for a moment. Black grunted disconsolately and I grinned at him and stepped down, untying him. "You old phony," I said, rubbing him between the eyes. "You'd grumble if you were the only stud in a field of mares and had a bait of oats at your beck and call."

Black shoved me with his nose. I laughed again and took

his reins and walked him across the parade ground to the re-mount stables. A burly man wearing a dirty pair of faded red longhandles worked an anvil on a blacksmith's bench. Heat from the forge rolled out in an acrid wave. A sorrel stood hip-shot next to him, head drooping in the heat as it waited patiently to be shod. He glanced up at me, then at Black, and shook his head. He spit a long stream of tobacco juice and shifted his cud past rubbery lips to the other cheek.

"That there ain't no army horse," he proclaimed.

"Nope," I said. "He's mine." I started to lead him into the stables beyond, but the smithy dropped his hammer and stepped in front of me, placing a soot-blackened hand against my chest to stop me.

"You ain't listening. Ain't no horse but army horses coming in here," he said. Sweat stood out in huge drops upon his face and I could smell the sour odor he hadn't washed off in at least a week. "I gotta 'nough to do with these damn sojers bringing in their nags what with having to deal with another's. Take him on down to Junction City and stable him there."

"I'm working here," I said quietly.

His eyes ran rudely up and down; then he laughed and shook his head. "Don't look like it to me. What you workin' at?"

"Deputy U.S. marshal," I said quietly.

"Uh-huh," he said, and shook his head. "But that ain't makin' cotton with me. You think you bringing that nag in here, you're barking at a knot, sure as a skunk smells."

"Couldn't smell any worse than you," I said impatiently. "Now step aside—"

I could see the punch coming in his eyes before he had time to draw back his fist. I twisted at the hips and threw a fist deep into his gut just above his belt buckle. He sucked in a gulp of air and the cud slipped down his gullet. His face turned a shade green as he sank to his knees and spewed a bile green and yellow mess onto the hard-packed dirt in front of the forge.

"Sorry," I said, "but I'm just too damn tired to waltz

around with you." I fished the badge out of my pocket and held it down in front of his watering eyes. "Now you paste an eyeball on this and take real good care of Black here. Nobody else is to ride him, and if they want to know why, you tell them Marshal Hickok has said no. Understand?"

He nodded, and strangled noises came from his throat. He gagged again and turned his head. The cud of tobacco plopped in the middle of the mess in front of him. "Ain't Wild Bill?" he gasped.

I sighed. "There's some who call me that. Good as name as any, I suppose."

I led Black down to a stall at the end of the stable and unsaddled him. I found a brush and worked him down as he contented himself with a small bait of oats. When I left the stable an hour later, I saw word of my arrival had spread. Soldiers watched curiously as I made my way back across the parade ground to the officers' bathhouse.

An orderly silently took my saddlebags and bedroll and said he would take them down to my quarters. I had the third room. He had drawn a bath for me, but he was afraid the water had cooled some. I told him that was all right and he left, grateful that I hadn't made him heat up more.

I stripped and eased myself into the tub and relaxed as much as I could. But at twenty-eight I was at nearly six-three and around a hundred eighty pounds, and tubs on army posts weren't made that size. Still, I was grateful and slowly soaked away the knots of travel.

CHAPTER

38

I LEFT the post at false light, riding the sorrel the smithy had been shoeing and tugging a high-stepping mule behind me with a camp pack tied tightly with a diamond hitch. The smithy was all apologies for his conduct the day before and quick to make amends, his eyes straying constantly to the twin Colts at my waist. I read his concern and tried to make him feel at ease but knew my reputation made him wonder if I was sincere.

I swung a wide loop around the post until I found the trail of the two deserters and the nine mules. I smiled to myself at their confidence, as they had made no attempt to hide it, electing instead to ride steadily toward the southwest. I sighed and settled back in the saddle and pointed the sorrel down the trail after them. I let the horse make his own track. I had a suspicion that the deserters would change mounts quite a few times among the mules, electing to ride steadily for a day or more before making camp, wishing to put as many miles between them and the fort as possible. I had only the sorrel and, in a pinch, the mule and was outhorsed.

But there's a funny thing about a man who thinks he's in the clear: He gets lazy, and I was counting on that happening, if not at the end of this day surely by the next or the one after that. The trick was not to wear my mounts out too early in case the deserters caught sight of me and made a run for it.

It took two days, and in the evening of the second I caught the flicker of a campfire tucked up in a stand of cottonwood trees on the banks of the Little Arkansas River. I reined in and tied the sorrel to a tree and settled down to wait for an hour or two.

When the half moon climbed up by the Dipper, I rose and made my way downstream. One of the mules caught my approach and snorted and I froze, my heart leaping; then I heard the twin snores coming from the blanket-wrapped forms curled around the embers of their fire. I shook my head; they were lucky a roving band of Indians hadn't come upon them. It was a misconception of most white men that Indians didn't fight at night. Something about their souls losing their way to the happy hunting grounds if they were killed in the dark. But that wasn't true; the happy hunting grounds didn't exist and most Indians had nothing against the cover of darkness.

I simply walked into the camp and dropped a couple of branches on the fire and waited until it flared up. Then I took a glowing branch and held it against the foot of one of the deserters. He yelped and came clawing up out of his blankets, grabbing his foot and howling as he rolled around on the ground.

The other sat up quickly, fumbling for his pistol, then froze as I stuck the barrel of one of the Navies between his eyes and rocked back the hammer.

"Uh-uh," I said quietly. "You don't want to do that."

"I don't want to do that," he parroted, his eyes crossed and staring hard down the shiny barrel.

I reached and took his pistol from him and stepped back. "Keep your hands in plain sight," I cautioned.

The other man was trying to blow on the bottom of his foot to cool it as he hopped down to the river. He fell on the clay bank and jabbed both feet in, puddling the burnt foot in the shallows to cool it. He sighed and looked back at me.

"What's the big idea?" he demanded, then saw the pistol in my hand, and his eyes widened. He raised his hands up to his shoulders. "Look, we ain't got much, mister, but you're welcome to it. Just leave us one mule, will you? It ain't civilized to leave a white man without a ride in hostile country."

"It's stupid for a white man to camp by a fire in hostile country, too," I said. "You should have had your dinner, then moved camp a few miles away. You're lucky to have your throat in one piece."

His hand automatically cupped his throat. "Who are you?"

"I'm Deputy U.S. Marshal James Butler Hickok and you two are under arrest for desertion and stealing army property," I said.

"Aw, shit," the other man said. "I told you we should've hid that trail. But no, you hadda ride on down. 'No one'll come after us,' you said. And now look at the mess we're in." He looked up at me. "Say, you wouldn't consider—"

"Nope," I said. "I wouldn't. Now let's just get ourselves ready to return to the fort, shall we?"

"It's the middle of the night!" the man with the burnt foot said.

"It is that," I answered. "And I want to put a little distance between us and this place just in case there's a hunting party of Indians out and about."

"I'll get my boots," he said, standing and wincing.

"Nope," I answered. "We'll just leave the two of you boot-less. Be a lot easier on me if you have to think about it before you decide to take off."

"This—this—ain't no white man treat another like this!" he sputtered.

"Yes, they would. Especially in this situation. Now un-hobble those mules and get up on one. Don't use a saddle. I want you riding bareback."

They looked at those mules with their sharp-ridged backs, and their shoulders slumped in dismay.

"Have a heart," the first man begged. "We go two miles rubbing up and down on those spines and we'll have sores to gall a grizzly."

"And no thoughts of running, either," I answered. I motioned with the pistol. "Let's get moving. Now."

CHAPTER

39

WE TOOK four days to get back to Fort Riley. One day we had to lay up in a little wash while we waited on a Kiowa hunting party to work its way by us—not that there was much to hunt, but the Kiowa were a long way from their hunting grounds and probably figured they'd better keep an eye open for the Comanches, who took a dim view of trespassers in general and thought the whole world was their walking ground. I couldn't blame them; from what I had seen, the white man wasn't far behind in making his claim, either.

When we finally rode in through Fort Riley's gates, Captain Owen grinned from ear to ear as he ordered the two weary troopers to be taken to the guardhouse. He glanced up at me and said, "You look like you could use a wash and a rub from the inside out."

I scrubbed my hand over my chin, grimacing at the rasp of bristles, and said, "Well, I allow as to how you're probably right, but I think I'd just as soon have a bath and shave and sleep for a day or two."

Captain Owen shook his head. "Not that I'm begrudging you that, but we have General Sherman here, since you've been gone. He's putting together an expedition up north and needs someone to guide him. Someone who knows that country," he added.

I swore and sagged in the saddle, feeling the weight of the miles like a steel anvil upon my shoulders. I shook my head. "When?"

"You have about six hours, I'd suspect," Captain Owen said. "Of course, who knows with that Blood and Thunder? He gets a burr under his saddle, he'll be wanting to go."

"Uh-huh," I grunted, and turned my horse away, heading toward the stables. "Well, you tell him that if he wants me to scout for him, to head due north if he wants to leave before I'm ready. I'll pick him up. He won't get into any trouble in that short distance."

"Tell Sherman?" Captain Owen asked incredulously. "Might as well tell the wind to stop blowing. You'd better be ready when he's ready. He waits on no one."

"Then you'd better get Cody to scout," I called over my shoulder.

"Cody's not here, dammit!" he said, raising his voice. "And I wouldn't want to be the one to tell the general anything he might not want to hear! Men have been ruined for less than that!"

And so, six hours later, I found myself on Black's back, gritty-eyed but washed, and heading north up toward the Rock Creek country I had left so long ago, as we made our way up to Fort McPherson with a detachment, including Dr. William Finlaw and his family. Dr. Finlaw was scheduled to be the new post surgeon, and Sherman decided that rather than send a separate troop to accompany him to the fort, we'd just make a little detour and drop Dr. Finlaw and his family off at McPherson on the way. This was typical of Sherman, though; impetuous and impatient at all times, he somehow managed to temper that with a bit of common sense at the crucial moments that kept him mortal and human.

The third night out, I was sitting with Dick Curtis, another scout, by our campfire when a small girl appeared hesitantly at the edge of the fire.

"Hello," Curtis said. "What's your name?"

I looked up and noticed the little girl staring solemnly at me. I smiled at her and went on with cleaning my Navy Colt, figuring that she was just wandering around before bedtime like most kids do when they're bored but don't want to go to bed.

"Sally," she said timidly.

"That's a pretty name," Curtis said. "Your mommy and daddy know where you are?"

She didn't answer and I looked up to catch her nodding, still staring at me. Then I realized it was my hair, which had grown long and now hung over my shoulders. I smiled again at her and suddenly remembered that I had a stick of peppermint candy in one of my saddlebags.

"You like peppermint?" I asked.

Her eyes lit up and she nodded. I smiled and slipped the cylinder back onto its axle and snapped the barrel in place. I laid the revolver aside and wiped my hands on a bit of rag before pulling my saddlebags to me. I rummaged around for a bit, then found the sack and pulled it out. I was wrong; there were two sticks of peppermint left.

"You been holding out on me, Bill!" Curtis said accusingly. I grinned at him and held the candy out to the girl. Most of the dime dreadfuls made a big deal about the drinking habits of the scouts and westerners, but few ever said that most of those who lived on the plains and in the mountains had a sweet tooth and often had a piece of hard rock candy whenever they sat down with a glass of whiskey. I was no different. There were times when rolling around a piece of candy in the cheek made one feel better after a long hard day on the trail when one really didn't dare drink.

"Well, to tell you the truth, Dick, I totally forgot I had it, what with the hurrying up and everything before we left the post," I said. The little girl fastened her eyes upon the bag but hesitated until I shook it at her. "Go on—take it," I said. "Better you should have it than this old man and me."

Timidly she came forward and took the candy from my hand, then surprised me by reaching out to touch my hair.

"It's like silk," she said solemnly. "Like Momma's. Why do you wear it like that? My daddy doesn't."

Curtis started chuckling and reached over to pour himself another cup of coffee from the pot we had placed next to the fire's coals to keep warm. "Now let's hear you with that one, Wild Bill," he said.

She glanced over at Curtis. "Why does he call you Wild Bill?" she asked me.

I shrugged. "It's just a name someone stuck on me. My name's really Jim."

"My daddy told me about you," she said, turning to look at me with wide cornflower blue eyes. "Did you really kill all those men?"

Curtis coughed, but I refused to rise to his snorting and chuckling. I shook my head. "Well, I don't know about all because I don't know what your daddy told you," I said. "And it really isn't important. I just do the job that I'm supposed to do."

"But you have killed some bad people," she persisted.

"Yes, I have shot some bad people," I said. "To keep them from hurting others."

"I guess that's all right," she answered, then turned to look back into the dusk as her mother called her name.

"I think I'd better go now," she said. "Momma gets worried if I don't come when she calls."

I rose and dusted off the seat of my trousers and held out my hand, bowing courteously. "Well, Mistress Sally, would you like me to walk you back to your wagon?"

She giggled. "You're silly," she said, but she placed her hand in mine and together we crossed the camp to the ambulance where Dr. Finlaw and his family had made their beds. A twinge of regret came over me as I felt her tiny hand in mine and I had a strange premonition that I would never have any children or know the warmth of a family of my own. By the time we arrived at the Finlaws' cook fire, a lonely melancholy had settled over me.

"Hello, Mr. Hickok," Dr. Finlaw said when he saw the two of us. He glanced at Sally, still clinging to my hand and sucking on one of the peppermint sticks. "What have you got there, Sally?"

"Wild Bill gave it to me," she said. She looked up at me. "Isn't that right?"

"Yes," I said, "but you could do me a big favor by calling me Jim."

"I like Bill better," she said.

"And Mr. Hickok would be even better," her mother said, coming up to gather her. She nodded politely at me. "I hope Sally didn't bother you, Mr. Hickok."

I shook my head. I sensed her concern behind her politeness and knew she worried as any mother would if she found her child in the presence of a man who had blood on his hands.

"I enjoyed her company," I said politely. "I don't get a chance to talk with children much. It's a relief."

She quirked an eyebrow at that, then said, "Tell Mr. Hickok good night, Sally. It's bedtime."

"Good night, Mr. Hickok," she said dutifully.

"Good night, Sally," I said.

"Will you stay here with us?"

I raised my eyebrows at that and glanced at her father. He smiled faintly and gave a tiny nod.

"Sally has nightmares when we're out here like this," he said. "She's afraid the Indians will sneak her away." He made a gesture. "It's all those stories she's heard."

"I wouldn't be afraid if Mr. Hickok was here," she said. "No Indian would want to come around someone named Wild Bill."

I smiled and went back to the fire I'd been sharing with Curtis and gathered my belongings and carried them back to the ambulance and spread out my bedroll under the wagon. I slept under that wagon for the rest of the trip, enjoying the time in the evening and early morning when Sally would stay close to me.

When we hit the Blue River, I took her bullfrogging in the sloughs and slipped and fell with a loud *ker-splash!* in the water when my foot rolled over a dead branch submerged in the shallows as I was reaching for a particularly large bullfrog. She laughed and laughed when I struggled up, a water lily hanging over my shoulder but still holding the squirming frog in one hand. I glared at him and said, "Well, you're one for the roasting pan!"

That set her off laughing until she had to hold her sides and sit on the bank. We caught a mess of bullfrogs and took them back to camp, where her mother rolled their legs in flour and fried them up for a fine supper.

All too soon, however, the trip came to an end and Sherman's expedition made its way up to Fort Kearney, where I scouted for some short patrols while Sherman debated about mounting a large expedition up into the Dakotas to chase the Sioux. I hoped the weather would start to change and hold him in the fort until spring. I knew what it was like being out on the prairie in winter and didn't relish trying to scout through drifts and spending my nights curled in blankets as close to a fire as possible, hoping my toes wouldn't be frozen by morning.

Common sense held Sherman out of the Dakotas, however, and he returned to Fort Riley. There I met Henry M. Stanley, who had come west as the correspondent of the *New York Herald.* We met in a saloon and I could tell right away that he was looking for stories and on impulse I spun him a few yarns, watching his eyes widen as he scribbled with a short pencil on a handful of papers he always carried in the pocket of his coat. Later I would remember that short pencil must have shortened his memory some, too, for when I read some of the dispatches he sent back to his paper I could scarce recognize the stories I had told him in the whoppers that emerged from those yellow pages. A careful check of records would have shown Stanley that I couldn't have been in two places at once, but those writers like Stanley are too impatient for that. They just want to see the story in print and find their pockets a little heavier with the jingle the stories bring.

While the army decided to settle in and began to winterize itself, I took advantage of the fall weather to make my way over to Kansas City for a last fling before the snow came. Market Square turned out to be quite a haven for others who were having their last fling as well. Buffalo hunters lounged around along with a lot of professional gamblers and some scouts like me. Wyatt Earp was there along with Luke Short, who liked to sit with me in the cool evenings, sharing a bottle or two while we discussed Shakespeare. I remember Short had a likening for *Henry V*, while I thought *Hamlet* was a better play. I was grateful that Dad had insisted we study Shakespeare and for the schooling I had, as, frankly, I took a better shine to Short than I did to some of the others who preferred to wrap their hands around bottles of whiskey and talk about what they'd left behind out west.

I also took to a new game I'd heard about but never seen—baseball. Kansas City had a team they called the Antelopes that played against other town teams on a field they'd made ready at Fourteenth and Oak streets. There was a great rivalry between the Antelopes and the Atchison Pomeroys, and when the Pomeroys came to town for a game a riot had evolved when the Pomeroys drove the umpire from the field, halting the game before either side had won. They decided to play the game again the next Saturday and this time find an umpire that couldn't be driven from the field.

I was sitting in Jake Fourcade's room at Fourth and Main, having a quiet game with Short, arguing about *Richard III,* when one of the city fathers came up and cleared his throat. I looked up and politely pushed my chair back from the table to hear what he had to say.

"Uh, Mr. Hickok, a couple of us have taken note that you've been coming to the Antelopes' games and . . ." He hesitated, swallowing nervously.

"Yes?" I said. "I hope that's all right. I'm kind of getting to like that game. Never saw it before."

"Yes, well, no," he stammered. "I mean, no, there's nothing wrong with that; it's just that— Look here, would you be willing to umpire a rematch with the Pomeroys next Saturday?" He fidgeted and sweat began to bead upon his forehead. "What I mean is, well, those rascals drove our umpire away just as we got up a couple of runs. We want someone that they won't drive away and will last until the game's over. It's a matter of pride," he said. "I mean honor."

"Well, Bill," Short laughed. "What would Richard do in a time like this?"

"I don't know," I said, "but I sure know Henry wouldn't run away."

He laughed again and pushed his chair back, tossing his cards into the middle of the table. He rose from the chair—he was short in more than just his name—and, placing his hand over his heart, gesturing like Booth with the other, declaimed:

> *"He which hath no stomach to this fight,*
> *Let him depart; his passport shall be made,*
> *And crowns for convoy put into his purse:*
> *We would not die in that man's company*
> *That fears his fellowship to die with us.*
> *This day is called the feast of Crispian:*
> *He that outlives this day and comes safe home,*
> *Will stand a tip-toe when this day is named,*
> *And rouse him at the name of Crispian.*
> *He that shall live this day, and see old age,*
> *Will yearly on the vigil feast his neighbours,*
> *And say, 'Tomorrow is Saint Crispian':*
> *Then will he strip his sleeve and show his scars,*
> *And say, 'These wounds I had on Crispian's day.'*
> *Old men forget: yet all shall be forgot,*
> *But he'll remember with advantages*
> *What feats he did that day. Then shall our names,*
> *Familiar in his mouth as household words,*
> *Harry the King, Bedford and Exeter,*
> *Warwick and Talbot, Salisbury and Gloucester,*
> *Be in their flowing cups freshly remembered.*
> *This story shall the good man teach his son;*

And Crispin Crispian shall ne'er go by,
From this day to the ending of the world,
But we in it shall be remembered;
We few, we happy few, we band of brothers;
For he to-day that sheds his blood with me
Shall be my brother; be he ne'er so vile
This day shall gentle his condition:

"And gentlemen in England, now a-bed
Shall think themselves accursed they were not here,
And hold their manhoods cheap whiles any speaks
That fought with us upon Saint Crispian's day."

"Damn," someone muttered, "but that Short has a way with the words."

Short grinned and cocked an expectant eye at me. I rose and gave a mock bow, sweeping my hat off, and, holding it over my breast, said:

"There's the respect
That makes calamity of so long life;
For who would bear the whips and scorns of time,
The oppressor's wrong, the proud man's contumely,
The pangs of deprized—"

"'Disprized,'" Short interrupted. "For Christ's sake, quote accurately."

"Shut up," I muttered, and continued:

"The insolence of office, and the spurns
That patient merit of the unworthy takes,
When he himself might his quietus make
With a bare bodkin? who would fardels bear,
To grunt and sweat under a weary life,
But that the dread of something after death,
The undiscovered country from whose bourn
No traveller returns, puzzles the will,
And makes us rather bear those ills we have,

> *Than fly to others that we know not of?*
> *Thus conscience doth make cowards of us all;*
> *And thus the native hue of resolution*
> *Is sicklied o'er with the pale cast of thought,*
> *And enterprises of great pith and moment*
> *With this regard their currents turn awry,*
> *And lose the name of action."*

"Shit, Hickok ain't no slouch at those words, either," the same man said loudly as a smattering of applause followed the end of my speech.

"Not bad," Short said grudgingly. "I always wondered: What are 'fardels'?"

I started to give him the definition Father had drummed into us, but the man beside me cleared his throat. I looked down at him.

"Excuse me," he said. "That was well done and all, but, er, what, that is, will you umpire the game?"

"Yes," Short said, drawing himself up as much as he could—his head came bare to my shoulder and damn if he didn't remind me then of a cocky rooster. "That's just what Wild Bill's been saying."

"Jim," I muttered, but to no effect. "Dammit—"

"A man is nothing but his name," Short said. "And Jim does not fit well with your demeanor. Rather a Bill—nay, a Wild Bill art thou!"

"Oh hell," I said. "Yes, I'll umpire your game."

The man beamed and shook my hand enthusiastically, pumping my arm as if trying to draw water from a reluctant well.

And so it came that I found myself behind the home plate that Saturday, umpiring a game I knew little about. Not knowing what an umpire should wear, I had decked myself out in a silk hat, brocaded vest, calfskin boots, a velvet-collared frock coat, and a fine shirt with starched ruffle. I wore a red sash around my waist and placed in it a pair of ivory-handled Colt Navies that had been given to me by Senator Henry Wilson after I had guided his party on a short trip into the plains. I have to admit that I certainly made the best-looking umpire the Antelopes ever hired—Short's words, not mine.

The game started and soon it was apparent that the Antelopes were the better team, and they jumped out to a big 15–0 lead. That was when the Pomeroys decided to try me a bit. A big, broad-shouldered man with hands like a blacksmith's came up to bat. Shorty Anderson was pitching for the Antelopes and whizzed one by the plate.

"Strike!" I called.

The batter stepped back away from the plate and glared at me. "That was nowhere near the base!" he snapped.

Shorty noticed the batter's attention was on me and took the opportunity to whip another ball across the plate.

"Strike two!" I called.

"What the hell?" the batter yelled. "Goddammit, I wasn't ready!"

"That's your problem, not mine!" I said. Out of the corner of my eye, I saw Shorty winding up to heave another ball across the plate. "But if I were you, I'd keep my eye on that pitcher."

"You sonofabitch! We're being homered!" he yelled at his teammates. He waved one huge fist under my nose.

I didn't wait; I hauled off and punched him on the buzzer, knocking him backward. He staggered, trying to keep his feet, but one foot rolled over a bat and he sat down abruptly on the ground as Shorty pitched another ball over the plate.

"Strike three! You're out!" I called.

The Pomeroys started out onto the field, but I stepped in front of the plate and hooked my hands around my pistols and stared at them.

"Something wrong with the call?" I asked innocently.

A couple started forward but were jerked back by their teammates. I glanced at the batter as he struggled to his feet, blood streaming down his nose.

"No, no," he mumbled. "Guess I should've been paying attention to the game."

He went back to his teammates as the Antelopes jogged in

to take their place batting. The game proceeded without a hitch to the end, and the Antelopes won, 48–28, and Short appeared with a carriage to give me a ride back to Market Square. People cheered as we rode slowly down the streets. It was one of my finest moments.

CHAPTER

40

ALL THINGS come to an end, however, and I had to make my way back to Fort Riley. I found the fort a changed place in the month I'd been gone. A new regiment of cavalry was being formed—the Seventh—with a new commander: Lieutenant Colonel George Armstrong Custer, who persisted in wearing the brevet rank of general he'd been given during the war. He was a colorful sort who appealed to me, wearing his blond hair nearly as long as I did (although I could tell his was thinning faster than mine on top), and had a liking for fringed buckskin coats with his general's stars sewn on the shoulders and a flashy red silk scarf around his neck.

But it was his wife, Elizabeth, that drew my attention more. Her eyes seemed to follow me around the room whenever I was in it, making me feel a bit hot and uncomfortable from the frank intensity of her stare. I hoped Custer wouldn't notice it, and as far as I know, he never did. But whenever his attention drifted, I found her standing close to me so that a feather would barely have been able to fit between us. She wore a cinnamon scent that seemed to roll up from her shoulders and high breasts, and there were times when I'd leave their home and make my way to the saloon to drink away the stirrings that she rose in me.

I spent most of my time, however, down in the Solomon River valley, which was a favorite hangout for the riffraff that were trying to strip the fort of its horses. Cody came to join me at the fort, and together we made a big dent in the thieves that had taken to settling in shanties and soddies in that valley.

But Cody couldn't be with me all the time and there came a time—December 22 in '67, I remember—when I found myself at a crossroads saloon somewhere in Jefferson County up in Nebraska. I had been following the trail of some horse thieves and the night came down cold with a hint of snow to it, so I decided to wait out the night in the saloon rather than get caught in a snowstorm along the trail.

It was a sad, evilly run place with barrels and stoned planks serving as a bar. Whiskey was drawn from a keg, the bartender ignoring the few dusty bottles that stood on a short plank table behind the bar. The walls were earth bricks and the chairs were old wooden boxes that were gathered around a potbellied stove at the back of the room.

Heads turned to look at me when I walked through the door. The hackles rose on the back of my neck as I recognized the unfriendliness of the herders who had made their way, like me, to the saloon to wait out the storm. For a moment I thought I didn't know anyone in that place and almost turned and left, but then I thought, *The hell with it.* The room was warm and I could keep my back against a wall. Then I saw Seth Beeber, Jack Slater, Frank Dowder, and Jack Harkness—four cusses who were friends of a couple of men I had taken to Fort Riley for stealing horses.

"Well, well," Beeber said when I stepped up to the bar, elbowing my way to the end to put the wall at my back. "Would you all look who came in?"

"Hickok," Slater answered. His ferret eyes stared unblinking at me. "Thought I heard you'd lost your fine hair down at Sandy Creek."

"You heard wrong," I said. I motioned to the bartender, who drew a glass of whiskey and placed it silently in front of me. I tasted it and my throat tried to close against the trickle going down. I frowned and said to the bartender, "What'd you do? Throw in a couple plugs of tobacco and some rattlesnake heads?" I pushed the glass away from me and pointed to the dusty bottles on the table. "Let's try one of those—unless it came from the same barrel."

"Cost is two bits more," he said. His teeth were blackened stumps in his mouth.

"And a clean glass," I said, noticing the rim of dirt around the one I'd just sipped from.

"What's the matter, Hickok?" Dowder sneered. "You don't want to drink with us?"

"No," I said frankly. "I'm particular about who I drink with."

I took the drink the bartender poured from one of the bottles and had started to raise it to my lips when Harkness suddenly reached out and gave me a shove. The whiskey splattered into my face. I dropped the glass and backhanded him across the face, splitting his lip, knocking him back and away from me.

"Better stop this before it gets serious," I said.

"Bastard!" Harkness yelped, and tugged at his gun. The other three went for their pistols at the same time. I flipped one of the Navies out and shot Harkness in the jaw. Beeber's bullet struck me in the right shoulder, staggering me. Two other bullets fanned the air where I'd been. I slipped the second pistol out with my left hand and fired rapidly. My first shot took Beeber in the head, snapping his head back. My second ripped a hole in Slater's throat. Dowder fired hurriedly and missed and I took the moment to put my bullet in the middle of his face. I glanced down at Harkness, but the fight had left him, as he gurgled and bawled, holding his shattered jaw in both hands.

I felt blood dripping down my shoulder and looked at the room, suddenly aware that I was vulnerable. A man rose from one of the tables and came over to me. I looked at him carefully and he pulled back his coattails to show he was unarmed.

"I helped doctors during the war," he said. "You want, I'll see to your shoulder." I followed him to a back room where he stripped the shirt back from my shoulder. The bullet had gone clean through and he clucked to himself as he took a clean towel and poured a generous dollop of whiskey on it.

"Lucky," he said. "I thought I might have to dig it out, and I ain't got no probe to be carving down in your shoulder with. It might have been messy."

He clapped that towel on my shoulder and I let out a yelp as the raw whiskey burnt into my shoulder, and wondered how much luckier I could have been. But he was a good man and I was lucky to find one in that place at that time.

But I've always been lucky in that respect. Whenever I've needed someone, I've had someone around to give me a hand. Lady Luck, however, is a fickle lady, and sometimes one can press her too much. But I was young and foolish then, and life seemed to be better when I pushed my luck. And I took great satisfaction when Lady Luck stayed with me through one narrow scrape after another and men would wag their heads in admiration and swear up and down that I had the luck of the angels riding with me and cast jealous glances in my direction. I didn't realize at the time that I was building a reputation that would make too many men jealous and wanting the same reputation for themselves and figure that going through me would be a shortcut to the reputation that they wanted. When I was older, I tried to explain that to a writing fellow once, but he wouldn't do the story I wanted because it didn't have the color that he thought people wanted to read. The truth never does and truth is an unwelcome bedfellow for the young.

I think the best example of Lady Luck probably came the time that Jack Harvey and I were making our way back to Fort Hays after we'd been sent out on a scout by Custer. About thirty miles west of Hays, we found a man who had stumbled across a band of Indians and had been cut and gashed and scalped. He was almost done with this life and looking into the darkness waiting for him, but he told us that he and five others had been attacked by a party of Indians numbering roughly fifteen. The men had split up, hoping to draw the Indians away from one another and hoping that the Indians would chase one or two for their sport and game, but the Indians came after him, then went after the others. He remembered hearing their screams; then he took one last deep breath and let it out in a wheezy gasp and died.

"Reckon it'd be best if we didn't stick around and bury him, Bill," Harvey said. I glanced up, irritated a bit, knowing that Harvey had a dim regard for life in general, but I saw that he was staring back along the trail that we had just left. I rose and looked over his shoulder at a dusty cloud rising and swore.

"I think I know what that is," Harvey said pointlessly. "And I don't really feel like tying into numbers that would raise a cloud like that."

"I agree," I said, and caught Black up by the reins, mounting. Harvey threw a leg over the buckskin he was riding and we made our way down to a small gully cutting south of where we had found the man. We reined up and crept up to peek over the rim of the gully to see what the Indians decided to do. I noticed that fresh scalps hung from the manes of their horses and figured they remembered that they had left that man alive and had come back for some more fun. Then one big fellow noticed our shod tracks leading away from the man's body, and he yelped something at the others and pointed in our general direction.

"Shit," Harvey muttered, and scuttled back away from the lip of the gully and leaped on his buckskin. He didn't wait to see if I was following him—truth be told, I wouldn't have waited for Harvey, either; common sense dictated the other would be following—but galloped away, bending low over his horse's back as the Indians came along the lip of the gully, trying to get close enough to shoot down upon us.

"At the next bend, turn around and shoot!" I hollered at Harvey as Black came up behind him.

"Fuck that!" Harvey shouted, bending lower.

"We need to stop them a bit somehow if we're to get out of this!" I yelled.

Harvey swore again, then whipped up his rifle as we thundered around the bend in the gully. I pulled my pistols from my belt and clamped Black's reins in my teeth. The Indians came recklessly around the bend after us and we opened fire, dropping two of them. I don't know who hit them and don't care. It was enough that two fell, as the Indians turned away and ran back to regroup and rethink their possibilities.

Harvey and I decided to leave them to their thinking and turned and galloped back on down that gully and Lady Luck was with us, as it widened out into a sandy bed of a dry river. We left the gully and took a wide detour around a stand of willows, heading toward Fort Hays. About that time, however, I reckon that big Indian managed to convince the others that only two horses had made the tracks they were chasing and here they came, yipping and yelping along our trail, hell-bent on having a bit more fun with a couple of white men.

"You got any more ideas, now would sure be a good time to use one!" Harvey yelled.

I glanced over my shoulder; the Indians were gaining on us and I could feel Black beginning to labor between my legs. I glanced at Harvey's buckskin and saw the foam-flecked sides and knew he wasn't going to be good for much longer. Then I remembered something I'd read during the war when Custer had said he always rode to the sound of the guns and that the best defense was an offense. When in doubt, charge.

"All right!" I shouted. Harvey gave me a quizzical look. "When I say, 'Now!' wheel that horse around and we'll charge them!"

Harvey's look turned to skepticism, then certainty that I was mad. "What? Are you out of your goddamned mind? We're a bit outnumbered here!"

"And our horses aren't going to last to the post at this pace!" I said. A reckless grin pulled at my lips. "So what have we got to lose?"

He shook his head and swore a long and blue streak, but his right hand plucked a Colt Army from its holster over his pommel.

"Let's do it, then, before common sense takes over!"

"Now!" I shouted, and wheeled Black hard to the left. The buckskin grunted and followed, and I let out a large yell and clamped my heels to Black's sides.

He gave a loud snort, his head came up, and I felt him reach down inside himself for that extra bit as we charged directly back at the Indians. I slipped the reins between my teeth and pulled my Colts and began shooting as rapidly as I could thumb the hammers. Beside me, Harvey's big Army boomed continuously.

A big hole appeared in the chest of the big Indian leading the others and his face took on a surprised look as he tumbled backward off his pony. The other Indians slowed, staring at us in wild surprise; then as one they wheeled their ponies and beat a hasty retreat. Another one threw up his arms and fell off his pony, bounced twice, then lay still, but no one turned to pick him up.

I pulled Black in and sat, breathing deeply, as Harvey came up beside me, gasping. His buckskin hung his head, sides heaving. Harvey glanced over at me.

"You are one lucky sumbitch," he said. He slammed the Army back into its scabbard. "But you're madder than a bee-stung wolf! Sometimes I think you gotta foot in heaven and hell and friends in both places!"

We made it back to Fort Hays without any problem.

CHAPTER

41

THE 1867 winter closed tightly over the prairies, and General Hancock, who'd been sent out to bring the Indian "troubles" to a close, was called back east to take up duties more suitable for his stodgy mind, and this time the army sent Major General Phil Sheridan out to take charge of the campaign against the "savages." But the army never gave Sheridan additional troops. He was still outnumbered roughly six-to-one. But Sheridan realized that he needed to compensate for his inferiority in numbers by setting up an intelligence system, and for that he relied upon his scouts.

When July came, the Indians broke out of their territory, the Cheyennes slipping away from their reservation near Fort Dodge and immediately cutting a large swath, murdering the settlers around the Council Grove area. Large bands of Comanche and Kiowa heard about their sudden success and slipped away to join them. Soon the valleys of the Saline, the Solomon, and the Republican had a gray haze from burning homesteads hanging over them.

Sheridan sent columns out in pursuit, but the Indians managed to give them a slip. The days slipped into weeks and the weeks into autumn, and only then did the attacks upon the settlers and ambushes upon patrols began to slacken. Sheridan then decided upon a winter campaign. Although the scouts tried to tell him that a winter campaign was a big mistake, Sheridan was adamant, as he was certain the soldier was better equipped than an Indian. He sent one column under Custer to strike at the Cheyenne villages along the Washita while another under Colonel A. W. Evans would come up from Fort Bascom. General Eugene Carr would lead a third column out from Fort Lyon in eastern Colorado. The plan was to push the Indians into a center somewhere and crush them, somewhere around the headwaters of the Red River. I was sent to the Fifth Cavalry at Fort Lyon and spent late autumn riding dispatch back and forth from Carr to Sheridan at Fort Hays.

Not long after I arrived at Fort Lyon, Carr sent me out on a lone scout to the north to see if rumors about Cheyenne raiding parties were true. I came across a burnt wagon on the grassy bank of Kiowa Creek with dead bodies lying naked and mutilated in splashes of blood. I could tell from the tracks that a large band of Indians had come through and that the tracks were fresh. Figuring that the Indians might be flush from their victory and a bit careless, I rode to Gomerville, fifty miles southeast of Denver, to get some volunteers to help me track down the band.

Gomerville was a small town that sprang up around a sawmill that had been built along a creek. Most of the men there knew someone or a family that had been killed by the recent marauding Indians, so I had little trouble in getting volunteers to ride with me. With thirty-four men, I rode rapidly to the area between Kiowa Creek and the Republican River, but the Indians seemed to have vanished into thin air.

For eight days we scouted that territory; then on the ninth we rode to a high table mesa near Sand Creek to use as a vantage point. That was a big mistake. The plain below us was covered with Cheyenne and no sooner did we appear on the top of the mesa than we were spotted.

"Jesus Christ!" Bob Anderson breathed as he saw all the Indians below us. There must have been nearly a thousand. "I think we're a bit outnumbered, Bill!"

"Jim," I said automatically. "Yessir, I'd say that we were. In fact, I think it would be best all around if we left just as quickly—"

"Bill!"

I craned my head and looked over at Johnny O'Dell, a young rancher. He was staring back at the trail we'd used to come up onto the mesa.

"I don't think you're gonna like this! I sure as hell don't!"

I nudged Black and rode back and looked down: A war party had come around the mesa and cut off our retreat. I shook my head. "Well, boys, I'd say we'd best get to work. All of you get something to dig with and start making a big hollow all around here. It's sandy enough that we should be able to get a good barricade up fast."

"I don't know," O'Dell said doubtfully. He squinted up at the sky. "There's a good two, three hours of daylight left. That's enough time for those reddies to make a couple of charges."

"Get to digging!" I snapped. I wheeled around. "Tom Riley, Bill Garrison, you two unlimber your rifles and keep those Indians down as much as possible. Remember that they have to come up the hill, so you have to lower your sights a bit. Aim for the horses. That'll slow them down some."

No sooner were the words out of my mouth than a small band of young warriors charged up the side of the mesa toward us. I slipped a Henry out of my saddle and stepped down from Black. Fred Gomer took the reins and led Black to the rear as I knelt behind a sandstone and began firing. I dropped two Indians from their horses before Riley and Garrison joined me. The next volley killed three more, and the others turned abruptly and rode back down to join their elders, sitting on horses and watching the rashness of youth.

The next three hours seemed to crawl by as the three of us moved from one side of the mesa to the other, shooting down to keep the Indians away while the others dug furiously to shelter the horses and men. At last, the sun began to slide down the horizon and I pulled the others together for a quick meeting.

"We have to face facts," I said. "We can't hold out here indefinitely. Someone's going to have to ride for help."

Garrison shook his head and looked down at the milling Indians. "I'd say anyone who tries that is bent for certain upon suicide. He might get through, but there's a better chance up here than down there. Who knows? They might get tired and go off and leave us. I've heard about that happening."

"True," I said, "but that happened where the defenders had food and plenty of water. We've got some food that we can ration out, but all the water is what we brought up here with us in our canteens. And I don't know if we have enough ammunition to hold out for any length of time." I pointed down at the Indians. "And don't think those Indians haven't got an idea what they're up against. They have a pretty good idea about our problem just as we do."

"So," Riley said, "who's going to go?"

They glanced around at each other, refusing to make eye contact. I gave a deep sigh. "Well then, I'll go. Black's had a bit of rest and he should be able to show those Indian ponies his heels."

"Ain't gonna say I wish you weren't going, Bill," Garrison said, shaking his head, "but I'm grateful that you're willing to give it a shot. I don't think much of your chances, though."

"Well," I said, straightening. "If I don't make it, one of you will have to try next. And another after him."

I walked over to Black and took my canteen from my saddle. I filled my hat full and let him drink, then smoothed the blanket under the saddle and tightened the cinch. Black's ears perked and I knew he knew that something grand was going to happen. He grumbled happily, deep in his throat.

"All right, old boy," I whispered, patting his neck and running my hand down his nose. "You're gonna have to fly like the wind. I hope you're ready."

He tossed his head and mouthed the bit as I climbed into the saddle. The sun had dropped full below the horizon and blue twilight was coming like a dark blanket over the land as I eased off the top of the mesa and began to walk Black down the steep side. Keeping a Navy in one hand, I let him pick his own way. I hoped we'd get down to the flats before being spotted. That'd give us a little more edge than coming at a gallop down the side of the mesa onto the flatland.

And Lady Luck was with us. We managed to get a couple hundred yards across the flats before an Indian spotted us. He gave a loud cry, and I put a bullet in his chest as I kicked Black hard in the ribs. Black screamed and charged forward. I heard an arrow sing past my ear and saw flashes of gunfire in the darkness. An Indian appeared in front of us, but Black hit him with his shoulder, spinning him away. Another tried to run his pony into us, but the pony was no match for Black. I fired at the gun flashes near us and ignored those that winked a short distance away. Suddenly I sensed we were beyond them. I held the reins in my teeth as I replaced the cylinder on the Navy with a fresh one and holstered it. Then I bent low over Black's neck and urged him on.

We had about fifty miles to go and I don't remember ever watching the moon skate so slowly over the night sky. But then we were in Gomerville and I was yelling for relief riders. About twenty-five saddled up, but when I tried to exchange Black for another horse, none were to be had. I patted his neck and gave him a hard look in his one good eye.

"You'll have to do it, boy," I said. "I don't like doing this, but we have no choice!" Black tossed his head again and nickered.

I mounted and led the men back toward the mesa. We rode hard, as I wanted to get back while night still hung over us so the Indians wouldn't see how small a party we were. It was a hard ride, even harder going back than coming, but it was still dark when we charged down upon the Indians, hollering for all we were worth, shooting everywhere. The Indians didn't bother making a stand but rode away from the valley as fast as they could go.

When we rode up to the top of the mesa, a quick glance told me no one had been killed. I swung down from Black as Garrison grabbed my hand and pumped it.

"Goddamn, Bill! I didn't think you could make it!"

I glanced at Black, legs trembling from the strain of the past hours, head hanging low. I could hear him gasping for air and loosened the saddle to give him all the slack he needed. But I knew that ride would have been too much for any horse, even Black. I shook my head and patted him along the neck, feeling tears spring to my eyes. Garrison moved up beside me and ran his hand down Black's back.

"I'm sorry as hell about your horse, Bill," he said. "Wind-broke, ain't he?"

I nodded, unable to speak.

"Well," Garrison said, "he's got a place in my home pasture and barn for as long as he lives. I promise you that. It's the least we could do."

So, thirty-four men were saved, but I lost Black, the best horse I've ever owned. I rode back there a few years later and Black was still alive, his muzzle gray now, but he recognized me and came up and nuzzled me and it was all I could do then to keep from crying like a baby.

Not long after that, I made my last ride for the army. I didn't know it at the time, of course, but it all happened when Cody and I found a bull train loaded with Mexican beer winding its way along an old trail. Cody and I watched that train for a couple of hours, then decided that it would be better if we took that train to the boys who most needed it: Carr and his troops, camped south along Turkey Creek from Fort Evans.

It didn't take much, just a bunch of hollering and shooting over their heads, to convince those Mexicans that they were set upon by bandits and raiders. They turned and ran back south, heading for the Rio Grande, leaving Cody and myself in command of the beer train.

We took that beer back to Carr's command and, well, we

made a little profit selling it in pint cups to those boys. Of course, it didn't take long before tempers started flaring here and there, and Cody and myself weren't helping matters along any, having sampled the beer along the way back to make certain it didn't "turn" on us.

Carr decided that Cody and I were a bad influence and set us to riding dispatch again. I was sent to Fort Wallace and made the whole trip without a hitch. I was returning to Fort Lyon when I saw a buffalo grazing near Sand Creek. Feeling a bit peckish, I dropped him and carved out a steak to broil over a driftwood fire on a gravel bar in the creek bed. I had just finished when suddenly seven Cheyenne warriors appeared on the bank above the stream and charged down toward me, shout and yelling as if the devil were at their hindmost.

I had no time to make it to cover but drew my revolvers and managed to drop four of them before one of the three remaining managed to get close enough to throw his lance into my right hip. I put a bullet in his head as I fell to the ground, spoiling the aim of the other two braves, who overshot me. As they wheeled their horses, I took advantage of the stationary targets and dropped them with a ball each.

I was sorely hurt, though. I tied up the wound as best I could, then started to ride back toward Fort Lyon. Every step that horse took jolted me so that I swore a thousand bees were taking a bite out of the raw edges of that wound. I'm not certain what happened finally, but I managed to come upon a small band of woodcutters not far from the fort but fell out of the saddle before they could help me.

I woke up in the fort's hospital with Cody sitting on a rough-hewn stool beside me. He grinned and held out a bottle of whiskey when he saw I was awake.

"Well, Bill, for a moment there, we all thought you were cashing in," he said. I took a small sip of whiskey and started hacking and coughing as it burnt its way down my throat. I gestured toward a cup of water and Cody held it while I drank thirstily.

"Tell you the truth," I said after opening my throat up with water, "I was certain about that, too."

Cody's eyes traveled to the lance I'd brought back with me. "Looks like a Dog Soldier's lance," he said. "How many were there?"

"Seven."

"And how many did you account for?"

"Seven."

He shook his head. "You're a regular hell on wheels, aren't you?" He took another drink from the bottle and smacked his lips. His pale blue eyes were as shiny as new-minted dollars. "What you going to do with that lance?"

"You want it?" I asked, reaching for the bottle of whiskey. I took a cautious sip and held my breath as it slid down my throat.

His eyes lit up. "You mean it?"

"It's yours. Just make certain that I have enough whiskey to get through this."

"It's a deal," he promised.

And he was as good as his word. But my hip refused to respond to treatment and became infected despite everything the army surgeon tried. At last, I decided I'd go home to recuperate and that spring found myself back in Troy Grove, where my sisters and mother spoiled me with cookies and pie and cake. But the wound became even more infected, and finally we had to call in the doctor from town to open the wound up again and scrape the bone.

After that, I healed rapidly and soon the old familiar restlessness came upon me again. When fall came, I bade everyone good-bye and made my way back to Fort Hays, thinking I'd pick up scouting again. But when I arrived, I found Hays City had grown into a bunch of saloons and dance halls with gaudily dressed women cavorting around in paint and ribbons among the board shanties and tents and false-fronted buildings. Hays set right on the old Santa Fe Trail, and long trains of canvas-topped freight wagons made their way up that trail from New Mexico on a regular basis, carrying trade goods, and Fort Hays had grown to include nearly two thousand soldiers, including the Seventh Cavalry.

Brawls were daily and numerous, and with the east–west railroad coming through, the town was booming and law was an afterthought. The day belonged to those who could take it.

CHAPTER

42

THE DOG days of August. And the day had been no exception to the rule—hot and muggy—sweat running in streams off a person who was hoping for night when surely it would be cooler but it wasn't and the dust hung like a brown curtain in the air that turned to muddy runnels when someone walked through the droplets that seemed to be hanging in the air and gathering granules like iron filings to a magnet and music bounced like leaden notes around the darkness off wooden storefronts and posts and windowpanes until it all seemed to merge into a jackannery of noise—

"Bill!"

I sighed and tossed my cards into the deadwood on the table. I took my hat off, pulled a handkerchief from an inside pocket of my coat, and mopped the perspiration from my forehead. I looked disgustedly at the brown tinge left on my handkerchief, folded it, and replaced it in my pocket.

"What is it?" I asked.

Jess Bowden stood just inside the doorway, gasping for

air, pointing frantically behind him. "Mulvey and some of his cronies got John Lee treed."

I shook my head tiredly, then rose from the table and made my way out of the saloon. I stood for a moment, letting my eyes adjust to the brightness while the sun beat down hard on me, setting my temples to pounding like a blacksmith's hammer on an anvil. The sun took the drench right out of a man and I felt the whiskey I had drunk while playing cards begin to churn in my stomach. I glanced down the street to where Bill Mulvey and some cowboys down on their luck had hoisted John Lee up in the air with a rope around his chest. They had thrown the other end over a rafter beam and tied it to a hitching post. They passed a bottle back and forth. One would take a drink, then step forward and slam a fist against John Lee.

I drew a deep slow breath, checked the ivory-handled .36 caliber Colt Navy pistols in their holsters, and started down toward them, my boot heels echoing hollowly on the boardwalk.

Mulvey saw me coming and stepped aside, lips peeling back from blackened teeth. He slipped a pistol from his holster and held it low by his side. "Well, well. Hickok. Wondered when you'd get down here."

I nodded at John Lee. "Cut him down, Mulvey."

His eyes narrowed. He took a long, deliberate drink from the bottle and tossed it to one of the others. He wiped his hand on his dirty shirt. "Uh-uh. Don't think so." His eyes went flat. "All we wanted was a bit of credit so we could get some supplies."

"That's why people have jobs," I said. "A man's reputation gets him credit. You can't expect something to be given to a nobody who can't even hold a job swamping out a saloon's spittoons."

I watched his eyes grow wide; then the dull liver red flush came suddenly into his face.

"Damn you—" he said thickly, and I flipped the pistols out of their holsters and fired. The bullets struck him in the belly. The pistol flew from his hand as he fell backward to the ground. For a brief moment he looked stunned; then the pain hit him and he screamed and clutched his belly and tried to press the pain away.

I looked at the others staring openmouthed at my pistols. "Well?" I asked softly.

The one holding the whiskey bottle swallowed with difficulty. "We was only funnin'," he said.

"Cut him down," I said. "I don't want to tell you again."

He nodded and pulled a knife from his pocket.

"Doctor! Help!" gasped Mulvey. "Christ! The pain! Ahh!"

The cowboy stepped over Mulvey and, hand shaking, cut the rope holding John Lee from where it was anchored to the hitching post. John Lee fell in a heap on the boardwalk.

The cowboy looked uncertainly at me, wet his lips, and glanced at Mulvey. His face turned dirty white under the grime and tan.

"Now what?" he asked.

"How fast can you run?" I asked.

"What?"

"I said"—thumbing the hammer back—"how fast can you run?"

You never saw the like of it in all your born days. The bottle fell from his hand, and before it hit the ground the cowboy and his friends were high-stepping it down the street, legging it for all they were worth toward the Hays City limits as if the hounds from hell were chomping on their heels, saliva dripping bloodily from their great jaws, sweat sluicing off their bodies and running in rivulets to muddy the street, horse apples flying behind the heels of their booted feet.

"Damn you, Hickok! You've . . . killed me!" Mulvey said from between teeth gritted against the pain.

I looked down at him as he gave a last terrified scream, eyes bulging in terror as they looked down the long, dark path into the abyss.

And I heard the running feet of the righteous coming down the street toward us.

"Migawd!" someone said in an awed voice.

I slipped the Colts back into their holsters. I pointed at Mulvey and ordered he be taken to Halloran's Funeral Parlor and John Lee to Doc Adams's office. I started to walk toward the jail and the crowd parted like the sea spreading before Moses.

"God, ain't he the cold one?" someone muttered.

But I ignored them all, forcing myself to walk nonchalantly to the jail. I opened the door and stepped in, shutting the door firmly behind me. Then I ran down the corridor to the back door letting out to the alley and barely made it before my gorge rose mightily and I vomited the leavings of my lunch and the whiskey I had drunk into the silted dust of the alley where none but a battered one-eyed cat could see the loss of dignity and the clay feet of the knight-errant that reminded him constantly that he was, after all, only a man.

For a while I thought that killing Mulvey would be the last of it, that word would spread and others would avoid me. Word spread, all right, but it had the opposite effect; it brought others to me, trying to be the one that took down Wild Bill Hickok. Always, though, I ruefully remembered the woods and Israel and Helen Caroline Ernst's words or the words that came from the vision she had woven magically around me and knew instinctively even while I hoped otherwise, that those who came to me were being brought to me for killing, as a sacrifice, if you will, to the god who would allow others to live on land fought for by others like those I would kill who did not want to give up what they had earned—not even for civilization, for it was a rebellion against civilization that had sent them out to the West in the first place. And now they were being told that they were no longer wanted: Move farther west, mister gunmanpathfinderhuntermountainmanadventurer, for the frontier is a frontier only briefly, a mere grain upon the sandy beach of time, and there is no longer any room for you here.

But I knew that it was for those who came after that I had been sent for and it was for them that I would fight even though my fighting would eventually mark even me as one who had to be banished in order for civilization to continue to grow. That is the make of humanity; it uses the people it needs for the moment, then discards them upon the refuse pile of time.

There wasn't much to Hays City, Kansas, although the city was growing rapidly. Buffalo hunters, skinners, hide pullers—all those connected with buffalo hunting used it as a place to sell the hides they had taken from butchered bison. Gamblers, pimps, and prostitutes began to flock to Hays City as well as did the soldiers who were stationed a mile away at Fort Hays. I read in the paper once where I told a reporter that "there was no Sunday west of Junction City, no law west of Hays City, and no God west of Carson City." But I don't remember ever saying anything like that and I didn't know the reporter from Adam.

Hays City was filled with mule whackers and stores filled with everything that would appeal to a man's pocketbook on payday. There was the huge Othero and Sellars warehouse that employed only Mexicans in its freighting business. North and South Main streets flanked the railroad track from Chestnut to about one-half of a block west of Fort Street. North Main held the Capless and Ryan Outfitting Store, Leavenworth Restaurant, Hound Saloon & Faro House, Hound Kelly's Saloon, the justice of the peace's office, M. E. Joyce, Tommy Drum's Saloon, Kate Coffee's Saloon, Mose Water's Saloon, R. W. Evans's Grocery Store and Post Office, Cohen's Clothing, the Perry Hotel, M. J. R. Treat's Candy and Peanut Stand, Cy Godard's Saloon & Dance Hall, and on the far corner "Nigger" White's barbershop. There were several places where the soiled doves roosted and stood on balconies, displaying their charms in their scanties, calling boldly down to riders.

Not long after I killed Mulvey, I was having a game in Tommy Drum's place when Jim Curry, an Irish locomotive engineer, saw me sitting with my back against the wall and stormed up to the table, waving a pistol, claiming he was going to shoot me. For a moment I thought I was going to have to draw on him, but Tommy Drum started dancing around us, jabbering about how this wasn't right and for Jim to put up his gun and that he'd buy champagne all around. I swear he looked just like an excited rooster prancing in a hen yard, and I burst out laughing. Jim goggled at my laughter, then glanced at Drum and started laughing as well and put up his gun, mumbling something about how Ida May wasn't worth it.

I knew then that Ida hadn't been the clean catch I had thought she was when I took her to my bed, and resolved then and there that I would be a bit more careful with another's charms in the future. I also knew grimly that I had better be in constant practice, for there would be some like Jim Curry who wouldn't want to kill me for the sake of a spurned love; there would be some who would be looking for the reputation that came with killing someone who had already killed another.

In September, Samuel Strawhun came to town, spoiling for trouble. I sighed when I saw him ride into town, knowing that we would be locking horns before long. I had known him in Ellsworth, where I had been living with Indian Annie. The sheriff, E. W. Kingsbury, had needed a bit of help one day when Strawhun and his cronies got drunk and tried to tree the town. We took their guns away and, since there were more than the jail could hold, tied them to a stock corral until they sobered up. The trouble was that some sobered up faster than others, but we didn't dare let one loose until all were sober enough to be let loose, for fear that the one untied would find a way to free the others who would still be drunk enough to want to finish the job they had set their minds to doing.

I was standing next to John Bittles when Strawhun rode into town. I heard John sigh and turned to look at him.

He shook his head and spit into the dust of the street. "Sam Strawhun. I knew things were too good to last."

"You know him?" I asked, surprised at his statement.

"Yeah," he said disgustedly. "I know him. Everyone in Hays knows him. He tried to take on A. B. Webster at the post office when A.B. told him that the vigilance committee had his name on the short list. He and a Weiss fellow went into the post office and banged around A.B. and then tried to kill him. But old A.B. isn't to be reckoned that way, you know. He managed to get to his pistol and put a pellet in Weiss's belly down low where it could do the most damage. Strawhun ran away and left Weiss on the floor. He's no damn good and as yellow as the day is long. Watch your back, Bill," John said warningly. "He won't come at you head-on unless he has a couple of boys with him. But he will lay for you."

"I'll remember that," I promised, and walked on down the street to where Strawhun had ridden in front of Odenfeld's Saloon on Fort Street. Strawhun had just swung down from his saddle and was tying his horse to the post in front of the saloon.

"Strawhun," I called.

He ducked under his horse's neck and peeped over the saddle at my approach. His brown eyes blinked nervously, shifting back and forth like a cornered lizard. He stepped out and around his horse, keeping his hands well away from his pistol.

"Hickok," he said. "I wondered where you had run to."

"Run? Why, you two-bit snake rustler, who ever had to run from you? Run?" I shook my head and planted my feet. He suddenly looked unhappy, shifting back and forth in his boots, badly scuffed and run-down at the heels. One pocket of his shirt, which had obviously been a stranger to the washboard since he bought it or stole it from a clothesline, had been partly ripped off. His pants bagged at the knees. "You've got iron. Settle your problem now."

His glance darted around at the curious on the boardwalk, a cowboy sitting on his pony in the street, warily watching the two of us. Strawhun tried to laugh, but it came out shrill, like a schoolgirl goosed by the class bully.

"Sure. Right. And which of these good folks would come to help you?" he sneered.

I stepped toward him. He backed away so rapidly that he ran into his horse. Startled, the horse lashed out with its left hoof, catching Strawhun in the buttocks, lifting him in the air, and throwing him forward. He landed *whumpp!* on his belly, his face slapping forward into a fresh pile of horse apples. He rolled over, gasping for air. I stepped forward and slipped his pistol from its holster.

"I'll leave this with the bartender in Odenfeld's, you sorry-assed cat—" I held my tongue, for I sensed ladies around, but Strawhun caught my drift. I could see it in his eyes, glittering mad, but he lacked the sand to do anything about the madness within him. "You can stay two days. One to wash the trail dust off, if you ever do"—I backed a step away from the stench lifting off him—"and another day to get yourself supplied. But then you got three options: hit the trail, take the train east or west, or go north." I nodded in the general direction of the cemetery. "That's it, Strawhun. Two days. No more."

I left him in the street dust and walked into Odenfeld's and handed his pistol—a Beals .36 caliber Remington that had seen much better days; its hammer looked like it had opened more than one can of beans—to Jackson, the bartender, with instructions to return it unloaded to Strawhun once he was certain that he was leaving town.

I should have been a bit more cautious, but I was too mad for horse sense, as Father used to claim I lacked. He was right; I have found Father to have grown wiser over the past twenty-some years. In fact, he seems to grow wiser each day—

Two days later, Strawhun and a couple of men he had befriended—hide hunters down on their luck—tried to clean out Odenfeld's Saloon. I suppose they meant to rob it as well, but Jackson sent the swamper out the back door to get me when he saw which way the stick was floating.

Glasses were flying out of the saloon as Rattlesnake Pete Lanihan, my deputy, and I came close to the saloon. I stopped and picked up a couple and handed them to Pete. "Watch yourself," I said softly, then stepped into the saloon about 1:00 p.m. and found one of the hide hunters standing in the middle of the floor, his face flushed with drink, weaving back and forth, his pistol swinging recklessly in his hand. Strawhun leaned against the bar, watching hungrily, his eyes glittering. I glanced around quickly, noticing the rest of the bar huddled behind the stove at my left, poised, ready to duck left or right if the hide hunter started shooting.

"Drop the pistol," I said loudly. He swung toward me, epithets falling foully from his lips. "Drop the pistol. Now."

He squinted, trying to make out who had the nerve to say anything to him. I stepped forward as he hesitated, caught his pistol by the barrel, and twisted it in his hand. His finger caught in the trigger guard and popped like a dry stick in winter. He screamed and staggered away, clutching his hand, the broken finger pointing crazily away at a right angle.

I nodded at Pete, who stepped to the bar with the glasses in his hand and placed them on top of the bar. I laughed and said, "Boys, you shouldn't treat a poor old man this way. Glasses are expensive."

"I'll throw them out again, if I want," Strawhun said.

I watched him out of the corner of my eye as I studied the other hide hunter. "Then they'll carry you out of here, Strawhun. I told you to leave in two days. Your time's up. Walk out, climb on your horse, and leave."

The other hide hunter raised his hands belt level, pulling his dirty coat aside to show me he hadn't a handgun. But I noticed his Sharps rifle leaning behind him against the bar. I heard a noise and I glanced over at Strawhun. He had stepped away from the bar, starting to draw his pistol, but froze in an awkward pose, his prominent Adam's apple swallowing with difficulty.

"Well," I said softly. I smiled at him and saw him cringe inwardly. A wild glee rose in me, then an icy calm. "You're halfway there, boy. You want to travel the rest of the way north?"

He wanted to give it a try—everyone in the saloon could see how hard he wanted to try—but he was about a quart low on nerve.

"Pull it or back off," I said. "I've got more to do than stand here jawing with a pig-sucking scum like you."

He shook his head and wet his lips nervously. "I don't go against a stacked deck." He glanced over his shoulder at Jackson, who raised his hands and moved down the bar, away from the action.

"Don't take no account of me," he said. "You're on your own."

I stood, silently waiting for Strawhun. I watched as he began to tremble.

"Who else is going to back you, Hickok?" he whined, trying for bravery, but everyone saw his fear. Someone chuckled and Strawhun's face turned dull red beneath the dirt and scraggly beard covering his weak chin. "Say something, damn you!"

I remained quiet, letting the silence build up between us. The room stayed quiet except for that one snicker. A light drift of cigar smoke wisped between us and the room began to narrow down to one thin shaft of light as I focused on his face. For an instant I smelled the sour odor of his fear; then his hand started moving. I flipped my right Colt Navy out of its holster, firing as it came level. The .36 caliber bullet struck him in the forehead. His head snapped back, suddenly becoming too heavy for his scrawny neck. He fell backward, dead.

"No!" Pete shouted. I turned to see the other hide hunter starting to lift his rifle, but he had forgotten Pete, who stepped forward and laid his pistol alongside the hide hunter's head. His eyes rolled for a minute; then he crumbled into the sawdust on the floor, out cold. I took a deep breath, smelling the acrid smoke left from my shot. *Brimstone, an old friend—*

"Good work," I said to Pete. I pointed at the hide hunter, who cradled his hand, whimpering from the pain of his broken finger. "You. Come here." For a moment he looked as if he was going to refuse; then he stumbled forward. I took a knife from his belt and pointed at his partner. "Drag him down to the jail."

"My hand—" he began, but I cut him off.

"That isn't a request," I said, tossing his pistol to Pete. He caught it deftly and held it down by his side, thumb ready on the hammer.

"Yes, sir," the hide hunter mumbled, and bent, grabbing his partner's leg with his uninjured hand, tucking it under his armpit. He leaned away from the weight, dragging the hide hunter toward the door.

I glanced over at the crowd. "Would a couple of you gentlemen mind dragging that man down to the undertaker's?"

Four men stepped forward and quietly bent to lift Strawhun from the floor. Outside, I heard the hide hunter's head *thunk-thunk* down the two steps to the street. Silence deepened; then Jackson stepped to the middle of the bar and announced the saloon was buying the next round. Slowly the others crossed to the bar, giving me a wide berth. I sighed and walked to the door, knowing that two killings in two months was going to draw criticism from some and hoping that the vigilance committee would back me against the angry voices that would soon be raised.

I stepped into the middle of the street and looked up at the stars. Suddenly I thought of Nichols's story and realized the grim fascination that as funny as we had taken it at the time, it was my death warrant. There would be others beside Strawhun who would be coming to town to make trouble, hoping to become famous through a shortcut.

I turned and walked heavily toward the jail, feeling a black depression begin to drop over me like a shroud.

I didn't have long to wait. The next night, a shot buzzed past my ear like an angry hornet as I made my rounds. I crouched, my pistols suddenly in my hand, as I faced the alley. I heard heavy footsteps pounding the dust. I straightened slowly, realizing what had happened. I looked down at the pistols in my hand, remembering the strange encounter I had during the war, the warning of the strange visitors. I sighed and carefully placed my Colt Navy pistols away.

I took to avoiding strong lights and dark alleys. I made my rounds down the center of the street. When I had to enter a saloon, I pushed the doors hard against the wall to make certain no one waited to catch me unaware. I always stepped in to the right or left, varying it at whim so no one could predict my movements upon entering, sliding along the wall so no one could get to my back. People noticed the change in my behavior, but there was a certain respect in their glances my way.

The good reverend tried to raise enough holy disgust at the two killings, but A. B. Webster and the others on the committee refused to listen to him. At one time, A.B. told the reverend—*Ticklor? Yes, Ticklor*—to mind his own flock and let the townsfolk herd their own sheep. Wolves were more common there than in the reverend's square building at the end of town.

But my time, I realized, was limited, as more and more problems came my way from Fort Hays. I had taken a warrant to the commander at the time, Colonel George Gibson, to take Bob Conners, who had murdered a drover near Pond City and was arrested by Deputy U.S. Marshal Jack Bridges and deposited in the stockade, to Topeka for trial. But Gibson refused to release Conners to me, claiming that I wasn't duly appointed by the governor.

The real reason, however, was that I had posted the town off-limits to the soldiers until Gibson decided to run a bit of discipline on the troopers, who had a history of raging through the town on payday. Finally tired of warning the soldiers to behave themselves, I tossed a couple of them in jail and held them over for trial. Gibson tried to take them out under his authority as commander of the fort. But I declined to release them to him, and when his adjutant tried to push his way into the jail I calmly told him that he could join them if he wished.

This made Gibson angry, and cooperation between the fort and the town fathers became lost in the shuffle. Grudgingly, however, Gibson issued orders to his men that they would serve time in the post guardhouse if they caused any trouble in town. This stopped the partying troopers in their tracks for a while, but it was an uneasy solution to the problem and I was very unpopular with the soldiers for quite a while.

My unpopularity didn't lift when General George Custer came to the post as commander, although George and I got along better than one would expect. George was intent upon making a name for himself with the papers back east and had no intention of letting the soldiers mar his reputation with a bit of drunken behavior.

It was his wife, Elizabeth, however, who intrigued me more, and that brought on more trouble from George's brother, Tom, who fawned over Elizabeth—Tom and George called her "Libby," but I always referred to her as Mrs. Custer when we were in company and later as Elizabeth whenever she came to town to shop, accompanying her whenever she took a ride out in the prairie.

I remember the day I met her at Fort Hays, riding my sorrel to the post after I figured the Custers had settled in to introduce myself, although George and I had known each other for years. I had worked briefly with George as a scout in '67. I didn't think George would remember me, but he did. That was one thing about George: He was quick about remembering people, because he never knew when they might be able to push his legend along a bit a ways down the line.

The day was bright and sunny and my sorrel had been groomed until his hide shone like polished leather. He was well fit from a good diet of oats and trim as I rode him out to Big Creek every day to practice with my pistols. Fort Hays had been at the mouth of North Fork of Big Creek where Smoky Hill Trail crossed the stream, but when the railroad came in the fort was moved fourteen miles up Big Creek. I no longer wore my buckskins, having traded them in for a Prince Albert coat and checkered pants, and had discarded my holsters—save for when I rode out on the prairie and was going to be gone for a while—for a red sash, as I could feel the pistols always that way and they came more readily to hand when I had to draw them than they did from the deep holsters. I always wore a broad-brimmed hat to keep the sun from my eyes.

This day, however, I planned on riding on out in the prairie to visit some homesteaders after my call at the post. I wore top boots, riding breeches, and a dark blue flannel shirt with a scarlet set in front to match the scarlet neckerchief that trailed down the side of my neck and chest. The sorrel was feeling his oats and pranced in a huff when I rode him to the Custers' home and dismounted.

Tom Custer opened the door when I knocked on it. His eyes widened slightly, then narrowed when I introduced myself again to him. Although George (his wife and friends called him Autie, but I could never for the life of me figure that one out) was always polite and never drank a drop of liquor, Tom was quite a randabout who got drunk quite frequently—a dangerous time, because there wasn't an ounce of fear in Tom and a man like that who got drunk could be a handful for anyone. I didn't know it, but a streak of cruelty ran in him, too, for a few weeks later I arrested him when he got drunk and rode his horse into a saloon in emulation of me in that damn Nichols's story and tried to make the horse climb up on the pool table. When the horse wouldn't, Tom pulled his pistol out and shot it, saying, "That'll teach the dumb son of a bitch!"

"It's the lawman from Hays: Hickok," he said over his shoulder.

A murmur came from within and he stepped grudgingly aside and motioned for me to enter. I removed my hat and stepped over the threshold and came face-to-face with a beautiful woman, realizing almost too late that it was George's wife. She had glossy auburn hair, gray eyes, and a waist I could easily span with two hands. Her eyes widened and a faint scent of lilacs came from her. I found later she wore lilac scent in the company of her husband, jasmine at other times—

"My sister-in-law; Mrs. Custer," Tom said sourly from my shoulder.

"Ma'am," I said, and made a small bow. She presented her hand and her eyes widened in surprise when I gently kissed it.

"My, a gentleman here, of all places!" she exclaimed, a lovely rosy flush touching her high cheekbones.

"I think he's here to see Autie," Tom said quietly.

"Of course," Elizabeth said, but her eyes held mine boldly, commanding. "Whatever would he be doing here otherwise?" I caught a glimpse of mischief in her smile at me; then what I came to call her political mask dropped over her face.

"Marshal Hickok?" a voice called from the other room.

I nodded at Elizabeth and stepped cautiously around her, conscious suddenly of her breasts pushing against her bodice. "Excuse me, ma'am," I said politely.

As I walked in his office George rose, extending his hand to me. I took it, remarking silently to myself on the strength of his grip. A self-assured mantle seemed draped over his shoulders and I recalled the stories I had heard about the boy general during the war who had fearlessly thrown his men into battle against the Confederates but also about his uncanny sense of attack that had him emerge victorious at every encounter.

"James, isn't it?" he said, catching me off-guard for a moment. I had been called "Bill" so long that my given name seemed foreign to my ears. Then I nodded and smiled back at him, feeling myself leaning toward the bright aura that seemed to be sparking from him. His golden hair lay as long as mine across his shoulders. He wore a bright red scarf at his throat and his uniform was freshly pressed. I had heard stories that he bathed every day, as I did—a fact that had started a new enterprise in Hays, as others had taken to following my example.

"General," I said, noting that he accepted the title as if he had been permanently posted in that rank and did not carry it as a brevet only—an honor that he clung to from the war even though he was technically only a lieutenant colonel commanding the Seventh Cavalry.

The room was a monument to his successes, souvenirs of battle hanging on the wall: a tattered Rebel guidon, Indian pipes, hatchets, a quilled breast guard, bows and arrows in deerskin quivers, photos of himself—he was a bit vain in that regard—and rifles. His dogs raised their heads at my entrance, eyeing me questioningly. One thumped its tail a few times on the floor and the others took this as a sign of good intent and went back to sleep in front of the small fire burning cheerfully in the fireplace.

"What can I do for you? Is this a formal visit?" he asked, motioning me to a chair. He offered a cigar, which I refused, and I noticed that he closed the humidor firmly before Tom's hand could reach into it.

"No, informal," I said easily, holding my hat in my hand. "I'd like your assurance that we won't have any repeat misbehavior of soldiers in Hays." His eyes narrowed and I hastened to add, "We've had a few unfortunate problems in the past with troopers getting drunk on payday and trying to force their, ah, attentions on some of the wives and daughters. Your predecessor gave us a bit of trouble with this, and I'm trying to stop any trouble before it gets a chance to start."

"You've got to expect some blowing off of steam," Tom said, butting into our conversation. I caught a hint of anger in his voice and turned to meet his stare.

"I'm not saying that they can't come into town," I began, but he interrupted.

"Yes, I'm certain of that. Hays makes quite a haul from the army payroll, doesn't it?"

I felt my shoulders stiffen with a sudden awareness of the animal anger beginning to seep from him. A challenge seemed to flicker from his eyes to mine and I nodded slowly.

"Very well," I said softly. "Have it your way." I stood, still looking at Tom but feeling George's annoyance behind me. "But anyone who causes trouble in Hays will visit my jail. Anyone," I repeated for emphasis. "Officer, enlisted man, hired help—I don't care. *And* they'll face charges in town, not here."

"You have no authority," Tom started, but this time I interrupted.

"I'm wearing my authority," I said.

His eyes dropped to my chest, but I was not wearing a badge. A puzzled look started to form in his eyes and I tapped the ivory handles of my Colts, drawing his attention to them. His face tightened with anger.

"That's enough, Captain," George said from behind me. The formality of his tone brought Tom to stiff attention. His eyes stared off into the distance, anger still sparking from them, but the rigorous discipline of the soldier held him in check.

"Marshal," George said authoritatively, and I turned to face him. "I thank you for your concern, and rest assured that punishment will be double that which you mete out in town for any who behave dishonorably. I will see to that personally," he added, staring hard at Tom. He was displeased with his brother's behavior, but he was a fellow officer *and* his brother and I knew that there would be exceptions made.

I made my thanks and took my leave. Outside, I found Elizabeth dressed in riding clothes, wearing a campaign hat over her auburn curls, a feminine copy of her husband's coat tailored to emphasize her breasts. She was mounted on a pretty sorrel mare.

"Marshal," she said warmly as I emerged from Custer's quarters. "Would you mind accompanying me on my morning ride?"

"I'll get my horse," Tom said brusquely from behind me. Her eyes flashed at him and then her husband's voice called for him from inside. He stared furiously at me for a long moment, then reentered the quarters, closing the door behind him.

"Be happy to," I said, untying the sorrel. I swung easily into the saddle and stared down at her. A flush began to climb the white column of her throat. She laughed throatily, and together we rode through the gate onto the prairie, following the creek south away from the fort.

* * *

A week later, the Seventh Cavalry took to the field and Elizabeth came to town, finding me in my office where I was filling out overdue paperwork. I looked up as she entered, wearing a pearl gray satin dress, her hair gathered at the back and falling in careful curls to her shoulders. She wore a tiny gray hat with a black band perched on her head. Her eyes were wide, and tiny lights glimmered from them.

I rose and said, "May I help you, Mrs. Custer?"

"Mrs. Custer?" She laughed. "Why don't you call me Libby? Everyone does."

"Then," I said gallantly, "I shall call you Elizabeth. I don't wish to be everyone."

An eyebrow arched as she studied me carefully. "Very gallant," she murmured. She pronounced it *"ga-lant"* and I felt a smile forming.

"Easy when I'm in the presence of a charming *woman*," I said. For a moment I almost said "lady" but changed my mind, emphasizing the latter.

"I have heard about you, Wild Bill," she said. I winced and she smiled a bit wickedly. "Yes, I heard my husband call you James. But Elizabeth deserves her Wild Bill." She took a deep breath as she spoke, and I motioned to a chair.

"Would you like to sit, Elizabeth?" I asked.

"No," she answered. "I think I would like to go for a drive. Would you mind accompanying me?"

"What about your brother-in-law?" I asked pointedly. "I understand he is your usual escort."

"My brother-in-law is a bit too enamored of me," she said matter-of-factly. "And he is out in the field with my husband. I'm alone."

Her eyes met mine with a studied frankness and I felt her magnetism deep inside me. I stepped around the desk and started to take my hat, but she came past me, shutting the door firmly. Then she turned and moved close to me, her arms slipping around my neck, pulling me down and kissing me firmly, pointedly.

I caught my breath and stood awkwardly, frozen by the suddenness of her action. She leaned back away from me and said breathlessly, "But there will be no complications, Wild Bill. None, do you understand? I will not leave Autie and we will be *very* discreet. There will be no scandal. Autie will be president someday and I will not permit anything to keep that from happening."

"But—" I started.

She laughed softly. "I know about his . . . liaisons," she said. "The weeks that he's been away—what soldier's wife doesn't expect that? He writes every day, but I can tell when he's been unfaithful. His letters have a certain regret about them, the words feel a bit ashamed when I read them, and I know."

"And that makes a difference?" I asked.

She shrugged and I felt her breasts move against my chest. "Of course it does," she said. "A woman is no different from a man." Her eyes darkened and I read the anger in their depths. "I am a woman, not an icon, despite what everyone tries to make of me. You know that. I can tell, so don't deny it. A woman has the same needs as a man. And I have no intention of—" But I bent and kissed her, shutting away further words that I did not want to know. Confession may be good for the soul, but not for embarking lovers. There must remain a mystery. And there remained a mystery between Elizabeth and myself, although given her wild abandon in bed, I wondered at Custer's willingness to chance losing her for the sake of a momentary fling. But Custer's arrogance would not let him think for a moment that he wasn't always in full command of every situation surrounding him. That would eventually be his downfall.

Tom, however, quickly sensed something was happening between Elizabeth and myself. I caught his glare whenever he rode into town or business took me to the fort. A couple of times, he pressed deliberately close to me, a challenge that most men would not ignore. But I kept away from him as much as possible. His attention to Elizabeth, however, forced us to be only that much more discreet in our affair and to take extra pains to keep it so secret that George and everyone else had not the slightest hint of Elizabeth's infidelities.

* * *

"Bill?" Elizabeth Custer asked. I turned, looking at her.

"Yes?"

She smiled at me, her generous lips curving up into twin dimples. Her eyes danced mischievously. "You look good today," she began. I looked automatically into the mirror she had hanging beside the door where Custer could check himself before stepping out into the fort where his admiring public waited. I did look good, I thought, studying my reflection: long blond hair brushed carefully, just touching my shoulders, a small-fringed buckskin jacket over a bright blue shirt that matched my blue-gray eyes, sash with my old army belt buckled over it and twin holsters that I wore when I went out scouting hanging on each side, the Navy Colts butt forward. A bowie knife nestled behind the left holster. I glanced on down at the leather trousers and Wellington boots I had brushed before coming to meet Custer at his quarters.

"You're another Narcissus," she said accusingly.

I flushed, recognizing how she had set me up by appealing to my vanity. And I was vain then. I knew it and wasn't bothered by it until someone brought it to my attention. Like Elizabeth. Or Bill Cody, who had been teasing me since I'd met him when he was a boy riding for the Pony Express. That had been a long time ago and many bottles of whiskey.

"The other day you called me 'Orpheus' when I was sawing away at my fiddle at the Officers' Dance," I said, smiling over at her.

"Ball." She grinned. "It was the Officers' Ball. You never did get that right, did you?"

"A dance is a dance, whatever you want to call it," I said, shrugging. I looked in the mirror again. Maybe I was a touch narcissistic, but what the hell? I looked damn good. Not as good as I looked in my marshaling outfit: cutaway coat, flowered vest, ruffled white shirt, salt-and-pepper trousers, string tie, high-heeled boots, and a broad-brimmed hat to keep the midnight sun out of my eyes. I wore the same outfit when I went to New York to meet Cody at the Brevoort Hotel. The damn cabdriver tried to charge me five dollars for a two-dollar fare and threatened to take three dollars out of my hide when I wouldn't pay the extortion. I left him on his back in the gutter.

"I guess it is at that," she laughed. She glanced around to see if her husband could see us, then stepped close, pressed her perky breasts against me, and gave me such a deep kiss that I thought I was going to pass out for lack of air.

I came up swimmingly just as Custer entered the room. Fortunately, Elizabeth had pulled away and was reknotting my red scarf around my neck. He grinned and crossed, kissing her on the back of her neck.

"Just can't resist mothering everyone, can you?" he said.

She smiled and gave him a quick kiss that wives long married give their husbands to bid them good-bye. "You men always need someone to look after you," she said. She pulled his shirt collar out from under his jacket. "I never saw a man who could take care of himself. You all need a woman around."

She glanced at me and gave me a wicked grin. "Right, Bill?"

I felt my face growing hot, remembering the last time we'd been together while her husband was out on patrol with Buffalo Chips White as his scout instead of me. Custer was a lucky man; Elizabeth was quite gifted in bed.

Elizabeth Custer answered when I knocked on the door to Custer's quarters. I took a step backward, unmanned to a degree by the force of her presence. Her round breasts pushed against the dress she had chosen that resembled an officer's uniform on top but then swept down into the generous curve of her hips before falling to the floor.

"Yes?" she asked. "What is it, Bill?"

I pulled my hat from my head and said, "I was told to report to General Custer as soon as I arrived," I said.

A faint smile touched her lips. "Well, he isn't here. He rode out this morning with Buffalo Chips. I understand he's going to be gone for a couple of weeks on patrol with White and Tom."

She meant Custer's brother Tom, who had been a pain in my side ever since coming to Fort Hays. There was something between the two of us that just rubbed each of us raw. I nodded and said, "Well, ma'am, if you'd be so kind, just tell him that I stopped by as he asked."

"Excuse me, Mr. Hickok, but I'm forgetting my manners. Won't you come in?" She stepped back into the house, swinging the door wide before I could refuse. I glanced around; nobody seemed to be paying us any particular attention, so I took a deep breath and stepped inside. She shut the door behind me and came around in front, taking my hat and hanging it on the hat rack.

"It's almost dinnertime and I'm dining alone," she said. "Won't you join me?"

"Well, Elizabeth, I'm afraid I haven't had a chance to bathe yet—"

"Nonsense, Bill, you are quite all right. But if it's a quick wash that you want"—she gestured toward the back—"you'll find a washroom at the rear."

"Thank you, ma'am," I said. I was splashing water on my face before I realized that she had taken control of the entire situation, assuming that refusal was not an option that I had. I grinned sourly at my reflection in the mirror. Why was it that women always try to take control? The hell with it. I slipped out the back and hotfooted it over to the post barber and bribed the boy to heat up some water for a quick bath.

I couldn't have been gone more than twenty minutes, but in that time the table had been set, the meal placed, candles lit, and the servants dismissed for the night. She waited primly on a Hepplewhite chair made from mahogany with a satinwood veneer. Her black satiny dress fell off her shoulders and tucked neatly up under her breasts to bring them bubbling over the top like ivory balls. The sleeves gigot sheers. I took a deep breath and smelled the light scent of roses.

"Well, Bill," she said lightly. "You seem to have been a while."

"Yes, ma'am," I said, standing awkwardly in front of her. "That I have." I tore my stare from her breasts and studied the various trophies Custer had hung on his walls. One wall was filled with horns: antelope, deer, a pair of elk, with framed photographs sprinkled between them.

"Autie likes his trophies," she said dryly.

Something in her voice drew my attention back to her. Her eyes looked brittle, unamused, for a moment; then laughter rolled back into them. "My husband is a hunter, Bill. Of any game."

"Yes, ma'am, I know that," I said. I glanced back at the trophies gathered on the wall. A buffalo head had been mounted close to the ceiling and threatened to dominate the room. I pointed at it. "I was with him when he collected that one."

She rose and came over to stand close to me. This close, her scent bewildered my senses.

"Yes, I know. In fact"—she waved a hand at all of them—"I know about them all. Even the one he gathered down on the Washita. But you weren't there then, were you, Bill?"

"Call me James," I said. "That's my name."

She shook her head. "No, but I will call you Bill. James suggests far more intimacy than I intend."

I stepped back and stared down at her. "Ma'am? I'm sorry, but I'm not much good at these parlor games."

Her laughter rang through the room. Then she placed her hands deliberately behind her. I heard buttons slipping through their holes in the fabric of her dress; then the gown gathered in a soft black cloud at her feet. My eyebrows nearly pushed themselves off my forehead. She stood naked except for a pair of black net stockings held on her alabaster thighs by white garters with tiny red rosebuds upon them.

I gulped and glanced at the door. She laughed deeply. "It's locked, Bill. Don't worry. We won't be interrupted."

"We won't?" I asked stupidly. I couldn't take my eyes off of Custer's luck. I had never seen anyone so closely resembling pictures of old Grecian sculptures of Aphrodite before. She could have modeled for any of them with her high breasts, rounded to perfection, with large nipples pointing toward me. Her waist tucked in, her belly flowing smoothly down to her thighs and her heavy red-gold triangle between her legs.

She crossed to me and stood close, her breasts rubbing gently over my stomach. "We have all night, Bill. *All night,*" she emphasized. Then she placed her arms around my neck and kissed me deeply and I forgot about everything except wondering where the damn bed was.

I awakened in the early morning, sated, Elizabeth's head tucked in the hollow of my shoulder, her leg thrown across my belly. I kissed her gently and she opened her eyes to smile at me. "Are you hungry yet?" she asked.

"Not for food," I said, nuzzling her cheek.

She slapped my arm playfully. "You're insatiable. I like that." Then she drew away from me and sat up, back on her heels, looking down at me. Her eyes went serious. "I like this, Bill, but this is all it will ever be."

"I know. We've had this conversation before."

She touched my lips with her forefinger and ran the nail down my neck and chest to my groin. I shivered She smiled. "Bear with me. I want to emphasize our relationship. I won't leave Custer," she said. "I *can't* leave Custer. Oh, I know he's cheated on me—especially with that Cheyenne girl that he brought back from the Washita River when he destroyed Black Kettle's village. They had a son, I believe. I don't know. I was back in Michigan visiting family during that time." Her lips hardened. "Do you know a woman can always tell when her man has slept with another woman?" I shook my head. "It's true. We can always tell. It was in his hesitance toward me. And then there was the quiet talking whenever I came around. Eventually a couple of friends discovered what had happened and told me. At first I was hurt, then thought I would leave him. But"—she shook her head—"I couldn't. I have become a part of the Custer legend, you see. Just as much as if I rode with him constantly. And there's a good chance that he'll be president someday. George Benton, the New York publisher, is already laying the groundwork for Autie. I can't jeopardize that. You understand?"

"You mean you haven't jeopardized it with this?" I gestured at the bed. She laughed merrily.

"No, I haven't. Who would believe you? And besides," she purred, settling down upon my chest, "I don't think you are looking for any long involvements, either. Or am I mistaken?"

"You minx," I said, laughing in spite of myself. "You planned this all along!"

"Yes, I did," she said.

"And Custer had not sent word for me to meet him as soon as I arrived from scouting?"

She shook her head, her tresses trailing over my bare chest. "No. Are you mad?"

"I should be."

"But you're not."

"No. No, I'm not."

And I pulled her close, devouring her anxious lips, feeling her hands move hotly over my body, her legs wrapping around my waist—

Almost as good as Agnes Lake Thatcher, whom I met later—

But trouble wasn't far down the line, and trouble always seems to put an end to everything pleasant with me. I lost the election to my own deputy, Rattlesnake Pete, although I was really ready to leave Hays anyway. The town and the county were slow in paying me, forcing me to send a demanding letter to them:

ELLIS COUNTY

To J. B. Hickok Dr.

To services as policeman 1 month and 19 days at $75.00 per month $122.50. I certify that the above account is correct and remains due and unpaid.

J. B. Hickok

But my salary was short in coming, and following my defeat at the polls I took a brief vacation in Topeka before returning to Hays to try to collect what I was owed.

Dust. I remember the dust of the day. Hot. Sweaty. July 17, 1870. I was frustrated at not receiving my money and went into Paddy Walsh's saloon to have a drink that evening. The air hung like a fur coat over everyone, stifling. Five or six soldiers sat in a corner nursing their beer. I ignored them and walked to the bar. Paddy met me, smiling a welcome.

"Bill," he said pleasingly. "Damn, but you're a sight for sore eyes."

"Paddy. How about joining me in a drink?"

He grinned. "Now isn't that a fine thing to be saying to an Irishman? And what fool would be ignoring an invitation like that?" He reached beneath the bar and pulled out a dark bottle, winking at me as he did. "And we'll just start with a nip from the private stock."

I laughed and took the glass he offered, sipping. "How have you been, Paddy?" I asked.

He drank and sighed, nodding slightly toward the soldiers in the corner. "There's been the ups and the downs. Oh, I'm saying nothing against Pete, you understand, but there's a bit of a problem between himself and the soldiers. Right now, he's out of town after the person who cut out a couple of Jake Mason's cattle and we've had a wee bit of trouble—"

"Here now, is that a bottle of whiskey from the good land?" a rough voice said at my shoulder.

I glanced over, recognizing Jerry Lonigan and John Kelly, both in uniform, the sleeves of Kelly's blouse showing where sergeant's stripes had recently been taken. He grinned at me, his red face bloated with drink. I sighed inwardly and casually moved a half step to my left, putting distance between the three of us. I had had trouble in the past from both of them and knew they were baiting me, trying to draw me into trouble.

"It is that," Paddy said quietly.

"Well then, let's be having a glass," Kelly said.

"'Tis a sharing I do only with my friends," Paddy said. He nodded toward the other soldiers in the corner. "Be a good lad and go back to your suds with your mates."

Lonigan placed both hands on the bar, leaning over it to glare at Paddy. "So you'll be having a drink with the little miss here and ignore the men? Now what would that be making you?"

"The owner of the bar who's telling you to take your business elsewhere," Paddy said, his voice tight with warning. One hand dropped down beneath the level of the bar and I knew if it came up there would be a wooden bung stopper—he called it a shillelagh—that had ended more than one would-be brawl in his saloon when he crowned the fighters with it.

Kelly looked over at me, his eyes moving slowly over my hair. "Y'right, Jerry, me friend. 'Tis a fine set of curls on that head. Now, d'yuh suppose he would be willing to treat us?"

I recognized the insult in his words. "Keep a civil tongue in your head, Kelly," I said.

He beamed and turned toward me, his hand reaching out to push me in my chest. He froze as I brought a pistol up, cocked and pointing at his bulbous nose that glowed like a red bull's-eye lantern. "All right, you bog jumper," I said softly. "You want trouble? You've got it."

His eyes narrowed as he looked down the barrel of my pistol. "'Tis not a gunman I am and you're no man if you won't be meetin' another with something 'sides iron."

"That's no problem," I said. "Put your pistol on the bar. You, too, Lanigan, then go back to your friends."

The two unbuckled their belts and laid them on the bar. Lanigan walked back to the table with the others and stood beside it, watching. I smiled at Kelly.

"Back off, Kelly. Five steps backward."

Grudgingly he moved. I slipped the other pistol from my sash and laid it on the bar, holding the other steady on him as I slipped the Prince Albert from my shoulders. I handed it across to Paddy along with my other pistol and stepped toward Kelly.

"Now you satisfied?"

"Lad, you just made the biggest mistake of your wee life," he said, and swung a meaty fist at my jaw.

I swayed back and away, then stepped forward, hooking him low in his big belly with my left, and when he bent forward raked the heel of my palm up and over his chin, splitting his lips wide, shoving him away from me. He staggered backward and I stepped forward, hitting him again in the belly and this time hooking sharply with my right to his jaw, holding my elbows close in at my sides. His head snapped backward, his eyes crossed. He swung another clumsy right at me, but I slipped under it and hit him twice in the belly and snapped my head up, catching him on the point of his jaw. His teeth came together with an audible *click!* and he fell backward like a cut tree, crashing into a table, upturning it.

"Well," I said, turning toward Paddy. "That's that."

He started to smile; then his eyes closed warningly. I started to turn, ducking at the same time. A beer mug caught me a glancing blow on my temple, dazing me. I caught myself against the bar.

"Here now! Fair play!" Paddy shouted.

But the soldiers ignored him, swarming over me. A fist caught me on the jaw, stunning me. Another struck me in the belly, but I had tensed myself as I fell back against the bar and little damage happened. Then another glass smashed against my forehead, and I felt a cut open above my eyebrow. I levered myself up with my elbows on the bar and kicked out blindly with both feet. I connected with someone, heard him yell, and for a second I had breathing room. I slipped down the bar, striking out instinctively as someone came in from my right side. With satisfaction I felt bone give way, followed by a yelp of pain; then I caught a glimpse of metal.

"Bill!"

I half-turned and caught my pistols as Paddy flipped them to me.

"Look out!" someone shouted.

I fired at the flash of metal and heard someone scream from pain. A shot snapped past my ear. I fired at the flash in the gray smoke that began to fill the space between me and the soldiers. I fired again and heard the wet *smack!* as my bullet hit someone, where I couldn't tell. Dimly I saw Kelly rise from the floor and grab at his pistol on the bar. I snapped a shot at him and saw the bullet take him in the belly. He staggered, screamed, and fell to the floor, his head going forward as he grabbed the pain.

And then, quiet.

I stared at the two soldiers still standing. I motioned at them angrily, indicating the wounded on the floor. "Pick up your people and get out of here," I said furiously. "You wanted to buy into this, now you pay the piper. Get back to the fort where you belong."

"And you'll not be coming in this place again!" Paddy said emphatically. I glanced over my shoulder and saw him shouldering a shotgun, the barrel cut down to eighteen inches or less, at the soldiers. One blast from that would take out everybody in the room, and the soldiers knew that. Silently they helped the others to their feet; then two of them hoisted Kelly between them and they left.

Paddy sighed and lowered the shotgun. He glanced at me. "You'll need a bit of patching, Bill," he said. He poured another glass and slid it over to me. "But if I were you, I wouldn't be wasting much time on my aches and pains in Hays. Soon as Tom Custer hears about this, he'll be in after you, and there's nothing you can do about that with Pete out on the trail. The army's the law when the law's gone."

"I know," I said quietly. I downed the drink, shuddered against its bite, and took my coat, shrugging into it. I slid the Colts back into the sash and took a towel from him, pressing it against my forehead to stop the bleeding. I glanced at the repeater clock on the wall, noting the time.

"Be seeing you," I said, and stepped outside. I walked down to the station and caught the 9:05 train heading toward Topeka. I didn't draw a clean breath until the train pulled away from the station, ten minutes late as usual.

I never saw Elizabeth again. Nor George or Tom Custer, for that matter, although I heard about them several times. I still remember her, though, the soft nights, her wild abandon, and her fanatical devotion to Custer. A strange combination never resolved.

CHAPTER

43

ABILENE—"CITY of the PLAIN"—was a typical town, running from the east to the west. Texas Street ran next to the railroad while Cedar Street truckled south from the railroad about five blocks from Mud Creek. But it was A Street that was most important, for this was where Joe McCoy built his Drover's Cottage, three stories with a hundred rooms for the cattlemen bringing herds up from Texas and the buyers waiting to bid hotly for the mossyhorns those Texas randies pulled out of the brush.

The Alamo was the best saloon, but there were plenty of others ready to splash tanglefoot out into shot glasses for the cowboys after they'd had long overdue baths and dipped their tallywhackers in willing cyprians down in the Devil's Addition where they held their red-light practice. The Alamo had three sets of double-glass doors that folded back, and large paintings of nude women with "more bounce to the ounce" hung on the walls. Yet there were other saloons suited more to the wild man's fancy, such as the Bull's Head, the Applejack, the Old Fruit, the Elkhorn, the Pearl, the

Lone Star, and the Longhorn. I don't think there was a cattle town in Kansas that didn't have a Longhorn Saloon.

The "proper folk" of Abilene tried to maintain law and order in their town by hiring Tom Smith to be marshal. Smith, however, didn't believe in using firearms, preferring to pound a sense of right and wrong into those who'd strayed with his huge fists. But fists don't match up well with guns, and Smith was soon killed while trying to arrest a ne'er-do-well.

About that same time, McCoy was elected mayor and sent Charlie Gross to find me at Fort Harker, where I was playing poker and running a losing streak. I was offered the job of marshal of Abilene at $150 a month and 25 percent of all fines collected in court. I took office on April 15, 1871.

I do not believe there are angels hovering protectively over us, but there well could be apostates walking in our shadows. They wait to take advantage of our mistakes—and we all make them.

I have.

Neither love nor prayer can bring Mike back since I put him by mistake in the earth.

That was indeed a grave night.

I remember everything about it from the taste of the peppermint candy I had eaten to calm my stomach after a supper of steak—I seem to taste the cloying flavor even now—to the tiny shadows dancing at the edge of my vision. Somewhere, someone was banging out "Buffalo Gals" on a piano badly out of tune and the boys were whooping it up in the thick of the night. A haze of dust hung in the gloaming, creating halos around the lighted windows.

A few of the stalwart stodgers were down in the church trying to drown out "Buffalo Gals" with "Rock of Ages," singing in ancient, reedy voices, but even if it had been Sunday there weren't enough Christian voices to drown out the songs of pleasure. A few black-garbed women had earlier marched down the street followed by old Mose Harper diligently pounding a bass drum so loudly that he drowned out the sheaves they were trying to bring in, much to the amusement of a few liquored-up cowboys who stood on the corner smoking hand-rolleds while catching their second wind to have another go at chasing the elephant.

Beside me, Joe, the fire dog that had adopted me, sat on his brown-spotted haunches and occasionally moaned a long, sad refrain to the music—much to the annoyance of the Ladies Brigade led by the mayor's wife, Ida.

She had a nose like a blue heron and a chin like a pelican followed by a goiter that turned liver red and flounced back and forth like a turkey's wattles when she got angry, which was most of the time—which was why the mayor spent as much time as he could sneak in at Mexican Lupe's small house down by the cattle pens. He figured he was safe enough down there because Ida was certain that all Mexicans were in league with the devil, and would rather be caught outside without her bustle than be within a hundred yards of Lupe's place.

Ida was always accompanied by the Widow Johnson—I swear, it seems like every town I've been in has a Widow Johnson in it and every one of them is scrawny-necked, pigeon-breasted, and has a face that looks like it's been savaged with an ice pick. The widow and Ida were quite a pair, each gifted with a tongue that could lash varnish off a mahogany bar. And given to using it with a frequency that challenged the rising of the moon.

I remember once when the Widow Johnson got to haranguing a pair of cowboys fresh from Texas without the trail dust washed off them yet and the back of their throats parched dry as the desert wind from New Mexico chasing tumbleweeds over the Chisholm Trail. They took it for a while—like most Texas cowboys, they had a healthy respect for women—but when she raised a question about their mothers (one *never* questions a Texan's mother whether one knew her or not) one of them draped a noose around her middle and pulled her squawking like an upended chicken into a water trough. When that failed to cool her ardor, they tired quickly of their game and raised her up over the Bull's Head saloon sign. One of them used his bowie knife to quickly divest her of dress, bustle, and, well, everything and left her dangling there, red-faced with embarrassment, turning this way and that, trying to hide her nakedness and not knowing which part, north or south, to cover first. The children got a quick education in the female anatomy—although since she had ventured on her own down toward the cattle pens, there weren't many children who lived there who hadn't had an eyeful of a naked woman more than once.

When I finally arrived there to cut her down, tears were flowing through the caked dust on her face, but I swear there was a new light in her eyes, hidden behind her fronted indignation—excitement, if I'm any judge (and I am)—and I reckon I was right on that, because this Widow Johnson left town on the next stage. I found her six months later in Wichita in one of the upstairs rooms of The Oriental, rouged and happy in her rebirth.

But Ida worried at my days and nights like a dog at a fresh butcher's bone, caterwauling about the degradation *proper women* (I know what that implies but hanged if I can *understand* the difference) had to undergo in that lawless and godless community. She enlisted the aid of just about every churchgoing woman in town, berating me for not doing my duty by shutting down the dens of iniquity flourishing in town. Finally, I tired of listening to her and her friends and did just what she and the others asked—much to the consternation of their husbands, who finally put their collective foot down and forbade their wives from dabbling in politics when the husbands discovered taxes would have to go up 3,000 percent to make up the differences in the budget normally covered by the "weekly fines" once levied upon the cyprian practitioners. In no uncertain terms, the ladies were told to concentrate on other godly activities, setting women's suffrage back a decade or so.

But all that happened long before I killed Mike by accident.

Sometimes I wonder if there is a God and if Father wasn't just whistling a hopeful tune in the dark with all his quiet lessons by the flickering firelight at night before the hearth after the supper dishes had been cleared and all of us had gathered to listen to him read from the Bible.

Funny that I should remember them now—why?—

I think it all began—I *know* it all began; what do I think I'm doing by pretending ignorance?—when the governor didn't act quickly enough to provide law for Hays City to satisfy the citizens who elected me to be the marshal or sheriff. I never was quite certain which office I legally held, but it was enough at the time to satisfy the citizens of Hays City, who really were interested in only two things in a sheriff: his reputation for handling pistols and his reputation as a man killer.

I had both. And it didn't take long for me to have to prove it. Once a person has a reputation for that type of work, someone is always trying to take it away from him. I have *never* understood why anyone would deliberately go out of his way to want such a reputation, but there are always those madmen who equate strength and power with murder.

The warm night spread over us like a soft blanket. I relaxed at the table in the back, my chair resting against the wall, watching the room contentedly, enjoying the night for what it was and trying to forget what it would become in a couple of days when the trail herds began pouring up in beefy waves like a sick cantankerous sea over the Chisholm Trail from Texas. Abilene waited impatiently, anxiously, for their arrival. The dry goods stores had filled their stock with the latest hats and shirts and pants and broadcloth coats, the women's shops had their hat stock with delicate feathers and veils and stylish sunbonnets refilled, with Chicago, Boston, and New York labels sewn in them by seamstresses in Cleveland to double their prices, the general stores had laid in supplies of preserved foods—namely, peaches, to satisfy the sweet tooth of some cowboys—and cases upon cases of liquor and countless barrels of beer had been stored in the back rooms of the saloons.

Unfortunately, the riffraff also arrived early, gamblers in velvet-collared pearl gray coats over brocade vests. Two gamblers sat a couple of tables away from me even now, practicing their deals. I watched as one tried to deal a hand of "seconds" around the edge of the table, and sighed, knowing he would be one I would have to deal with sooner or later if he tried that trick on a sharp-eyed Texas cowboy who knew his game—and practically all of them did. I hoped it wouldn't end in a burial, but, I shrugged philosophically, that was a risk one took when one played with such foolishness.

The door pushed open and "Pie" Downstreet, the "printer's devil" we called him, although he was the editor of the local paper, staggered in, eyes peering redly through the dim light left by the burning peg lamps on the walls. His long coat hung loosely on his narrow shoulders hunched like a vulture's wings. His white shirt was ink-stained, but his string tie had been carefully knotted at his throat. He needed a shave, but he wore his derby cocked at a dignified slant over his forehead. Tufts of graying blond hair stuck out from under the brim. He weaved for a moment in the doorway, then made his way to the mahogany bar, freshly waxed and gleaming wetly. He tapped with a finger on the bar and Muggins, the barkeep, looked up from his place at the end where he had been polishing glasses with a dirty towel to remove water spots.

"What can I do for you, Pie?" he asked solicitously.

"A little whiskey if you will, my good man," Pie said, forming the words carefully. "This is a sad day for all." He squinted through the gloom and shook his head. "And there's not a man jack of you knows why."

One of the gamblers looked up, showing mild interest. "Someone die?"

Pie nodded and slowly picked up the glass poured him by Muggins. He turned it slowly, admiring the way the light refracted off the whiskey's amber surface. "Yes. A lot of people." His eyes looked into the distance for a moment; then he said solemnly, "Here's to the death of the sovereign state of Georgia."

"Aw, hell," the gambler said, disappointed. "Another damn Southerner."

I sighed again and picked up my glass, draining it. I rose,

settling my coat over my shoulders and loosening my pistols in the red sash around my waist. Pie was normally an easy-goer, but when he had "drink taken"—as he put it—a craziness would come over him at times and he became sullen and morose and belligerent, taking offense easily.

He drained the glass quickly and set it precisely in the middle of the bar. Muggins took one look at Pie's face and reached under the bar for the sawed-off billiard cue he kept there.

"Pie," he said warningly. "Let's not do anything we'll be sorry for. I'll give you a final tot on the house and you make it a night. What do you say?"

Pie gave him a long dignified look, then drew himself up and straightened the settle of his coat over his shoulders. "I thank you for your hospitality, Mr. Muggins, and the libation offer, but there's a little matter of an insult to settle."

He started to turn from the bar. Muggins began to raise his stick, but I shook my head warningly and stepped up beside Pie, laying my hand on his shoulder, pressing him back against the bar, keeping him from turning.

"Now, Pie, I don't want trouble tonight. I'll have enough of that in a few days. So let's have a quiet drink and then I'll walk you home. After," I said, turning pointedly toward the outspoken gambler, "this gentleman conveys his apology."

The gambler frowned and leaned back in his chair, his hands slipping under the edge of the table. "I don't apologize to drunks. Especially Southern trash," he said.

Beside me, Pie took a deep breath, air whistling through his teeth. He tried to turn again, but by now I had the collar of his coat in a firm grasp.

"Mister," I said softly, "that wasn't an option. You made a mistake. Own up to it. And"—I glanced at the edge of the table to where his hands had disappeared—"don't be foolish enough to compound it. Bring your hands up slowly." I rested the palm of my right hand lightly on the pistol nestling butt forward, my wrist curved slightly for a twist-draw if needed.

Indecision flickered in his eyes and briefly I felt a cold

chill run through me. Then Muggins spoke up from behind my left shoulder.

"You want I should throw them out, Marshal Hickok?"

The gambler's face turned pasty white. He swallowed with difficulty and carefully raised his trembling hands above the edge of the table and rested them on the green felt surface. They twitched as if he had palsy.

"Hickok. Sorry. I didn't know."

I shook my head. "Shouldn't have mattered," I said. "Now it does. You've got three choices: Take the first train east or the first train west. Miss either one and you go north next."

"North?" A puzzled look came over his face. His partner coughed. The first gambler looked questioningly at him.

"He means Boot Hill," the second said apologetically.

The first gambler's head swiveled back to me. "You throwing me out of town? Last I heard, this was a free country. Lincoln made it that way when he freed all the niggers and we beat the hell out of those Southern bastards who didn't believe he could do that."

"The country is," I said gently. "But this town isn't. Here I make the rules who stays and who moves on. You've got the mark of trouble about you, and that I don't need. Now or later. So I'm just taking care of that now." I looked at the clock on the far wall. "I think you've got about an hour to get your things together. The nine-oh-five is due through then." I waited for a moment, but he continued to stare at me. I released Pie's collar and took a step away from him. I shifted my balance to the balls of my feet, feeling the cold chill race through me again, prickling my skin.

"It's not much of a choice, but it's the only smart one to make," I said softly.

His partner cleared his throat noisily and I divided my attention between the two of them.

"I heard about what you did at Rock Creek Station," he said. I waited, remaining silent, watching. It was his game now. I was just one of the players. He waited for me to answer, and when I didn't he rubbed his nose with the heel of his hand. "I heard about that shot you made at Hawkin's

Ridge in the war. How far was it? Some say a mile, but that seems a bit far to me. Probably an exaggeration, I'm thinking. Right?"

"Damn fool," Pie muttered from beside me. The gambler's eyes crossed to him, growing ugly. "You're talking yourself into being brave and right into your grave."

Then, just as suddenly, it was over. The gambler threw up his hands. "Not me," he said quickly. "I was just making small talk. You know?" he added, looking my way.

I nodded. "Yes. I know. It's dangerous talk, though. You go along with your friend now, and don't come back to Abilene again. Understand?" Indecision flickered in their eyes. "We don't know your names, so there's no shame to follow you. But again, there'll be only 'Anonymous' on your headboard if you push this. Nobody will know what happened here unless you tell them."

Silently they rose and quietly left the saloon. I waited for a minute in case one of them suddenly found his nerve up again, then relaxed and turned back to the bar.

Wordlessly Muggins slid a tumbler of whiskey in front of me and one in front of Pie. He poured a third glass for himself.

"Well, I'm glad that came to nothing," he said. He raised his glass to ours, and we drank to our good fortune.

"No loss with those two," he said, lowering his glass. "I marked them for trouble when they first came in. They were too smug, you know? As if they already had the game they were planning on playing won." He closed one eye and leaned his elbow on the bar. "You handled that real well, Marshal. And I thank you."

"My job," I said, finishing my drink.

He shook his head and made a motion with the whiskey bottle, but I placed my hand over my glass.

"No, sir," he said. "You could have killed them and no one would have faulted you for that. You'd have been doing your job that way, too." He nodded, pressing his lips together. "And most would have—'cept for Tom Smith, I reckon. He would have just used those big fists upon them." He shook his head. "Glad to see it end the way it did."

"A killing doesn't solve anything," I said. A faint picture of Father appeared at the edge of my thoughts. A bitter smile crossed my lips.

Remember, James, he who lives by the sword dies by the sword. But sometimes there are those who are destined to that life. There was a time when even God needed the warrior Michael and Charlemagne his paladins. Sometimes, a certain man is needed, but that doesn't mean he gets a free ride out of it. A killing is always a killing whether it is needed or not. And few escape a return stroke once they swing their sword.

"You all right?" Pie said curiously from beside me.

I blinked my way back to the present. I frowned, shaking my head. This drifting was happening more and more lately. A dangerous time for someone marked by others. I glanced into the mirror behind the bar and for a brief moment felt a shock run through me at the recognition of the lined face staring back from what looked like a soft halo. My eyes had been bothering me lately, aching. When had those creases started to appear? I couldn't remember although I stared into the shaving mirror every day.

"Come on," I said roughly to Pie. "I'd better walk you home before you take it in your head to lick half of Abilene."

He finished his drink and handed the glass to Muggins. "Ah, that's kind of you, Marshal, but the night still has heels on it and hasn't started yet to tiptoe into dawn. And I, for one, am thinking a trip to Mrs. Mack's fine house would be a fine way of settling the hours into a calming state." He produced a battered pewter flask and handed it to Muggins. "Fill it up, sir, to give us the strength for our journey to the fine manse where the good widow still directs others into how to lock their shins around a man's worthy middle."

Muggins raised his eyebrow at this but took the flask, stoppered it with a small funnel, and filled it with the good whiskey he kept beneath the bar, Tennessee samplings left behind by traveling salesmen trying to increase their territory.

I shook my head. "I think not, Pie. But I'll walk you to Mrs. Mack's if that's where you want to go."

He blinked watering eyes at me and took his flask from Muggins, carefully restoring it to the inside pocket from whence it came.

"A gentleman indeed!" Pie exclaimed. He turned, sliding one hand under my elbow, gesturing eloquently like a Cicero with the other. *"Vidi aquam egredientem de templo a latere dextro. Alleluia!"*

Muggins leaned forward, beckoned, and whispered across the bar. "Do you understand him when he gets into that?"

"Yes," I replied. "It's loneliness. And fear."

"Fear?" He frowned. "Of what?"

I shook my head. "I don't know. It's general among all men. For some, it's growing old." I couldn't help glancing again at my reflection in the mirror. Muggins caught my look and nodded.

"I understand," he said. "Especially when you're alone, right?"

I smiled, following Pie's gentle pulling on my arm. "Yes. Especially when you're alone."

"Salvi facti i sunt. Ad deam qui laetificat juventuteng meam," he slurred.

"Damned if I know what you're saying. I take it you were an altar boy," I said. I stumbled a bit, trying to match my step to his shambling stride. He laughed at what he thought to be my clumsiness.

"Come, Marshal, let us make our way to Mrs. Mack's mantrap," he said.

I glanced back at Muggins, who shook his head and made his way from around the edge of the bar. "I think I'll just close up," he said resignedly.

"It's a bit early for a saloon to be closing, isn't it?" I asked.

"Yeah," he grunted. "But tonight's a bit empty." He glanced around. "Besides, there's nothing more lonely than being alone in an empty saloon at night. I think I might just call it an evening and get some rest while I can."

Pie and I made our way down the boardwalk. When we passed the Bull's Head tavern, a voice came from the shadows, caressing us with false interest. "Hello, boys. You interested in searching out maidenheads?"

Pie paused, weaving slightly as he tried to peer into the shadows. "That you, Cissy?" he asked.

"Go to hell, Pie," the voice said. "I'da known it was you, I woulda kept my mouth shut."

"La belle dame sans merci," Pie said, placing his hand over his heart. He doffed his derby in her direction.

"Don't be doffing that come-to-bed hat of yours to *me*!" she said sharply. Then a note of new interest came into her voice. "But who's that with you, Pie? What long drink of water is that beside you?"

She came swaying out of the shadows into the pale moonlight. Her crimson dress shone wetly like dark blood. Her net stockings looked like spiderwebs wrapped around her thin legs. She eyed me boldly, but for all her pretending, I knew she recognized me. She bent forward, pretending to study me, allowing her bodice to drape open and her buddies to move tantalizingly like old ivory cones in the moonlight.

"Ah now, Cissy, you know full well this man," Pie said. He wagged an admonishing finger at her. "You're being a bit frivol', aren't you? Looking for a bit of a roll with the good marshal here? A nip and tuck? A quickie in the alley?"

She ignored him, her black eyes boldly eyeing me. "My goodness! So it *is* the marshal. My, my, my." She straightened, arching her shoulders back, posing provocatively. "I hope I didn't say anything wrong." She slipped her pulpy tongue between her lips as if pretending to offer me a kiss, but I knew the fakery in her gesture for the reality she meant.

"No," I said, my lips spreading into a grin. "You've said nothing wrong. But I'm not interested. Sorry."

She pouted and threw her head back, making her hair flounce at the back of her neck. Then she laughed throatily.

"So," she said. "You're after helping this old rousty down to the red house, eh? Down to old Mrs. Mack's? Well." She cocked her head to the side, eyeing me saucily. "You might go that far and fare the worse for your walking."

"Not tonight, fair Cissy," Pie said hastily.

"And why not tonight?" she snapped back, annoyed. "Do you think you hold the hours in your hand to dole out when you want like pennies to a beggar?" She thumped herself between her breasts with her thumb. "I can walk where I want without begging your permission, you old pirate! I haven't forgotten how you left me in the morning hours without so much as a kiss for my time!" She looked at me, pointing an accusing finger at Pie, now rocking back on his heels to put as much distance as he could between him and her fury. "I demand you arrest this man, Marshal!"

"Oh?" I struggled to hold myself serious. "And what charges should I bring against him?"

"He stole . . . He stole . . ." She paused, shaking her head. "First, he took advantage of my 'charms,'" she said delicately, "when I was in a soft moment. Then, he left me without so much as a thank-you and . . . he stole my garter. Black with tiny red rosebuds upon it! But"—her eyes grew steely—"he raised dangerous feelings I didn't know I had!"

I looked at Pie, who was squirming in embarrassment. "Did you do that, Pie?"

"Ah now, that was a goodly time ago and I can't remember everything that's happened since the end of the war—"

"Ah," she said disgustedly, making a gesture as if brushing him from the night. "You're like all the rest of them who fought, always blaming the war for something you don't want to have anything to do with! When are you going to forget the war and get on with your life? Besides," she continued, "you are a liar!" She stepped boldly up to him, backing him to a porch post. "You are a lying whoreson—"

"'Tis the pot calling the kettle black!" he said. He swung around behind the post, placing it protectively between them. "Keep her away from me, Marshal! Before I lose my temper! A woman with an adder's tongue has a bite to her as well! She speaks poniards, and every word stabs: If her breath were as terrible as her terminations, there were no living near her; she infects to the North Star!"

She spun on her heels and stared up angrily at me. "Well?" she demanded. "Are you going to arrest this romper or not?"

I shook my head. "Not," I said.

She stared at me in disbelief, then threw up her hands, spitting the word, "Men!" as if it was a curse that had been placed upon the whole earth. Then, turning, she stomped back into the shadows.

"Whew!" Pie said. He pulled a dirty handkerchief from the sleeve of his coat and wiped his face. "That harridan will be the death of me yet!"

"Maybe you should just give back her garter," I suggested. "And perhaps a little something to soothe her ruffled feathers?"

"There's wisdom in the simile," he said solemnly. "But for all of that, she's a whore. Still . . ." His voice trailed off musingly as he looked in the dark where she had disappeared. He pulled the flask almost absentmindedly from his pocket and took a drink. He offered it to me, but I shook my head and he returned it to his pocket. "Still," he repeated, "in a way so are we all."

Then he brightened and, holding his hat to his head, craned his head upward, studying the heavens. " 'Tis nearing the very witching time of night when the churchyards yawn and graves gape wide and hell breathes out a contagion to the world!" He grabbed my arm, pulling me urgently down the street. "And it's best the time for all who would run the wild-goose chase to take themselves well away to the hellsgate and Queen Mack."

"Yes," I said. "I think that would be most prudent—to get you off the street."

"I sense a mockery in your words, Marshal, but no matter. Time marches on and opportunity with it. We must hasten to catch it!"

I sensed a strange urgency to his words and remained

silent, following him as we hurried down the street to Mrs. Mack's house. The whorehouse sat on the edge of the town on a little rise above the streams that trickled from the cattle pens draining into the creek. Stones had been haphazardly placed to guide the unwary foot over the soggy ground. A rich smell rose from the streams and grounds, raw and nearly overpowering, but Mrs. Mack had directed the planting of rosebushes and lilac bushes, jack-in-the-pulpits, lilies of the valley, rose of Sharons, mimosa, all scented flowers that bloomed continuously until the first killing frost, masking the cattle smell effectively, creating a tasteful garden in the middle of swamp and squalor.

"Ah, the abode of Circe!" Pie said as we approached.

The three-story house gleamed whitely like a marble tomb, although lights shone cheerfully from many windows and a strange cascade of notes fell from inside in a series of five. I couldn't recognize the song, but the line was simple enough that I wished for my fiddle, wanting to join the anonymous player in a tune or two.

We stumbled up onto the porch and Pie hammered on the freshly enameled red door. It opened quickly and Mrs. Mack stood in front of us, dressed in a blue silk gown that did much to hide her age. She held a drink in one hand and stared affectionately at Pie.

"Well," she said, the word rasping in her throat. "I was wondering if you were going to make it tonight." She glanced at me and her smile tightened perceptively as she recognized me. "Are you helping him, too, Marshal?"

My eyebrows rose in puzzlement. She nodded and her smile slipped to sadness. "You don't know. I see. Well, come on in, you wastrel boys!" She stood back, throwing the door open wide. I caught a glimpse of an emaciated black man sitting at the piano, improvising, the sleeves of his red pin-striped shirt held tightly to his thin biceps with red garters. A young cowboy, his hair still gleaming from his recent bath, sprawled on a lion-footed couch with a fleshy blond whore on one arm and a sober-faced Indian, long glossy hair as shiny as a raven's wing falling to her waist, on the other. Both were half-naked.

Pie stepped through the doorway, lifting his hat from his head, piously intoning, "*Introibo ad altare Dei.*" He stopped in the center of the room, blessing the four cardinal directions and, by default, all in the room.

The blonde beside the cowboy gave a squeal upon hearing him and leaped away from the side of the cowboy, hopping across the red and gray Oriental rug to throw her arms around Pie's neck, hugging him tightly.

"Pie!" she said happily.

"Ah, Zoë," he said, patting her rump affectionately.

The cowboy looked annoyed and started to gather his legs to rise. I stepped through the door still held open by Mrs. Mack. The cowboy glanced at me, then paused and looked again. I saw within him the same hellfires that burned within me. But I did not see a shadow of goodness that could cool those raging fires and turn the man-host away from his trespasses.

"I know you?" he asked, a touch of insolence to his voice.

"You don't know how long I've been waiting for you!" Zoë exclaimed.

"Ah, yes. 'Tis nice to be missed," Pie said.

"Perhaps," I answered easily. "Where you from, cowboy?"

He stiffened, his face closing tightly with anger. I couldn't blame him; it wasn't a question that one asked another in the West until they had ridden together for a month or two—and perhaps even not then. I knew a couple of old-timers high on the divide who didn't know each other's given name, yet they had been together in that cabin for the better part of twenty years. But it was a question a marshal had to ask—or *better* ask—from time to time simply to be prudent. There was no reason not to answer the question when an officer of the law asked it—unless there was a cloud along a person's back trail or, more often I had found, he wanted to create the *illusion* of a cloud to impress someone, usually a young woman. But the women in Mrs. Mack's had known those men who did not need to impress anyone, and looked upon such youthful posing as pure posturing.

"Getting a bit personal, aren't you?" he asked.

"Goes with the job, kid. Take it easy," I said.

He flushed. "I ain't a kid and you can stuff easy up your butt!" he said hotly, his face red like spoiled liver with anger.

Pie cocked a red-flashed eye over Zoë's bare shoulder. "Now there stands a man whose empty words threaten to loose a hurricane!"

The cowboy flushed fiery red, going all hot around the eyes as anger flexed through him. "Shut up, you old fool! I don't need no lip from you, either!"

"Oh?" Pie asked, raising his eyebrows innocently. "And what do you need from me?"

The cowboy started forward, his fists clenched tightly at his sides.

"And you don't need nothing here, either!" Mrs. Mack said, stepping forward, blocking him. "Get your hat, cowboy, and hit the trail!"

He swayed for a moment, his lips curling into a sneer. "You're throwing me out of a whorehouse? Nobody throws me out of a whorehouse! Especially an old whore like you!"

"Get out," Mrs. Mack snapped. "You can just go on down to Buck's Livery. He's got a nanny goat out back. Either that or go back to pulling your tallywhacker on the trail, 'cause it ain't gonna get pulled in here!"

"That's it!" I said. I grabbed him by the shoulder and spun him toward the door. He turned back, swinging wildly. I shifted my weight, dropped my left, and when his eyes followed it automatically threw an overhand right hard against his jaw. He dropped like a sledgehammered steer. I grabbed his feet and pulled him out of the room. His head bounced like a nursery ball down the three steps from Mrs. Mack's porch. I dragged him over to the corner of the yard and left him under the lilac bushes planted there and went back inside.

"Well played, thou just and faithful servant!" Pie cried, peeling Zoë from around his neck and applauding.

A cuckoo clock on the wall began crying: *Cuckoo! Cuckoo! Cuckoo!*—

I glanced at it: eleven.

Mrs. Mack stepped forward, her fingers touching me lightly on my cheeks. Rice powder seemed ingrained in every pore of her face. She had blended kohl half moons under her eyes and deeply rouged her lips and cheeks scarlet. Her hennaed hair had a fresh look and the scent she wore had an expensive musk to it.

I could tell she was old by the tired lines she had artfully hidden and the world-weary knowledge that she kept half-hidden behind green eyes. Yet she carried a sensuality with her like the mantle of Aphrodite discreetly draped over her shoulders.

She smiled gently, and I knew she had seen interest quicken in my eyes, but she shook her head.

"Thank you again, Marshal. A woman—even an old whore—likes to be reminded she is still wanted. But tonight belongs to Pie."

Zoë immediately stepped back, looking chagrined. "I'm sorry, Pie. I didn't know what day it was."

I frowned, looking at the old editor and the tears gathering in his eyes and sprinkling his cheeks like diamonds. He nodded, patting her gently on the shoulder.

"June seventeenth," he said kindly. "I don't expect you to remember, my dear. It's enough that I do." He looked at Mrs. Mack and corrected himself. "*We* do."

"Yes," Mrs. Mack said softly, placing her hand gently on his arm. Zoë took his hat from him and stepped back respectfully, courteously waiting.

"Thank you, Zoë," Pie said. He smiled at Mrs. Mack.

"Ned," she said. The piano player looked over his shoulder. His eyes were puffy and yellow, and I knew if I stood next to him I would smell the sick-sweet scent of opium.

"Yas 'um?" he mumbled.

"Play 'The Drover's Waltz,' " she said.

A look of mild surprise came into his eyes. "It that time o'year, 'gin?" he mumbled. Then, his fingers stretched and flexed and the groups of five rolled sweetly into the waltz. Pie held his arms out and Mrs. Mack gathered the hem of her gown in one hand and stepped into them. They swayed together for a second, picking up the rhythm, then slipped gracefully into the dance.

Dimly I was aware of time shifting, Pie wearing a frock coat with watered-silk facings, a starched shirt with mother-of-pearl studs, long trousers ironed tightly, with his feet encased in highly polished Congress boots; she in a moonlit blue gown with matching shoes, dance card held around one wrist by a gold ribbon, her gloved fingers resting lightly on Pie's gloved palm. The years fell away, and I heard the strings of an orchestra, the low murmur of polite talk, yet Pie and Mrs. Mack were oblivious to it all, lost in the world of their own making. I sensed coaches waiting, carefully groomed horses restlessly shuffling hooves on cobblestones, uniformed men cordoning off a crowd of the curious pressing close to catch with eager eyes a glimpse of the world they could never have. Then others danced by—one who could only be a mayor or governor or senator or perhaps all three, with a plump, partridge-pouting-breasted dowager in black in his arms.

And then they were gone.

As were Pie and Mrs. Mack.

I blinked, then felt a small hand in my own, leading me to the spangled couch. Zoë smiled gently up at me as we sat together. Her hand slipped over my thigh as she leaned into me, twisting her shoulders so my hand seemed to naturally cup her breast and her nipple pressed urgently against my palm. Her breath had a faint hint of garlic to it, not unpleasant. Her forehead was smooth alabaster, her nose aquiline, hooked slightly at the end above bow-shaped lips. A tiny mole stood at the corner of one eye, both eyes the color of deep-blue mountain lakes.

"What is so special about the day?" I asked.

She sighed and tiny tears squeezed out of those deep-blue eyes. She snuggled closer to me and her hand slipped between my thighs.

"It's the night when Pie's wife died trying to give birth," she said lowly. "Both of them. The baby, too, I mean. At midnight."

"And what does that have to do with Mrs. Mack?"

"She was, is, his wife's sister."

"Sister?"

"Happened fifteen years or so ago this very night," she said. "Ever since, they have spent the night together."

"Fifteen years? How would you know all that? You're not that old."

She smiled sadly. "There's not a whore anywhere doesn't know that story. It happened in Atlanta during the war. It's sort of like real love, you see?"

"No," I said. "I don't see that. I just see two tired old folks trying to remember better times."

"Maybe," she said. She lay quietly against me, fondling me absentmindedly, her thoughts elsewhere.

Ned shifted his song again into the handful of five notes he had been noodling with earlier. I wished again for my fiddle. Then a song began to emerge from the abstract chords and runs. I closed my eyes, concentrating, trying to remember.

James.

The word whispered softly from the air. I opened my eyes, seeking the speaker.

James.

A command then. The voice familiar. Then, suddenly, Father stood before me, black burial suit moldering, his face leper gray, blue-circled hollow eyes staring mesmerizingly into mine.

James. Repent. Now. Leave this den of iniquity.

"I cannot," I said.

"Pardon?" Zoë said.

You fornicated while I lay dying.

"Accident," I muttered. "Who can tell the comings and goings of man?"

"Are you all right, Marshal?"

You learned your lessons well. But you were the death of me.

"No."

"Shall I get you a drink?"

Yes. With your disobedience. Now I say to you: Leave this whoresden and return to your mother.

I shook my head. "Too late for that."

"For a drink?"

Too late? It is never too late to repent. Lift up your eyes unto the Lord. Knock upon the door and it shall be opened unto you.

"And the wicked if I leave? Will they inherit the earth? No, Father, it is too late to repent, too late to begin again."

"Oh, Marshal. What is it?"

And his face seemed to soften under its gray shade and then I felt the ache of his love come across the room between us on his ashen breath. He began to slowly weave back and forth like the shadows of dappled leaves in a sunlit slow breeze.

James. James. James.

"I'm Bill now, Father. James is no more."

No more.

"Remember? Once upon a time a knight—"

Not long now, James.

My mouth felt dry. "Father?"

Slowly the specter faded, leaving behind only the hint of a whispered, *Not long.* I started, leaping to my feet. Zoë fell away, clutching the arm of the couch to keep from tumbling to the floor.

"What—" she began, confused.

I looked across the room into the mirror bracketed with deer antlers. My features looked drawn and gray and old. Cuckolded by fate. An antique smell of mold and dank earth permeated the room. I recognized the smell: like old battlefields filled with rotting bodies and covered with heavy, cold fog.

I walked shakily to the window and looked out. Zoë came with me and anxiously pressed against me. My face felt damp from perspiration. I looked out into the darkness, glancing toward the lilac bushes where I had unceremoniously dumped the young cowboy. The ground was vacant beneath the bushes. I nodded toward them.

"Did that cowboy give his name?"

"Calls himself John Wesley Hardin," she said. I glanced down at her. She frowned, concerned. "Why? Do you know him?"

I shook my head. "Never heard of him."

She looked relieved. "He said his boss sent him ahead of the herd to look things over. I think he was lining up buyers."

I nodded. The name of a minister, but there was hell in that boy, and a coldness in the pit of my stomach told me I would be seeing him again, soon.

Cuckoo. Cuckoo. Cuckoo—

"Bill?"

I looked down at her face, blurred around the edges now in the half shadows by the window. She looked soft and vulnerable, needing.

"It's after midnight. Do you want to go to bed?"

I glanced at the stairway, then overhead. I felt the need, too.

"Yes," I said softly. "Yes. I think I would like that."

She sighed and snuggled her head against my chest. I placed my arm around her, holding tightly to her youth as we climbed the stairs to her room beneath the eaves.

CHAPTER

44

THE HOUSE seemed empty when I came down two hours later from Zoë's room. I felt strangely nervous, on edge, although there was no reason for me to feel that way. The whiskey had worn off, and although I was tired, everything appeared bright and lucid. The piano player was gone; the whores were gone. I breathed deeply through my nose, smelling the cheap perfume, whiskey, other strange scents that were not strange in that house. I glanced into the mirror between the antlered hat rack on the wall beside the door to check my dress. A tired old man looked back, and briefly, for a scant moment that burned itself into my mind, I saw the face of my father in mine.

"Cuckolded by fate, aren't we, Father?" I murmured. Then the image changed and I saw myself with fine lines criss-crossing my forehead like a scout's rudely drawn map. Suddenly I felt old, as old as the hills, and the weight of time burying itself upon my shoulders like the stone of Sisyphus. And, like Sisyphus, I felt as if all I was trying to do kept rolling back down on top of me, burying me.

Briefly I saw hills studded with dark pines, a gulch with a small stream running like a snake through it, tents and quick buildings tossed up to serve the citizens slogging through muddy streets, and dimly I heard strained-string twanging of banjos playing "Buffalo Gals" and an out-of-tune piano or two rattling out jangling noise that only the player could appreciate.

> *"Buffalo gals, won't you come out tonight . . ."*

merged with

> *"Once in the dear, dead days beyond recall*
> *When on the world the mists began to fall."*

I crossed to the window and looked out again at the lilac bushes, half-expecting to see the cowboy I had lain there still there, although I knew he had been long gone. A strange premonition came over me. I felt empty, brooding, as if something vital had been taken from me.

I sensed someone beside me and looked down at the Indian woman I had seen earlier on the couch with Zoë and the cowboy. She looked tired, with bruised half moons under her eyes. A tiny red mark appeared on the side of her neck. I glanced around the room, but we were alone.

"You don't remember me, do you?" she asked, her full lips smiling slightly, ironically.

I studied her carefully—her skin shone like burnished copper, her breasts full, aureoles large and nearly purple, legs short and muscular but finely shaped. There *was* something familiar about her. But what? Slowly I shook my head.

"I'm sorry," I said regretfully. "Should I?"

"Annie was my sister," she said softly, her lips curling back from white teeth.

Indian Annie. Annie Liffey.

Ellsworth, 1867. Smoky fall had draped itself upon us and I breathed deeply as I rode on Black into Ellsworth, a quarter of an antelope tied behind my saddle. I rose early that

morning and saddled Black, riding out mainly to clean the
sour saloon taste from my mouth and the cigar smoke fog
from my lungs. I breathed deeply of the cold air on the
prairie and lifted the reins. Black needed no further urging
and broke into a ground-gaining lope that he could carry all
day if necessary. I sensed the joy in the one-eyed horse as he
shook his head, his long mane flashing in the gray light as he
sensed the open space in front of us.

I let him run for a long while, until his skin was shiny with
sweat, but his breathing was still deep and easy. I turned him
away from the road. He plunged with joy into the deep buffalo grass and grama grass that swept in undulating waves in
front of us. We moved up and down the hills. I let him pick
his own way. Finally, he came to Fossil Creek and dropped
down into a trot until he came to the edge of the water. Then
he snorted and bent his head, drinking the cold, clear water.
I sensed movement at the edge of my vision and turned to
see a small herd of antelope coming down a ridgeline a short
distance away.

On an impulse, I slipped from the saddle, sliding my
Henry out of its scabbard. Black froze as the reins hit the
water in front of him, standing rigid as a statue. I faded away
from his side into a stand of willow beside a thick bunch of
bluestem grass. I settled into the grass and quietly levered a
round into the Henry's chamber. I waited patiently as the antelope continued down the ridge, moving toward the stream.
Then the leader saw Black and stopped, his head coming up
swiftly. His tail raised warningly like a rabbit's scut. The
others behind him scattered left and right. I drew a bead on
his chest, held high, and squeezed the trigger. The bullet
took him in the white blaze of his chest. He took a wild leap
left, ran a few paces, then dropped, sliding on the thick
grass.

I rose and watched the other antelope race away. Black
snorted and tossed his head, turning to stare from his good
eye, trying to see what had happened. I crossed and slid the
Henry back into its scabbard and patted Black on his shoulder.

"Meat, boy," I said, and mounted, riding him over to the dead antelope.

And now I came in the back way to Ellsworth, making my way to a small shack at the back of the Grand Central Hotel. A cold wind started skating down from the north across the treeless prairie. I reined in beside the shack and sat for a moment, wondering why I still stayed in Ellsworth after losing the election for sheriff. I had carried the town—perhaps that was why I still stayed—but the rest of the county had decided E. W. Kingsbury would be the better man. I knew the good captain—an honorary self-appointment, I suspected—and I suppose for the county he was. Cattle rustling had risen along with horse theft, and I had a hunch it wouldn't be long before the entire country broke wide open.

I sighed and stepped down from Black and untied the antelope quarter and carried it inside. Annie turned from the table where she had been making bread, her forearms white with flour, a smudge alongside one high cheekbone. I paused, staring fondly at her. Her lips spread in a smile. Her eyes dropped down to the antelope quarter. She nodded approvingly.

"Fresh meat. We'll have stew or steaks tonight?"

I laughed delightedly at the way she made a statement a question. "Steak," I said.

She nodded. "Stew tomorrow." She came forward to take the quarter from me, pausing to kiss me quickly.

I grabbed her and kissed her deeply until I could feel the passion move up inside her. Then I released her and stepped back and away from her. Her eyes glinted blackly at me, her nose widening as if gathering scent on a breeze. Then she lunged forward, catching me unaware. Her momentum drove me backward until the backs of my knees caught the edge of the bed. I fell backward and she tumbled onto me.

"You don't get away that easily," she muttered darkly.

"Didn't think I would." I grinned.

"Damn you," she breathed. . . .

"Sophie?" I said.

She nodded. "You do remember. Just needed a little nudging?"

A wave of nostalgia washed over me as I recognized the habit of her sister ingrained in her, the making of a statement into a question. Images flitted across my memory, then fluttered away on bat's wings.

"Yes," I said. "I remember you. But not like this."

She shook her head. "Times are hard. Especially for half breeds. That damn Custer and his men. You know?"

I nodded. I knew. Everyone knew about the Washita and how the Seventh Cavalry had massacred the Cheyenne and some odd hangers-on despite their peaceful lodging under the American flag that Black Kettle flew religiously outside his tepee under the mistaken guise that it offered protection from xenophobic Americans. The newspapers had made it out to be a major victory for Custer, thanks to his pet reporters he took with him on all his campaigns. He had learned early the advantage of publicity.

"Not everyone's a Custer," I said. "There are quite a few good men around."

She gave me a strange look. "Yes. I didn't mean to hurt you. What was between you and Annie was between you and Annie. Besides"—her lips split in a rueful smile—"who am I to point a finger and shout about whoresons?"

I shrugged. "Who is anyone?" I cupped my hand under her chin and lifted it and kissed her gently on the lips. Her eyes shone up at me and then a tear ran slowly over her high cheekbones and down her golden skin.

We didn't become lovers that night but soon after. Zoë was a bit miffed for a while, but Judd Harkin started paying her a moon-eyed attention, riding in from his ranch two or three times a week, and her attentions turned elsewhere.

Sometimes, though, when the pale moonlight slanted in just right through Sophie's window and caught her face in a certain light I would see Mary's face and then a great sadness would well over me again at what I had lost and the world would seem a sadder place for me and I had a hint of what Pie was going through each June.

Once I tried to talk to him about this, but he cut me short, saying with a twisted grin, "All the world's a stage and we're all playing various roles upon it. Didn't you know that, Bill?"

CHAPTER

45

I WAS walking past the stage when a woman stepped in front of me. I touched the brim of my hat automatically and made to step around her, but she stepped back in front of me. I frowned and took a half step back, studying her carefully; then a smile broke over her generous lips.

"James Butler Hickok, you mean to say that you don't recognize me? And after all we were to each other once?" she said, pouting. She arched her shoulders back, bringing her breasts up brazenly, and I smiled.

"Hello, Susannah Moore," I said. "It's been a long time since Springfield."

"Six years," she said, her voice low and husky as I remembered it. My stomach felt weak and I grinned.

"Six long years," I said musingly. Lights glittered in her eyes and her pink tongue flickered out like an adder and damn if those six years didn't seem to melt away. She and I had set up housekeeping in a small cottage south of the tracks, but I could tell that there wasn't anything to us other than a healthy desire for each other's bodies. When we weren't making love, we fought like cats and dogs, and then she took to taunting me about Dave Tutt, and, well, I had put her on the next train going west, figuring she would find herself another "house" somewhere down the line. When that train finally rolled out of sight, I had breathed a long sigh of relief.

I strolled on down to the Alamo Saloon and went in to have a drink to celebrate my good fortune. Mayor Joe McCoy was having a midafternoon toddy and offered to buy a round for the two of us, saying he had a little thing he wanted to discuss with me.

"By the way, Jim," the mayor said, "we will have a circus in town next week."

"A circus?" I shook my head. "You're asking for trouble, Joe. A circus always brings shills and crooked games with it."

"There will be a lot of spending, too, though," McCoy said.

I stared into his eyes and knew that any further argument was useless. The mayor and other businessmen had already imagined the money they would deposit in the bank during the week that the circus was in town. For that they would put up with minor nuisances, which would really be my problem anyway. Yet I had to voice my opposition, if only to be on the record if something drastic went wrong.

"I'm going to be pretty shorthanded next week," I said. "I have to send some prisoners over to Abilene with a couple of deputies. All of us will be pulling double duty as it is without the problem of the circus being in town. This is a bad time for it to be here."

McCoy frowned at me. "Would there ever be a good time for you, Mr. Hickok?"

"Frankly, no," I said, honest to a fault. "Circus people cause more trouble than they're worth."

"People need an outlet for amusement, Mr. Hickok," Ted Henry said. I turned my attention to him. "The normal mundane passing of life must have a few thrills to it."

I laughed. "I thought we had that when the trail herds came through. Wasn't that enough excitement for everyone?"

McCoy sighed and stared at me. "What do you have against a circus?" he asked.

"I have nothing against the circus coming to town," I said patiently. "I just want to wait until my deputies are all ready. We're shorthanded enough since I had to send a deputy down to Wichita and bring back Tom Jackson for stealing that homesteader's horse, and my other out trying to track down that cowboy who put the knife to the parson's hand when he tried to hit him."

"The parson going to be all right?"

"Yes," I said, shaking my head. "But he thinks that little cut on his hand has marked him like the wounds of Christ. He's going to be big trouble unless someone has a talk with him."

"By 'someone' I suppose you mean me."

"Who better?"

He shook his head. "I hate talking to Parson Jonas more than I did taking a dose of salts as a kid. Well—"

The sun was beginning to slip over the horizon as I decided it was time to make my way to the circus tent pitched outside of town. I really didn't want to go, but my deputies were busy checking the saloons and whorehouses down by the cattle pens, so the lot fell to me. I promised that I would make a quick appearance to remind people that the law was still around despite roustabouts who seemed to carry a carefree, romantic reckless abandon for rules and regulations. When I was a child, I had loved the carnivals and circuses when they came to the county, but I knew as an adult, as an officer of the law, that petty thievery often accompanied the circus on its rounds, with pickpockets and pitchmen often teaming together to relieve a person of his hard-earned wages. An appearance was needed to cast a bit of doubt into their minds. Yet I did not delude myself; my appearance would not keep absolute order. I would have to deal with several complaints before the circus left town.

I stepped inside the tent, pausing to let my eyes adjust to the flickering light coming from torches strategically placed around the periphery of the tent. Someone in the crowd spied me and called out.

"Bill!"

"Wild Bill!"

"It's Wild Bill!"

I nodded at the calls, for the banter that greeted me was nothing new. I glanced around at the crowd seated beneath the tent, flattered at their recognition, yet a strange premonition seemed to lodge within me. Something timeless upon the gray warm air within the circus tent, fluid and personal. The dim noise of the crowd rolled over me like waves and I looked up at the roof of the tent and saw a man in tights flying through the air from one trapeze bar to be caught by the hands of another and thrown back to the bar he had just left.

For some inexplicable reason, my heart trembled and I felt my breath come faster as a wild spirit seemed to pass over my limbs. I felt as if I, too, was soaring upward and outward, rising to meet the sun beyond the canvas limit of the tent. I felt . . . purified? Yes, purified and radiant, and my soul seemed to rise from the lethargy of my dull spirit that had lodged within me for days, weeks, and months.

"Ladies and gentlemen! Mrs. Agnes Lake Thatcher!"

My eyes flicked back to the center ring and a dizziness swept over me as I saw a woman standing beside a horse. She wore a pair of crimson tights that failed to hide her sweeping muscular thighs, her hips, the smoothness of her belly and rise of her breasts. She wore her auburn hair up on top of her head. One arm stretched toward the applauding crowd. Then she leaped gracefully upon the back of the horse and urged it into a lope around the center ring. She seemed magically changed from the human to a part of the horse. Her long, muscular legs gripping the sides of the horse moved rhythmically with the horse, her hips riding gently with the rise and fall of the horse. A small black-fringed skirt around her hips seemed like the feathering of soft down as it fluttered. Her breasts moved tantalizingly beneath her thighs. Her face became flushed and her lips parted with excitement as she rose to her feet on her horse's back, her feet confidently gripping the horse's hips. A strand of hair slipped free and curled over her forehead. She brushed it away irritably.

Then she leaped up in the air and flipped her feet gracefully over her head, landing gently upon the back of the loping horse, her arms spread for balance. And then she was in constant movement, like quicksilver, flowing over the horse's back from one side to the other. The crowd applauded wildly and I felt my heart hammering in my chest. I touched the pistols at my waist, calming myself with their familiarity.

And then her eyes met mine accidentally in quiet sufferance of my stare. She withdrew her eyes, then suddenly looked back, her eyes widening, holding mine, and I felt a force pass between us as if she had allowed my image to pass into her soul. She curled herself around on the back of the horse, gracefully crossing one leg over the other as she brought the horse to a stop in the center of the ring. Her heel nudged the side of the horse and I saw her rich, full lips part as she murmured and the horse bowed to the crowd.

And then she was gone, riding across the ring away from me, waving at the crowd. She disappeared through an opening in the tent across the ground from me. I took a deep breath and, turning, went back outside. I paused in the coolness of the evening and glanced back into the flickering torchlight inside the tent. A couple of painted clowns in baggy clothes had moved into the center ring, arguing with each other.

I turned and walked away from the tent, heading back to town. A rim of the new moon rose into the black waste of the sky, throwing silver light upon the road leading into town. I walked along the edge to keep the dust off the shine of my boots. A new, wild life seemed to be singing in my veins.

I made my way behind the big tent to where a small caravan had arranged its wagons in a tight circle to form a miniature hamlet. I paused uncertainly, then caught a passing clown and asked where I might find the Thatcher wagon. He gave me a narrow look, glanced at the marshal's badge on my vest, then pointed wordlessly at a large wagon near the center of the hamlet. I could feel his hostility seeping from him in waves but couldn't blame him. I was certain that they had been rousted several times by other marshals during the past few years. But then I couldn't blame the marshals, either; I understood their reluctance to put up with circus folks. There had been too many cases of riotous behavior in some towns that had allowed the circuses to pitch tents on the outskirts. Usually it began in saloons when some of the roustabouts decided to "let down their hair" after a performance—usually the last one after they had packed and were getting ready to pull out. Sometimes they had left wreckage in their wake, disappearing in the night when the law tried to find them. A couple of times, banks had been robbed. Or saloon owners. Or both. I had no intention of letting any of that happen in Abilene. I figured the best way was to let the circus owners know to head off trouble before it got a chance to start. Besides, I couldn't get the picture of Mrs. Thatcher out of my head.

I shook my head as I approached the wagon. *Quit this nonsense. You're only asking for trouble. Rule one: Never fool around with a married woman. Leave that for Cody and the others.*

I knocked politely on the door and heard a voice call out to come in. I opened the door and stepped inside. She was alone in the wagon, costumes and the careless litter of a single person scattered throughout the living space. The crimson tights had been tossed on a small bed attached to one side of the wagon. She sat at the long end in front of a mirror and tiny table littered with makeup, powder, brushes, and rouge pots. She leaned forward, looking in the mirror as she wiped the stage makeup from her face. The robe she wore gaped wide and I had a quick look at her generous breasts before she looked up at me, gasped, and leaned back away from the mirror, her hands quickly pulling the robe closed around her neck.

"Yes? What is it?" she asked anxiously.

"I'm Marshal Hickok, ma'am," I said politely, removing my broad-brimmed hat. I brushed my hand quickly over my hair, smoothing it. I straightened my shoulders, and my head bumped against the ceiling. I felt cramped in the narrow space. "Mind if we have a little talk?"

Her eyes narrowed, the flesh drawing tight across her high cheekbones. "And if I did?"

"Well," I said quietly, "I reckon we'd have it anyway. Is your husband about somewhere?"

She sighed and stood up. I was surprised at how short she was. She had looked taller in the ring. She had a lot of spring in her legs, I thought, looking down automatically. Her bare feet were highly arched, her ankles well formed.

"Sorry, my husband died a few years ago. I own the show now. Marshal?"

I glanced up, feeling my ears begin to burn, realizing that she had caught my stare and read my thoughts. "Sorry, ma'am," I said. "But I thought I would have a bit of a talk with you and make certain that nothing goes wrong during your stay in Abilene."

"I see," she said. Her eyes shone brightly at me. I could feel the anger behind them. "So you are warning us to stay out of your town?"

"No, ma'am," I said, shaking my head. "But I don't want your people going up above the Deadline."

"Deadline?" she asked, puzzled.

I nodded. "This is a drovers' town, ma'am. A lot of cattle herds come up to be shipped back east. We've got a section of town reserved for them. I reckon it'll do for you folks as well."

"And if we need supplies?"

"There's a couple of general stores there that outfit the cowboys and outfits that come in. Some saloons as well and"—I flushed—"more than a few houses for the men if," my face burned, "they, well, you know," I finished lamely.

A tiny smile curved her generous lips. "You mean whorehouses, Marshal."

"Yes, ma'am, I reckon that's what I mean," I said, suddenly irritated by her boldness.

"And if we decide we want to go up into the other part of

town where the 'respectable' folk live? What then?" Her voice dripped with contempt.

"I'll arrest them," I said quietly. "This isn't an option I'm offering, ma'am. It's a telling. Don't go above the Deadline. You have no reason to go up there. And," I added deliberately, "that doesn't mean you get a free rein below the Deadline, either. The same rules apply to you folks as to the cowboys when they come up from Texas. No guns. No fighting. I'm not saying you can't have fun, but don't let it get out of hand."

She eyed me narrowly for a long moment, then said, "How many deputies do you have, Marshal?"

"Three," I said. "But don't let it come down to that, ma'am. You'll lose."

"I think we have you outnumbered," she said.

I sighed and replaced my hat. Her eyes widened slightly at my deliberate movement. I touched the ivory handles of the Navy Colts in my sash, drawing her eyes to them. "The choice is yours, ma'am. And your people. I'm giving you fair warning. Don't go above the Deadline."

"Have you spoken to the mayor about this?" she asked challengingly.

"I don't need to, ma'am," I said.

"It seems to me that you might be overstepping your bounds, Marshal," she said. "You aren't—"

"But I am, ma'am," I said, interrupting her. I met her hard stare. "Don't go above the Deadline."

"Good day, Marshal," she said firmly.

I nodded. "Good day, ma'am. Enjoy your stay in Abilene."

I opened the door and stepped outside, closing it gently but firmly behind me. I stood for a moment in the afternoon sun, thinking regretfully about the need to be the law and how my life wasn't mine own to live as I wished. I looked thoughtfully at the closed door, then walked away from the temporary hamlet. I had a hunch that I hadn't seen the last of Mrs. Thatcher. There was a lot of strength in that woman. She didn't like limitations being put upon her. I had made a mistake asking for her husband. That was carelessness upon my part. A couple of questions put to circus folks would have told me everything I needed to know. But what is done cannot be undone.

I was right, though. The next day I came across Mrs. Thatcher coming out of a dress shop above the Deadline. She threw her head back, green eyes looking at me challengingly. "Good morning, Marshal," she said.

"Good morning, Mrs. Thatcher," I answered. "I think you have strayed a bit."

"Have I?"

"Yes, ma'am." I pointed down the street to where a sign stood in the middle, dividing the town in half. The Deadline. "That's where the line ends. Where the sign is."

"I can read, Marshal," she said.

"Then you know that you are above the Deadline."

"Yes." She gave me a defiant look. "It isn't fair, Marshal. We have the same rights as everybody."

"That's true, ma'am," I answered. "But your rights end at the Deadline. It's not that I have anything personal against you, ma'am, but if I allow you to come across the Deadline, that sends a signal to your people that it's all right for them to come across as well. And that could mean trouble later. I don't intend on having trouble later. Preventive medicine is always better than the sickness."

She flushed and bit her full lower lip. "Are you saying that we're a sickness upon the fair people of Abilene?"

"No, ma'am. But you could be. I'm just quarantining you, that's all. Just like a doctor would the measles, cholera, or typhoid."

She swung her hand to slap me, but I was too quick. I caught her wrist and held it tightly as she tried to pull back away from me.

"And you're under arrest, ma'am, for violating the Deadline and for attempting to assault an officer of the law," I said, turning and pulling her toward the jail.

"Oh! You . . . you . . . brute!"

"Yes, ma'am," I said. I lengthened my stride deliberately to keep her off-balance, stumbling after me. People turned to stare at us as we passed, but I hurried along, ignoring their questioning looks.

I opened the door to the jail and pushed her inside. She recovered her balance like a cat and, turning, lashed out again at me. This time, however, I failed to catch her wrist and her hand struck me stingingly across the face. Without thinking, I slapped her back, staggering her. I reached out, grabbed her shoulder, pulled her reticule from her, tossed it on my desk, and propelled her toward the cells. We were alone, the night drunks having been cleared out and taken to court for fining earlier by one of my deputies before he went off-duty from the graveyard hours. I scooped the keys off the top of the desk and pushed her into the first cell, locking the door firmly behind her. She spun and threw her weight against the bars.

"This—this is intolerable!" she said angrily. Her eyes were bright with frustrated tears.

"No, ma'am," I said. "This is what happens when you don't follow the instructions of the law. I won't have anarchy in my town. Even from a beautiful lady."

The last caught her up for a moment; then she remembered herself and said, "I demand to see the mayor!"

"After you see the judge, ma'am," I said.

"Very well. Let me see the judge then."

"As soon as you cool off, ma'am," I said. I turned and walked behind my desk, seating myself. I opened the drawer, removed the ledger in which we kept our arrest reports, and dropped the keys into the drawer before shutting it. I opened the ledger, took up a pen, dipped it, and began to fill out the report.

"Your full name, ma'am?" I asked.

"You know my name!"

I sighed and leaned back in my chair. "Ma'am, I know your name, but this is a formality. I don't mean any offense, although," I added, "you certainly have given me enough cause not to treat you like a lady."

A hot retort leaped to her lips, but she pressed them tightly together, staring at me. I waited. At last, she said, "Mrs. Agnes Lake Thatcher. Widow."

"Thank you, ma'am," I said, leaning forward, writing. "Age?"

"That, sir, is an impertinence!"

"Shall we say twenty-five?"

That caught her up short. I knew she was older than that; I could see it behind those green eyes that stared hypnotically into mine. Her features softened and she turned away, crossing to the narrow cot. She sat gingerly on the edge.

"Whatever you say, Marshal," she said wearily.

I started to fill out the report, then stopped and drew a line through her name. I closed the ledger and stared thoughtfully at her. Her eyes met mine; then a wry smile came across her lips.

"I'm sorry, Marshal. I was wrong."

I nodded, waiting.

"I should have stayed below the Deadline," she said. "But a person gets tired of always being regarded as a second-class citizen. I guess I was warned by one sheriff or marshal too many. But you could at least have given us the benefit of the doubt until we did something to give you reason for warning us like you did."

"That's the point, ma'am," I said. "I didn't want it to come to this. I didn't want any unpleasantness like this. Below the Deadline's not all that bad."

"But it isn't right—"

"Yes, ma'am, it is right. Folk have a right to live the way they want. You chose your life just like these folks chose theirs. I wouldn't put up with anyone going down across the Deadline to cause trouble down there any more than I would having folks from below the Deadline come up and cause trouble up here. The fathers of this town have decided how they want to live and I enforce what they have made law. Doesn't matter if I agree with it or not. That's not my job. I was hired to enforce the law, not to stand judgment against it. That's what I do. That's all I do," I said deliberately.

She nodded slowly. "I said I was sorry, Marshal. Very well. I'll stay below the Deadline and I'll keep the circus people down there. Does your law have compassion for someone who apologizes?"

"Yes, ma'am," I said. "I can give you another chance to stay below the Deadline."

She glanced at the jail door when I didn't move toward it. A tiny frown marred the space between her eyebrows. "Well then?"

"There's still the charge of attempting to assault an officer of the law," I said. "That's a more serious matter."

Her shoulders slumped. "All right. Let's go see the judge and get it over with."

"I can fine you, ma'am, if you wish to plead guilty. We won't need to go before the judge unless you wish."

"Yes, yes," she said, waving her hand. "I plead guilty. How much is the fine?"

"Dinner tonight with me at the Drover's House," I said.

Her head jerked up and she stared through the cell bars at me, her green eyes boring into mine.

"Dinner," I repeated. "Nothing more. Just dinner."

She studied me carefully, then nodded, a slight smile softening her features more. "You are an enigma, Marshal. That means—"

"I know what it means, ma'am," I said, rising and taking the keys from the drawer and crossing to her cell. "I can read."

Her smile widened, bringing a strange, ethereal beauty to her features, taking the hardness from behind her eyes. "My words come back to haunt me," she said musingly. "Very well, Marshal. Dinner. After the last show?"

"Yes, ma'am," I said opening the door to let her out. "And it's James, please."

"I think I prefer Bill," she said, stepping out of the cell. She stood close to me for a moment. I could smell the cologne she had used and a hint of Pears Soap behind it. Tiny wrinkles slipped out of the corners of her eyes and her forehead had a fine trace of wrinkles across it. A tiny softness appeared below her chin. I was conscious of the swell of her breast and how tiny her waist was—I felt as if I could span it with my two hands, although I knew I couldn't—and a womanly swell to her hips.

"May I have my reticule, Bill?" she asked softly.

"Yes, ma'am," I said, stepping away from her and taking it from my desk. I handed it to her. Our fingers touched and she held the touch a second longer than necessary to keep it from being an accident.

"Agnes, please," she said. "Call me Agnes. I'm old enough for that." She walked to the door, then looked back over her shoulder. "And it's been a while since I've seen twenty-five."

I shook my head slightly. "Not for me it hasn't."

She laughed, deeply, richly. "You are a strange one, Bill."

And that began our affair. Not that night, though. But the next night she came to my room, and when she slipped out of her clothes my breath caught achingly in my chest as she stood naked in front of me, her full breasts dropping a little to one side after being freed from their restraint, her belly smoothed, curving down into the dimple of her navel, then a slight swell down to where tiny lights from the lamp in the room glinted off the red-gold triangle between her legs, heavy, muscular thighs swelling, then dropping down to well-formed calves, and then she stepped forward, pressing herself against me, and I thought back to the first night with Josephine and Hannah and now it felt like the first night again and a shyness came over me, startling me with its urgency, and I remembered all the other women briefly, their faces and bodies flitting like shadows across my memory like Annie's and her features appeared before me and then faded blurred by the thoughtlessness of time and slowly other images appeared slipping in and out of memory and then it was autumn and Lorenzo coming to see me to tell me not to marry Mary and oh God I thought I was going to burst when Josephine and I tumbled upon the bed of leaves beside Tomahawk Creek for the first time and I thought then that I didn't love her and that it probably wasn't fair that I would do that with her and know I wasn't going to marry her but then I thought as well as her as another and I knew then that I wasn't the first in that well-plowed field and I knew that it was all right because she was enjoying herself as much as I and teaching me a lot more than I had ever known even after watching the cows and pigs and horses and I felt a stallion myself as we slipped naked and sweaty beneath the dappled leaf shadows and again in the gentle running waters of Tomahawk Creek and again and again until I felt knowing and experienced and everything became easier and the firelight flickering over Hannah's dusky body turning it almost golden and and I felt the deep urgency of Agnes and knew it to be far more than the urgencies I had felt before with the others and I felt her mouth against mine and her tongue pressing gently against my lips and then I tasted a bit·of the cinnamon and hint of apple on her tongue from the pie she had had for dessert and Hannah's deep kiss that almost drove me out of my mind with desire and then I felt Agnes's hands unknotting the sash from around my waist and then unfastening my belt and my salt-and-pepper trousers fell to the floor and she was sliding my coat off my shoulders and suddenly we were naked on the bed and a fire seemed to be licking across my flesh and . . .

CHAPTER

46

PIE AND I were strolling by the stream behind Mrs. Mack's place, enjoying an after-supper cigar, when her scream rent the night, tearing the moon to tatters. Even over the lowing of the cattle upstream I could hear the shouts and felt the terror racing through the dark. Then out of the dark stumbled Ned, Mrs. Mack's piano player, holding a matted cloth dripping red—black in the moonlight—tightly against his cheek.

"It Mrs. Mack's, Marshal," he said as loudly as he could. He winced but gritted his teeth and continued. "I tried to stop him, but he git me with a skinnin' knife! He got Zoë upstairs in onna dem rooms doin' turble things to her!"

I swore and threw my cigar away, racing for Mrs. Mack's. I heard Pie lumbering along at my boot heels, wheezing as he ran as fast as he could. My boots thundered across the porch boards and I threw open the door. Sophie saw me and nodded solemnly, pointing toward the stairwell.

"Third door from the left on the second floor," she said as I pushed my way through the crowd hovering like carrion eaters at the foot of the steps. I shoved the mayor away. He cursed as he stumbled and sat down abruptly. I ignored him and took the stairs two at a time.

I pulled a pistol from my sash, simultaneously slamming my foot against the lock, breaking the door out of the frame. Zoë lay curled into a fetal ball on the floor. Over her stood a hulking buffalo hunter, fresh from a bath, but the stink still clung to him like rancid suet. He held a braided rawhide quirt in one hand, a knife in the other, the quirt singing as he smacked into her flesh. Blood spurted from the bruised flesh and she screamed again.

"Hold it!" I yelled. He looked up, wild-eyed, then back down at Zoë. His arm slashed her again. "Goddamnit, I said stop!" I roared.

He paused for a moment, staring at me, then kicked her once with his round-toed boots. She moaned and tried to roll away from him. He lashed her twice with the quirt.

I swore and stepped forward, swinging the barrel of my revolver hard against his nose. He yelped and stumbled backward. The backs of his knees hit the bed. His arms windmilled as he tried to keep his balance, but I had followed him and struck him again on his nose. He fell backward, the knife flying into a corner. He raised both hands to his nose, holding it.

"Guddam yuh, yu bwoke muh nood," he muttered. Blood ran between his palms, dripping onto his shirt.

"Next time, stop when a lawman tells you," I said.

"Whyg? Sheg onlyg a whoge," he said.

A wave of anger came over me as I listened to him claim his rights for having bought her services for the night. I had heard this before when buffalo hunters bragged how they had bought an Indian squaw for some of the meat from buffalo they had slaughtered, then left her without her nose in the middle of the prairie. This wasn't the first time I had had to come into a whorehouse, either, to set things right with a customer who thought his two dollars entitled him to a slave for the night.

I glanced down at Zoë. She stared up at me, both eyes

nearly swollen shut. Her nose bent off to the left and there were cigar burns over her arms and shoulders. She cupped one hand close to her naked breasts, but I could see that at least two of the fingers in the hand had been broken. Her back and stomach had bloody welts from the quirt and there was one long cut down a thigh that had to have come from the knife in the corner.

I felt the muscles in my jaws work as I turned back to the buffalo hunter. "You are one sorry son of a bitch," I said softly. "Get up. You're under arrest."

He stared dumbfounded at me, not believing what he was hearing. "I'm arrested for the likes of her?" He jabbed a thick forefinger at Zoë on the floor. "Since when's it against the law to take what's coming to you?"

"What's coming to you?"

"I bought her! She owes me!"

"I didn't want to do it, Bill," Zoë sobbed. "He wanted me to whip him, but I couldn't do it. I offered to give him his money back, but he wouldn't take it! Said a deal struck was it and if I wouldn't do him, then he'd do me." She sobbed.

"Get up," I said.

A sullen look came into his eye. "You wouldn't be so much without your pretty pistols, would you?" he said contemptuously.

"Now you've really done it," Pie said from the doorway. "You sorry bastard, you're gonna get what's coming to you now."

I stepped forward and jammed my pistol hard in the hollow of the buffalo hunter's throat. He gagged, then froze as I cocked the Navy. "Get up. Real slow, but get up."

He rose, the quirt dangling from his wrist.

"Take that off and toss it on the bed."

He slipped it off his wrist and dropped it on the bed.

"Turn around."

He frowned but did what I told him. I jammed the pistol barrel against the back of his neck to let him know it was still there. Then I reached down and gathered the quirt and nudged him toward the doorway. The crowd gathered stepped back hurriedly as we came slowly out of the room.

He reached the head of the stairs and I placed my foot on his butt and pushed. He stumbled forward, then rolled head over heels down the stairs. I was right behind him, and when he pushed himself up, shaking his head, I jerked him onto his feet and whipped the barrel of my pistol back and forth across his face, letting the pistol sight rake across his flesh, tearing it. He yelled and stumbled backward, his hands trying to block and catch my hands.

"You asshole!" he screamed.

He turned and ran for the door, jerked it open, and stepped outside. I followed him, and when he had taken a few steps I put a bullet in the ground next to him.

"The next one's in your back!" I shouted.

He froze, then slowly turned as I stepped down, coming toward him. A cold recklessness came over me as contempt for him welled up from deep inside of me, burning like a paschal fire. I jammed my pistol back into my sash and walked slowly up to him, rolling my shoulders, loosening them. He frowned when he saw the pistol put away.

"All right, you wanted it," I said.

His eyes narrowed suspiciously; then a leer came over his ripped lips. "You ain't gonna get away now, Marshal. This is my game!"

He threw a lumbering right hook. I leaned back away from it, then stepped left and away from the left he tried to sneak behind the hook. He grunted as his fist caught nothing but air, swishing around to his right and throwing him a bit off-balance. I swayed forward, digging my right hand into his short ribs, feeling them give way. He gasped and reeled, then tried to back-heel me. I stepped away from his foot and kicked him hard up between the legs. He screamed and fell to his knees, hunching forward, head slamming hard into the sloppy ground. His shoulders heaved as he tried to draw a breath past the pain in his groin. I reached down and raised him up by his collar, and when he stood half-erect I looped a left under his cheek, straightening him. A quick left-right-left combination drove him backward. He fell down again. This time I put my boots to him, kicking him again and again as he tried to roll away from me.

"'Nough!" he gasped.

"I'll bet that's what Zoë said, too, didn't she?" I said.

I let him climb to his feet, then stepped in and beat him again, dodging as he tried to swing two heavy fists at me. He came up against a corral, and I wedged him there, settling into a rhythm as I hit him with short, hard blows, keeping him from falling, drawing back just enough to punish him without putting him out.

Suddenly he bawled loudly like a bull calf just castrated and rushed forward. I stepped away, balancing myself on my toes, expecting him to turn, but he ran instead for the stream. I drew my pistol and, taking careful aim, shot him in the ass. He screamed and fell forward into the stream.

The crowd rushed forward, but he never showed again. Later, when I tried to track him in the daylight, I found where he had come out of the stream near a stand of willows, but I lost him when he went across the cattle trail. It didn't matter. By then, the anger had left me and all I wanted was a prisoner to take before the judge.

But when I turned back toward Mrs. Mack, the crowd watched silently as I made my way through them to the whorehouse. They remained silent while I passed, but I could feel the uneasiness spreading through them as they wondered what had been unleashed in their town. Yes, I wanted to tell them, it was below the Deadline, but it was still Abilene and if it happened down there, couldn't it happen up where the respectable folks lived?

I kept silent, letting them puzzle it out on their own. I went up the stairs to where Zoë now lay on the bed, the other whores gathered around. Sophie was carefully washing away the blood with a clean towel when I entered.

"I saw what you did," Mrs. Mack said, stepping forward. She nodded at the other girls. "Most here did. Thank you, Marshal. It's been a long time since someone stood up for us."

I shrugged. "There's no difference between you and others, Mrs. Mack. You chose your profession and it's an honorable one as far as I'm concerned. You have the same rights as others."

I walked toward the bed, but she placed her hand on mine, stopping me.

"Anything you want anytime, Marshal, you come here and we'll get it for you," she said emphatically. "And you can leave your wallet at home, if you know what I mean."

A murmur of assent rose from the other girls. I nodded and turned my attention back to Zoë as Pie came through the door. He took one look at Zoë and shook his head.

"Ah, yes," he said. He swayed a bit from all the drink he had taken. "It's a sad affair of which we speak. But weep no more, my dear, for he has walked through the watery floor of the river, baptizing himself by walking through the waves. One can forgive him his Bluebeard tendencies as he tried to mount his way to the heights of Olympus, there to encounter his own furry Aphrodite. He did not, my dear Zoë, mean to harm you. He sought, instead, penance from your hands. You should have been quicker in giving it to him, but his Greek ways would not allow him to accept that which he asked."

"Oh, shut up, Pie; you're not making any sense," I said. "You want to do something useful, quit your nattering like an old washerwoman and go fetch the doctor."

Pie drew himself upright, gripping the lapel of his long coat in his right hand as if he intended on delivering an oration. His eyes blinked lazily, owlishly, but bright lights sparkled in their depths.

"I don't want to hear it, Pie," I said quietly. "Not now. Nor does Zoë."

He frowned, then glanced again at Zoë's battered features and nodded. He hurried away. I turned my attention back to Zoë.

"She going to be all right?" I asked Sophie.

Sophie turned her dark eyes upon me. I nearly fell into their depths, but she nodded and went back to cleaning Zoë's wounds.

"She will need to have a doctor's care for a while," Sophie

said. She touched Zoë's thigh. Zoë moaned in pain. "That will have to be looked after. Stitches, I'm afraid. But there is more that you cannot see. He used that whip inside her, too."

A quick gasp came behind me. I glanced at the women standing around the bed, their hands pressed against their mouths, their eyes as they stared at the battered figure on the bed.

"Don't you worry, honey," Mrs. Mack said, patting Zoë's hand. "We'll take care of you."

"She can't hear you," Sophie said.

"Well, we will!" Mrs. Mack said as if Sophie had been doubting her word.

I sighed and pushed my hat to the back of my head. I glanced around the room and saw the man's saddlebags lying in the corner of the room. I crossed to them and opened them. They were filled with money. I stood and carried it back to the bed.

"It looks like he came straight here after selling his hides," I said. I opened the bags so Mrs. Mack could see. Her left eyebrow twitched and she nodded.

"Well, it all goes to Zoë," she said stoutly. "She deserves it after all this."

"Yes, she does," I said. I closed the saddlebags and draped them over my shoulder. "Tomorrow I'll put it in the bank in her name. Meanwhile, after the doctor has seen her, we'll move her up to the Drover's House, where she can rest."

"That's over the Deadline," Mrs. Mack said, eyeing me narrowly.

"Yes," I said, turning toward the door. "It is. I'll have a room made ready for her and send a buggy down to bring her up. Better yet, tell the doctor I said for him to take her up there himself."

I walked out of the room and down the stairs, heading for the Drover's House. The mayor caught up with me halfway there.

"I heard what you were intending on doing," he said, breathing heavily from his run. "I don't think that's such a great idea."

I stopped and stared at him. He walked on two more paces before he realized I wasn't beside him. He stopped and turned back, a puzzled look on his face.

"You make one exception, you're opening the door," he said. "The law's the law and—"

"There'll be about ten more trail herds coming through here in the next month," I said. "You want my badge now? Because it won't make any difference one way or the other. She's going up to the Drover's whether it's a good idea or not. The question is, do you want me as the law or just another citizen taking her up there. Your choice."

He stared at me, then drew a deep breath. "You're a hard man, Hickok."

"That I am, Mayor," I said, walking around him. "That I am."

The Drover's didn't want to rent a room for Zoë until I leaned over the counter and stared hard at the clerk for a moment, letting the quiet do my talking for me. Finally, he flushed and mumbled how he was probably going to be fired for it but pushed the register across to me. I nodded and wrote "Zoë Butler" in the register.

"That her real name?" he asked, reading upside down.

I stared at him again. He turned nervously to the keys and took down No. 8. "It's at the end of the hallway upstairs," he said. "It'll be quiet there."

"And pretty much away from the rest of the guests, that it?" I asked, taking the key from his fingers.

"You can't go pushing people around like this, Marshal," he protested, his nerves finally easing off.

"Yes, I can," I said quietly. "I don't like to do it, but I can only take so much hypocrisy in one town and Abilene's just used up its quota. Anyone says anything, you refer them to me. Otherwise, just leave her alone. The doctor will be giving her some prescriptions and directions of things to do. She needs anything, I expect you'll do her running for her. Right?" He hesitated. I drew a deep breath and tapped the key against the handle of one of my pistols. "Do you want to compound the mistakes made this evening?"

"Yes, sir," he said glumly, "I'll take care of her."

"That's good," I said softly. "And if you run into any trouble or someone tries to trouble her, I want you to get me immediately. Night or day. Doesn't matter. That woman's been through more than any woman should have to. *Any* woman," I said slowly, emphatically. "And keep those damned sky pilots away from her. They want to save her soul, tell them I said to get down on their knees in their own church and do the praying there."

"Yes, sir," he repeated. "I'll do what you say."

"I know you will, Harvey," I said kindly. "You're too smart to do otherwise. When do you go off?"

He glanced at the repeater hanging on the wall. "Midnight. In two hours."

"Swing on down to Muggins's place," I said. "I'll buy you a drink."

His eyes brightened and he looked much happier as I stepped out of the Drover's and made my way back toward Mrs. Mack's place, pausing at the livery stable to tell Stumpy Waters to hitch up the doctor's horse and buggy and bring them down to Mrs. Mack's.

Zoë healed slowly, and I made certain that it was a peaceful healing. I let her friends come up from below the Deadline, and when the Ladies Brigade tried to object I told them they would be better off in the church asking God to forgive them for their hypocrisy for trying to keep sinners away from his divine judgment. For the next few weeks every time I encountered one of them on the street, she turned her head, pretending not to see me from under her parasol.

Then came the time when Doc Blake came to me and told me there was nothing else he could do for her, but that she needed the help of some specialists back in Chicago.

"Sorry, Bill," he said, rubbing his hands across his tired face. "But there's only so much I can do here. Gunshot wounds, sewing up a few knife cuts, delivering a baby now and then, listening to the reverend's wife complain about her womanly problems, that I can handle. But whatever that buffalo hunter did to her up inside's going to have to be fixed by someone who knows his way around in there better than I do. This is going to take a specialist. Now there are a couple I know about back in Chicago, but . . . well"—he scrubbed the knuckles of his hand furiously across his scalp—"how's she going to get there? It's going to be expensive, too. We're not talking about anything simple here."

"Don't worry about it," I said. "I'll take care of it."

"You?"

I nodded at the skepticism in his voice. He started to say something else, then shrugged and left, making his way across the street to the Drover's House. I sighed and rose, settling my pistols in my sash. I took my hat off its peg by the door, flicked some dust off its brim, and left for Mrs. Mack's place. I had an idea but wasn't certain if I could swing it. I knew, however, that Mrs. Mack hadn't always been in the business, not until it became the only option left to her. I swung by the newspaper office to catch Pie up on the problems. He promised to put a plea in the paper but warned me that probably not much would come from it.

"These people have their own standards," he explained, wiping ink off the tips of his fingers with a rag soaked in kerosene. "And their standards don't dip low enough to include whores. Sorry, but that's the way it is. I got a couple hundred I can let her have. That's the best I can do."

"It's a start," I said, and left, continuing on my way to Mrs. Mack's.

I shouldn't have worried. All that woman needed was a cause to get her lickerish up and moving. By the end of the week, she had deposited about seven thousand dollars in Zoë's account and her girls were looking hollow-eyed and sore from helping in their own way. Pie was right; the good folks of Abilene hadn't raised even a thousand toward helping Zoë. But with what had been in the buffalo hunter's saddlebags, Zoë was well off.

When I put her on the train heading east she began crying and clung to me, pleading with me to go with her. But I didn't. I watched as the train chugged out of sight, taking her away from Abilene. Inside I felt a small loneliness in the hollow of my stomach, the type one feels when a good friend moves away. We hadn't been friends, but Zoë had come to mean something to me. I hadn't figured out just what yet, but I knew there was something special that had just left my life, and a sadness came over my spirits.

CHAPTER

47

FIREFLIES DOTTED the streets at the corners as we made our way through the deserted streets. Faint piano notes tinkled in the night so faintly that they seemed imaginary. The whole town seemed to breathe shallowly, like a giant beast awaiting its prey that it knew would be coming— wolves at a water hole, waiting for the sick to make their way to it.

From beneath the boardwalk in front of the Bull's Head, Dooley the Dwarf, his hair like twists of dry straw, crawled. His mad eyes flickered left and right, anxiously seeking the children, the bane of his existence. A scabbed weal over one eye told of their cruelty. His eyes caught us and he winced, crawling backward in puffs of dust until he was half-again into his den. Then he paused, raising his head, sniffing the air questioningly.

"Grrahut?" he said, hawking and spitting phlegm in the dust before him.

"One must always honor the idiots," Pie said. "They are

today's jesters who formerly advised kings with their merriment."

"Grabst. Kthogue arat lacht mucht grimbacuch gluch clach bucht—"

"Yes, yes," Pie said, nodding seriously as Dooley spoke urgently, his hands twisting and jerking passionately with his speech. Pie reached into a pocket, removed a small coin, and handed it to Dooley. The idiot took it, his eyes slanting this way and that slyly. He bit the coin experimentally, nodded, and it quickly disappeared among his rags. He looked questioningly at me.

"Grubh vohim?" he said.

I reached into my vest pocket, removed a dollar, and handed it to him. He snatched it eagerly and slipped it somewhere upon his person. Then he lay his fingers aside his nose conspiratorially and said, "Ban, ban, Ca-Caliban."

"You've made an invaluable friend with your generosity," Pie said. "Most noble of you."

Dooley nodded vigorously and scuttled backward, disappearing under the boardwalk.

Pie nodded, patting my shoulder, knighting me as a comrade in adventure. "I'm proud of you, Bill."

"He's an idiot." I shrugged.

Pie gave me a look of disappointment. " 'Tis better to be lowly born, and range with humble lives in content, than to be picked up in a glistening grief and wear a golden sorrow."

I shook my head. "All right, Pie. You've lost me."

Pie looked at me solemnly. "I wonder at times whether men really trust themselves with men. All too often, men satisfy themselves with the foppery of the world that makes them react like fools when they are sick in fortune." He gestured toward the boardwalk where Dooley had disappeared. "One must never challenge the fates, Marshal. A man's good fortune at times comes at his heels. Mad people often have great wit and others look away from them, for they do not understand their thoughts, and because they do not understand, they fear them and drive them away if they can. If not, they ignore them and pretend that they are not there. They become shadows, and as shadows they are privy to the secrets of others. One must never take the station of others for granted lest one become the fool and the fool the sane."

"If you say so," I said solicitously. I wanted no argument with a drunken man. One never wins. And an *intelligent* drunken man always emerges victorious. When Bacchus touches a man on his shoulders, he imparts as well a semblance of truth.

CHAPTER

48

I HEARD a noise and, turning, spied Dooley stumbling down the street, toting a grimy flour sack of rags, bones, and old pieces of metal that clinked and clanked with his step. He stopped before me and grinned, his teeth blackened stumps in his mouth. An overwhelming stench seeped from his open mouth. I averted my face, nodding at him, and tried to step around him, but he stepped in front of me, shaking his head.

"Gach! Gach!" he said urgently, his eyebrows waggling seriously. I remembered Pie's words and inwardly sighed. I smiled pleasantly at Dooley and took another dollar from my vest pocket. I tried to hand it to him, but he shook his head violently.

"Gach! Gach!" he said emphatically. He pointed toward the Bull's Head and then pantomined shooting me. I slowly nodded.

"Yes, I know there are people there who would like to kill me. But I am ready for them," I said slowly, patting the revolvers at my waist.

He shook his head, muttering quickly some unintelligible noise, then glanced around covertly and scuttled sideways around me like a broken-legged crab. He jabbed me hard in the back with his forefinger, simulating gunfire. Then he came around in front of me again, bowing and nodding grimly, pointing again at the saloon.

I frowned. "Someone is planning to murder me? Shoot me in the back?" For a second I felt ridiculous, talking to an idiot as if he were an equal. But he nodded and I knew then that madness is only a matter of perspective.

"Would you happen to know who?"

He nodded vigorously and pretended to deal cards, then pulled an imaginary pistol from a shoulder holster. He rolled his shoulders, threw his chin toward the sky, and swaggered around in a circle, smoothing his cravat, had he worn one.

"Phil Coe?"

He stopped and nodded solemnly at me. I patted his shoulder gratefully, conscious that it was the same gesture I used on Joe, my dog, who sat panting patiently at my heels. Dooley grinned and twisted his shoulders pleasantly.

"All right. Thank you, Dooley," I said. I again offered him the dollar, but a hurt look came into his eyes and he turned away from me. For a moment I was puzzled; then I had a rare insight: Dooley didn't want my money; he wanted my friendship.

"Dooley." He glanced over his shoulder at me. "Would you like to have dinner with me tonight?" A sudden light of hopefulness shone in his eyes. He nodded. "Very well," I said. "Meet me at the Chinaman's at six this evening. All right?"

He grinned and nodded and turned to go.

"Dooley."

He glanced back.

"It would be nice if you would bathe first. Here." I again stretched the dollar out to him. His eyes narrowed. "No, no," I said. I pointed across the street to the barbershop. "I want you to get a shave and a haircut and a bath. I'll stop by and have Mr. Goldman bring you some new clothes. All right?"

He frowned for a moment, sticking his tongue into his cheek, thinking.

"It would be a favor to me," I said.

His lips split into a grin, and he nodded, clapping his hands with excitement. He took the dollar, touched his forehead with a dirty finger, and scurried across the street toward the barbershop. I walked down the street to Goldman's Store.

The bell jangled as I walked inside. Goldman looked up from the ledger where he had been entering figures. He nodded, carefully marked his place with a pencil, and closed the ledger. He rose, pulling his sleeve guards off as he came toward me.

"Yes, Marshal? How may I help you?"

"Hello, Samuel," I said. I glanced over at the counter where he had neatly folded pants and shirts. "I need some new clothes. But they're not for me." He nodded, hands folded patiently in front of him, waiting for me to explain. "They're for Dooley." His eyebrows rose. "I'm taking him for dinner tonight. Would you be so kind as to take him an outfit? He's over at the barbershop getting cleaned up."

"You surprise me, Marshal," he said.

I raised a quizzical eyebrow. "Why's that?"

"I didn't expect to find compassion in you, given your reputation," he said bluntly. "There's not many would do anything for the unfortunate among us despite their . . . 'Christian' pretenses." He spread his hands. "Of course I'll follow your wishes, Marshal."

"And bill me," I said.

"At half-price," he said. He smiled faintly at my surprise. "If you are willing to help Mr. Dooley, then who am I to take advantage of your generosity? We have a story about that among my people."

"The Good Samaritan?" I asked.

He shook his head. "I see you are familiar with more than I thought. No, but it will do as a simile." I turned to go, but he stopped me, saying, "Do you know where Abilene takes its name?"

"Luke three one?" I said.

He smiled faintly. "That I would not know. But it is a region west of Damascus where one finds the tomb of Nebytlabil—the tomb of Abel, slain by Cain. The first murder, Marshal."

"Yes," I said. "Too bad it wasn't the last. But men are more prone to follow bad examples than good. That's why there's a need for people like me."

"Yes, perhaps. But I still think it would be best for all concerned if there were no more guns at all—even yours, Marshal."

A heavy weight seemed to descend upon my shoulders and I felt the years press heavily upon me like the weight of the stars upon the shoulders of Atlas. I nodded respectfully and left, pausing outside to let my eyes adjust to the harsh sunlight.

A group of cowboys galloped recklessly by, raising a cloud of dust, weaving around two women and a child crossing the street. One woman screamed, throwing her hands fearfully in front of her. The second hunched protectively over the child.

The cowboys reined in in front of the Bull's Head. Laughing and calling coarsely to each other, they flipped the reins of their horses over the hitching rail in front of the saloon and swaggered in, clapping each other on the shoulder as if they had just pulled a successful prank.

I sighed and crossed the street toward the Bull's Head, pausing to check at the barbershop and tell Clem that Samuel Goldman would be bringing clothes around for Dooley.

"Goldman?" Clem asked, moving carefully around a patron's lathered chin with his razor. "The Jew?"

"Yes, the Jew," I said calmly.

"I hope he doesn't want a bath," Clem complained. "He'll leave a line of grease around the tub! Damn Jew!"

"Leaving it dirtier than those buffalo hunters coming in?" I asked, irked by his prejudice. He winked at me, supposing he had found a like believer.

"Far as I can tell, one and the same. Grease is grease and it takes a heap of scrubbing to get something like that clean," he said, nodding his head like a weather vane in rhythm to his own words.

"You might try climbing into it yourself now and then, Clem," I said. He glanced suspiciously at me. "You can't keep getting by with the lavender bottle."

He started to reply, but a gunshot cut off his words. I turned and stepped cautiously from the barbershop, my hands hovering around my pistol butts. Across the street, a small crowd of cowboys had gathered outside the Bull's Head. In front of them stood Phil Coe, Ben Thompson, and the young man I had rousted out of Mrs. Mack's place. I couldn't see any pistols out, but that meant nothing in the Devil's Addition, where gamblers and cowboys had pretty much a free hand—as long as they didn't terrorize the citizens by galloping through town on their way to the saloons and bawdy houses.

I sighed and strolled across, noting my deputy, Mike Williams, shadowing me from the boardwalk opposite. Mike was a good man who usually stayed in the jail, but we had emptied the jail that morning, taking the drunks and cowboys to court. Now he watched my back as I strolled up to the small crowd of men. Ben Thompson gave me a cool grin, but Coe's eyes burned with a maniacal hatred. I understood where that hatred came from: A young lady, Susannah Moore, had left him and moved in with me when I left the Drover's Cottage for a small two-story house at the south end of town. But we had argued constantly, as she was in the market for a husband and I wasn't looking for a wife—it wouldn't have been fair, given how tenuous marshaling was—and she soon moved out for another gambler who had a small house in the Devil's Addition.

Damned, though, if the red-haired lady who was living with Coe at the time didn't show up on my doorstep a couple of days after Susannah left—*what was her name? Beth? No, Bessie, I think. It could have been Emma Williams, but I think she was more in Hays or Ellsworth*—and that pretty much was the last nail in the coffin for Phil Coe. I had taken to watching my step carefully around him.

Now Thompson was another sort. I had hauled his faro table out of the back room a week before when I found out they were using a San Francisco shoe in the game—a slap on top released a spring that allowed the dealer to slip out the second card or third card, if he wished, leaving the winner on top a loser if the bets were in favor of one way or the other. Things didn't improve, either, when I had the Bull's Head sign altered somewhat to make it more appeasing to the gentle sensibilities by painting out the genitalia. Coe was little more than an obnoxious drunk, but obnoxious drunks are dangerous when they get a load on and sense their own invulnerability. I had more respect for Thompson, who had shown how deadly he could be with his pistols.

"Hello, Ben," I said, coming up to them. I stopped about eight feet short of the crowd, far enough that I could keep all hands in view. I recognized the young cowboy from Mrs. Mack's. He wore a brace of pistols in brazen view against the posted policy. Thompson nodded at me.

"What's going on, Ben?" I asked, keeping my voice light but firm.

"Damn dog," Thompson said, smiling widely. He pointed across the street. I knew without turning he was pointing at Joe, my dog. "Thought I'd get rid of it." He shrugged and nodded at the young cowboy. "I pointed him out to Wes here, but he missed."

"Lucky," I said, eyeing him steadily. "That happens to be my dog, Ben. And you know it. What are you up for?"

The young cowboy stirred and strutted forward. "All this over a goddamned dog?" He laughed. "Why, back home in Texas we'd shoot anything that wasn't where it was supposed to be. Dogs or niggers. Makes no difference. Come to think of it, Mesicans come under that, too."

He eyed me boldly, challengingly. I smiled at him. "I think you'd be better advised leaving your guns somewhere they won't get you in trouble. This bunch could cause you a bit of a problem."

"I can take care of myself," he boasted, standing as tall as he could. His eyes shone like agates. "Course, you want, you could take them. If you think you're man enough."

"Foolish talk," I said. "I'm not impressed, and if you get killed trying it, these folks aren't going to be impressed, either."

"I don't plan on being the one dying," he said. He hunched his shoulders dangerously. "I don't know what you plan."

"On living," I said.

"Kill him," someone said—I thought I recognized Coe's voice—and the young cowboy started to draw, but by that time I had flipped the Navies out of my sash and had one cocked and leveled at the center of his face. The other I kept pointed between Thompson and Coe.

"Bad mistake," I said.

"You think you can get all of us?" he blustered.

"I don't have to," I replied, feeling a trickle of sweat drop down my spine. "All I have to do is kill you and these other two. The others won't want a piece of that. And if they do"—I shrugged—"you won't know about it. That worth dying for?"

He half-pulled his pistols and I rocked the hammer back on the Navy with my thumb. "Another inch," I said softly. "Another inch and you're dead. Make no mistake about it. Anyone shoot me or not, you're dead. Just as certain as the sun. You want that?"

He shook his head and let his pistols drop into their holsters, slipping the thong over the hammers to secure them. I nodded but kept the pistol leveled at his face.

"What's your name?"

"John Wesley Hardin," he said sullenly. "Some folks call me Little Arkansas."

"I got paper on someone that fits your description," I said. "I'd think it a wise choice if you'd climb into your leather and head out of town."

"Now?"

"Better now than never, don't you think?" I asked.

His face flushed. "This is the second time—"

"And there won't be a third," I said, fixing him coldly with my eyes. I lowered my voice so only the two of us could hear. "The next time, I'll kill you. Make no mistake about it. This isn't a game for me despite what you think. You can say whatever you want to whomever you want once you're out of Abilene. Doesn't make any matter to me."

He turned silently and walked to his horse tied to the hitching rail in front of the Bull's Head, mounted, and rode out of town. I had a strange premonition that I would be hearing about him again before long, but at the moment I was more concerned with Thompson and Coe. I lowered the hammer on the Navy and turned to face them, keeping my pistols in my hands.

"You are one sorry son of a bitch, Thompson," I said, looking down on the pudgy gambler. "You and that pretty boy partner of yours—"

"Who the hell you calling a 'pretty boy'?" demanded Coe, taking a half step forward. I brought the pistol up slightly and he stopped, glaring at me.

"I'll pluck that beard of yours hair by hair, you don't shut up right now," I warned. I looked back at Thompson. "Next time, try and do your own dirty work instead of getting a half-cocked kid to walk your talk," I said.

"Maybe I will," he said, his face flushed beet red.

"Uh-huh. And pigs will fly," I said.

I was pushing and I knew it, but things had come to a head enough that it was time to make an example of someone and I couldn't think of anyone who might make a better example than the two in front of me at the moment. But I knew, even as I spoke I knew, that neither one of them would make a move toward his pistols and their standing among the Texas boys had just gone down a peg or two. That was enough for now.

I slipped the pistols back into my sash and backed away a

couple of steps, then turned and made my way down the middle of the street. I heard muttering behind me but couldn't make out the words and knew that I had nothing to worry about. Only after the muttering stopped. But it didn't and I walked confidently down the street away from them.

CHAPTER

49

IT DIDN'T take long, however, before things came to a head, and quickly. Thompson left town to meet his wife and children in Kansas City. The town council told me to shut down the Bull's Head but decided to leave it open after Coe sold out to Tom Sheran. But Coe didn't leave town. He hung around the fringes, gambling a little here and there. Once, when he was roaring drunk, he announced to the world that he was going to kill me before frost, and I had no illusions that it was only drunk talk. Coe would do that, but not where anyone could see him.

The city council had dismissed all of my deputies save Mike Williams, who had taken to walking the rounds with me at night until the hours settled a bit. I was grateful for his company, as it gave me another pair of eyes when I walked down through the Devil's Addition.

I remember the night.

October 5.

Mike and I had stopped for a nightcap at the bar in the Novelty Theater when I heard a gunshot come from the

Alamo on Cedar Street. I knew there was bad trouble, as the Alamo catered to a different clientele than the other saloons. The Alamo had three sets of double-glass doors that were folded back on hot nights. Several paintings of voluptuous nudes lolling on velvet settees hung around the walls. The bar was one of the longest in town, with a gleaming mahogany top fitted with brass. It was a place where the stockmen played, not penny-ante gamblers.

"Stay here," I said to Mike as I moved away from the bar.

"You need someone at your back," he protested, starting forward. I stopped him.

"No, not tonight," I said "I'd just as soon you stay out of the way."

I hurried across the street, slipping into the back door of the Alamo and pushing my way out through the front. I saw a mob of Texans, mostly drunk, weaving in the street around Phil Coe, who stood in the middle of the street, waving a pistol. I took a deep breath and stepped down to face him.

"You fire that shot, Coe?" I asked.

"Damn dogs around here," he said, grinning broadly. "I almost got him, too."

"What dog?" I asked coldly, feeling the hatred welling from the crowd like a flood wave. "Where?"

"Well, hell, he got away," Coe said. "But what the hell? A dog is only a dog. Right?"

"All right," I said quietly. "Drop your gun on the ground. All of you drop your guns," I repeated, raising my voice. "Drop your guns and leave town. And you don't come back, Coe. I've had enough of you."

"*Damn* you!" he exploded, and started to raise his pistol.

I flipped the pistols out of my sash and fired as they came level. The bullets took Coe in the abdomen. He dropped the pistols and sank forward, his hands pressing against the sudden pain that stabbed hard deep inside him.

"The rest of you—"

A shadow flitted at the corner of my eye. I saw light glinting from a pistol barrel and whirled and fired. Mike grunted as the bullets hit him in the chest. He fell dead to the ground.

"My God," someone said in the sudden hush. "He's kilt them both. An' one a friend."

Rage rushed through me as I saw Mike stretched lifeless on the ground. I turned slowly to the crowd, rocking the hammers back on both pistols, a hot recklessness driving rational thought from me.

"You all have just thirty seconds to get out of town," I said. "Then I'm going to kill every man jack of you. This town is closed to your type. Now, you coon-swyving sons-a-bitches, play your hands!"

They scattered like pasteboards in a whirlwind, leaping upon horses and galloping out of town. Within minutes, I was alone in the street with the dead Mike Williams and the dying Coe. "You . . . killed . . . me . . ." Coe gasped.

"I reckon so," I said. A bartender peeked out of the Alamo. "Go get the preacher. Get the doctor, too, if you want. It won't make a damn bit of difference. But before you do, close and lock your doors. This town is shut down."

And with that, I roared through the town, shutting down all the saloons and gambling houses. Even Mrs. Mack's place locked its doors. Within an hour, I walked the silent streets. Coe had been taken to his cottage near the schoolhouse in the southwest part of town. He was a while dying, but I couldn't feel any remorse for him. I had Mike placed in a coffin and sent home to his wife and family in Kansas City.

Two months later, I resigned, knowing full well that I no longer had the heart for the job. Whenever I went to arrest someone, I sensed Mike coming to help me out of the shadows. A couple of times, I narrowly escaped injury when the shadows coming from the corner of my vision turned out to be friends of the man I was arresting. I knew I no longer had the heart for the job. But the days of the cattle drive were pretty much over anyway by this time. I left Abilene and went to visit Colorado Charley Utter for Christmas. I loved the mountains during Christmas—the snowcapped peaks, the sharp, crisp smell with a hint of pine. I think it was the nostalgia of Christmas as well that held me as it always did, for I could never pass a Christmas without remembering the ones I had had as a boy back in Homer. Charley opened his house to me. And then shortly after that I went to Springfield, where Cody found me.

CHAPTER

50

"BILL," CODY said, coming into my dressing room at Niblo's Gardens—New York, I think it was. Cody had found me in Springfield, where I was broke and trying to make a living gambling, which is hard when you're broke and gambling has been declared illegal by the Springfield blue bloods. He had sidled up to me at the bar and told me he was putting together a Combination, acting out stories of the Wild West.

That threw me for a minute and I looked at him closely and asked, "The Wild West?" Cody always seemed to speak in capital letters. "What do you mean, the 'Wild West'?"

But he waved away my question impatiently and went on about how a fellow named Ned Buntline had put together this show and it was tailor-made for people like us and we would make more money than we could burn in a lifetime of autumns if we went on with it. My options were kind of thin at the moment, so, with some misgivings, I said yes.

I should have realized what the East was like when a cabbie took me from the train station to the hotel where Cody was staying and tried to charge me double. When I refused, the cabbie tried to pound it out of my hide and I left him unconscious in the gutter. Cody had bailed me out of that one, so I thought I would give the show a try.

I glanced in the mirror at him, standing behind me. He closed the door gently behind him and I sighed, knowing what was coming. Last night had been a disaster. I had a mental blackout and couldn't remember my lines. Ned Buntline had been furious, but Texas Jack Ohumurado had thought it funny and regaled the patrons in the many saloons we had passed through in New York City after the show with accounts of my ad-libbing.

"Bill," Cody said in a stage whisper. "I don't like it. I think there're Injuns around. I gotta funny feeling on the back of my neck."

The spotlight hit me in my eyes. I saw twin halos spinning in front of me like comets. "You want to take that damn light out of my eyes?" I asked, shading them with my hand and looking up at the operator managing the light from the balcony.

Cody looked baffled for a moment. The actors playing Indians froze in tableau around the stake to which they'd tied Molly—what the hell was her last name?—artfully enough so her breasts were all but hanging free, and I had to admit that they were good-looking breasts, as I'd seen them on the times when she managed to slip away from her husband and make it to my room, which was every time when we didn't have an afternoon performance.

"What say, Bill?" Cody said, stalling for time.

"I said to take that damn light out of my eyes," I said irritably.

"Why, Bill, 'tisn't a light but the sun," he said. I recognized Kate's line, but damn if I could remember what I was supposed to say next.

"Well, it sure ain't the moon," I said, trying hard to remember the foolish line Buntline had written. I still couldn't. Something like, "Well, I reckon we ought to scout around and see if we can find those rascals." But the line just wouldn't come. My eyes were beginning to ache from the harsh light shining into them. The audience tittered, recognizing that I was lost in the wilderness of bantering words.

"Well, my neck's just a-itching," Cody said, coming back to the script.

"Hell," I muttered, "maybe you should wash it now and then."

The audience roared with laughter. Texas Jack nearly doubled over, his voice keening with his giggling behind us. Molly hooted from the stake. Even the Indian actors were trying not to break into hooraws, desperately holding on to their stage stoicism. Buntline's eyes glittered with anger when I glanced at him. But I stood nearly a foot taller than him and had once upended him in a rain barrel when he got a little cocky like the bantam he was.

Cody, however, was another story and he wasn't laughing as he stared somberly into the mirror at me. I could smell the whiskey he had drunk "to clear his pipes" as he readied himself for the matinee.

"I know," I said. "But that damn light shining in my eyes just drove the words out of my head. Besides, they're just crap anyway. You and I know that isn't what happened. Hell, you never killed Yellow Knife anyway in a duel. You shot him with your Sharps from a hundred yards away."

"That doesn't show very well on the stage," Cody said. He lifted his hand automatically, smoothing his goatee, running his thumb along his mustache on his upper lip. His eyes were red-lined from the night's drinking and foolish with the blue smudges he insisted on putting around them and the heavy rice powder he had dusted his face with to cut down the glare from the stage lights. He looked like an old whore. I told him so.

"Now, you see, Bill, that's just what I mean!" he said, annoyed. Cody was a good man, but he just never seemed to come down off the stage at that time. He even held his character when he called it a season and went back to North Platte to his Scout's Ranch. He was always Buffalo Bill Cody and whatever the hell he had decided to be the next season: Indian Fighter, Man-Hunter, Chief Scout of the Plains—whatever.

"You've got to learn what people want and give it to them. Their heroes have to be larger than ordinary men and that's what we are supposed to be out there." He flung his buckskin arm dramatically toward the stage behind the door and slid one booted foot forward. I glanced at the thigh-high boots he ordered specially made for him from Fort Worth. Texas Jack always swung by to pick up his leather order when he came north to join Bill in Kansas City, where they met each year to put the show together.

"You've got to give people what they want," he said.

I remembered when I thought that was what I was doing when I was marshaling. That was before the fracas in Abilene when I killed Mike accidentally. Those were good times, if a bit stressful, always watching my back, automatically reading the shadows when I made my rounds late at night through the streets, waiting for cowboys to make up their minds when I braced them for stepping over the bounds I allowed as to whether they were going to turn their pistols in or use them, Phil Coe—

"Bill," Cody said impatiently. "Bill, are you listening to me?"

I shook my head and glanced up at him in the mirror, then back at myself, seeing the tired lines drawing my face tight, my hairline beginning to track up on my forehead, remembering when I tried to open *The Great Buffalo Chase at Niagara Falls* and going bust—a thousand dollars in the hole—getting drunk as a skunk when my creditors foreclosed on the show and letting a cinnamon bear we had brought along as an exhibit out of his cage to roam the streets, laughing insanely as people ran screaming from him as he ambled through the streets, pausing to gobble down a bunch of sausage an Italian had on a pushcart. The Italian tried to shoo the bear away, but the bear, who had been around humans since a motherless cub when Red Feather had found him and raised him—I never figured out why he did that; I would have given odds that he, being an Indian and all, would have killed the cub and used his fur for something—but the bear grabbed the Italian and licked him affectionately, positive that he had found a friend in that friendless city where people had been poking him through the cage bars with pointed sticks when one of us wasn't watching. A bunch of bystanders managed to free them, and the bear, sorrowful at losing a friend, ambled down the alleys, scavenging garbage bins for food. I remembered the look on the three policemen's faces when I told them to put up their pistols when they drew them to shoot the bear and hoping that they would do it and not make me live up to my reputation by using the pistols beneath my hands and the bear going *Umph! Umph!* behind me as he grunted his way through some spoiled meat outside Delmonico's. The judge took a dim view of my actions although the bear was safe by that time in a cage at the zoo.

That did it for me until Cody found me, broke in Springfield and no way to make a stake at the tables after a bunch of rich wives with nothing else to do pushed through a reform policy that outlawed gambling. Cody found me lounging around Market Square, looking for something to do. I damn near didn't recognize him in a long fur-trimmed coat that he'd had copied after a picture of some lord or baron in a magazine, a brocaded vest with a gold watch chain spread across his belly. The links on that chain were heavy enough to pull a ferry across the Mississippi River.

"Bill," he said, leaning an elbow comfortably on the bar, a tumbler full of whiskey close at hand. "Bill, I'd like to have you come back to New York with me. Buntline's putting together a play he's calling *Scouts of the Prairie*. There'll be me, him, Texas Jack, and Colorado Charley in it. You'll make up the fifth. We'll have a gay time of it all."

"Have it," I grunted, draining my glass of whiskey. "I've had it with show business. I lost my shirt on that Wild West show I tried to take back east."

He shook his head, glancing sideways at his profile in the mirror behind the bar. "Hell, Bill, there'll be no risk to you.

You'll draw a salary of a hundred a week to start. More later, I expect, after it becomes a hit."

A hit. Well, I never could say that Cody didn't have confidence. He never did think that he'd come out on the short end of a rope in anything he did. I guess that's why he managed to live grandly even when he had no money. He managed to convince everyone around him that there was gold in buffalo chips.

I started to say no, but then I remembered I was thirty-six and didn't want to spend any more time scouting for the army and tired of bending a pistol barrel over some cowboy's hard head. So here I was, giving out such lines as, "The Indians are upon us!" and "Fear not, fair maid! By heavens, you are safe at last with Wild Bill, who is ever ready to risk his life and die, if need be, in defense of weak and defenseless womanhood," which caused a bit of snickering and such from drinkers at whatever bar I wandered through.

"Goddamnit, Bill!" Cody said, exasperated.

"Yeah, I hear you," I said. "Hell, everyone in the theater hears you."

"Well?"

"Well what?" I asked.

He rolled his eyes and stuck a fist on his hip, glaring at me in the mirror. "What are you going to do? Buntline's having a litter of kittens over your actions last night. And that ain't—isn't the first time. You're getting worse as we go along instead of better. You're losing it."

"Well, whatever 'it' is that I'm supposed to be losing I don't know. But this 'play' "—I made my voice heavy with sarcasm—"is nothing more than a pile of manure. Why don't you give the people the truth?"

"I just told you—"

"I heard you. But they seemed to enjoy themselves last night. They laughed," I said defensively.

"This isn't supposed to be a comedy," he said patiently. "People know the West isn't funny. It's serious. People die out there. Horribly. Indian attacks—"

"Save it," I sighed. "I know what goes on out there as well

as you do. It's not all killing Indians and outlaws. Hell, I play my fiddle about as much as I shoot my pistols. Say, you remember that dance we threw together at that church social—where was it? Wichita?—when you disappeared with the good reverend's wife and those kids found you a humping away down by the river like two jackrabbits and she yelled that you trapped her? That reverend sure was mad as hell at you! I think if he'd had a pistol he would have blown a hole clean through you."

"I remember you laying a pistol alongside his head to stop him from slapping his wife around—damn it, Bill! This is serious!" he said. But I could tell that his heart wasn't behind his words. For all of his pretending and posturing, Cody was a plainsman and damn good at it when he didn't have an audience around demanding that he be Buffalo Bill and not Cody. "Buntline is threatening to take us to court!"

I studied him for a moment, until he flushed and looked away, his hand straying once again to stroke his goatee, thumb his mustache. "And what," I asked softly, "is Buntline going to take us to court on? Being too stupid to learn lines? Why did he hire us anyway?"

"You know why he hired us," Cody mumbled, looking away. "You got any whiskey in here?"

"You've already loosened your pipes enough," I said dryly.

He ignored me and went to a small table by a chair in the room where I had left a whiskey bottle and tumbler. He poured a tumbler full, sipped it. His eyes raised in surprise. "Tennessee sipping whiskey? Since when have you drunk anything other than Monongahela?" He took another appreciative drink.

"Since a few people like my performances," I said, motioning to the tiny bar in the corner where my costumes hung behind a dressing screen.

He crossed over and drew the curtain, his eyebrows rising nearly to his failing hairline. "Glory be to Bob!" he breathed. Cases upon cases of whiskey had been stacked back there. He opened one idly, almost reverently. Then he turned and pointed an accusing finger at me.

"All this gold and you weren't going to share with your old pard?" he said, the words rolling in proper declamation from his lips. "After all we've been through together?"

I shook my head. "We weren't really pards, Cody. You went your own way most of the time, leaving me to mine. Help yourself. I can't drink it all."

He took two bottles from the case and stuck one in a pocket on each side of the long fringed buckskin coat that hung nearly to his knees. He cleared his throat and drained the glass, placing it back on the small stand.

He shook his head. "Try, will you, Bill? Buntline takes himself seriously, and that's a dangerous man."

"Any man is dangerous who takes foolishness seriously," I said. I held up my hands as his lips pressed together angrily. "I'll try. I promise. I'll try."

He nodded and crossed to the door, pausing to say, "I know you will, Bill. I know this isn't exactly your campfire, either, but there's a lot of money here if we play our cards right. A lot of *easy* money. Easier than we ever made in all our lives."

"My father used to say that easy money usually had the devil behind the door, spending it," I murmured.

He stared soberly at my eyes in the mirror, then nodded slowly. "Your father was undoubtedly a wise man. But money spends the same no matter where it comes from. It ain't, doesn't, got a conscience. See you onstage."

He closed the door behind him as I continued eyeing the reflection of a young middle-aged man growing rapidly older before his time. I noticed the soft blurring around the edges of the figure in the mirror and wondered idly if it was a problem with the refraction of the mirror or if it was an ominous sign of the time coming when I would slip into the other world behind the mirror.

That night, while Buntline was declaiming about "dirty redskins" and how we (the white men) had to get rid of the varmints if we wanted to civilize the West, the spotlight operator made the mistake of shifting the light to shine in my face. I was ready for him this time and drew my pistol and shot the light out.

The pistol shot, coming at that particular time, when Buntline was waxing eloquent in some speech he had cribbed from Shakespeare, took him by surprise and the beans and steak he had eaten for dinner took that moment to explode from his concentration. A loud *brrraaaaakkkk* followed hard on the heels of the pistol shot like a distant echo. The audience collapsed. Even the fabled stoicism of the "Indians" broke apart onstage and Molly, tied to the stake (I never could figure out why, as she was playing an Indian woman named Dove Eyes) and supposedly filled with fear, laughed so hard that tears dug gullies through her thick pancake makeup. Cody turned his back to the audience, his heavy shoulders shaking with deep barrel laughter, while Texas Jack sank on his heels, his high-pitched giggling sounding over the guffaws onstage. Charley Utter snickered and ran offstage, holding his nose, which only made the audience laugh harder.

Buntline stormed over to me, his face livid with laughter. "You son of a bitch, that's it! I'm not putting up with another goddamn thing from you!"

I looked down at him. "I warned you about that before, you cocky little bastard."

Enraged, he drew back his fist and swung at me. I leaned back away from it and jabbed him in the nose with a quick left. His nose popped like an overripened tomato and blood spattered his beaded buckskins. He staggered backward, lost his balance, and fell solidly on his butt. A stunned look spread over his face; then he scrambled to his feet and ran at me, fists flailing wildly.

I stepped in and dug a right into his belly. That did it for his insides. He bent double, gasping for air while air ripped out through his butt.

Brrrrrrraaaaaaaaaaaaaaaccccccccchhhhh! Pft! Pft!

That was pretty much the end of the play that night, as the stage manager wisely dropped the curtain over the whole fiasco, symbolically dropping it over my stage career as well. I didn't wait for Buntline to fire me or file charges on me. I left the stage, grabbed the few possessions I had in my dressing room, and headed back to my hotel room.

I checked out, leaving the room charges in Buntline's name, and worked my way through the saloons over to the train station. In the last one, an Englishman came up and touched my long hair wonderingly, saying, "I say, are you an Indian or a white man?"

Which affront I was drunk enough not to take. I knocked him flat, announcing to an openmouthed crowd, "That's what I am."

I walked across the street and took a train to Topeka, breathing a deep sigh of relief only when the train thundered across the trestle over the Ohio River, feeling the tightness of the past months seep from my shoulders, my very bones. The two bottles of whiskey I had drained by then helped, too. I didn't come away from that trip with much of anything except blue-tinged glasses I had to wear after a footlight exploded near me when all the scouts were supposedly snuggled around a campfire on the plains, listening to me tell a story.

CHAPTER

51

FOR A while I moved around the place and finally got word from Cody and Colorado Charley that they were planning on doing a bit of hunting and if I could meet them in Cheyenne—

The message came at the right time. I needed to get away from Kansas, where I was getting tired of trying to cool off the hotheaded youngsters looking for a fast way to get a reputation, without killing them. I usually managed to get close enough to bang them on the head with one of my pistols—which was a good thing for me, as my eyes had gotten to the point where I wasn't sure anymore who was friend and who I should shoot if they yelled my name from more than twenty-five feet away.

So there I was stepping down from the train in Cheyenne, wearing my dark glasses to keep the sun from burning my eyes, squinting, trying to find the damn Republican Hotel, where I was to meet Colorado Charley. I finally found the damn thing, checked in, and made my way back downstairs. I was heading for the bar when I heard a gasp and then, "James? Is that you?"

I turned and peered through the permanent gloom and saw a shapely figure hurrying toward me. I could tell by the skirts that it had to be a woman—I thought I knew the voice, but time places a trick on a man's memory in more ways than one—but I didn't know her until she was standing in front of me.

"Agnes?" I said hesitantly.

She laughed and I watched the color come up into her cheeks. Her eyes sparkled and she put out a hand to touch my arm. "I thought that was you—"

I was glad to see her, and all ideas of exploring the bar pushed themselves right out of my head. We went over to a corner and sat, I taking the edge, where I could keep as much of the room in focus as I could. We talked for hours, then went to eat, and then I escorted her to the house where she was staying with her friend Minnie Moyer.

"Why don't we get married?" she asked suddenly. A mischievous smile curved into dimples.

I was a bit taken aback at this and hemmed and hawed, trying to find a way of stepping back from the proposal in a gentlemanly way, but suddenly I remembered everything that had come up since Abilene—my fling in show business, gambling, drinking—and I wondered why I should not have what other men my age had.

"I don't know," I said, giving her a chance to back away. But she didn't. She stepped in close and I smelled the lilac of her perfume and I remembered the fine time we had had in Abilene and the letters that she wrote to me at least once every two months and everything I had for myself after all those years in the West and suddenly nothing seemed as important as marrying her and nothing seemed to make more sense than marrying her, and I figured, *Hell, that's two out of three or four, and what better odds could a person ask for?* Better than hunting for a third or fourth queen on a new deal from a fresh deck, and it had been a long time since I had seen a fresh deck.

"All right," I said.

A stunned look came over her face; then she squealed

with joy and leaped into my arms and the next day, March 5, 1876, Agnes and I were married by Reverend Warren in S. L. Moyer's home, and after spending the night in the Republican Hotel Agnes and I headed for Cincinnati for our honeymoon and where I thought, briefly thought, I suppose in the passion of the moment, that I would be able to hang up my guns.

I didn't find out until much later that Agnes had known I was going to be in Cheyenne because she ran into Cody, who had been drinking all day and told her in a rash moment that he was meeting me in Cheyenne to go hunting. Agnes beat him to Cheyenne on her own hunting party and bagged her own game. She was hesitant to tell me, but when a couple shares a wedding bed there comes a time eventually when one has to rest, and that means talk. At first she was afraid I would be angry, but after I thought it over for a second I realized that I was pretty fortunate to have someone like Agnes go to all that trouble for a broken-down gunfighter.

"Bill," she said after a little over a week in Cincinnati, "I heard about an eye doctor in town who has had pretty good luck treating folks with eye problems. Why don't you go to see what he has to say?"

I pushed the newspaper away from my face and stared across the room at her. She sat in front of the window in a soft halo that outlined her. I didn't say anything while I thought over what she had said. I really didn't want to go to the doctor—I suppose I already knew what he was going to tell me: that I should have been a bit more careful with consorting with cyprian devotees—but I really couldn't think of a good excuse to give Agnes without hurting her feelings. And that I wasn't going to do.

So Agnes made an appointment for me, and the next day but two I found my way to a Dr. Roderick Thorpe's office, where he examined me and then said, "Mr. Hickok, I'm afraid I have bad news for you."

"Uh-huh," I grunted, reaching for my hat. "I reckon I have a good idea what it is you're going to say."

He caught my hand for a moment and quickly released it

when I turned to stare at him. He was close enough that I could see how unhappy he was about having to give me the news and how nervous he was by the perspiration popping out on his forehead.

"I am sorry, Mr. Hickok, but you have what is called glaucoma. You probably got it from your mother or father and they from theirs. We don't know much about it; I can give you some drops against the pain, but"—he shrugged his shoulders—"there really isn't anything we can do about it. Usually we find this in older people, but that doesn't mean that it can't occur in young men, either."

"I understand," I said, turning away from him.

"I would like you to see another man, however," he said, following me to the door. He shoved a piece of paper in my hand. "A doctor in Kansas City on the Missouri side—Dr. Joshua Thorne—who might have a different opinion and who might have a remedy or can offer you some more advice. I am sorry, sir."

"It isn't your fault," I said, and gave him a smile.

The smile disappeared, however, when I stepped down into the cold wind whistling through the Cincinnati streets. I had no illusion at all about what the good doctor was trying to tell me gently: I was going blind and I didn't have that much time until I would be completely blind. I think I knew I was heading that way when I was in Hays City and noticed how some people had gentle halos around them like angels and perhaps I should have mentioned that before, but at the time and in that place it would have been deadly to let it get out that Wild Bill Hickok had eye problems. I would have been dead in a week.

"Well, of course we must go to Kansas City," Agnes said when I told her what Dr. Thorpe had said. "We'll leave on the train the first thing in the morning."

I reached out and pulled her to me and kissed her as gently as I could. I felt the slight tremble of surprise on her lips and I think she knew even then what I was going to say. But I said it anyway, telling her that I wanted to go to Kansas City alone and then go back to Cheyenne and from there up into Deadwood, where the latest gold strike had been discovered. I worked hard at convincing her to let me go alone, telling her that I had better see if I could find some quick money up there against the time when I would be blind and unable to find any work. Finally she agreed to my suggestion when I told her I would only be gone six months at the most.

The next day she saw me off on the train to Chicago, where I would change over for one to Kansas City. She cried when we left and held close to me and finally walked away, her shoulders shaking. For a moment I was tempted to go after her and tell her that I had changed my mind, but I didn't. I already knew no jobs waited for me in Cincinnati regardless of whether I had healthy eyes or not. And I already knew—even before the train chugged out of the station—that I couldn't let myself be a burden to her. I loved her too much for that.

PART FOUR

Legend

All ashes to the taste

CHAPTER

52

THE TRAIN pulled into the station in Chicago. I stepped down stiffly and sighed, looking around. I had a long wait until the next train left for Kansas City and wondered what I would do to kill the time. There were always bars, but I felt a certain reluctance about going into a bar. I half-smiled at the strange change in me that seemed to have come since my marriage to Agnes, but there it was. I knew that I would eventually be back in the bars and back to playing poker, but in the meantime, I didn't want to have anything to do with the strange company of men that I knew I would find there.

I walked out of the train station into the cold, gray weather, shivering slightly when the cold struck me. I turned and walked briskly down the street, intending on stretching my legs for a couple of hours, and thought I might as well see what sights I could.

I had just turned up Michigan Avenue when I heard a woman's voice behind me.

"James? That you?"

I glanced over my shoulder at a well-dressed woman

standing in a doorway, a package under her arm. I took my hat off my head and gave a half bow. "Yes, ma'am. It is. But it's a long time since anyone called me by that name except my mother and brothers."

She laughed, the sound tinkling like silver bells. "You don't remember me, do you?"

I frowned, stepping closer so that I could bring her more in focus through the blue-tinted glasses I was wearing after Dr. Thorpe recommended that I wear those until after I had seen Dr. Thorne.

Vanity.

I shook my head.

"I'm Zoë."

For a moment I was confused; then I remembered the battered woman I had put on the train in Abilene so many years before. *How many? How many?*

"I'll be damned," I said. I started to hold out my hand, muttering the pleasantries one makes in such situations, but she stepped close and stood on tiptoes to kiss my cheek.

"It's been a long time, James," she said.

I felt a moment's confusion, then realized that she had never before called me James. Always Bill. Always. I smiled at her. "Yes, it has."

She cocked her head on the side like a towhee and regarded me for a second before saying, "I heard about your little escapades in the theater."

I laughed. "Well," I said ruefully, "there's some that just weren't made for traipsing the boards. That's what they call it, acting, I mean."

"I know," she said. I realized the changes in her, the sophistication that came only after long study. I was impressed.

"So what have you been doing with yourself?" I asked in the sudden awkwardness that fell between us.

"Not much," she said, smoothing her dress in front of her with that automatic gesture she had used so many times when she wore nothing but a wrapper and stockings held up with red ribbons. A pang of memory came flashing back to me, but I pushed it away. "I invested a bit of money with a 'friend,' " she finished.

I nodded. "Good for you. You're doing well then?"

"Oh yes. Nothing to want." But her eyes said something different. I pretended not to notice.

"Married?"

"No, you?"

I nodded and watched her face tighten for a minute; then she laughed. "Well, would you think it bad if a woman like me would invite you for dinner?"

I shook my head. "I would be honored to have dinner with a woman like you, Zoë."

A wetness sparkled in her eyes for a second; then she laughed and stepped next to me, tucking her hand beneath my arm. "Then come on. We'll find a cab and go home. It's the maid's day off, but I can—"

"Why don't we eat at a restaurant? No sense you going to any trouble," I said.

She cocked her head at me like a towhee again. "You afraid to be alone with me, James?"

You little minx. "No," I said. "All right. If that's what you want."

"I owe you that, James," she breathed quietly. A dark shadow slipped down over her eyes and between us.

"You don't owe me anything, Zoë," I said. "Let's not think about that, all right?"

"All right," she answered, her eyes sparkling again. "Let's enjoy ourselves."

I laughed and we walked to the corner, where we found a cab, and took it to her house. I sat in the kitchen enjoying a glass of whiskey with her while she cooked. Then she opened a bottle of wine and we ate—

We were sitting on the couch when she turned to me and said, "Why did you marry, James?"

I was nodding sleepily from the meal and wine and felt a moment's confusion. Then I realized what she was asking.

"Because . . . I fell in love," I finished lamely. But she had caught the hesitation in my voice and smiled sadly.

"That's not it, is it?" she asked.

I shook my head.

She regarded me silently for a second, then said,

> *"Can I be less desirable than she?*
> *Less interesting? Less beautiful? Can mortals*
> *Compare with goddesses in grace and form?"*

"No," I replied. "When my Agnes walks, she treads upon the ground. But I was not meant to belong in the East; I do not belong here; I belong where I am needed."

Angry lights glinted in her eyes. "Have you looked at yourself lately?" she demanded. "You are nearly blind and whiskey-bloated. You are right; you are not Odysseus. You look more like Falstaff, staggering around, proclaiming your honor. But"—her gaze softened but not the intensity of her words—"you are no longer the young man who tamed Hays City and Abilene and scouted for Custer. You have earned your rest." She fell on her knees in front of me. "The West is for young men, James. At least those who do what you do. Put away your guns."

I squinted at her, working hard to bring her into focus. The lamps in the room had a soft glow around them. Her golden hair shone softly around her like a halo. I shook my head regretfully. She sighed and rose, walking to the window.

"Is it because of me?" she asked lowly. "Because of what I once was?"

I glanced involuntarily at the nude painting of her hanging on the wall and remembered the photograph she had had made of her naked and given to me after I had shot the man who had beaten her while she was at Mrs. Mack's house.

"No, that has nothing to do with it," I said.

She turned from the window and pressed her hands together tightly in the folds of her dress. She gave me a crooked smile, but it had no happiness in it.

"They say once a man has tasted the forbidden fruit it no longer holds a fascination for him."

"And some men like a fine whiskey that's been well aged in oaken barrels."

She stared at me for a long time, her hair, newly cut in the day's fashion, seemed to glow around her again, and I sighed and pressed the pads of my fingers against my eyes, rubbing softly at the ache, softly rubbing the pain away from the muscles of my face.

"James," she began, but I interrupted her.

"I no longer know the boy who was James," I said softly.

"You told me once—"

"James is dead, Zoë. Can't you see that? Only Bill is left." I shook my head. "When a wolf gets too old for the pack, he must leave or be killed. I don't have that luxury."

"You have become your own legend," she said slowly.

I nodded. "Whatever Bill is. Wherever I go, I'll always be Wild Bill."

"I think that's what you want," she said, an angry note creeping into her voice. "You *want* to be the legend. All your life you have been building the legend. Well, now you have it!

"How does it feel to be Wild Bill?"

I shook my head and felt the years pressing hard upon me. My knees ached, and whenever the weather changed I felt the pain throughout my body, the old wounds reminding me constantly that they were there. My hands—I glanced down at them, spreading my fingers, studying the large knuckles, the slight involuntary trembling, critically—had lately been giving me trouble in the mornings. Sometimes they were so stiff that I could barely buckle my belt. I rolled a poker chip back and forth over my knuckles to keep them from becoming stiff during the day. Even my feet were prone to swelling during the night, so much so that I could no longer order boots from Fort Worth—the last the boot-maker had made so many years ago belonged to a younger man, to James, not me.

"It's what James wanted," I said. "Bill wants to be James."

She came back to the couch and sank down beside me. I

lifted my arm and placed it around her, pulling her close. This close, I could see the tears welling in her eyes.

"Funny, isn't it?" I said. "A boy wants to be a man, but the man wants to be the boy."

"It wouldn't make any difference if you could reverse the sands of time," she said. "You would always be what people want, what people need you to be. What I needed you to be back in Abilene." She sighed. "I'm sorry for being ungrateful. If you hadn't helped me then, I wouldn't be here now."

"I don't know about that," I said. I touched the tip of her nose and used my thumb to wipe away the tears. "I have a hunch you would have been here now anyway. You weren't made to be a happy whore, Zoë."

"I wish it could be Zoë Hickok," she said mournfully. "But that wouldn't do, would it?"

I grinned and shook my head. "Some writer would get to investigating and find out about Abilene. Here you are invited to the theater and into the proper houses. You're much better off being Zoë Butler than Mrs. Hickok. But," I added as her full lips drew down into a pout, "you could be Mrs. Butler." She frowned, uncomprehending. I smiled and gently touched the softness under her chin. "My full name is James Butler Hickok."

A new dawning crept into her eyes. She wrapped her arms around my neck and kissed me gently upon my lips. I rose, picking her up in my arms, and carried her into her bedroom, pausing just before the threshold. Her opulent curves pressed against my chest. I felt the trembling of her heart, and the answering beat of my heart begin to thud faster in my chest. On her mantel, the clock struck gently the witching hour of the night.

"It's the best I can offer," I said, hesitating.

"It's enough," she said. Her lips brushed my neck just above the collar. "But just tell me you love me. You don't have to mean it. Just once is all I ask. That's enough."

"Zoë, I love you," I said, and for that moment, I did. I carried her over the threshold as a new bride and gently laid her on her bed behind the lacy bed curtains. I bent and kissed her, long and deep, as tenderly as I could. The quickening of her breath ruffled the hairs of my mustache.

"Yes," she said breathlessly. "Yes, James, I will be your bride. Yes, you will always have Mrs. Butler to come back for. Yes, I will. Yes."

Later I rose in the dark of her bedroom, slipping from beneath the quilted comforter and walking naked as Adam before the serpent's teasing across the floor to the window. I parted the curtains cautiously. Snow fell, big flakes tapping gently upon the windowpanes. Spring snow. A bad time, but the time had come for me to set out upon my journey westward. I looked back at Zoë sleeping peacefully from our newly wedded lovemaking, curled into a warm ball beneath the comforter. I studied her face and her hair and wondered what she had been like in her youth, in the first bloom of her girlish beauty. A strange but friendly pity entered me, and I felt tears forming in my eyes and I touched them wonderingly, trying to remember when last I had shed a tear. I looked to where our clothes lay in a marriage mix upon the floor. A petticoat string lay across the floor from beneath the ball of my checkered trousers. I couldn't remember any tears before this and thought that this must be love and perhaps I had not lied when I had told her I loved her—as much as James could have loved her, perhaps, before he became Wild Bill, who only had left the moment to pass boldly into the dark of the other world, which was better for him than to fade and wither dismally with age.

I became aware of the air of the room chilling my shoulders and pulled the curtains tightly closed to shut out the night and crossed through the room's dark, quietly feeling my way back to bed with my knobby toes.

Yes, I thought, slipping under the comforter and stretching out beside her. It was time to begin my journey to the West. But not tonight. Nor tomorrow. Nor, perhaps, the next day. No, not the next day. Before then. Otherwise I would stay and age dismally until I became a dried pod, but in that time I would forget the joy of being James one last time and Bill would destroy what was between us at this moment, this *fi-*

nal moment, when James had come back into the world but even now was already beginning to slip away into the dark as Bill thought of his westward journey.

I turned in to her, kissing her eyes until their lids butterflied beneath my lips, wanting her at that moment desperately to help push away the final dark for one brief moment until James entered it forever.

She smiled up at me sleepily, her bare arms rising to caress my shoulders. "James—"

CHAPTER

53

DEADWOOD.

No light, rather darkness visible.

A gray day spreads over the gulch as I saunter down the muddy road. Frost was on the surface of the water barrel when I rolled out from under Colorado Charley Utter's wagon and washed my face and shaved. I dressed and then nudged the pile of blankets heaped over Charley. Soft snoring ceased. His head poked cautiously out and dark eyes blinked heavily at me.

"What the hell you doing up in the middle of the night?" he demanded, yawning.

"Day's half spent and you're still lolling around like a whore after an all-night party. And you call yourself a mountain man," I scoffed. I nudged him again with my toe. "Come on," I said. "Let's go down to the Chinaman's and get a hot bath. My bones are creaking and need a bit of lubricating."

He yawned again and motioned vaguely at the wagon box overhead. "There's a bottle in the back left. Under the tarp.

Lubricate and be happy." He started to pull the blankets back over him, but I bent and yanked them off. He yelped.

"Goddamnit, Bill! It's the middle of the foggin' night!" he complained, shivering in the cold morning air.

"It's late," I said sternly. "If you're going to go tomcattin' all night long, you can damn well get up and earn the day."

He sighed and grabbed a blanket to wrap around him as he rolled out from under the wagon. He stood, swearing softly as he worked the night out of his muscles. His legs were a mass of scars from the unwelcome attention of a bear and at least two arrowheads and a rifle ball that he still carried somewhere. He limped in a tiny circle, then went to the barrel and panned water. He splashed it vigorously on his face and chest, then toweled dry. He picked up his razor and stared at it for a moment before shaking his head.

"All right, we'll go to the Chinaman's," he said. "I can't face a cold shave today." He yawned and stretched again, looking around our campsite on the creek above the town. "There's something about the day that ain't right, Bill."

"What do you mean?" I asked, feeling the bristles rise on the back of my neck. I shivered suddenly and looked around the camp. Thirty feet away, most everything was a blur, and I stared hard, trying to focus upon the brush.

"I dunno," he said, shaking his head. "But something feels bad about the day." He glanced at me. "Stop squinting. It's a feeling, that's all. Like the day was made for something that's yet to happen and something that you won't like."

I nodded, taking him seriously. A man who had lived life like Charley seemed to develop a sixth sense that warned him about things that were about to happen. That's why men like Charley had managed to keep their hair as long as they had despite the years they spent in the high mountain country and around Indian camps and mining towns. It came from being away from man for long periods at a time. I had had it once when I was scouting for the army and in the war, but I had spent so much time since then in towns that it had slipped away from me. Or maybe I was just too damn tired anymore to pay attention to it. I felt like I was a hundred years old lately, my hands stiff in early morning, aches where I had never had aches before, and times were at night when I would sometimes wish wistfully for a bed and mattress instead of the cold ground under my blankets.

I shivered. "Well, you get any more specifics, you let me know," I said. "Get dressed now. Let's go to the Chinaman's. I need a long hot soak."

He turned away, grumbling to himself about how damn men were inconsiderate of another who had spent a long day's night familiarizing himself with the layout. I laughed as he stood on a camp stool and reached over the tailgate of the wagon and pulled a bottle of Old Hermitage out from under a tarp. He pulled the cork, took two long swallows, then replaced the cork and tossed the bottle to me. I damn near missed it, fumbling with it before wrapping both hands around it.

"Getting old, Bill. Time was you could have caught that with one hand without looking," Charley said, stepping gingerly down from the stool. He squatted and retrieved his clothes from where he had neatly folded them under the wagon.

"You're no spring chicken yourself," I said. I took a long drink from the bottle. "I've never seen anyone gimp around as much as you in the morning, complaining about this and that. You'd think the world had been made for you and the rest of us are just trespassing."

"Uh-huh," Charley said, pulling his leather britches on and slipping the fringed shirt over his head. "Well, we have to look at things from a practical side. I've known you what? Ten years? At least all of that. And you been burning that candle from both ends. I think your wick has finally found the flame in the middle. Look at you: damn near blind—don't worry; I won't let anyone know; my mother raised no stupid children 'cept my brother—and you're still playing Wild Bill. Why don't you cut your damn hair, put away your pistols, and enjoy what time you have left?"

I laughed and turned away, heading up the gulch toward the town where "Chinese Bob" had build a bathhouse next to the creek. I could hear Charley muttering to himself as he struggled to catch up. I passed him the bottle as he came close. He took another drink and shuddered. "I could use a steak," he said.

"We'll go get something after the bath," I said firmly. "You're beginning to ripen a bit yourself."

"Uh-huh," he said. He sniffed at his armpits and frowned. "You may be right about that."

I smiled and kept silent. Charley was one of the most fastidious men I had ever seen. Next to myself, of course. I never had liked being dirty—a strange dislike for one who lived on the frontier, where bathhouses were few and far between. But I had taken more cold baths and washes in streams and creeks than I could ever remember in a month of Sundays even if I was inclined to put my mind to it, which I wasn't.

We steamed a long time in the Chinaman's house, feeling the whiskey work its way out of our pores. After a half hour, both of us felt a bit more human and we made our way down to Alice's Restaurant, where we ate steak and potatoes and drank a pot of coffee. Charley decided he was going upriver to Lead and check on some property up there—he had this idea about making a fancy house for those miners who wanted something other than a tumble and poke with overworked girls in Deadwood—and I decided to go on down to McNutt's place and see if I couldn't scare up a game.

A dog yelps in an alley next to me and my hand reaches reflexively for one of the ivory-handled Colt Navies in a sash around my waist. The alley is just a blur in the gray light, and I tense for a moment, ready to draw, then relax and chuckle silently to myself. "You're jumping at moonbeams," I say.

I continue on down the street to Saloon No. 10 and enter. The saloon is a bit crowded for this early in the day, but not as bad as it had been the night before. Red, the bartender, notices me and waves me over, placing a glass of whiskey and an egg in front of me.

"On the house, Bill," he says.

I nod. Red has taken to me since I drove a brace of drunken miners and a wolfer out who had decided to take issue with his speed of service a week back. Fact is, I had to be careful, since he refused to take my money and wanted to keep my glass full all the time. I thank him and crack the egg and drop it into the glass. I drink it in one pull, replace the glass, but before I can put my hand over it, Red fills it again from the private bottle he keeps under the bar.

"Thanks, Red," I say.

He brushes away my words with a quick wave of his hand. "My pleasure, Mr. Hickok," he says. A miner calls for another round from down the bar. Red shakes his head and turns away from me. "The game's still going," he says over his shoulder, and nods toward the back of the room.

I turn and see Captain Frank Massey, a Missouri River pilot, still at the poker table from the night before along with Charlie Rich and Carl Mann, one of the owners of No. 10. I wasn't surprised; that game had been going on steadily for about a week now, with one or the other of us slipping away for a day or so but always returning. I walk back to the table.

"Well, look who just rolled in," Massey says, winking at the others. "You going to give us a chance to win back our money?"

I laugh. I had been a big winner the night before and there had been general grousing about me leaving the game with half the money from the table. A squint-eyed man with a broken nose who called himself Jack McCall had been busted flat and had pushed himself away from the table as I stood to leave.

"Well, you left me empty," he said sourly.

I handed him a dollar. "I never leave a man busted. At least get yourself something to eat."

He glared at me. "I don't need your handout," he said, a dull flush coming under the black beard stubble. He jammed his hands into his pockets, but his eyes fixed on the coin in my hand. I laughed and reached out and tucked it into his pocket.

"Man's got to eat," I said. "I'll be damned if I let a man go away from the table without a bit of jingle in his pocket to see him through at least one day."

Anger flashed in his eyes and his shoulders had hunched as he clenched his fists inside his pockets, but he turned away, muscles in the corners of his jaws working furiously.

"I don't believe he cared much for your gesture, Bill," said Mann.

"Some people just ain't grateful," Rich answered.

I sighed and stood, stretching. Knots popped in my back and I could feel the weariness settle between my shoulder blades. "Well, doesn't matter much to me," I said. "I just know it makes me feel better."

Mann shook his head. "Some people get insulted at gestures like that, Bill," he warned. "I'd be a bit more careful if I were you."

I laughed and sauntered out, making my way down to Alice's to get a bite to eat.

Now I laugh with the others and look at Massey. "All right, I'll give you a chance," I say. "Trade places with me."

"Superstitious, are you?" Massey jokes.

"All gamblers are," I say, grinning. "But I really don't like leaving the room at my back."

Massey nudges Mann with his elbow and winks. "Well, you can't have this one. My luck's running good with this seat and I don't want to change."

I shrug and start to turn away, but Massey says, "What's the matter, Bill? You finally afraid of something?"

I turn slowly and stare at him. A silence falls over the table as the others look nervously from one to the other, wondering how I'm going to take the accusation. I pull a stool away from the table and sit, being careful that enough space is left between the edge of the table and my pistols to clear.

"All right," I say quietly. "I'll play your game. But it better be a good one."

The others heave sighs of relief and play resumes, more subdued than before, as a nervousness settles over the table that inhibits talk. The cards run against me almost immediately, probably because I'm nervous about my back naked to the room and find it difficult to pay attention to the play. Soon I've played the last of the coin in my pockets and I turn to Red and ask him to bring me fifty dollars in chips. He waves and I turn back to the table, staring across at Massey.

"Deal," I say quietly.

"Cards running against you, Bill?" he taunts.

I nod, knowing that it takes only one hand for Lady Luck to change her fancy, usually against those who take her for granted. She's a fickle lady and not given to those who do not acknowledge her with a touch of humility.

Massey flushes, then begins to deal.

Dimly I hear a drunken harlot singing to a beggar-man whose raggedy clothes show his sunburnt ass hanging like sourdough starter from his breeches:

> *"I have met them all, Cody and Bill,*
> *And had both of them in an hour.*
> *I adore their wonderful eyes, but still*
> *I cannot grip their thighs. . . ."*

But song is a lie. I am troubled, though, for who will remember the man behind the raunchy lines in a dance hall girl's song? A man's honor is all that survives him past the grave.

Is that the sole reality of what men like and loathe? Lies instead of truth? Dishonor instead of honor?

I am an old man looking backward upon life. It's not the years; it's the mileage in a world gone into the midnight of madness—

Eight of spades

and then there was Cheyenne and Colorado Charley and together we took a wagon train along the trail to the Black Hills following up and into the Hills to a gulch stripped of wood and called Deadwood by those who were mining the gold from the sides of the gulch and a fall rain had left the main street full of mud so that the horses and stage had a hard time coming through and then Doc Holliday climbed

*off the stage and Jane found him Calamity Jane who wanted
to be more to me than I could take and had come overland
from Cheyenne with us but she wasn't much of a beauty and
didn't have the manner or features or contours that a fellow
might conjure up on a lonely night and savor and she wasn't
tall and leggy or even shapely at all and her nose was a bit
flat and a little canted off to one side as if it had gotten in
the way of someone a time or two in the past and her eyes
were deep-set and green with lips that were thin enough with
a touch of pout to the lower but still unvoluptuous and a little jowl and high cheekbones that would have been fashion-
able on anyone but her and her auburn hair had full red tints
to it and was seldom waved or curled and cut short to hang
just below her neck and occasionally she would let it grow
longer but then it would appear greasy and gray the red dull
like rust and she carried no shame of her sex with her as
many women did then which made her strangely in a way
pretty and vivacious but her escapades shocked the Baptist
righteous who allowed a person little leeway between this
world and the next and she had a way of moving her head to
toss her hair back and forth away from her face but the
strangest thing was how she could switch from an alley cat
ready to dig your eyes out with dirty claws to a Persian kitten
cuddly and warm and with a gesture leave you with an insinuation of beauty and grace that would hang momentarily in
the air like lavender scent and leave a man hungry for more
and she knew this because she had learned enough of what
she needed to make man a fool of himself by fabricating
whatever charm she instinctively knew would appeal to him
but it was all sport to her regardless how seriously others
might take her flirtations and I didn't take them seriously
enough to suit her and she became moody but always appeared at my elbow like a cat cuddling up to its master for a
saucer of milk except Jane's milk was whiskey which she
drank hard and fast like a man and then the words and stories would pour boastfully from her mouth and often I would
leave her there spinning yarns to whoever would buy her a*

glass of whiskey while I made my way back down the creek to where Charley and I had set up camp

Jack of diamonds

and the next morning the two of us would go to the China-man's place where we'd get a bath and have a few drinks while the Chinaman fixed us steaks and eggs and then Charley would go around looking for claims to buy and up to Lead where he finally took on a house and then decided to run a pony mail service between Cheyenne and Deadwood while I limped my way around with an old billiard cue as a cane to help me with my rheumatism that had crept up on me during the overland trip halfheartedly looking for a claim and more often than not finding a card game in a saloon with some who wanted to play with Wild Bill Hickok who was tired of being Wild Bill Hickok and who had to squint to make out his cards as his eyes were going bad until everyone looked soft with a halo around them like angels except there weren't angels in that gold camp and I knew it for there weren't no angels anywhere even in Cheyenne where I had met Agnes Lake Thatcher and married her and then went with her to Cincinnati where I thought we would be happy but we weren't happy there couldn't be happy there because I knew that I no longer had a place in this world but I couldn't tell Agnes that and that I would have to go back to the West again

Ace of clubs

and when the Deadwood strike came around I told her that I would go there and make a fortune and then we could go anywhere we wanted and she pretended to believe me and that night we made love as if we invented it and the next day I was on the train for Chicago and then back to Cheyenne where I met Charley and we put together the wagon train to go to Deadwood and found Jane at John Hunton's ranch where she got drunk and ran naked through our camp and tried to climb into bed with me and then passed out and some of the girls in the train bound for Deadwood Big Dol-lie Dirty Emma Tit Bit Smooth Bore and Sizzling Kate all

took her into their wagon and she rode the rest of the way to
Deadwood with them past Jack Boman's ranch at Hat Creek
where Cody met us and told us that Custer and his men had
been killed at the Little Big Horn

Eight of clubs

*that sobered us up as we rode the rest of the way looking
for the Sioux and Crazy Horse and Gall and Sitting Bull or
White Owl to come down upon us a-whooping and a-
hollering and trying to kill us but we made it to Deadwood
and I could tell it was the last town for me as I rode into that
town that wound along the creek like a snake between the
hills and saw Charlie Storms and Jim Levy prowling around
and wondered how they managed to get away from not being
hanged all these years and I felt Death walking in that gulch
and said to Charley Charley I feel this is going to be my last
camp and I won't leave it alive but Charley just laughed as
the others did who heard about that and I sat down and
wrote a letter out to Agnes using a stump for a desk saying
Agnes Darling if such should be we never meet again while
firing my last shot I will gently breathe the name of my
wife—Agnes—and with wishes even for my enemies I will
make the plunge and try to swim to the other shore and I
walked down and posted it to her then went to Nuttall and
Mann's No. 10 Saloon where Harry Sam Young shouted his
cheery greeting when I came in the door and got into a poker
game with Captain Frank Massey a Missouri River pilot who
had to drop out and get something to eat and then a ferret-
faced man calling himself Jack McCall sat down and tried to
play poker but he was too aggressive and had to buy in on
every pot and before long he was broke and when he left the
table I handed him some money and told him that I never left
a man without a meal and he gave me a hard look and
looked around the table and I thought then that I had insulted him and knew that he had played in the game only so
he could say that he had played in a game with Wild Bill
Hickok but he took the money and left and a couple of days
later I came back into the No. 10 and came over to where
Carl Mann Charlie Rich and Captain Massey were playing*

and asked if Mann would change seats with me so I could put my back against the wall but he laughed and teased me and I decided the hell with it and took the chair that left my back to the room and played some and lost some and then asked Red to bring me fifty dollars in pocket checks until I could get money from the camp and then I saw Jack McCall come in and look around and thought for a moment that he looked like a cornered rat

Ace of spades

but then the cards came and I laughed and said that the old duffer he broke me on the last hand but this one was going to be different then McCall shouted damn you take that and

A HISTORICAL NOTE

Jack McCall shot James Butler "Wild Bill" Hickok in the back of the head in Saloon No. 10 on August 2, 1876. Hickok was thirty-nine years old and rapidly going blind from "ophthalmia"—a rather broad term that covers a lot of diseases, but Hickok's apparently was a type of glaucoma or granular conjunctivitis or trachoma. The general assumption by ophthalmologists consulted in regard to the descriptions of Hickok's affliction is that Hickok suffered from gonorrheal ophthalmia. McCall was subsequently brought to trial in a miners' court in Deadwood and found "not guilty" and promptly left town for Cheyenne and Laramie. There McCall took to bragging about how he had murdered Hickok with one lucky shot—out of the six rounds in his pistol, the only one that worked was the one that killed Hickok. He was promptly arrested by Deputy U.S. Marshal Balcombe and taken to Yankton in the Dakota Territory, where he was brought to trial again. This time, he was found guilty and hanged on March 1, 1877. It was the first legal hanging in the territory. Although it would appear that McCall was the victim of "double jeopardy," this was not the case, as the court in Deadwood had no legal jurisdiction and was, consequently, an illegal court. Deadwood was an "outlaw town" in that the citizens had no right to be in the territory at the time, as the Black Hills were still legally an Indian reservation and only a federal court had legal jurisdiction.

The legend that has sprung up in regards to Calamity Jane and Wild Bill Hickok is precisely that: a legend. Despite Calamity Jane's claim that she and Hickok were secretly married, much evidence exists that shows this was an invention of hers and Hickok was not associated other than as a casual acquaintance with Jane. He was married to Agnes Lake Thatcher on March 5, 1876. She had a daughter, Emma, by a previous marriage who took Hickok's name when she entered show business. No records of any children sired by James Butler Hickok have yet come to light.

R.L.E.

LOOK FOR

The Quick
and the Dead

BY RANDY LEE EICHOFF

Available in hardcover July 2005
by Tom Doherty Associates